PENGUIN CRIME FICTION

A DOG'S RANSOM

Patricia Highsmith was born in Fort Worth, Texas, in 1921. Her parents moved to New York City when she was six, and she at tended Julia Richman High School and Barnard College. She edited the school magazine and at the age of sixteen decided to become a writer. Her first novel, *Strangers on a Train*, was filmed by Alfred Hitchcock, and her third, *The Talented Mr Ripley*, was awarded the Edgar Allan Poe Scroll by the Mystery Writers of America. In her spare time Ms. Highsmith enjoys gardening, carpentering, painting, and sculpture; some of her works have been exhibited. She now lives in France. Her other books include *The Animal Lover's Book of Beastly Murder*, *The Boy Who Followed Ripley*, *The Cry of the Owl*, *Deep Water*, *Edith's Diary*, *Eleven*, *The Glass Cell*, *Little Tales of Misogyny*, *Ripley's Underground*, *Ripley's Game*, *A Suspension of Mercy*, and *This Sweet Sickness*.

Patricia Highsmith

A Dog's Ransom

Penguin Books

Penguin Books Ltd, Harmondsworth,
Middlesex, England
Penguin Books, 625 Madison Avenue,
New York, New York 10022, U.S.A.
Penguin Books Australia Ltd, Ringwood,
Victoria, Australia
Penguin Books Canada Limited, 2801 John Street,
Markham, Ontario, Canada L3R 1B4
Penguin Books (N.Z.) Ltd, 182–190 Wairau Road,
Auckland 10, New Zealand

First published in Great Britain by
William Heinemann 1972
First published in the United States of America by
Alfred A. Knopf, Inc., 1972
Published in Penguin Books 1975
Reprinted 1978, 1980, 1981

Printed in the United States of America by
George Banta Co., Inc., Harrisonburg, Virginia
Set in Linotype Granjon

For my father
Jay Bernard Plangman
with affection

I

Greta showed Ed the letter as soon as he came in the door. 'I couldn't help opening it, Eddie, because I knew it was from this – that creep.'

The envelope was addressed to Mr Edward Reynolds, as usual. It was the third letter. Greta had rung him up at the office about it, though she had not wanted to read it over the telephone. The letter, printed with a ball-point pen, said:

DEAR SIR OR 'GENTLEMAN':

I SUPPOSE YOU ARE PRETTY PLEASED WITH YOURSELF? PEOPLE LIKE YOU DISGUST ME AND NOT ONLY ME BUT A HELL OF A LOT OF OTHER PEOPLE IN THIS WORLD. YOU ARE SMUG, YOU ARE SELF-SUFICIANT YOU THINK. SUPERIOR TO EVERY- ONE ELSE YOU *THINK*. A FANCY APARTMENT AND A SNOB DOG. YOU ARE A DISGUSTING LITTLE MACHINE, NOTHING ELSE. YOUR DAYS ARE NUMBERED. WHAT RIGHT HAVE YOU GOT TO BE 'SUPERIOR'?

ANON (AS IN 'SEE YOU ANON' HA!)

'Oh, my God,' Ed said, smiled uncertainly at his wife, and handed the letter and the envelope back to her. Since Greta didn't extend a hand, he laid them on the top of the baby grand piano on his left. 'Hi, Lisa, hello!' Ed said, bending at last to take the front paws of the black French poodle dancing around him.

Greta removed the letter and envelope from the piano, as if they might contaminate the instrument. 'You don't think we should tell the police?'

'No. No, really, darling. And don't you worry. These people vent themselves – in writing letters, that's all. They're irritat- ing, but they can't really hurt you.' Ed hung up his topcoat, then went into the bathroom to wash his hands. He had just come from th. office, and as he let the water rinse away the soap, he thought, *I'm washing my hands of the subway and also of that damned letter*. Who was writing the letters? Someone who lived in his neighbourhood, probably. Ed two weeks ago had asked George, one of the doormen downstairs, if any stranger had asked for his name, if he'd seen anyone odd hanging around, male or female, and George had said no. Ed was sure George had asked the other doormen the same question. Was it someone in his office? Inconceivable, Ed thought. Yet one never knew, did one? A poison-pen letter-writer didn't necessarily stare at you, wouldn't be obviously an enemy. On the other hand, Anon's letters seemed genuinely dim-witted, not like anyone at C. & D., even the clean-up men. The letters annoyed Ed, but they frightened Greta, and Ed didn't want to show even his annoyance too much, lest it augment her fear. And perhaps he was a little afraid, too. Someone had singled him out to write to. Or was he the only recipient? Were there other people in his neighbourhood just as annoyed as he was?

'Want a drink, darling? Lisa can wait a minute,' Greta said.

'All right. I'll start one. A small one.' Sometimes he took Lisa out as soon as he got home, sometimes after a pre-dinner drink.

Greta went into the kitchen. 'A lousy day or a good day?'

'Mixed. Meeting today. Lasted all afternoon.'

Lisa rushed up to Ed with a teasing 'Wurf!' because she knew she was due for an airing. She was a miniature poodle, not of the very best kennel, but still a pure poodle, with dark-golden eyes, and she was sensitive and polite – evidently born polite, because neither Ed nor Greta had spent much time training her.

'So? The meeting today?' Greta handed Ed a scotch and water with ice.

'It wasn't bad. No big arguments.' It had been the monthly Editorial Meeting. Ed knew Greta was troubled by the letter from Anon, and was trying to make this interval between his homecoming and dinner like that of any other evening. Ed worked at Cross and Dickinson on Lexington Avenue, and was senior editor in the non-fiction department. He was forty-two and had been with the publishing house for six years. He sat down on the dark-green sofa and patted the pillow once, which was an okay for Lisa who wanted to leap up. 'Want me to pick up something?' Ed asked, as he nearly always did.

'Ah, yes, darling, some sour cream. I forgot it. It goes with our dessert.'

There was a delicatessen on Broadway.

'What's for dinner?'

'Corned beef. You didn't smell it?' Greta laughed.

Ed had smelt it, and forgot. One of his favourite dishes. 'It's because you didn't put the cabbage on yet.' He set his drink down and stood up. 'Okay, Lisa?'

Lisa leapt off the sofa and scurried around in the foyer, as if looking for her own leash, which hung inside the hall closet door.

'Back in twenty minutes,' Ed said. He started to take his topcoat, and decided not to.

The elevator was self-operating, but there was a doorman below – George tonight, a husky black fellow.

'How you, Lisa?' George said, and bent to pat her, but Lisa was in such a hurry to see the great outdoors, she gave him only a perfunctory salute with front paws raised in a capriole, then strained at her leash to get to the sidewalk.

That evening, Ed envied Lisa's energy. He felt tired, and vaguely depressed. Lisa went to the right, towards West End and the delicatessen, and paused to crouch and pee in the gutter. Ed considered going to the delicatessen first, then decided to take Lisa to Riverside Park now for her usual run. He went down the stone steps ornamented by the equestrian statue of Franz Sigel, crossed the Drive with the light, and let Lisa off her leash. Dusk was falling quickly. It was just after 7 p.m., and the month was October. Across the Hudson River, a couple of lighted advertisements had come on. This time last year, Ed thought, Margaret had been alive. His daughter. *Don't think any more about that,* he told himself. Aged eighteen. What a shame and all that. Oddly the conventional phrases were the most comforting. It was because, he knew, he could not bring himself to think profoundly about her death, her absence, the waste, the shame and all that. That was, if he was even capable of thinking profoundly, about anything. Maybe he wasn't. Maybe that was why he didn't try, didn't dare, to think about his promising daughter who had fallen in with a lot of young crumbs and died of drugs – no, rather she'd been shot in a brawl. Why had he thought of drugs? She'd been trying drugs, yes, that was true, but the drugs had not killed her. The shot had killed her. In a bar in Greenwich Village. The police had rounded up the boys with the guns, but it had been extremely vague just who fired that particular shot, and in a way it didn't matter, to Ed. The bar was called The Plastic Arms. Disgusting. Not even a funny joke, that name. They had changed the name since the night of the police raid, the brawl, the shooting.

Ed said in a firm voice, 'Lisa, old girl, you're going to bring something back tonight.'

But he hadn't brought her blue rubber ball. He didn't want to throw a stone, which Lisa would have gladly fetched, because stones were bad for her teeth.

'Lisa, dammit, I forgot your ball.'

Lisa looked at him expectantly, and barked. 'Throw *something*!'

Ed picked up a stick, a short thick piece heavy enough to be thrown some distance. Lisa went after it like a shot, and brought it back, teasing him for the first seconds, as if she would not let it go, but at last she put it down, because she wanted it to be thrown again.

Ed threw it. The sour cream, he thought. Mustn't forget.

'Okay, Lisa!' Ed clapped his hands. He was shouting towards some dark bushes where Lisa had disappeared in quest of the stick. Since the dog didn't appear, Ed trudged towards the bushes. 'Give it up, old girl.' She had no doubt lost the stick and was sniffing around for it.

He didn't see her. Ed turned around. 'Lisa?' He whistled.

There was a *zoo-oom* of automobile engines as a red light changed to green on Riverside Drive.

'*Lisa!*'

Ed went up to the street level, and looked on the pavement. But what would Lisa be doing up here? He turned back down the grassy slope, back to the clump of trees and bushes where she had disappeared. 'Lisa, come!'

It had grown much darker suddenly.

Ed walked back the way he had come, parallel with the horse statue. *'Lisa!'*

Had she gone back to the house? Absurd. Still, he crossed the Drive, and ran along the pavement to his door. To George, in the lobby, he said:

'I can't find Lisa. If she comes back here, can you keep her in the lobby?' He swung the leash towards George, then realized he would have need of it himself, if he found Lisa on the street.

'Can't find her?'

'She was chasing something. Didn't come back. See you in a few minutes!' Ed hurried down the same steps, was halted by what seemed a very long green light, then crossed the Drive.

'Lisa! – Where are you?' He suddenly had hope. She'd have given up the search for her stick by now.

But the darkness, the black clump of bushes was silent. Maybe the poison-pen fellow got her, Ed thought. No, ridiculous. How could anyone 'get' Lisa – unless by shooting her, and he certainly hadn't heard a shot. Nearly ten minutes had passed since he missed her. What the hell to do? Tell a policeman on the beat? Yes. Ed walked up the steps towards the sidewalk. No policeman in sight. Only three or four people, walking separately.

Ed went back to his apartment house.

'No sign of her,' George said, holding the door open for an elderly woman who was going out. 'What're you gonna do, Mr Reynolds?'

'Dunno just yet. Keep looking.' Ed nervously pressed the elevator button three times. He lived on the eighth floor.

'You forgot the sour cream,' Greta said when he came in. 'What's the matter?'

'I can't find Lisa. I threw something in the Park – and she didn't come back. I'd better go down again, darling. I'd better stay till I find her. I'll take the flashlight.' He got it from a drawer in the hall table.

'I'll go with you. Let me turn something off.' Greta disappeared into the kitchen.

As they went down in the elevator, Ed said, 'You go down the steps by Sigel. I'll walk up further and go into the Park, then I'll walk down and we'll meet each other.'

They did this, and a few minutes later met each other in the Park, near the clump of bushes where Lisa had disappeared. Here Ed searched the ground with the aid of the flashlight. No sign of Lisa, no spots where she might have scratched the soil, nothing.

'It was here,' Ed said.

'I think we should tell the police,' said Greta.

Ed supposed she was right. They walked back towards the house, both calling Lisa to the last moment before they crossed the Drive.

Ed looked up the nearest precinct and telephoned, and was passed on to a second man, to whom he gave a description of the dog. Yes, she had a licence tag on her collar and also an identification tag with 'Lisa' on it, also Ed's name and address and telephone number. Plus the word 'Reward', Ed recalled, but he did not think that worth mentioning.

It was a brief and unhappy dinner, with Ed wondering what he ought to do next, and Greta assuring him twice that they would go down again, both of them, and look the neighbourhood over. The telephone rang just as Ed lit a cigarette, and he leapt up, hoping it might be about Lisa, but it was a friend of Greta's, Lilly Brandstrum. Ed passed the telephone to Greta.

A few minutes later, Greta's words broke into his thoughts: 'Listen! Tonight we are very upset because Lisa's missing ... Yes ... So I can't talk long.'

Advertise, Ed thought. If they didn't find her downstairs in a few minutes, he'd ring up the *Times* and put an ad in. He could see himself doing that by midnight, and he began to compose the 'lost or strayed' item while Greta was still on the telephone.

2

Lisa had disappeared on a Wednesday evening. Thursday morning early, Ed returned to Riverside Drive and the Park and looked over the ground. Now he even looked for blood. He did not know what to think, what he should imagine. He saw no odd signs on the ground, yet he realized it was absurd to look for disturbed leaves, even a scrape in the earth, in a public park like this. It wasn't exactly virgin territory where one could read a broken twig, in case one noticed one. He felt compelled to look along the kerb of the street above, to see if Lisa had been hit by a car and her body possibly not yet removed.

He went back to the apartment to report to Greta that he hadn't found anything. Greta gave him another half cup of coffee. The *Times* had arrived, delivered to the door by George, but the notice about Lisa would not be in until tomorrow, Friday. Ed had arranged to run it for three days unless he cancelled. He could have put an ad in the *Post* too, he realized.

'Don't worry so, Eddie. Maybe someone found her last night and didn't telephone because it was late. Maybe this morning I'll hear something.' Greta had said she was going to stay in all day.

'Call me, would you ? – Call me anyway this afternoon.'

'Of course.'

Greta was just over five feet, and rather plump, German-Jewish, and born in Hamburg. She had slightly buck teeth with a space between them, reddish-brown hair that was fine and short-cut, eyes that could look green or light brown. She played the piano well, and had been a concert pianist with a philharmonic orchestra until she married Ed thirteen years ago. Her marriage had put a stop to her concert career, but she did not regret it, or had ever seemed to, to Ed. Her early life had been rough, exile with her parents first into France, where she had gone to school until 1940, then America where her parents had had a difficult time settling and making a living in Philadelphia. Ed always thought of Greta as older than himself, but she was forty while he was forty-two. She was older in experience, Ed felt. Anyway, he liked to think of her as older, it made her more attractive to him. She was not the mother of his daughter Margaret. Margaret was the only child of a marriage Ed had made when he was twenty-two, an unwise marriage.

Ed did not want to leave the apartment, and left as late as he dared, 9.12. He had a 9.30 appointment, and treated himself to a taxi. In the taxi, he thought, 'Something ghastly has happened, and we'll never see Lisa again.'

Then after a good lunch with a writer named MacCauley, and Ed's secretary Frances Vernon, Ed's spirits lifted. As he puffed a cigar (he smoked about four a week) and laughed at a story MacCauley had told, he thought, 'There'll be news this afternoon or tonight about Lisa for sure.'

But that evening brought nothing. Eric Schaffner – a retired professor of art history who had been a friend of Greta's father – came for drinks and as usual Greta urged him to stay for dinner. Ed was glad he declined.

'Oh, you'll get Lisa back,' said Eric with confidence.

Sometimes Greta and Eric lapsed into German, which Ed did not understand, though he had picked up a few phrases from Greta. That evening he did not try to understand and was slightly irked by their German.

'Darling, tomorrow is another day, and tomorrow the ad is in,' Greta said, when Eric had gone.

'Even tonight it's in,' Ed said. 'By around ten the papers are on the stands.'

But the telephone did not ring that evening.

Ed took his time Friday morning. The mail came around 9.30. He had no appointment until 11.30. 'I want to wait for the mail,' Ed said in answer to Greta's remark about his lateness. It was then ten past nine. George or Mark, another doorman who was white, delivered the mail under people's doors. 'I think I'll go down, in fact.' He avoided looking at Greta, and in a deliberately casual way walked to the door.

Ed had been braced for the clumsy printing on the cheap envelope, but the sight of the envelope when Mark handed it to him downstairs – along with three other items – sent a shock of dread through him.

'No word about your dog, Mr Reynolds?' Mark asked.

'No, not yet,' Ed said.

'We're certainly keeping a look-out down here. I even told the delicatessen fellow and his wife this morning.'

'Good. Thanks,' Ed said. He wanted to get to the safety of his apartment before he opened the letter, but on the other hand Greta was there – and he wanted to spare her. He opened the letter in the moving elevator.

DEAR SIR:

I HAVE YOUR DOG LISA. SHE IS WELL AND HAPPY. BUT IF YOU WANT HER BACK LEAVE $1,000 (ONE THOUSAND DOLLARS) BE-TWEEN ELEVENTH AND TWELFT PIKES OF FENCE EAST SIDE OF YORK AVENUE BETWEEN 61 & 62 ST FRIDAY NITE AT 11 P.M. IN NEWSPAPER WRAPPING IN BILLS OF NOT BIGGER THAN TEN DOLLARS. IF YOU DONT LEAVE THIS MONEY THE DOG WILL BE KILLED. I GATHER THE DOG IS IMPORTANT TO YOU? WE'LL SEE! A NICE LITTLE DOG. MAYBE NICER THAN YOU.

ANON

LISA WILL BE TIED TO SAME PIKE ABOUT ONE HOUR LATER. NO COPS PLEASE – OR ELSE.

So there it was. The nightmare had come true, Ed thought – a phrase that reminded him of clichés in the not very good books he sometimes had to read. He let himself into the apartment.

'Eddie –'

Ed supposed he was white in the face. 'Well, I know where Lisa is. My dear, I could use a neat scotch – despite the hour.'

'What's happened? Where is she?'

'The poison-pen guy has her.' Ed went to the kitchen, bent over the sink and with his free hand splashed water on his face.

'He wrote another letter?' Greta brought a scotch in a tumbler.

'Yes. He wants a ransom by tonight. A thousand dollars.'

'A thousand *dollars*!' Greta said in a tone of astonishment, but Ed knew it wasn't the sum so much as the crazy situation that shocked her. 'Should we do it? Where is she? – Who is he?'

Ed sipped the scotch and held on to the sink. The crumpled letter was now on the drainboard. 'I'll have to think.'

'A thousand dollars. It's insane.'

'This guy's insane,' Ed said.

'Eddie, we've got to tell the police.'

'That's sometimes the way to lose something – something kidnapped,' Ed said. 'If the fellow gets scared – I mean if he sees police waiting for him –' But a plainclothesman, Ed thought, with a gun, might be different. Telling the police might not be a bad idea.

'I want to see the letter.' Greta took it and read it. 'Oh, my God,' she said softly.

Ed had a vision of Lisa breaking away from the leash or whatever Anon was holding her with, running to him on the dark sidewalk of York Avenue at 61st Street tonight at midnight. What made sense? Should he get the money? The returning of the dog one hour later, written at the bottom of the letter, seemed an aftermath, something Anon might not mean.

'Darling you should get the police to watch that spot and don't fool around with the money,' Greta said earnestly.

'If we get Lisa back, isn't it worth a thousand dollars?'

'Of course she's worth it! That isn't the point! I'm not trying to save a thousand dollars!'

'I've got to think about it. I'd better get to the office.' He was thinking, if he got the cash, he would have to go to the bank before 3 p.m. He felt he would go to the bank. He could always decide about the police after he got the money. Ed wished, not for the first time, that he was a type who became angry quickly, made a decision quickly, based on the right, as he saw it. Even if such a person were occasionally wrong, he had at least acted, decided, because of what he thought right. *I hesitate, without any of the eloquence of Hamlet,* Ed thought with a faint amusement, but he did not smile.

'Will you telephone me this morning?' Greta asked, following him to the door.

Ed realized she was physically afraid here in the apartment. And what was more logical, because Anon probably knew Greta by sight as well as himself. Ed had an impulse to stay home. He said with difficulty, 'Don't go out, darling. And don't open the door to anyone. I'll speak to Mark downstairs. I'll tell him not to let anyone up to see you. All right? Do you have to go out for anything?'

'No. I had sort of a lunch date with Lilly, but I can cancel it.'

'Cancel it. I'll call you during the morning. Bye-bye, darling.'

That morning, during a Publishing Committee meeting – which was so full of agenda it would be resumed in the afternoon – half Ed's mind was on the Lisa situation. By 11.30 a.m. he had decided that to have a plainclothesman, who might insist on trailing Anon after he collected the money, would jeopardize Lisa's life: Anon might realize he was being trailed and be afraid to return an hour later with the dog, or to have anyone else bring the dog. So when Ed telephoned Greta just before he went out to lunch, he told her that he had decided to get the money and to have no police. Greta was still in favour of a plainclothesman.

'If we lose, we've lost only a thousand bucks, darling. I mean if we can't identify him later and so forth. There's more chance of losing the other way – losing the dog.'

Greta sighed. 'Could you telephone me again this afternoon, Eddie? I am worried.'

'I'll call you twice if I can.'

He and Greta had four letters from Anon now. If he took them to the police, which he certainly intended to do eventually, the police might have in their files letters to other people from the same Anon. Identifying printing was just as easy as identifying script writing. If Lisa were dead or alive, Anon would be found and stopped. Even his own letters were bound to provide a clue. And yet – just how exactly?

After a quick lunch alone at the Brass Rail on Fifth Avenue,

Ed walked to his bank and withdrew a thousand dollars in ten-dollar bills. He had foreseen the bulk and brought his black briefcase. As he left the bank, Ed wondered if he was being watched even now by Anon? Ed did not glance at anyone on the street and made his way at a moderate pace back to his office. It was a fine, crisp day full of sunshine. He wondered if Lisa were outdoors or in at this moment? Surely she'd bark, surely she was unhappy and mystified. How had the bastard grabbed her? *How?* It was quite possible she was dead, Ed realized.

When Ed came home, with the briefcase, Greta said she had had no telephone calls other than Ed's and one from Eric who wanted to know the news about Lisa.

They had a simple dinner. Greta was depressed about the money, and didn't want to look at the briefcase. But she wanted to go with him at 11 p.m. Ed tried to dissuade her. Where would she wait for him?

'Oh, there are bars on York Avenue. Or Third. I'll order a drink. I'll ask Eric to come. Sure!' she interrupted his protest. 'Why not? What's the harm? Do you think I want to leave you alone with this bastard?'

Ed laughed for the first time since Lisa had disappeared.

Greta telephoned Eric, who was nearly always in. Ed had not been able to stop her from telling Eric his mission, and maybe it wasn't a bad idea, Ed thought, if Eric came.

It was ten to 11 p.m., when Ed went out the door of a bar on Third Avenue and 60th Street, leaving Greta and Eric on their scotch and sodas. He carried the newspaper-wrapped parcel under his left arm. The parcel was held by two big rubber bands. He was to rejoin Greta and Eric in about fifteen minutes – and Ed did find it comforting to have a date with them. He walked slowly, but not too slowly, eastward, and at York Avenue crossed to its east side and continued north. He was not anticipating a physical encounter, but one never knew with a psychopath, he supposed. However, he pictured Anon as a short fellow, fortyish, maybe even fifty, a weakling, a coward. Anyway, Ed was five feet ten, sturdily enough built – in fact he had to watch his waist-line – and in college, Columbia University, he had boxed for a year or so, and played football, though neither with much enthusiasm. Ed took a breath and walked straighter. Now he could see the rail fence across 61st Street.

Ahead of him, a slender figure of a young man walked, hands in coat pockets, away from Ed, northward. Trees along the kerb shaded the sidewalk from the street lights. Behind the rail fence was some kind of medical research centre, Ed recalled vaguely. Ed glanced behind him, and seeing nothing to worry about, began to count off the pikes. Between the eleventh and twelft (he remembered the spelling) he stuck the newspaper-wrapped bundle, pushing it so that nothing of it projected, yet it was right there, not in danger of falling to the ground behind, but resting on the cement.

Ed turned, and feeling that this was no time to look around if he was to be a good sport, retraced his steps towards 60th Street and crossed discreetly with the light. He entered the red-neon bar casually.

Greta waved to him with a gleeful face from a booth on the right. Eric half rose, beaming to see him back.

'Nothing at all,' Ed said as he sat down beside Eric. Suddenly all his muscles ached.

Greta was gripping his forearm. 'You didn't see anything? No one?'

'No one.' Ed sighed and looked at his wrist-watch. Five minutes past eleven. 'Be nice to have a scotch.'

'A double!' Eric said gaily.

A single, Ed thought, then reflected that he could make a double last a long time with water. He had nearly an hour to wait.

Ed hardly listened to what Eric and Greta were saying. Greta was talking about seeing Lisa tonight, and Ed realized from her confidence that she was either feeling her drinks or was a bit hysterical. Eric was optimistic, and the same time trying to be sensible: 'You can't tell with psychotics. It is foolish to be *over* confident. *Wahnsinnig!* What a crazy story!'

Yes, Ed thought, and Eric looked as entertained as if he were watching a TV show instead of being present at something real. Ed kept glancing at the wall clock, which seemed to be stuck at 11.23, so he stopped looking at it. Now Greta was spinning out her own drink with water. She believed she would see Lisa tonight. Ed could see that. She had been very stoic, or brave, since Wednesday night: not a sentimental word in regard to Lisa. All bottled up, Ed thought. She adored Lisa as much as he. And maybe Anon would be a good egg, and have Lisa tied to the rail by two minutes to midnight. Ed was going to appear on the dot of midnight and not before. Even if he saw Anon, and took the dog's leash from his hands, Ed thought, he wouldn't try to remember Anon's face so that he could run him in. No, he'd be too glad just to see Lisa again. Ed found himself grinning at a joke Eric had told Greta, which Ed hadn't even listened to.

'We are watching the clock,' Eric said in his smiling, precise way.

The minutes before midnight went swiftly. Ed stood up at six minutes to twelve.

'See you soon again!' Ed said.

Greta's face looked strained, not hopeful now. 'You'll come back when?' she demanded.

'Twelve-twenty at the latest,' Ed said for at least the third time. They had arranged that if Lisa wasn't there, he was to return and tell them, though Ed was prepared to go back and wait longer. Eric and Greta had of course wanted to accompany him to get Lisa, but Ed thought it a bad idea, because Anon might notice them (however much they tried to make themselves inconspicuous) and veer away.

Ed walked more quickly now, and only on the east side of York slowed up and peered ahead in the darkness. He was trying to see the black four-legged dot of Lisa near the fence, perhaps alone and straining first in one direction then the other to see who was coming to untie her. It was too dark to see anything really, and when Ed paused to read his watch under a streetlamp, he saw it was only three minutes to midnight. He stopped in the block between 61st and 62nd Streets, leaned on one hand against a tree, and waited. How easy it was to wait now. Anon ought to blow himself to a taxi, and maybe he had done, and got out north of here, and was walking Lisa downtown. Just as likely the reverse, Ed thought, and quickly turned to look downtown. Nothing on the east side of the pavement that he could see. He looked across the street and his heart gave a jump at a dog on a leash, but it was a white dog of some kind, led by a woman. Wouldn't it be odd if Anon were a woman?

It became five past midnight. Ed went closer to the rails where he had left the packet of money, and saw that it was gone. That was splendid! Ed looked up and down for taxis that might be slowing, letting out a man with a dog. He saw none.

At eighteen past, as he had promised Greta, he left his place and walked quickly back to the bar. He raised his hand and smiled a little as he approached Greta and Eric. But he sat down before he spoke. 'The money's gone, but no dog as yet. Sorry.'

'Oh, Eddie,' Greta said. All hope seemed to pour out of her.

'He could be late,' Ed said. 'I'm going back, of course.'

'A schnapps first,' Eric said. 'A coffee maybe.'

'Oh, no. Thanks.' Ed didn't want to waste the time. He stood up. 'I'll give it till one.'

'And then it'll be two, then three,' Greta said.

'We'll come with you,' Eric said. 'If he's *bringing* Lisa –'

'I'd better be alone, really, Eric. I'll be back by one, but I'd better go back now.' Ed walked to the door.

Again the sidewalk by the fence was deserted. It was 12.32 a.m. Ed tried to be calm. Give it till 1 a.m., fine. Maybe there'd been some delay, difficulty in getting a taxi. If the fellow, for instance, lived in Greenwich Village and had to take the money all the way back there – or even uptown west towards Riverside Drive –

By ten of 1, Ed began to realize he'd been hoaxed. His eyes smarted from straining. Two minutes to 1. Then 1 a.m., and Ed walked restlessly to the corner where he might have crossed York, but he could not bring himself to leave. At ten past 1, Ed saw Greta and Eric crossing York Avenue. Ed had thought they might come.

'Nothing?' Greta said when she was still several feet away.

'No. Nothing.'

She gave a groan. 'Eddie, it's a trick.'

'Maybe,' Ed said.

'Where was the money? Show me,' Eric said.

Ed counted off the rails, more or less, and pointed.

'What a bastard! It is disgusting! One thousand dollars. Now I hope you'll go to the police.'

Ed was still looking into the dark distances, ready to ask Greta and Eric to walk away in case he saw Lisa. Now the presence of Eric and Greta annoyed him.

'Eddie, how long are you going to wait?' Greta asked him.

'I'll smoke a cigarette,' Ed said. It was his last cigarette. He lit it with his lighter. Suddenly he felt tired and angry. 'Yes, I'll tell the police. You bet I will.'

But when Eric and Greta made a move to leave, to find a taxi, Ed said, 'Look, I want to wait another half-hour.'

'He knows where to find you if he's late,' Greta said. 'He could *telephone* us.'

That was true. Ed yielded. It was like defeat, like death, Lisa's death, as he moved towards the taxi and got into it with Eric and Greta. They dropped Eric off at his apartment building on East 79th Street, then drove homeward.

The telephone was ringing as they entered their apartment, and Ed made a dive for it.

'Hello, Ed. Lilly. Any luck?' she asked eagerly.

Ed let his breath out. 'No ... Yes.' (Yes he had delivered the money.)

'Oh. I *am* sorry. It's a criminal act! *Definitely!*'

'Would you like to speak with Greta?'

Ed wanted very much to ring the police tonight. The police could keep a watch on York Avenue all night, a plainclothesman. But Ed was afraid he couldn't explain it all clearly enough tonight. He realized he was angry, confused, and very tired. Better to start tomorrow morning early.

3

Ed could not get to sleep, and when Greta became aware of this (though he had been lying motionless), she suggested a sleeping-pill, but he declined it. He wanted to fall asleep with his arms around Greta, but he couldn't. Everything seemed suspended, unfinished. Greta found his hand, squeezed it and held it. Why was he so badly upset? Well, Lisa's death, possibly. And the money lost. No, that wasn't it, they could afford it. It was the evil. It was Lisa's absence, the emptiness in the house. As when Margaret had died: she had disappeared for four days, and they had rung all her friends whose telephone numbers they knew. Then from the police had come the news of her death, the news that her body was at the morgue. Ed remembered the silence of the apartment afterwards. Greta had cleared Margaret's room, the room across the hall from the bedroom, shifted the furniture of the whole house so that everything looked completely different. And still, now and then when he walked past the open door of Margaret's room (it was now a reading-room, or guest-room, there were two tanks of goldfish in it, Greta's painting things and her sewing-machine), he felt a shock of loss, as if her death had just happened. She had been in her second year at N.Y.U. Ed had wanted her to go to Barnard, since his school was Columbia, but she'd had more friends from high school going to N.Y.U. Ed remembered expecting the sound of Margaret's key in the door, expecting her to walk into the foyer, full of energy and news, or hungry, and now it was the same with Lisa's absense, absurd as it might be. He waited for Lisa to trot in from some room, to look at him and give the grunt-growl which meant it was time to be taken out. Lisa kept track of time better than Ed. Lisa's bowl of water was still on the floor in the kitchen, and tonight before going out to make contact with Anon, Ed had changed the water because of a compulsion, a compulsion which he had thought might bring bad luck, but on the other hand he didn't believe in luck.

At some point, he slept.

By a quarter past 8 a.m., Ed was at the precinct station on 109th Street, equipped with the four letters from Anon, each in its proper envelope. Ed was taken to the office of a Captain MacGregor to whom he told his story and showed the letters. The letters were not dated by Anon, but Ed had dated the last two, guessed at the dates of the first two, and written them at the top of the pages. The letters spread over thirty-five days.

MacGregor, a lean man of about fifty with close-cut dark blond hair, looked over the letters while standing at his desk.

'I thought,' Ed said, 'you might have had complaints from people who'd received the same kind of letters. From the same man.'

'I don't *think* so,' said MacGregor. 'Can you come with me please? The file for this kind of thing is in another room.'

Ed followed him. They went into a larger office whose door was open. A plump cop sat at a desk with a telephone at his ear. There were lots of files. In another smaller room towards the rear of the station, Ed saw an electric burner with an old-fashioned grey metal percolator on it. Two young patrolmen were standing in the room. MacGregor was looking through a big green file in a corner. The cop on the phone was saying nothing but letters and numbers, and an occasional 'Right'. MacGregor wouldn't be overly interested in a dog, Ed supposed. Until they did something like kidnapping a child, or setting a house on fire, anonymous letter-writers were merely nuisances. Ed felt also that MacGregor thought him an ass for having come forth with the money.

MacGregor came over with a folder. 'This isn't exhaustive by any means. Just our precinct. The real files are at Centre Street. I don't see anything resembling that printing here. Best we can do is photostat your letters and send the originals to Centre Street for checking out.'

The fat officer hung up, and MacGregor said to him: 'Seen anything like this before, Frank?' He laid one of the letters on the officer's desk.

The officer sighed, planted his hands on the desk and peered at the block-lettered page. 'No. – Nope. Lives in this neighbourhood?'

'We don't know. Seems like it. This gentleman Mr –'

'Reynolds,' Ed said.

'– lives on a Hundred and sixth. These four letters came to him, last one asking a thousand dollars' ransom for a dog. Missing since Wednesday night, was it?'

'Yes.'

'Mr Reynolds last night delivered a thousand dollars in ten-dollar bills, left them where the letter says here, money was picked up – and no dog.'

The fat officer's black eyebrows went up at the mention of the thousand dollars being paid, and they stayed up. On a block of wood on his desk was printed LT FRANK SANTINI. 'Any strange telephone calls?'

'No,' Ed said.

'We can check this printing out,' said Santini. 'Can you give us your name and address, Mr Reynolds? Or have you got that, Mac?'

MacGregor hadn't, or wasn't sure they had it, and Santini took it. Ed gave also his business address and telephone number. 'I'd like to give you a description of the dog. French poodle, miniature, black with light brown eyes – aged four. Dutch cut –'

'What's that?'

'She's trimmed. It's a style of trimming. Answers to the name Lisa. L-i-s-a. Identification and licence on her collar.'

'Last seen where?'

The telephone rang, and Santini took it.

'Riverside Park at a Hundred and sixth Street, Wednesday night, October fourteenth around seven-thirty.'

MacGregor wrote this, closed the notebook and pushed it back on Santini's desk. Ed felt that the information on Lisa was lost among its pages. MacGregor was now absorbed in what Santini was saying on the telephone, giving him urgent instructions about something.

'All right, where was the squad car?' Santini said. '*We* sent a squad car . . . Don't tell *us*!'

The two younger patrolmen stood patiently near a wall, as if awaiting orders from their superiors. One of them looked very young, and more like a college student than a cop.

When Santini had finished speaking, Ed said, addressing both him and MacGregor, 'I hope you can find out something soon. The main thing is, I want to get my dog back alive. I'm not concerned about the money. Can I telephone later today and see if you've found out anything?'

Santini glanced up at MacGregor. He had long crocodile lips, neither quite smiling nor cynical.

MacGregor seemed to fumble for something to say. 'Sure. Certainly. We'll get these to Centre Street today and ask for a quick reply.'

MacGregor walked with Ed to the front door of the station house. A shambles of a man, who looked as if he had been drunk for days, was sitting on a bench just inside the door. He had a wounded cheek and swollen, half-closed eyes, and was evidently too far gone to warrant surveillance, because there was no guard around.

'Not a pretty sight, eh?' said MacGregor, noticing Ed's glance. 'You'd think it was the old Bowery here sometimes.'

Ed turned on the front steps. 'Do you think you can find the man?' he asked, trying not to sound unreasonably insist-ent. 'What're the odds? I'd like to know, honestly.'

'Fifty-fifty. Maybe worse, Mr Reynolds. Honestly. That's all I can tell you. We'll keep in touch.'

Ed walked homeward. The last phrase sounded about as promising as the phrase, the same phrase, that people gave to people who came asking for a job. Ed found himself looking at other people on the street, watching to see if any gave him more than the absent, involuntary glance that the average per-son gave a passer-by. He saw none, but in one of these build-ings with all the windows behind which people quarrelled, laughed, made love, ate meals, or fretted waiting for some-one who was late – behind one of those windows lived Anon. He must be someone in the neighbourhood. This thought made Ed feel momentarily naked and afraid, even now in daylight, gave him a sense of impotence and danger. The kid-napper knew him, but he didn't know the kidnapper. One of the two or three men now walking towards him, apparently paying no attention to him, might be the kidnapper chuckling inwardly at the sight of him alone and without his dog.

This was Saturday morning. Sunny again. Not even nine o'clock. What could he buy to pick Greta up? Maybe a coffee ring from the good bakery on Broadway, a Jewish bakery, more or less. He turned towards Broadway. He still glanced at people he passed, wondering if they might be Anon, but now his face was confident and almost cheerful. After all, he'd laid his case before the police.

The young blonde girl in the bakery knew him and Greta, and gave Ed a big smile. 'Hello, Mr Reynolds. How're you? And how's your wife?'

'She's all right, thank you,' Ed said, smiling too. 'Can I have one of your — a coffee ring, please.' The shop smelled of fresh, buttery baking, of cinnamon and baba *au rhum*.

The girl reached for a coffee ring with wax paper in each hand, then paused. 'Oh, someone told me about *Lisa*! Have you had any news?'

'No. But just now I spoke with the police,' Ed said, smiling. 'We're hopeful. I'll take a couple of croissants, too, please.'

Then he bought three packs of cigarettes from the store in the middle of the block, in case something happened today and Greta or he couldn't get to the supermarket for the usual Saturday morning shopping.

'Ah, Mark was telling me you're missing your dog, Mr Reynolds,' said the cigar-shop man, a thin Irishman of about sixty.

'Yes, since Wednesday night. I've told the police. But keep your eye out for her, would you? I'd appreciate it.'

'Sure I will!'

Ed left the shop feeling that he lived among friends in this neighbourhood — even if Anon lived in it, too.

'Let's have a nice lazy breakfast,' Ed said as he came in.

Greta had put on black slacks, red flat sandals, a gay blouse with a floral pattern. 'Did you hear *news*?'

'No. That I'm afraid I didn't. But I spoke with them. The police.' He held up the paper box from the bakery by its string.

'Goodies.' He made his way to the kitchen. 'I could use another good coffee.'

'What did they say?'

Ed lit the gas under the big glass pot. 'Well – I spoke with two men. I told them where I could be found and all that. Told them you were here most of the time. I left the letters.'

'But do they *know* this creep?'

'No, they don't seem to. But they're sending the letters to the main office on Centre Street. I'm going to phone them back today.' He put an arm around her shoulders and kissed her cheek. 'I know it isn't much, my pet, but what else can I do just now?' Walk around the neighbourhood, Ed thought, put on different clothes, a false moustache, and try to spot someone who was maybe slyly watching his building? 'Open the cake box. Let's put the coffee ring in the oven for a minute.'

With a movement of her shoulder, Greta pushed herself from the door jamb that she had been leaning against. 'Peter called you. A few minutes ago.'

'Already? Um-m.' Peter Cole, a young and eager editor of C. & D., took home manuscripts on week-ends and telephoned Ed nearly every Saturday or Sunday to ask some question not always of importance. Ed remembered he had also brought a manuscript to read, a biography. 'I suppose he wants me to call him back?'

'I forgot. I don't know. Sorry, darling.' Absently, she adjusted the coffee-pot over the flame.

Ed and Greta sat in the dining area off the L-shaped living-room. It had windows that overlooked their street, and from where Ed sat, facing the Hudson River, he could look down on part of the long strip of green that formed Riverside Park. Was Anon down there now, strolling about? Would he be loitering around the supermarket on Broadway, probably knowing they went there, he and Greta or one of them, every Saturday morning around eleven? Often they took Lisa with them and tied her outside to a rail.

Greta propped her face on one hand. 'Oh, Eddie, I'm discouraged.'

'I know, darling. I'm going to ring them back, the police. If they sound vague, I'll go to Centre Street myself.'

'Three days now almost. I wonder if they give her enough to eat?'

Ed was glad Greta assumed Lisa was still alive. 'Don't worry about that. She's in good health.'

Greta put her cigarette down and covered her eyes with her finger-tips. 'If she's dead, I don't know what I'll do, Eddie,' she said in a voice squeaky with tears.

Ed knelt beside her. He wanted to say, 'We'll get another dog, right away,' but it wasn't time to say that – a statement that would sound as if Lisa were definitely gone.

'She's such a darling. As a dog, she is perfect, you know?'

Lots of their friends said that. As a puppy, even, she had not chewed up shoes, only chewed – with the greatest pleasure – the silly things they sold in pet shops for puppies to teethe on. Ed laughed. 'Yes, she's perfect, and I love her, too, darling! – Dry your eyes and we'll think about the shopping. Got a list? Then –' He remembered he had to read the biography this week-end, and it was a thick one. Well, he'd sit up at night doing it, if he had to. 'How about a movie this afternoon? Or would you rather go tonight? What was that thing we wanted to see? *Catamaran*, no? I'll look up the time.'

Greta came out of it slowly. Her face was still unhappy, but she was probably already composing her shopping list. Usually on Sunday they had a good lunch at two or three, and a snack in the evening. 'I think I'll make a *Sauerbraten*. Marinate it overnight, you know?'

They went to the supermarket together, Ed first taking the laundry in two pillowcases to the launderette near the supermarket on Broadway. Then he joined Greta in the supermarket and held a place on the line with her nearly full carrier cart while she came and went, adding small items like tinned crabmeat or *pâté*. There were simpler ways of shopping and doing chores, Ed supposed, and men in his position didn't usually frequent supermarkets, but Ed and Greta had shopped together in the same way when they first met, and Ed still liked it. They bought their meat at a shop on the other side of Broadway. Ed told himself that when they walked out of the supermarket in a couple of minutes, he wasn't going to think of Lisa tied to the rail, brightening at the sight of them. A dog wasn't everything in life. It was just that Lisa took the place of a child now, for both of them. That was obvious.

'Okay, okay!' said the check-out operator, because Ed was a few seconds slow in starting to unload his carrier on to the belt, which at once began to move. He looked around for Greta, and was relieved to see her approaching, carrying a pineapple in her hands, a smile on her face as she looked at him, as if to say, 'An extravagance, I know, but I want it.' She squeezed in behind Ed, unperturbed by a woman behind her who was annoyed by their manoeuvres.

At 5 p.m., Ed telephoned the police station. They had sent the letters to Centre Street, but as yet no report, the man said.

'Is this Captain MacGregor?'

'No, he's not on duty now.'

'When will they know anything?'

The man sighed audibly. 'That I can't tell you, sir.'

'Can I call Centre Street?'

'Well, no, they don't like that. – You wouldn't know who to talk to. Even I don't.'

'When can I know something? Tomorrow?'

Ed was given to understand there was less staff on Centre Street on Sundays, or something like that. Especially painful to Ed was the idea of waiting till Monday for information.

'It's not just the letters, you know. My dog has been stolen. I explained all that to Captain MacGregor and – an officer named Santini.'

'Oh. Yeah,' said the voice without a hint of remembrance or concern.

'So I'm in a hurry. I don't want my dog to die. The letter-writer's got my dog. I don't give a damn who he *is*, really I just want my dog back, you see.

'Yeah, I see but –'

'Can you possibly find out something *tonight*?' Ed asked politely but with determination. 'Can I call you back around ten, say?' Ed wished he could offer them money to speed things up, but one didn't do that, he supposed. 'Could *you* possibly ring up Centre Street now and ask what they've found out?'

'Yeah.' But the tone was not reassuring.

'All right, then I'll ring you back later.'

Ed and Greta were going to the 6.30 performance of *Catamaran* on West 57th Street. An adventure story – Pacific seas, danger, exotic islands, a triumph of heroism against elements and odds. For long intervals Ed was distracted from his own thoughts, from his life. Perhaps Greta was too. After the film, they had excellent hamburgers and red wine at a nearby steakhouse, and came home a little before ten.

Ed rang the precinct station, and said he was supposed to telephone this evening in regard to his missing dog and some anonymous letters. Once more he had a strange voice at the other end, and had to repeat the facts.

'There's no report come in from Centre Street . . .'

Ed could have banged the telephone down, but he hung on politely during a few more inconsequential exchanges. He was sorry, in a way, that he'd given them the damned letters. The letters had been something to hang on to, somehow. Or was he losing his mind?

'So?' Greta asked.

'So, nothing. I'll try them again tomorrow. I'd better get back to that biography.'

'Are you going to read late? Want some coffee?'

Ed hesitated between coffee and a drink. He preferred coffee. Or maybe both. Or would coffee keep him awake tonight? 'Do you want coffee?'

Greta usually wanted coffee. She liked it strong, and it almost never interfered with her sleep. It was miraculous, or her nerves were. 'I do, because I am going to sew a little bit.'

'Fine. Coffee.' Ed smiled, sank into the sofa, and pulled the paperbound manuscript off the coffee-table on to his lap.

The biography was of John Phelps Henry, an obscure English sea-captain of the mid-eighteenth century who had become an optician in his forties, after quitting the sea. So far, halfway into the book, Ed was not enthusiastic about its publication. It was a recent idea of Bruthers, one of the chairmen of Cross and Dickinson and a Senior Editor more senior than Ed, that C. & D. ought to bring out a series of biographies of little-known people of the past. It reminded Ed of 'minor poets', who were minor, Ed thought, for the good reason that their talents were minor. Not even the prose of this biography was noteworthy, not even ex-Captain Henry's sex life was lively. Who on earth would buy it, Ed wondered. But he ploughed on dutifully. He wanted to be able to say to Bruthers, honestly, that he had read it.

Greta's coffee arrived.

Then he heard the cosy, intermittent hum of her sewing-machine from the room that had been Margaret's.

Ed continued to read, or at least his eyes moved over the interminable pages. A hundred and seventy-odd more to go. It would be ridiculous to go back to York Avenue and 61st Street tonight, he supposed. He was glad Greta hadn't mentioned it, hadn't said it might be a good idea, because then he would have gone. If Anon was serious about returning the dog, Anon could telephone.

The telephone rang – just before midnight – and Ed jumped with a happy premonition. This was going to be *something*, some bit of news – probably from the police, but maybe from Anon.

'Hello. Is this Mr Reynolds?'

'Yes.'

'This is Patrolman Duhamell, Clarence Duhamell. You came to the precinct house this morning.'

'Yes?' Ed gripped the telephone.

'I was in the room when you were speaking with Captain MacGregor. I –'

'You have some news?'

Greta had come to the hall door and was listening.

'No, I'm sorry I haven't. But I'd like to see you. If I may. The point is – I happen to know the men are very busy at the precinct house just now. There've been a lot of house robberies, whereas – I have the night patrol post starting tomorrow. I think it's a good idea to look in the neighbourhood.'

'Yes.' Ed was disappointed at the absence of news, but grateful for this interest in his problem.

'Could I come to see you tomorrow morning?' the young voice asked on a more definite note.

'Yes, of course. You've got the address?'

'Oh, yes. I took it down. Tomorrow morning around eleven?'

'Very good.'

'Who was that?' Greta asked.

'A policeman from the station house where I went today. He wants to come to see us tomorrow morning at eleven.'

'He's got some news?'

'No, he said he hadn't. Sounds as if he's coming on his own.' Ed shrugged. 'But it's something. At least they're making an effort.'

4

Patrolman Clarence Pope Duhamell was twenty-four years old, a graduate of Cornell University where he had majored in psychology, though with no definite idea of what he wanted to do with it when he left university. Military service had followed, and he had sat for two years in four camps in the United States as a Placement Counsellor for draftees. Then honourably discharged, and having escaped Vietnam much to the relief of his parents, Clarence had taken a job in the personnel department of a large New York bank which had some eighty branches throughout the city. Clarence after six months had found the work surprisingly dull. The Preferential Hiring Law of the Human Rights Commission forced him to recommend people of 'minority races' whatever their lack of qualifications, and he and the higher-up hiring officers had been blamed when accounts later got fouled up in the bank. It was good for a laugh, perhaps, and Clarence could still remember Bernie Alpert in the office saying: 'Don't take it so *personnally*, Clare, you're just out of the army and you're just obeying orders, no?' Thus the bank personnel job had been not only unsatisfying to Clarence, but it had seemed an impasse: he was not even permitted to choose the best, the right person, and that was presumably what he had been trained to do. Casting about with a completely open mind – Clarence tried to keep an open mind about everything – he had read about police recruitment. Into the office at the Merchant and Bankers Trust Company's personnel headquarters itself, in fact, had come some brochures in regard to joining the police force, which might have been dropped there by some hand of Providence, Clarence had felt, for bewildered people like himself. The variety of police work, the benefits, the pensions, the challenges had been set forth in a most attractive way. These brochures emphasized the service a young man could render his city and mankind, and stated that a policeman today was in a unique position to make contact with his fellow men, and to steer wavering individuals and families back into a happier path. To Clarence Duhamell had come the realization that a policeman need not be a dim-wit flatfoot, or a Mafia member, but might be a college graduate like himself, a man who knew his Krafft-Ebing and Freud as well as his Dostoievski and Proust. So Clarence had joined up with New York's finest.

Clarence had been brought up in Astoria, Long Island, where his parents still lived. On his mother's side, Clarence was Anglo-Irish, and on his father's remotely French and the rest German-English. After a year with the New York Police, Clarence was reasonably satisfied. He had been disillusioned in some ways: there had not been enough contact with individuals (delinquents or criminals of whatever age), and a stretch with a downtown East Side precinct house had brought such violent incidents that Clarence (with a walky-talky) had had to run for cover and telephone for the squad cars several times. It had been his orders from the precinct captain to keep himself in fit condition for action, and to summon assistance at once in all circumstances in which he thought a gun might be used. Well and good, but Clarence had finally asked to be transferred, not out of fear, but because he felt about as useful as a streetlamp on that patrol beat. The upper West Side precinct where he was now based was little better, but for different reasons: the fellows were not so friendly, nor were the superior officers. Clarence was no longer a rookie. At the same time he was still young and idealistic enough not to accept kickbacks, even the two-dollar-a-week kickbacks some stores offered cops in order not to be· fined for, or to correct, petty infractions. Some cops got a lot more, Clarence knew, some up to eight hundred or a thousand dollars a month from pay-offs. Clarence had always known pay-offs existed in the force, and he wasn't trying to reform anyone or to inform on anyone, but it became known that he didn't take kickbacks and so the cops who did – the majority – tended to avoid Clarence. He wasn't fraternity material. Clarence was consistently polite (no harm in that) but he was afraid to be chummy unless the other cop was chummy first. The cops in Riverside Drive precinct house were not a chummy lot. Clarence did not want to ask for another transfer. A man had to make his own opportunities. To stay in a rut was easy for everyone, Clarence thought, and the majority lived out their lives in a secure groove, not venturing anything. If he didn't like the force in another year, Clarence intended to quit.

Because he mistrusted routine — ruts could never reveal an individual's destiny — he had telephoned Edward Reynolds, who had seemed to him a decent man with an interesting problem which his precinct wasn't going to pay much attention to. Such people as Edward Reynolds didn't turn up every day. In fact the main reason for Clarence's boredom was the similarity of the crimes and the criminals, the petty house robberies, the car thefts, the handbag snatches, the complaints of shoplifting, the muggers who were never caught — and neither were most of the shoplifters caught, even if they were seen by a dozen people running down the street with their loot.

When Clarence had taken the personnel job at the bank, he had leased an apartment on East 19th Street, a walk-up on the fourth floor. This one-room, kitchenette and bath he still had, and the rent was cheap, a hundred and thirty-seven dollars per month. Clarence kept most of his clothes here, but for the past three or four months he had been spending most nights with his girl-friend Marylyn Coomes, who had an apartment on Macdougal Street in the Village. Marylyn was twenty-two, had dropped out of N.Y.U., and was a freelance secretary-typist, though she took a regular job often enough to augment her income considerably by claiming unemployment after she quit it. 'Soak the Government, they're loaded,' said Marylyn. She got away with murder. Marylyn plainly lied, and Clarence did not admire her ethics, and tried to put them out of his mind. Marylyn was very left, much more so than Clarence, and he considered himself left. Marylyn believed in destroying everything and starting everything afresh. Clarence thought that things could be improved, using the structures that already existed. This was the great difference between them. But far more important, Clarence was in love with Marylyn, and she had accepted him as her lover. Clarence was the only one, of that he was ninety-nine per cent sure, and he often thought the one per cent doubt was only his imagination. Clarence had had two affairs before, neither worth mentioning by comparison with the apricot-haired Marylyn. The other girls – one had been young, timid, acting as if she were ashamed of him, and the second had been a bit tough and casual, and Clarence had known he wasn't the only man in her life, which had been an impossible situation for him. He put both those affairs down to experience. Marylyn was different. He had quarrelled with Marylyn at least four times, and yet he had gone back to her after staying away perhaps five days. At least four times he had asked Marylyn to marry him, but she didn't want to marry just yet. 'Maybe never, who knows? Marriage is an out-moded institution, don't you know that?' She was hopeless with money. If she had twenty-eight dollars from a typing job, she would blow it the same day she got it – on a groovy coat from a thrift shop, a potted plant, or a couple of books. She seemed to pay her rent all right. Her money was her money, and Clarence didn't mind how she spent it, but once he had seen a couple of dollar bills actually *falling* out of her raincoat pocket as she went down the stairs in front of him. She didn't like blind-folds. Now he slept more often at Marylyn's apartment than on East 19th Street. This was not kosher by Police Department rules, Clarence supposed, but on the rare occasions when he might be summoned by an emergency call, he had taken the trouble to sleep in his own apartment. The emergency calls had never come, but one never knew.

On the Sunday morning that Clarence was supposed to call on Edward Reynolds, he awakened in Marylyn's bed on Mac-dougal Street. He had told her about his appointment with the man whose dog had been stolen. Clarence made a coffee and orange juice from a frozen tin, and brought it on a tray to Marylyn who was still in bed.

'Working on Sunday,' Marylyn said in a sleep-husky voice, and yawned with a lazy hand over her mouth. Her long red-dish-blonde hair was all over the pillow like a halo. She had a few freckles on her nose.

'Not working, darling. No one's ordering me to see Mr

Reynolds.' As Clarence adjusted the tray so it wouldn't tip on the bed, he caught a delicious hint of her perfume, of the warmth of the sheets that he had left a few minutes ago, and he would happily have plunged back into bed, and it even crossed his mind to do so, after ringing Mr Reynolds and asking if he could come at noon instead of eleven. However, best to start off on the right foot. 'I'll be back before one, I'm sure.'

'You're free this afternoon – and tonight?'

Clarence hesitated, briefly. 'I'm on tonight at eight. New shift.' The shifts changed every three weeks. Clarence disliked the 8 p.m. to 4 a.m. shift, because it kept him from seeing Marylyn in the evenings. It was the third time he had had such a shift. Clarence sipped his coffee. Marylyn had given a slight groan at his news. She wasn't fully awake yet. Clarence glanced at his wrist-watch, then at the straight chair in front of Marylyn's dressing-table, half expecting to see his trousers and jacket there, but he had hung them up last evening, and over the chair-back now was a black bra, and on the seat of the chair a public library book open and face down. Marylyn was not very neat. But it could be worse, Clarence thought, she could be sharing the apartment with another girl, and then things would have been hell.

Clarence took a shower in the small bathroom, shaved with the razor he kept there, and dressed in his ordinary clothes – a dark-blue suit, white shirt, a discreet tie, oxblood shoes of which he was especially fond and which he now wiped vigorously with a rag he found under the kitchen sink. Then Clarence combed his hair in Marylyn's bathroom mirror. He had blue eyes that were a little pale. He kept his light-brown hair as unshort as possible, though the force was surprisingly lenient about that. His upper lip was almost as full as his lower – a pleasant, tolerant mouth, he liked to think. Seldom grim, anyway.

'Want me to buy something for lunch, or want to go out?' Clarence seated himself, gently, on the edge of the bed.

Marylyn had put the tray aside, on Clarence's side of the bed, and had turned over face down. She liked to lie in bed a half-hour or so after her coffee – thinking, she said. 'I told you I had that chicken,' Marylyn mumbled into the pillow. 'Come back and come to bed and then I'll cook it.'

His heart gave a leap and he smiled. He stretched out beside her, kissed the side of her head, but was careful not to stay long enough to wrinkle his shirt front. 'Bye, darling.'

He arrived at the Reynolds's apartment house at one minute to eleven, and asked the doorman to ring up Mr Edward Reynolds, who was expecting him – Clarence Duhamell. After an affirmative word from the doorman with the telephone, Clarence took an elevator to the eighth floor.

Mr Reynolds had the door open for him, and looked surprised to see him in civilian clothes.

'Good morning. Clarence Duhamell,' Clarence said.

'Morning. Come in.'

Clarence walked into a large living-room where there was a piano, paintings on the wall, and lots of books. Clarence at first did not notice the woman sitting in a corner of the big sofa.

'My wife, Greta,' Mr Reynolds said.

'How do you do?' said Clarence.

'How do you do?' She had a slight accent.

'Won't you sit down? Anywhere you like,' Mr Reynolds said casually. He was wearing a dark-blue sportshirt and unpressed flannel trousers.

Clarence sat down on a straight chair which had arms. 'I'm not sure I can help with your problem,' Clarence began, 'but I'd like to try. I heard you say at the precinct house that you had four letters.'

'Yes. I left them at your precinct house. And evidently the writer of the letters has our dog.'

'Just how was the dog stolen?'

Ed explained. 'I didn't hear any noise, any barking. It was pretty dark. But I can't imagine how anyone got hold of the dog.'

'A French poodle,' Clarence said.

'Black. About so high.' Mr Reynolds held out a hand less than two feet from the floor, palm down. 'Her name's Lisa. Not the kind to go off with strangers. She's four years old.'

Clarence took this in carefully. Mr Reynolds was pessimistic about him, Clarence sensed. Clarence felt that Mr Reynolds was a rather sad man, and he wondered why? He had dark eyes, a firm mouth that had the capacity for smiling, for laughter, but the mouth was sad now. He would be a reasonable and patient man, Clarence thought. 'And you paid the thousand dollars.' Clarence had overheard it in the Desk Officer's room.

'Yes. Obviously a mistake. I got a letter asking for it, you see. The dog was to be returned an hour later after the money was collected – on York Avenue and Sixty-first Street. – Would you like a cup of coffee ?'

Mrs Reynolds got up. 'I'll heat the coffee. It's quite fresh, because we got up late,' she said to Clarence with a smile.

'Thank you,' said Clarence. 'Have you got any enemies – someone you might suspect, Mr Reynolds ?'

Mr Reynolds laughed. 'Maybe enemies – non-friends – but not like this. This fellow's cracked, I think. You saw the letters ?'

'I'm sorry, I didn't.' Clarence felt at once stupid and at a disadvantage. He should have asked to see the precinct's photostats. Clarence had been shy about asking to see them, and now he reproached himself. 'I can look at the photostats tonight. I go on duty at eight tonight. My shift just changed.'

Mr Reynolds was silent.

'Is there any person in the neighbourhood you've noticed,' Clarence asked, 'watching you ?'

'No. Sorry. I've tried to think.'

Mr Reynolds had a large head with thick, straight black hair that had a few fine lines of grey in it. It was coarse, unruly hair that did not want to lie down, though there was a side parting in it. His nose was strong and straight, not handsome, though his dark eyes and his mouth were handsome, in Clarence's opinion. He made Clarence think of a Roman general – maybe Mark Antony.

Mrs Reynolds came in with a tray of coffee and Danish pastry. Her accent was German, Clarence thought. She looked Jewish, or partly Jewish.

'I intend to keep an eye out for people in this neighbourhood,' Clarence said. 'It must be someone in this neighbourhood. May I ask what time you go to work and come home, Mr Reynolds ?'

'Oh – I take off just before nine and come home around

40

six, six-fifteen. You know, I'd like this cleared up quickly, if possible,' Ed said, squirming with sudden impatience. 'Our dog is the important thing, to hell with the thousand dollars. I don't know what conditions this moron is keeping the dog under, but it can't go on for ever.' He glanced at Greta, who was making a silent 'Sh-h' to calm him down.

'I understand.' Clarence tried to think what to do, what to say next. He was afraid he had not made the best impression, not the excellent impression he had wished to make.

'I hope the police are checking to see if any anonymous letter-writers live in this neighbourhood. Seems to me that's the obvious thing to do.' Ed sipped his coffee.

'I'm sure they are. I'll call up Centre Street and see what I can find out.'

'More coffee, Mr Duhamell?' asked Mrs Reynolds, pronouncing his name as if she knew how to spell it.

'No, thank you. Have you a picture of the dog?'

'Oh, lots,' said Ed.

Greta went to a tall bookcase and out of nowhere, it seemed, produced a photograph in a white cardboard folder.

It was a colour photograph of a black poodle sitting beside a table-leg, the dog's eyes blue-white from the camera's flash.

'Poodles look all alike to people who don't know them,' said Greta Reynolds. 'But I would know Lisa from two blocks away – as far as I could see her!' She laughed.

She had a warm laugh, a friendly smile.

Clarence stood up and handed the photograph back. 'Thank you. I'll also prod the fellows at the precinct house. The trouble is – we're swamped with routine things now, like the robberies by junkies –'

'Ah, the junkies,' said Ed with a sigh.

'Thank you very much for seeing me,' Clarence said.

'We thank *you*,' Ed said, getting up. 'Really, we hadn't expected any personal attention. Apropos, what about a private detective? Or am I being naïve? Could a private detective do anything more than the police?' Mr Reynolds smiled his twisted, discouraged smile.

'I doubt it. We've got the files on such letter-writers, after all. The important thing is to work on it,' Clarence said.

They saw him to the door.

'I'll be in touch as soon as I know anything,' Clarence said.

It was chilly, and Clarence wished he had brought his overcoat from Marylyn's. He walked slowly towards Broadway, looking on both sides of the street for loiterers or anyone who seemed to be watching the Reynolds's building. Clarence didn't like the Riverside Drive area, because the big apartment buildings looked gloomy even in daytime. No shops anywhere until Broadway, no colour, just big concrete blocks of apartments that looked as if they'd been standing for eighty years or more. Most of the people also seemed old, and Jewish or foreign, and somehow sad and discouraged. However, the Reynolds were different, and their apartment certainly wasn't a bourgeois museum. There were modern paintings on the walls, interesting-looking books, and a piano that looked as if it were played – sheet music on it as well as Chopin and Brahms books. Clarence walked up one block on Broadway, then turned west, shoving his hands into his trouser pockets against the wind that came suddenly from the Hudson River. He wanted to see where Mr Reynolds had lost his dog Lisa.

He skipped down the stone steps at 106th Street, past the statue of Franz Sigel on horseback – a Civil War soldier, Clarence recalled, a helper of the North – and crossed the Drive. Clarence walked into the park, turned north, and blew on his hands. There were clumps of bushes, small trees that would have given shelter to someone hiding. It was almost noon. Should he go up to the precinct house and ask about those letters now?

No, don't go, he told himself. At the same time, he was walking uptown on the west side of the Drive now, still keeping his eye out for the possible letter-writer, a man who'd be alone probably, looking furtive, suspicious of everyone. Or would he be cocky? Don't go into the precinct house, he thought, because tough-boy Santini might be on. Asking for the letters might irritate him. On the other hand why should he care if he irritated Santini?

Clarence made for the precinct house.

An elderly black cop whose name was Sam or Sims or Simmy, Clarence wasn't sure, was sitting on a camp stool inside the door, reading a comic book. 'Well, well. Morning, Mr Clarence.'

'Morning to you,' Clarence said, smiling. He went into the first office on the left.

It was not Santini at the desk — Santini could be in the next room where the files were — but a lieutenant named Boulton, a rather friendly fellow.

'Well, well,' said Boulton, in the same tone as Sam.

'Good morning, sir. I'm not on till eight tonight, but I wonder if those letters — the anonymous letters addressed to Reynolds — Could I have a look at the photostats? It's the man whose dog was kidnapped.'

'Reynolds,' said Boulton, gazing at a wire drawer heavy with clipped pages on his desk. He pulled the wire thing towards him. 'Jesus, if anything — Yesterday, yes. Stuff ought to be filed. What we need is a girl around here.'

Clarence laughed a little. The letters certainly weren't in that wire drawer.

'Reynolds. Yes, I recall.' He reached for a stack of papers on his desk, picked it up, then said, 'Why do you want them?'

'I was interested. I heard the man's story when he came in yesterday. His dog's still missing, so I thought it wouldn't hurt if I saw the letters — or the photostats.'

The lieutenant flipped through the miscellaneous papers, and pulled out some clipped-together photostatted sheets. Just then, the telephone rang, and Boulton flopped into his chair and reached for it.

There were four letters, all dated by another hand, possibly Mr Reynolds's, and they were in chronological order. The first had a September date and said:

DEAR SNOB,
   I DONT LIKE SMUG PEOPLE. WHO DOES? I SUPPOSE YOU CON-
SIDER YOURSELF A SUCCESS? WATCH OUT. THE AX CAN FALL.
LIFE IS NOT ALL SMOOTH GROVES WITH LITTLE COGS IN THEM
LIKE YOU. I HAPPEN TO BE A FAR MORE INTERESTING AND
IMPORTANT PERSON THAN YOU ARE. ONE DAY WE MAY MEET —
UNPLEASANTLY.
                                          ANON

The letter must have been a nasty thing to receive, Clarence thought, and shifted on his feet before he read the next one, dated a few days later. Lieutenant Boulton was still on the phone.

WELL SIR,

STILL AT IT? YOU ARE A LITTLE MACHINE. YOU THINK THE MAJORITY IS WITH YOU. NOT SO! SINCE WHEN ARE YOU SO *RIGHT*? JUST BECAUSE YOU HAVE A JOB AND A WIFE AND A SNOB DOG LIKE YOURSELF? IT NEED NOT GO ON FOREVER TILL YOU CREEP INTO YOUR GRAVE. THINK AGAIN AND THINK CAREFULLY.

ANON

He progressed to the next two letters, the fourth about the dog Lisa. It was quite shocking to Clarence, having met the decent Mr and Mrs Reynolds. Boulton was off the phone now.

'Thank you, sir.' Clarence handed the folder back. 'See you tonight, sir.'

'Not me. Not tonight,' replied the lieutenant with a smile, as if he had a big date and wouldn't dream of working this evening.

Clarence walked back along Riverside Drive, watching for people – men – who might be staring at him a little too long. Clarence felt happy and excited. He wanted to ring up his mother. That would please her. Except that just now, at a quarter to one, she and his father were probably sitting down to Sunday dinner, maybe with a couple of neighbours as guests.

What about the little man in the dark grey overcoat and old shoes, shambling along, hugging the side of a building? The man didn't look at him. Clarence had a glimpse of a stubble of beard on his face. No, this man was too fallen apart, Clarence thought. The poison-pen letter-writer couldn't spell, but there was some demonic organization in him, he could get an address right (the envelopes had been photostatted beneath each letter), his bitterness seemed to have a certain drive. What kind of job would he have, if any? A lot of kooky characters were on relief, or over sixty-five and just making it on Social Security. Was this one over sixty-five? And what about the dog Lisa? That was the important thing, as Mr Reynolds had said.

Clarence impulsively hailed a taxi. He wasn't in a mood to take the subway. Marylyn would still be in bed, probably reading the Sunday *Times* which he had bought late last night. At 8th Street, Clarence said, 'Can you let me out here?'

He went into the drugstore at 8th and Sixth Avenue and telephoned his parents in Astoria.

'So how's it going, Clare?' asked his father. 'Are you okay?'

'Everything's okay. I just wanted to say hello.'

Clarence spoke also with his mother, who made sure there was not a bullet through an arm or a leg, then she dashed off to turn something off on the stove. When was he coming out to see them? It had been so long since he'd been out.

It had been about three weeks. 'I dunno. Soon, Mother.' He started to say he was on night shift again, but his mother would worry about that.

'Is your girl-friend taking *all* your time, Clary? Bring her out!'

The usual conversation, but Clarence felt better after he had hung up. His parents hadn't yet met Marylyn. Clarence, unable to repress a desire to speak of her, had deliberately repressed his enthusiasm about her, but it hadn't escaped his father, who was now asking when were they going to meet his betrothed and all that. His father liked to use archaic expressions.

At a delicatessen on Sixth Avenue, Clarence bought frozen strawberries and a can of cranberry sauce for the chicken, and also bread which Marylyn was always out of, mainly because Clarence ate a lot of bread. Clarence had the two keys to Marylyn's house, one for the front door, one for her apartment door. Having let himself in, he knocked on her apartment door.

'Clare? – Come in.'

Marylyn was in bed with the papers, looking beautiful, though she hadn't even combed her hair. 'How was it?'

Clarence knelt by the bed, the delicatessen bag on the floor. 'Interesting,' he mumbled. His face was buried in the warm sheets over her bosom. He inhaled deeply. 'Very interesting. It's important.'

'Why?' She mussed his hair with her fingers, pushing his

head away. 'Good God, I never thought I'd get mixed up with fuzz. Do you really take all this stuff seriously?'

He sat back on the floor, watched her as she got out of bed and crossed the room to the bathroom. Her words were a shock, even though he knew she was kidding. She was of a different world, and she didn't understand a thing, Clarence thought, about his life. In a curious way, Marylyn didn't even believe in law and order. 'I do!' he said to the closed door. He crossed his feet and got up nimbly from the floor. 'They're such nice people, the Reynolds.' He smiled, at himself, and took off his jacket and tie. In bed, he and Marylyn understood each other very well. Not even any words needed.

5

At the moment when Clarence was slipping naked into bed with Marylyn on Macdougal Street, Kenneth Rowajinski on West End Avenue and 103rd Street was putting ball-point pen to paper to write a second ransom note. He was not sure he would send it. He wrote many letters that he didn't send to people. Simply writing the letters gave him pleasure. After writing 'NEW YORK' at the top of the page, he rested his elbow, pen aloft, and gazed into space, vaguely smiling.

He was a short man of fifty-one, chunky but in good health. He limped, however, on his right foot. Four years ago the drum of a cement-mixer had fallen on his instep, breaking the metatarsals, and further complications had caused the amputation of his great toe and the toe next to it. For this reason Kenneth got two hundred and sixty dollars per month: he had been a semi-skilled labourer in construction work, good at pipe-laying, a good foreman in the sense that some men are good army sergeants though they may never rise higher. Kenneth had been lucky in claiming, via his lawyer, a skilled status with promise of immediate advancement when the accident had happened, so his compensation had been generous. But now Kenneth could never again (he thought with a kind of pride, self-pity and curious glory) jump about spryly on scaffoldings as he had once done, and for this he had been rightly recompensed.

His face and head were round, his cheeks inclined to be ruddy, his nose bulbous and crude. Either his expression was jolly, or it was tense and suspicious, full of menace, and there was little between. When he relaxed as in sleep, even, his face was vaguely smiling. And his expression could vary in a trice — smiling, for instance, as he mused over a letter he was composing, scowling and hostile if there came a knock on his door for any reason, or even if he heard a footfall beyond his door. Kenneth lived in a semi-basement, corner apartment that consisted of one huge room and an absurdly small W.C. behind a door in one corner. There was a basin with a mirror above it, but there was no tub, and Kenneth washed himself, at least twice a week, standing nude on newspapers in front of the basin. The room, because never any sunlight came in, required electric light at all times, but Kenneth didn't mind that. The windows were half-windows that started four feet up the wall and opened (but Kenneth never opened them) on West End Avenue. He could often see people's legs, up to the hips, walking by, and occasionally a heel made a clink or a scrape on a metal grille in the sidewalk there. An ironing-board always stood ready in a front corner of the room, with a shabby standing lamp beside it. Newspapers, folded and open, half-read, lay singly or in little stacks here and there on the floor, in corners, beside the limp bed which Kenneth sometimes made and more often didn't. The kitchen consisted of a smallish stove with two burners and an oven against the wall and to the left of where Kenneth now sat at his table. Similarly, his closet was not enclosed, but was a rod suspended on two wires from a shelf against the wall. Kenneth had few clothes, however, three pairs of trousers, two jackets, an overcoat and a raincoat, and four pairs of shoes – one pair so old he knew he would never put them on again. He had a transistor, but it had become broken months ago, and he had never bothered getting it repaired. Just outside his door was a corridor that led to some steps that went straight up to the street door, and also there were steps to the right leading to the level of his landlady's ground-floor apartment. The garbage bins and ashcans were left in Kenneth's corridor, which was why he sometimes heard the footsteps of his landlady's giant idiot of a son, who wrestled them forward and up the front steps. Kenneth suspected that the oafish son came into the corridor to spy on him through his keyhole, so for this reason Kenneth used a flap of tin (he'd found just the thing in a gutter) eight inches long and two inches wide. The top of this flap was nailed into the door above the lock, and the bottom part he kept slid behind the bolt that closed his door below the keyhole. This way, even if the son (whose name was Orrin) pushed the flap with something through the keyhole, the flap could not move sideways and permit a view of the room – because it was nailed with two nails at the top and therefore did not swivel. Also, from the inside, by pulling the flexible tin out of the bolt, Kenneth could lock his door from the inside, once he had come in.

Kenneth was the middle offspring of three children of a Polish immigrant who had come to America just before the First World War and married a German girl. Kenneth's sister Anna lived in Pennsylvania, and they almost never wrote to each other. His younger brother Paul now lived in California, and Kenneth had nothing to do with him. This brother was a bit of a snob, had made a little money, had two children nearly grown, and he had refused to lend (much less give) Kenneth any money on two occasions, when Kenneth had needed it, because work was slow. Kenneth had finally written Paul a blistering letter, after which there'd been not a word from Paul. Good riddance.

There were times when Kenneth considered himself lucky to be, in a sense, independent of mankind, of the New York populace, because of his two hundred and sixty dollars per month income. At other moments, he felt sorry for himself, alone, with a limp, living in a not very nice place. Then sometimes he would love his big room and his free existence all over again. These happy moments were usually after a good meal of *Knackwurst* and *Sauerkraut*. Then Kenneth would lean back in his straight chair, pat his belly, and smile up at his ceiling with the naked lightbulb hanging from it.

DEAR SIR:

YOUR DOG IS ALIVE AND WELL BUT I HAVE DECIDED THE SITUATION WARRENTS ANOTHER $1,000 (THOUSAND DOLLARS) WHICH I FEEL SURE A MAN IN YOUR POSITION CAN AFFORD.

Kenneth wanted to say that he himself needed another thousand dollars, but he could not put this in an elegant enough way, and he did not want to sound like a beggar.

THEREFORE WILL YOU AGAIN AT II P.M. TUESDAY EVENING LEAVE A THOUSAND DOLLARS IN TEN-DOLLAR BILLS AS BEFORE BETWEEN SAME PIKES IN THE FENCE ON YORK AVENUE. THIS

TIME I GUARANTEE THE DOG WILL BE TIED TO SAME PIKE AN
HOUR LATER, SEIZE THE MOMENT!

ANON

Perfect, Kenneth thought. No need to copy it over. He stood
up and went to reward himself with a beer from the small
refrigerator by the stove, but there was only half a small bottle
left, and that flat. Six or more empties stood on the floor. He'd
have to buy more. Well, he could certainly afford to! Kenneth with the bottle of stale beer in his hand turned and smiled
at his unmade bed. Between the sheets, at the foot of the bed,
was something like nine hundred and fifty dollars wrapped in
a dishtowel with a rubber band around it. Kenneth also had a
savings account with a few hundred in it, but had no intention
of making unusual deposits just now.

Edward Reynolds was good for another thousand, no doubt
about that. But Kenneth did not want the police crashing in
on him. Could he afford to risk it? He knew Reynolds had
been to the police, because he had trailed Reynolds from his
apartment house on Saturday morning. Kenneth congratulated
himself that he had guessed more or less when Reynolds would
actually go to the police – Saturday morning – though he had
also spied the previous morning and evening.

What a useless thing! The dog, the snob dog, had been
dead since Wednesday night. Crouching with a rock in his
hand, Kenneth had hit her fair and square on top of the head
as she had come galloping into the bushes there. A most wonderful piece of luck, Kenneth thought, not to mention that it
had been a nice piece of skill on his part to konk a moving
dog and knock her out at the first blow and without even a
yip from her. Or had there been a yip, camouflaged perhaps
by a chorus of carhorns just then, by a surge of traffic on the
Drive? At any rate, Kenneth had gathered the dog up in his
arms and gone on, northward, towards the next clump of
bushes where he had delivered a second blow that surely finished the bitch off. Then, in the darkness, Kenneth had made
his way up to the sidewalk, and by a somewhat devious route
to the corner house where he lived. He had removed in the
Park the dog's collar and stuffed it into his pocket, and he had
wanted to dump the dog into some rubbish container, but the

containers were wire and one could see through them. Kenneth had taken the animal to his room. Only one or two people had glanced at it in his arms – Kenneth had kept away from streetlamps, of course – and those people hadn't said anything, even though the dog's head had been dripping a little blood. At home, Kenneth had wrapped the dog in one of his bed-sheets, the oldest one he had. Then he had walked with this nearly twenty blocks uptown to the Spic district and got rid of it in a rubbish basket – a wire one, but it didn't matter with the dog in a sheet and in that neighbourhood, littered with newspapers and garbage, and those people tossed newborn babies into rubbish baskets, so who was going to make a fuss about a dog?

Then Kenneth remembered feeling the dog's collar in his pocket as he walked home, and how he had not wanted to look at it, to read it – though he had, as he killed the dog, imagined examining this complicated collar at home and at leisure. It had dangling tags, a name plate, a couple of metal rings, studs, and the yellow leather was stiff and good. Kenneth had whipped it out of his pocket and flung it down a drain in a gutter.

He had intended to ask a ransom of Reynolds, and now he had it. He had annoyed Reynolds, causing him to put an ad in the paper. He had deflated the pompous Edward Reynolds who wore swanky dark-blue overcoats and expensive shoes and sometimes gloves when it wasn't particularly cold. And he had put an end to the dog who wore a plaid raincoat in bad weather and a red turtleneck sweater when it was cold.

Kenneth liked to take walks, even aimless walks. His foot did not hurt when he walked, and his limp was caused mainly by the absence of toes there, but Kenneth occasionally exaggerated the limp, he even admitted to himself, when he could use a little extra consideration from people, or when he badly wanted a seat on a bus or a subway. Not that anyone had ever got up and given him a seat, but in case he was competing with someone for an empty seat, a limp helped. Kenneth liked his walks, because his mind raced madly, inspired by the ever-changing objects that his eyes fell upon – a baby carriage, a policeman, a couple of overdressed women glimpsed briefly in a taxi, a fat woman lugging home still more to eat in huge grocery bags, and the smug people into whose living-room windows he could see – men in shirt-sleeves watching television, a wife coming in with a tray of beers, warm yellow lights falling on bookshelves and framed pictures. Snobs. Crooks, too, otherwise how'd they get so rich, how'd they get a woman to live with them and serve them? Kenneth had little use for women, and believed they gravitated only towards men with money to buy them and to spend on them. He was convinced women had no sexual drive at all, or not enough to warrant mentioning, and that they used their physical charms merely to lure men towards them.

Besides Edward Reynolds, there were a couple of other people whom Kenneth watched now, one a woman with a *white* poodle, as it happened, smaller than the Reynolds's dog, and she wore high-heeled shoes and had dyed black hair as frizzled as her dog's, and she met, now and then, a tall, flashily dressed man who was probably her boy-friend-unbeknownst-to-her-husband on a corner of Broadway and 105th Street, then they went either to a bar on Broadway or back to the woman's house, where they stayed for about an hour. Another person he watched was a well-dressed but sad-looking adolescent boy who plodded every morning at 8.15 towards the 103rd Street subway. He looked somehow vulnerable. It had crossed Kenneth's mind to kidnap the white poodle of the woman (once in a while she took it to Riverside Park and let it off the leash) and he might have done this, except for one small thing: one morning as Reynolds (whose name Kenneth hadn't known then) came out of his building, he had opened a letter and dropped the envelope into a trash basket at Broadway and 106th. Kenneth had cautiously followed, and had taken the envelope out of the basket. Thus he had learned Reynolds's name. This enabled Kenneth to write letters to Reynolds. Letters gave Kenneth pleasure, because he knew he got his message across, and knew he upset people. He was also aware that the letters were dangerous for him, but Kenneth's attitude was that the pleasure that letters gave him made them worth it. He had written thirty or forty letters, he supposed, to a dozen people. Some of these people he had watched afterwards, as they came out of their apartment houses, and it amused Kenneth to see their frightened expressions as they looked around on the street, sometimes looking right at him. He got some names by seeing them on parcels being delivered to apartment buildings. He assumed the people were well-to-do, which meant any kind of threat could scare them.

Now, Kenneth knew that since Reynolds had spoken to the police at the local precinct house, it was dangerous for him to cruise in that neighbourhood, yet Kenneth knew that he would take walks, just around there. Would they put any extra police on to watch out for 'suspicious characters'? Kenneth doubted that. The police had other jobs to do – yes, indeed, like sitting on their asses in the hamburger shop on Broadway, guns, notebooks, nightsticks and asses draped on either side of the stools as they slurped coffee and gobbled banana pie *à la mode*.

Sunday evening, Kenneth strolled westward towards Riverside Drive around 8 p.m., the time when Reynolds or his wife had used to air Lisa. Maybe tonight he'd see Reynolds and wife, walking along the Drive in a melancholic way, without their Lisa. On either side of him, on 106th Street, the yellow squares of light in people's windows were coming on. Castles, fortresses of snobs. You couldn't get past their doormen to get at them, a thief couldn't, or someone who might want to murder them. However, *some* thieves did. Kenneth smiled to himself, his pink lips curling up at the corners. Murder wasn't his dish. He liked more subtle means. Slow torture.

There was a cop. The tall blondish fellow Kenneth had seen three or four times before. Kenneth deliberately did not look at him as they passed each other on the east side of the Drive, only six feet apart on the pavement. But Kenneth felt the cop's eyes on him. Kenneth much wanted to cross the Drive, to stroll down to 100th Street before making his way home, and there was no reason *not* to cross the Drive, in fact. Kenneth hesitated with one foot off the kerb, his good foot on it, and the light was with him, but he hesitated. He was at 108th Street now, and he looked to his left, down the Riverside Drive pavement, to see if the policeman was going on southward. The policeman had stopped and was looking back, at him, Kenneth thought. Kenneth turned and walked east into 108th Street.

Mustn't go straight home, Kenneth thought, in case the cop

decided to follow him. The street was rather dark. Kenneth concealed his limp as much as possible. He wanted to kill some time in a coffee-shop, or by buying beer and eggs in a delicatessen, but these places had lights, and if the cop did come in, he didn't want the cop to have a good look at him. He wished very much to know if the cop was following him or not.

Kenneth reached Broadway and turned downtown, walking on the east side of the street. At 105th Street, Kenneth stopped and casually looked behind him. There were at least eight people on the sidewalk, but no cop. Good. Kenneth decided to head for home. He had a sense of fleeing now, but also a sense of being in the clear. He let himself in the front door and slammed it, then limped to his own door and unlocked it.

He was safe.

Kenneth went to his table and hastily folded the page he had written to Reynolds. He put it in the top drawer of his chest of drawers under some articles of clothing. He looked at the unmade bed, thinking of the money. Relax, he told himself. Have a beer. But there wasn't any beer. Now he didn't dare go out again. Just do without, unfortunately. He set about making his dinner.

Open a can of beans. He had a specially good brand of beans a little more expensive than Heinz, and that was one small treat for tonight. Kenneth read the paper, which he had already looked at, while he ate. Politics scarcely interested him. International conferences, even wars, were like things going on thousands of miles away from him, not touching his life at all — any more than a stage production could touch a person's actual life. Sometimes a news item captured his attention, a woman mugged in a doorway on 95th Street, or a suicide found in a New York apartment, and he read every word of these things.

Kenneth had tidied up and was stripped to the waist, washing himself at his basin, when there came a knock at his door. Because of the running water, he hadn't heard any steps. Kenneth cursed, feeling extreme annoyance and slight fear. He buttoned his shirt again, but left it hanging out of his trousers.

'Who is it?' he called sharply to the door.

'Mrs Williams!' came the assertive voice, as if the name

itself were enough to gain admittance. It was his landlady.

Kenneth irritably unlocked his door and slid the bolt back.

Mrs Williams was tallish, stout, shapeless. Her hair was grey, her expression anxious and sour. Under her arched eye-sockets her pinkish eyes were always stretched wide, as if she had just been affronted. 'Are you in any trouble, Mr Rowajinski?' She had an abominable way of pronouncing his name.

'I am *not.*'

She came back at him: 'Because if you are, you're getting out, do you understand? I'm not so fond of you, you know, or of your twenty dollars a week. I'm not going to have any doubtful characters on *my* property.' And so forth.

Kenneth wondered what had happened.

At last she came to it. 'A *policeman* was just here asking me what your name was and what you did for a living.'

'A policeman?'

'He didn't say what it was about. I'm asking *you.*'

'How should I know? I haven't done anything.'

'You sure you haven't? Spying in people's windows or something like that?'

'Did you come here to insult me?' said Kenneth, drawing himself up a little. 'If you –'

'A policeman doesn't come asking questions unless there's a reason,' she interrupted him. 'I'm not having any creeps in my house, Mr Rowajinski, because I don't have to have them, there's too many decent people in the world. If that policeman comes again, I'm putting you out, you hear me?'

She'd have to give him some notice, Kenneth thought, but he was too taken aback to point this out. 'All right, Mrs Williams!' he said bitterly. He was holding his doorknob so fiercely his fingers had begun to hurt.

'I just want you to know.' She turned and went.

Kenneth closed the door firmly and relocked it. Well! At least the cop hadn't asked to see him, hadn't wanted to talk to him or search his room. Or was he coming back with a search warrant? This thought caused perspiration to break out on Kenneth's body. The rest of the evening was miserable for him. He took the folded letter from his top drawer and destroyed it. He kept listening for footsteps, even when he was in bed.

6

Clarence had been on the brink of asking to see the little man called Kenneth Rowajinski, but by that time it was nearly nine, and Clarence had not yet covered his beat once on foot, and he was to be rejoined by his partner for that night, a fellow named Cobb. Cops went in pairs after nightfall. MacGregor had told him and Cobb at the briefing to pay special attention to 105th Street tonight, because a woman had reported a strange man today in her apartment building, a man who had entered in some way other than by passing the doorman, and maybe he was in hiding there still, or maybe he had been casing the place for a robbery. Since 8 p.m. when he had gone on duty, however, Clarence had had eyes only for possible poison-pen letter-writers—that was to say odd- or furtive-looking people, and parting from Cobb for a few minutes, he had followed a stooped man, who did look very furtive, to a house on West 95th Street.

This man was an Italian named John Vanetti, aged sixty or more, who didn't speak English very well, and seemed to have a speech impediment besides. He had been terrified by Clarence's following him, of his insistence on coming into his apartment, although Clarence had been as polite and gentle as anyone could possibly have been.

'I'm going to ask you to print something for me.'

'What? What?' The Italian had been shaking.

'Write. Please. Just print. "Dear Sir. Will you meet me at York Avenue ..."' It had been difficult, agonizing.

The old fellow was a shoe repairman and worked in a shop on Broadway. Of this Clarence was sure. There were some cobbler's tools in his crummy little one-room place. The man could hardly print at all, and kept making letters in script, so that Clarence was positive he was not 'Anon'. Clarence had apologized and left. Astounding, Clarence thought, that old guys like that still existed in New York. He had thought they had died out in his childhood.

After that, back with Cobb, Clarence had spotted the cripple, and at the sight of him Clarence felt that he had seen him before in the neighbourhood. This was a quicker, brighter type than the Italian, with a slight limp and something about him made the word 'eccentric' come to mind. That was the type he was after. Clarence had followed him and spoken to his landlady. But by then it was nearly nine, and Clarence had to make his hourly call to the precinct house on the hour to-night, so he had rejoined Cobb. But he knew the name now, Rowajinski, and where he lived, and he intended to come back tomorrow.

To Clarence and Cobb, 105th Street looked as usual. They stopped to ask the doorman at the apartment house if all was well. The doorman seemed glad to see them. All was well, he said, as far as he knew.

Just after 10 p.m., Clarence again parted from Cobb and went to Mr Reynolds's building. He asked the doorman to ring the Reynolds apartment. Mr Reynolds answered.

'This is Patrolman Duhamell. I wondered if you've had any messages. Any news.'

'No, we haven't. And you?'

'Nothing. No clues from the letters, sir. I'll check with you again tomorrow.' Clarence had rung Centre Street, but they said they had no letters in a similar handwriting.

'Thanks. Thanks very much.'

Clarence was touched by the disappointment in Mr Reynolds's voice.

The next afternoon, Monday, around 4 p.m., Clarence went to the house of Kenneth Rowajinski. He was in civilian clothes. The landlady answered, and Clarence was in luck: she said Mr Rowajinski was in. She showed him through a door and then down some steps into a hall. Then she recognized him from yesterday.

'You're the *policeman*!' she said, and seemed to be horrified.

'Yes.' Clarence smiled. 'I spoke with you yesterday.' It was astonishing the difference a uniform made. People seemed to think cops weren't human, or didn't own any ordinary clothing.

'Tell me,' she whispered, 'has this man done anything wrong? Because if he has –'

'No. I just want to speak with him.'

Clarence could see that she was dying to ask about what, but she led him to the pale-green door.

'It's here.' She knocked. 'Mr Rowajinski?'

Kenneth opened the door, after sliding some bolts. 'What is it?' He jumped back a little at the sight of Clarence.

'Patrolman Duhamell,' Clarence said, and produced his billfold with his police card visible. 'Can I talk to you for a few minutes?'

Mrs Williams gave a jerky nod at Rowajinski, as if to say now you're going to get it. Clarence went into the man's apartment. Mrs Williams was still standing there when Rowajinski closed the door. He bolted it, and slid some kind of metal piece back through the bolt. It was a depressing, untidy room, quite big but ugly with grime and unfinished paint efforts. There was no sign of a dog.

'What is it?' asked Rowajinski.

Clarence looked at him directly and pleasantly. 'We're looking for someone – in this neighbourhood – who has kidnapped a dog. Naturally we have to talk to a lot of people.' Clarence hesitated, startled a little by the man's eyes that had grown suddenly sharp, but his dark pink lips were almost smiling. 'Do you mind printing something for me? Just a few words?'

Rowajinski shrugged, fidgeted, half turned away, and turned back. 'Why should I?'

Clarence didn't know how he meant that. But he decided to assume it was an affirmative, so he pulled a notebook from his inside pocket and took it to the table, where lay a soiled plate, a fork, pens, pencils, a couple of newspapers. The man whisked the dirty plate away.

He accepted the ball-point pen Clarence handed him, and sat down.

'Please print,' Clarence said, 'in block letters, "Dear Sir. Will you meet me at York Avenue."'

Kenneth had every intention of disguising his printing and started out with a D that swept back at top and bottom, followed by a small e, but by the time he got to 'meet me at' he was printing the way he usually did, almost, and his heart was racing. It was curiously pleasant, as a sensation, and at the same time terrifying. He had been discovered, found out. No doubt about that. After 'AVENUE' he handed the paper to the young man, trembling. He saw the recognition in the blue eyes.

'Mr Rowolowski —'

'Mr Rowajinski — uh — I'll have to ask you some more questions.' Clarence pulled a straight chair near the table and sat down. 'Your writing has a similarity to the letters at the station house. You wrote, didn't you, to a Mr Edward Reynolds, who lives at a Hundred and sixth Street?'

Kenneth was trembling slightly. There was no way out now. 'I did,' he replied, though not in a tone of total surrender.

'And you have Mr Reynolds's dog?' Clarence asked on a gentler note. 'Mr Reynolds is mainly interested in getting his dog back.'

Kenneth smiled slightly, stalling for time. Tell a story, he thought, prolong it. An idea was coming to him, out of the blue. 'The dog is with my sister. In Long Island. The dog is all right.' At the same time, Kenneth realized it was an awful admittance: he had just admitted kidnapping the dog. The same as admitting he had pocketed a thousand dollars.

'I suggest you get that dog here as quickly as possible,' Clarence stood up, smiling.

The cop looked triumphant, Kenneth thought. Kenneth rubbed his chin.

'Will you give me your sister's address, Mr — Rowajinski? I can pick up the dog right away.'

'No,' said Kenneth quickly.

'What do you mean "no"?' Clarence frowned. 'I want that dog today and no nonsense about it! What's your sister's address?'

'Queens.'

'Has she got a phone?'

'No.'

'What's her name? Her married name? — Look, Mr So-and-so, I'm not going to fool around with this. I want the answers, you get me?' Clarence took a menacing step towards him, and could have shaken the hell out of him by his shirt-front so eager was he to get on with it, but he was afraid this wasn't quite the right moment, that he might gain more by a few minutes' patience. 'Let's have her name and address.'

'I would like another thousand dollars,' said Kenneth.

Clarence gave a laugh. 'Mr Rowalski or whatever, I'm going to turn this place upside-down and get her address — now — or you're going to the precinct house where you'll get worse treatment. So let's have it.'

Kenneth was still seated at the table, and now he folded his arms. He was braced for slaps, blows, whatever. 'You won't find her address in this house,' he said rather grandly. 'Also she knows if I do not receive another thousand dollars by tomorrow night, the dog is to be killed.'

Clarence laughed again. He put his hands on his hips and surveyed the room, turning. 'You can start by opening that chest of drawers or whatever it is,' said Clarence. 'Okay, start.' He gestured.

Kenneth got up. He had to. At that moment, no doubt because of their raised voices in the last seconds, footsteps sounded in the hall, the busy carpet-slipper-shuffling footsteps of the old bag Mrs Williams, also the clump of Orrin whom she had probably summoned. They were going to listen outside the door, damn them. Kenneth went to his low chest which had three long drawers in it.

'Empty your pockets first, would you?'

'Have you got a search warrant? I'd like to see it.'

'I'll go on that,' Clarence replied, pointing to the paper Kenneth had printed, which lay on the table.

As Kenneth moved towards it, Clarence leapt for it, folded it and pocketed it.

Clarence assisted the man in hauling things out of his pockets — some wadded bills, keyring, filthy handkerchief, a couple of grimy shopping lists. Clarence was interested only in the address of the sister, and was already imagining having to search New York census departments to get it. 'Haven't you got a wallet? An address book?'

'No.' Kenneth pulled out the third drawer. He hated that anyone saw and also touched his belongings.

Next the table. It had a drawer, but in it were mainly knives and forks and spoons, some stolen from Horn and Hardart, a can-opener, and in one corner Kenneth's Social Security card and papers pertaining to his disability money. The policeman copied his Social Security number.

Now the books. Kenneth had eight or ten paperbacks and a couple of books from the public library on the floor under the front window. Clarence flipped through them. He also looked under the bed, and pulled the bed out so he could see behind it. He looked in the toilet, and also on the kitchen shelf above Kenneth's hanging clothes, and in the pockets of all the clothes there.

'I suppose the address is in your head,' Clarence said, frustrated and angry now, because he hadn't found the money either.

'My sister has instructions,' said Kenneth, 'to kill the dog tomorrow night unless I have the thousand dollars by 11 p.m.'

'And you expect to get away with this? And get *more* money? You've written another letter to Mr Reynolds?'

'I was going to phone him,' Kenneth said boldly, 'at his house. If he wants his dog –' Kenneth's temper burst forth. 'The address of my sister *is* in my head and you'll never get it!'

Torture it out of the bastard, Clarence thought. He lit a cigarette. Haul him in, Clarence thought. Let a tough guy like Santini or Manzoni work him over. But how far would Santini or Manzoni bother going? One would have to whet their appetite somehow. Suppose they weren't interested? Suppose Rowajinski didn't crack? Could he himself crack Rowajinski? Here or at the precinct house? Would MacGregor let him, for instance? 'Who's bringing the dog over from Queens?'

'My – my sister. I'll meet her somewhere.'

'She has a car? Her husband?'

'She'll come with her husband in their car.'

What a fine family you have, Clarence wanted to say, but

was afraid of antagonizing the man any further. The important thing, as Mr Reynolds had said, was to get the dog back alive. But was he to believe this story? 'Your sister lives in an apartment?'

'A little house,' said Kenneth.

'Can you give me some kind of guarantee?'

'What kind?'

'That's for you to think of. Maybe I can speak with your sister on the telephone, make sure the dog's alive, that she'll bring it. Can I?'

'I told you my sister has no telephone. I don't want my sister involved!'

The guy was really cracked. For the first time since he had been questioning him, Clarence averted his eyes out of a curious fear. Insane people – well, they disturbed him. You never knew what they were going to do. This fact reminded him that he had better keep his eyes on Rowajinski. But Clarence, much as he wanted the distinction of having found his man by his own effort, realized with comfort that he wasn't alone. He'd ask Santini or MacGregor to have him worked over for the sister's address. Meanwhile he would tell the Reynolds he'd caught the kidnapper. His gloom lifted at the thought.

'Mr Rowajinski, you'll please come with me to the station house,' Clarence said.

There were protests. What a bore the man was!

'Get your coat!' Clarence said.

Kenneth was on the defensive, yet he felt a core of security in himself. How could they find a sister? At least on Long Island? His sister was in Pennsylvania. Kenneth once had her address somewhere, but he had lost it, and it certainly wasn't in his head. 'You will see it's no use, if you want the dog. My sister will kill the dog by tomorrow night at six, if I don't tell her the money is coming.'

'How're you going to communicate with her?'

'I'll call her some place. We have an arrangement.'

Clarence hesitated. Was it true? The man hadn't sent a letter to Mr Reynolds, but it might be true that he was going to telephone him, and if he didn't get the money, inform his sister. What did he have to lose by waiting another eighteen or twenty hours, Clarence asked himself. He put on an air of contempt and self-assurance. Officially, he should report Rowajinski at once at the precinct. But Reynolds wanted his dog. If the sister heard nothing, she would probably just kill the dog to be rid of it.

'You see what I mean,' said Kenneth, pressing his advantage. The dog's life was indeed a great weapon. 'You know very well Mr Reynolds can pay another thousand dollars. I promised my sister.'

Work him over here, Clarence thought, and tried to gather his anger, his resolution. Wasn't it what any of the fellows at the precinct would do, beat him up? Clarence was also convinced of his greater strength, though the Pole was a sturdy fellow. He walked towards Rowajinski slowly. 'But there's no harm in telling me where your sister is, is there? Let's have it, mister!' Clarence slapped the Pole's face with a half-closed fist.

Rowajinski's pink lips shook with the impact and he looked startled.

Clarence grabbed the Pole's clothes over his stomach and pushed him back against the wall. Clarence caught a whiff of frankfurter. He was doing what the books didn't advise and what every cop did, under certain circumstances. He slapped downward on the bridge of the Pole's nose. Clarence had seen Manzoni do it in a back room.

'I'm not telling you! She'll kill the dog!' Rowajinski said in a suddenly shrill voice.

Clarence dropped his hands, and took his first breath in several seconds. He glanced at his watch. He ought to speak with Mr Reynolds, he thought. 'How did you catch the dog?'

The Pole squirmed with pleasure, it seemed, and relaxed.

'Oh, she just came. She's a friendly dog. Just walked away with me. – I got in a taxi. I took the dog to Long Island.'

'Your sister has a garden there?'

Hesitation. 'No, an apartment.'

'You said a little house before.'

'It's an apartment.'

'What area in Queens?'

'I'm not saying!'

Clarence thought of alerting the Queens patrol cars in re-

gard to a black miniature poodle answering to the name Lisa.
Wouldn't the woman have to air the dog? Unfortunately not
necessarily. And Queens was huge. 'I want this dog delivered
safe and sound. You understand?'

'Of course.'

'I'll speak with you in a few minutes. I'll be back.'

Rowajinski looked suddenly suspicious, turning his head,
peering with one eye at Clarence like a bird. 'You'll come back
here?'

'Yes.' Clarence went to the door and started to slide the bolt
with the metal behind it.

Rowajinski helped him. One had to pull out the metal before the bolt could slide. Clarence was thinking he should have
tapped around the floorboards for the money, or what was
left of it. Yet how could the bastard get away with it? If the
sister was keeping the money, which was likely, the police
could trace her – even if she wasn't his sister. Torture it out of
the Pole, once the dog was back.

As Clarence went into the hall, the door to the right, up the
steps, was closing. The landlady had been listening, of course.
He heard the Pole locking and bolting his door as he went up
the steps to the outside door.

Clarence ran across the streets to the Reynolds's apartment
house. It was now ten past 5 p.m. Mr Reynolds wouldn't be
home from work. Breathless, Clarence asked the black doorman please to ring the Reynolds's apartment.

'Mrs Reynolds? Clarence Duhamell here. Can I come up
to see you?'

'Of course! Come up, please.'

Clarence rode up and pressed the bell on the eighth floor.
When she opened the door, Clarence went into the foyer,
turned and smiled. 'I've found the man. The letter-writer.'

'You *found* him! And where is Lisa?'

'He says the dog is with his sister on Long Island. He won't
say just where. He's a man with a Polish name, lives on West
End and a Hundred and third Street. The problem is, he wants
another thousand dollars by tomorrow night, or his sister will
kill the dog, he says.'

'Oh, *mein Gott* !'

'So I've come to discuss this with you. I'd like very much to speak with your husband, too. Can he come here? Now?'

'Oh, I can call him. Sure!' She looked at the telephone. 'But I'm sure he will say yes, give it. Is that the problem? — Oh, I don't understand!'

'I wish you would call him, Mrs Reynolds – anyway.'

She dialled a number, and asked to speak to Edward Reynolds. 'Hello, Frances? Greta. Listen, I must speak with Ed. It is urgent ... It's more important than an interview. You must interrupt him.' A longer pause.

Clarence waited nervously with his hands in his pockets. Greta was staring at the floor, biting her underlip.

'Hello, Eddie! The policeman is here. They have found the man! ... Yes! Now can you come home at once because there is something we must discuss ... I can't explain now but you must come ...'

Clarence wanted to settle it by telephone, but apparently Ed could leave his office at once.

'He will be here in about fifteen minutes,' Greta said to Clarence. 'He is very pleased. Won't you sit down, Mr Duhamell?'

Clarence sat down on the edge of a chair.

'How did you find him?'

Clarence told her about trailing him to the house on 103rd Street. 'I had him print something. This.' He pulled the folded paper from his inside pocket and stood up to hand it to her.

'*Ach, ja!* It's the same!'

'Oh, yes. I'm positive.'

'It's not possible to *make* him tell where his sister is? They can make people tell things, can't they?'

'Oh, yes. Usually. I'd like to take him to the station house, but I'm not sure the fellows there would bother, frankly. I don't know if he would crack. He's an oddball.'

It crossed Clarence's mind that Greta might have been put to the torture herself, in her youth. Maybe she'd been held by the Germans, or her parents had. Greta got the ice bucket from the kitchen and asked Clarence if he would like a drink, or a coffee. Clarence declined. He wanted to get back to the Pole's house.

Then he heard a key in the lock, and Mr Reynolds came in.

'Hello! So you found the man.'

'Yes. A Pole named Kenneth Rowajinski,' Clarence said, remembering now even the spelling.

'Darling, he wants another thousand dollars,' Greta said.

'Well – tell me more.' Ed dropped a briefcase on the sofa.

'He wants you to leave a thousand dollars tomorrow night at eleven in the same place as before,' Clarence said. 'Lisa's now with the Pole's sister in Queens. Or so he says.'

'Um-m,' Ed groaned. 'Did you speak with his sister?'

'That's the trouble. He won't say where his sister lives, or her name. So there's no way of telling if the dog is there. He says his sister will – she'll kill the dog tomorrow night by six unless the money is promised. Now my –'

'It's unbelievable!' Ed said.

'My idea,' Clarence continued, 'is to try to trace the sister and meanwhile promise him that you'll give the money tomorrow night. If we can find the sister between now and tomorrow night, we'll get the dog and there's no money involved. He's supposed to confirm the money to his sister by – by tomorrow afternoon.'

'Good God,' Ed murmured. He took the drink that Greta offered him. 'Thanks, my dear. Now why won't this Pole – What's he like?'

Clarence described him, and wrote the Pole's name and address on a piece of paper torn from his notebook. 'I searched the room for the sister's address, but I couldn't find anything. Not the money, either, the money you gave him.'

'Oh, the money!' Ed said with impatience.

'I had him print this.' Clarence took the piece of paper from the coffee-table, and showed it to Ed. 'So I know he's our man.'

'Ye-es,' said Ed, and gave it back.

'What shall we do, Eddie? It's worth a try, no?' Greta asked.

'Sure.' Ed sipped his drink. 'I'm to get a letter tomorrow morning about this?'

'He said he'd telephone you.'

'Where is he now?'

'At his apartment. That's why I have to go back. To arrange something. To tell him if you're in agreement about the money.'

Ed smiled and shrugged. 'You could've told him I was whether I was or not. Then look for the sister.' Ed was at once sorry he had said that. The young man was so proud of having found the man. And Ed knew he should be grateful. 'You can tell him I'll have the money. Do you think he'll telephone me anyway?'

'I don't know, sir.'

'The same place, same time? Between the eleventh and twelfth spikes in that fence?'

'The same time, he said, anyway. May I use your telephone, sir? Then I'll take off.'

Ed gestured to the telephone. 'Help yourself.'

Clarence dialled Centre Street and identified himself. 'I would like to find the whereabouts of the sister of Kenneth Rowajinski...' He spelt it. 'Sister or sisters, possibly in Long Island.' Clarence gave Rowajinski's address, his approximate age, and his Social Security number. Clarence said he would like the information as soon as possible to be telephoned in to his precinct house.

'Who wants it? Your captain?'

'Give the information to anybody there but be sure they take it down. It's urgent.'

Clarence turned back to the Reynolds. 'I hope to get some information about the sister tonight.' Clarence was inspired to extend his hand to Mr Reynolds.

Ed took his hand. The young man's grip was firmer, more confident than his own.

'This is the first interesting case I've had in a year. I hope to achieve something,' Clarence said.

'Call us back tonight,' Ed said, 'even if nothing happens. Doesn't matter how late it is. Call us.'

Clarence departed. Three minutes later he was knocking on the green door, down the few steps from street level, which opened to Rowajinski's basement hall. Clarence knocked again, sure that Rowajinski could hear him, because his window was only three feet away in the front wall. Then the main door up the front steps opened, and Clarence went round on the sidewalk, and up the front steps to confront the landlady.

'I've put him out. He's gone.'

'When? Just now?' Clarence looked up and down the street. 'He's *gone*? Where?'

'I haven't the slightest idea, but he's out of my house!'

'He took a – suitcase–?'

'I think he had a suitcase. Good riddance! Trouble with the police! That's all I need!'

'Can I see his room?'

'Why should you? No.'

Clarence stammered, 'Madam – if you please – I'm a police officer. I'm not going to damage anything.'

Mrs Williams opened the door wider, muttering something. She and Clarence went down the hall, and she unlocked the green door. 'Filthy mess. Disgusting! What's he done?'

Clarence looked around him in astonishment. The drawers in the chest hung open, and some articles of grey-white were draped over them. The unmade bed looked the same. A dirty trodden-on tie sprawled across the floor. A couple of cans of something remained on the shelf by the stove.

'Did he say anything about Queens?' Clarence asked.

'Queens?'

'Long Island. About going there?'

'I don't know where he's gone. He didn't owe me any rent, that's all I can say for him. And what's he in trouble about?'

'Can't say just now, ma'am,' Clarence said quickly. 'Did he ever speak to you about his sister?'

'No. Never anything about a family.'

Clarence believed her. 'How long was he living here?'

'Seven months. Seven months too long.'

Clarence backed towards the door. 'Good-bye, ma'am. Thank you. Oh – your name, please?'

'Mrs Helen Williams,' she asserted, as if it were nothing to be ashamed of.

Clarence took a taxi downtown. It was a diagonal journey to Marylyn's, and hell on the subway at rush hour. God damn it, he thought, Rowajinski gone! How would he find him in New York? If he asked for the help of the precinct house, the fellows would say (if they bothered to say anything) 'What a dope! Found the guy and let him get away! Dummox Dummell!' Rowajinski would come to York Avenue tomorrow night for his money, however, of that Clarence was pretty sure. Pick him up then. All was not lost.

'This is *it*, isn't it?' asked the taxi driver, impatient.

Clarence had thought they'd been sitting at a red light, but they had arrived at Macdougal Street, and he hastened to pull out his money.

Marylyn was in. 'What's up?' she asked when she saw him.

'Nothing,' Clarence said. Seeing her, he woke a little from his trance. He had told her about Edward Reynolds and his wife. It had been something interesting for a change, and success had come – and now this. Clarence looked at the telephone, wondering again if he should alert his precinct house to look for Kenneth Rowajinski. But Rowajinski wouldn't communicate with his sister if they picked him up.

'Something about the man with the kidnapped dog?' Marylyn asked. 'You went to see him again?' Marylyn was sitting on her sofa, sewing a zipper into something.

'Yes.'

'Any news about the dog?'

'I found the guy who stole the dog and he got away. That's the trouble.'

'Got away?'

'He moved out of his lousy joint – while I was speaking with the Reynolds. Just cleared out.'

'He's got the *dog*?' Marylyn dropped her sewing in her lap.

'He said the dog's with his sister in Long Island. I don't know whether to believe him. He wants another thousand. Mr Reynolds is willing to give it. Tomorrow night. But now if I tell him the guy's disappeared –'

'You mean he's supposed to collect *another* thousand tomorrow night?'

'Yes.'

'He's a blackmailer! I bet he hasn't got the dog. What did you tell Mr Reynolds to do?'

'I didn't tell him to do anything. I asked him – if he was willing, you see.'

'Wow!' Marylyn shook her head. 'So the guy's loose! And you're all looking for him?'

'I didn't tell anyone yet. I'm going to try to find him myself first. He's got to communicate with Mr Reynolds tomorrow to ask for the money. He only told me, not Mr Reynolds. He's got to go to York Avenue again to pick it up. We can get him then. On the other hand, he might drop the idea of the second thousand since he knows I'm on to him.'

'Oof. – How'd you find him?'

Clarence told her.

Marylyn listened, and blinked. 'He's the type who carries a gun?'

Clarence heard an anxiety in her voice. 'No, not the type, I think.' Clarence smiled. 'I looked over his pad. He's just a creep. A nut.' Clarence sat down on the foot of the double bed, facing Marylyn. He felt that he had failed, and he had had to come downtown to Macdougal to tell Marylyn about that failure.

'It seems to me it's dangerous for you.'

'Me?' Clarence said.

'He might have friends. Aren't you the only one who knows about him now? You and the Reynolds? He might try to waste you, Clare.'

Clarence was pleased by her concern. 'I'm not worried. Don't you worry.' He stood up. 'I'd better take off, my sweet. On duty at eight.'

'Cuppa before you go? Instant?'

'No, but – Can I phone the Reynolds? I ought to.'

'Go ahead.'

The Reynolds's number had gone out of his head, and he had to look it up. He felt Marylyn watching him.

Mrs Reynolds answered.

'This is Clarence Duhamell. Is – is Mr Reynolds there.'

He was. He came on. 'Hello?'

'Mr Reynolds. Some bad news. When I went back to Rowajinski's house – just now – he'd cleared out. I don't know where he is now.'

'Cleared out?'

'He may still telephone you about the dog, but of course I can't be sure about that. Will you let me know at the station house if he tries to get in touch with you? I go on duty at eight tonight, but tomorrow, just tell the station house.'

'Well – no. If he gets in touch, I don't want the police in on it till I give it a chance with the dog. You surely understand that.'

'Mr Reynolds – we *will* do our best.'

Edward Reynolds fairly hung up on him. Clarence felt awful. He turned to Marylyn and said, 'Mr Reynolds doesn't want the police in on it, in case this guy contacts him. Jesus!'

'Oh, honey!' Marylyn sounded sympathetic, but she didn't drop her sewing, didn't say anything more.

She didn't understand the importance of it, Clarence thought. 'I've got to go. I'll see you later, darling.' He meant after 4 a.m. 'I'll be quiet coming in.'

'Don't take it so hard, Clare! You act like it's the end of the world!'

7

Kenneth Rowajinski, at twenty minutes to 6 p.m. on Monday evening, had lugged his suitcase up the steps of Mrs Williams's house, and treated himself to the first taxi he saw. 'In trouble with the police! You're a creep, a nasty old man, Mr. Rowajinski!' Mrs Williams had screamed after him. The bitch had four days' worth of his money besides, because his rent was paid through Saturday.

Kenneth had thought there were some inexpensive hotels in the University Place district, so he told the driver to go to University Place and Eighth Street. This area turned out to look rather swank, so he walked uptown towards 14th Street, and at last found what he wanted in the Hotel George, a dark greyish corner building some seven storeys high. Rooms were twelve dollars per night. Seventy-two dollars per week if one paid by the week, which was more than Kenneth had expected. He said he would pay by the day, because he was not sure he would be here more than two or three days.

'Can we have the three days now?' asked the man rudely.

'*Two* days maybe?' Kenneth could bargain as well as the next.

The man accepted two days' money, twenty-four dollars.

'Want to fill this out?' He shoved a registration form towards Kenneth.

Kenneth wrote after Name: Charles Ricker. Home address: Huntington, Long Island, a town that sprang to Kenneth's mind for no reason that he knew.

'Street address there? For Huntington?'

Kenneth invented one, and wrote it.

A coloured bellhop took him to his room on the fifth floor and carried his suitcase. Kenneth did not tip. Service was supposed to be included.

Then with his door closed, the extra button flicked so no one could open the door with a key from outside, Kenneth felt better, safe, even a trifle elegant. He had a private bath, a big white tub with shower, a clean basin with a little cake of soap wrapped in green paper. Kenneth opened his suitcase, made sure his money was still there, then he had a shower and shaved. He had nine hundred and twenty-odd dollars in his suitcase, and tomorrow he'd have a thousand dollars more. What was he worried about? That young cop? He'd shaken him.

Kenneth was hungry. He'd have to go out for something. He thought of putting his roll of money in the bed, but would they open or do anything to the bed tonight before he came back? Kenneth pulled the dark red, not exactly clean bed-spread back, and saw that the two pillows were fresh. Better here than in his suitcase, he thought, and he took the money and shoved it deep into a pillowcase, and replaced the bed spread neatly.

At Howard Johnson's on Sixth Avenue, Kenneth had a delicious hamburger with French fries and coffee. Then Kenneth went to a telephone booth on a corner and looked up Reynolds's number. He'd looked it up for curiosity days ago and forgot it. He put a dime in and dialled.

A woman's voice answered.

'Can I speak with Mr Reynolds?'

'Just a minute.'

Kenneth could tell she knew who he was. 'Hello, Mr Reynolds. I've got your dog. Lisa.'

'Where is she – please?'

'She is in Long Island. Absolutely okay. Now Mr Reynolds, I would like another thousand dollars. My sister insists on it, see? So tomorrow night at eleven, same place, same – small bills, all right? Then you will get your dog an hour later.'

'All right. – But what guarantee can you give me? Can I speak with your sister? Where is she?'

'In Long Island. No, you can't speak with her. She wants nothing to do with this. And listen, Mr – Reynolds, no one with you tomorrow night. No one following me. Okay? Because if that happens – you won't get any dog. You understand?'

'Yes, of course.'

'I have your promise?'

'Yes. – Where are you calling –'

Kenneth hung up. He was smiling, feeling triumphant.

The money was still in the pillow when he returned to his hotel room.

The next morning around nine, Kenneth left his room with a hundred and eighty dollars in his pocket, and walked to 14th Street in quest of clothing. His grey overcoat was pretty shabby, and he could afford to throw it away, he thought. Kenneth bought a suit for forty-nine dollars and ninety-five cents, and an overcoat of brown tweed for sixty-three fifty. He would have to come back in the afternoon for the suit, because the sleeves had to be shortened. Then he bought black shoes for eight ninety-five. The tweed overcoat was handsome, and stiff with newness. With his new coat and shoes on, his contempt for the people around him began to flood him again – a strong and reassuring emotion. They were all human cogs in a machine, never thinking about anything, just working, eating, sleeping, breeding. In another shop Kenneth bought a hat. He liked to wear hats and felt unprotected without one, and his old dark grey hat looked disgraceful in comparison with the overcoat.

Kenneth bought the *Times* and the *Post* and returned to his hotel to read, perhaps snooze, until he became hungry again. But with the future in mind he had bought a frankfurter on a roll at a stand-up coffee-shop, slathered it with mustard and relish, and wrapped it in a couple of paper napkins. In the lobby of the Hotel George, Kenneth had looked around for a policeman – or the young cop in uniform or not. He saw no one who seemed interested in him. Maybe the young cop had torn up his old room at Mrs Williams's, looking for the money, looking for clues as to where he was. Lots of luck! And it would certainly annoy Mrs Williams. *Good!* Then Kenneth realized that Mrs Williams would have to forward his monthly compensation checks to him somewhere. Or should he give the government office his savings bank address? Time enough to think about that, another two weeks till it was due. But it was a problem. Awkward. Because the police could trace him if he ever stepped into his savings bank (where he kept his bank book), if the police had troubled to find out that he had an account at the Union Dime Savings at 40th Street and Sixth Avenue. The police could ask the bank to detain him, and there was always an armed guard in the bank. But fortunately there was not much money there, and he could live on the ransom money for quite a time.

As the day wore on, Kenneth became a little nervous. 7 p.m. now. He wanted to leave his hotel, feeling that he'd be safer on the loose, walking around, and yet the walls of his room offered a kind of protection, too, and it was raining slightly. By five minutes to ten, Kenneth could stay in his room no longer, and he put on his old raincoat, which he had carried over his arm when he left Mrs Williams's. He had gone back to the clothing shop at 4 p.m. for his new suit, but because it was raining, he wore his old clothes.

He imagined the young cop having to tell Mr Reynolds — last night — that Kenneth Rowajinski had disappeared from his apartment. Mr Reynolds must have known this when Kenneth spoke to him. If so, it hadn't seemed to influence Edward Reynolds about coming up with the money. Kenneth took a crosstown bus on 8th Street to First Avenue, then an uptown bus. He got off at the 57th Street stop.

The rain still dribbled. On York Avenue, Kenneth walked slowly, looking everywhere for enemies, as he had done on Friday night. But he didn't think Reynolds would have allowed the police to come, really. Reynolds wanted his dog back. At 59th Street, Kenneth turned west, intending to make a circle to the north and approach the spot on York Avenue from uptown at, say, ten minutes past eleven. On 59th Street, Kenneth actually passed a pair of strolling cops. The cops paid him no mind.

But now Kenneth imagined cops converging in a ring on the York Avenue spot. It *wasn't* true, he told himself, but no harm in imagining, because it made him more cautious. If he saw a single figure that looked suspicious in that area, he intended to walk away.

But so far no one looked suspicious. Kenneth could not trust his wrist-watch, so he peered into a bar, then a grocery store – closed but he could see the clock on the wall – and saw that it was five minutes past 11. Kenneth crossed to the east side of York and walked downtown. The high fence, sunk into a cement base a few feet high, came into view, then Kenneth was walking along it, limping as little as possible. His small grey eyes darted in every direction. Reynolds should have come and gone. Kenneth tried to count the pikes off, but there was no need, because he saw the pale bundle from a distance of ten feet. He reached out and took it, not even coming to a complete stop. The bundle was thicker, perhaps because Reynolds had put more paper around it against the rain. Kenneth carried it with his right hand inside his raincoat. He crossed 60th Street, then 59th Street, looking for a taxi. He passed only two people on his side of the Avenue, a young man whistling and walking fast, a woman who did not glance at him.

At 57th Street, Kenneth found a taxi.

'Hotel George,' Kenneth said. 'University Place. Just below Fourteenth Street.'

He was safe. The clicks of the taxi's meter were counting off the fractions of miles between him and the danger uptown. Kenneth put the bundle in his lap while he paid the driver, then put the bundle back under his raincoat. He walked into his lobby. Again all was tranquil.

'You've been out in the rain,' said the black elevator operator as they rode up.

'A little walk,' said Kenneth non-committally. Kenneth disliked chumminess.

Kenneth went into his room and again double-locked his door with the button on the inside. Then he removed his shoes, also his socks, which were damp, and put on other socks. An idea had come to him in the last minutes, a protective idea. He could put the thumbscrews on the young cop, in case he ran into him again. After all, the cop had let him *go*, hadn't he? Kenneth's idea was to say the cop had agreed to let him escape, if he got some of the money of the second ransom payment. This idea was a bit fuzzy in Kenneth's head, but he sensed that essentially it was sound. To make it sounder, Kenneth intended to burn some of the money, destroy it. Kenneth was staring at the damp bundle on the round wooden table as his thoughts jumped this way and that. He was also prolonging the moments before he had the pleasure of looking at the money. At last Kenneth washed his hands in the bathroom, dried them on a fresh towel, and opened his package. There it was again, stacks and clumps of greenbacks, all tens, five bundles of twenty tens each !

He intended to burn five hundred dollars. It was a shocking thing and above all strange, but before he could think too much about it (because he was sure he was right), Kenneth slipped the rubber bands off two bundles and counted off ten ten-dollar bills from a third bundle. He tried it first in an ashtray, but it went slowly, and he decided on the basin.

The bills were surprisingly resistant to fire, but at last he could get five or six going at once in the basin, and soon he had to pause and collect the ashes in pieces of newspaper. It took him nearly a quarter of an hour to burn them all, and it was curiously exciting, all that money, that power, that *freedom* going up in smoke, turning to nothing. He rinsed the basin, and opened both the window in his bathroom and the window in the bedroom to get the smoke out. He had been enjoying the smoke, but he didn't want the hotel people to think a fire had broken out.

This possibility made him rush to the remaining money on his table and stow it away with the other money in case anybody insisted on coming into the room. He had stuck the money now in a folded sweater in one of the drawers, since he thought women might come in to fuss around with the bed while he was out. But when he slept, he thought it wisest to keep the money in a pillowcase.

Now it was five past midnight. He imagined Edward Reynolds waiting at York and 61st Street, waiting for the dog. In the rain. How long would he wait ? Kenneth smiled a little, feeling no mercy at all. Let the snob buy another dog. He could afford to. Reynolds was really a dope to have paid *two* thousand dollars. That made Kenneth feel superior. He might not have as much money as Reynolds, but it was plain that he had more brains.

8

Clarence's new 8 p.m. to 4 a.m. shift gave him Tuesdays and Wednesdays off for the next three weeks. Tuesday noon, he rang his precinct house to ask if there had been any message from Edward Reynolds. The Desk Officer, whose voice Clarence didn't recognize, said no.

'Are you sure? It's about a dog theft. A ransom.'

'Absolutely not, my friend.'

Clarence was at Marylyn's apartment. She had gone out at 10 a.m. for a dictation job on Perry Street. He had no plans with her for the day, because she said she wasn't sure she would have any time for lunch. Clarence made some scrambled eggs for himself. He walked around the Village, up to 10th Street, finally took a Sixth Avenue bus uptown, and stared out the window all the way, looking for a short, chunky, limping type like Rowajinski. Clarence rode to 116th Street, then walked to his precinct house. He asked what they had found out about a sister of Kenneth Rowajinski.

A young patrolman whom Clarence had seen only once or twice before looked it up for him and said: 'One sister named Anna Gottstein. Lives in Doylestown, Pennsylvania.'

Clarence wrote down her address and telephone number which was under her husband's name, Robert L. Gottstein. 'Thanks very much,' Clarence said.

Pennsylvania now, not Long Island.

Clarence took the subway back downtown, looking over all the passengers, everywhere. What else could he do?

He thought of ringing Edward Reynolds at his office around 4 p.m. to ask if he had heard yet from Rowajinski, but he was afraid Mr Reynolds would think he was meddling too much: after all, Mr Reynolds had made it plain that he didn't want police in on the affair even if Rowajinski contacted him and asked for a second thousand.

A little after four, Marylyn's telephone rang and Clarence answered it.

'My mother wants to see me tonight, Clare,' Marylyn said. 'You know – I told you I might have to go out. I called her but I really can't get out of it.'

She meant she had to go to Brooklyn Heights. Tuesday evening was her regular evening to have dinner with her mother, so Clarence could hardly complain. But he was disappointed and felt cut adrift.

At 6.30 p.m., Clarence rang his precinct house again. Lieutenant Santini was there, and Clarence spoke with him. Santini said there had been no message from an Edward Reynolds.

Again Clarence repressed his urge to ring up the Reynolds's apartment. But maybe Rowajinski hadn't dared ask for the second thousand. But if so, how was he going to get the dog to the Reynolds? Or was the dog alive?

Marylyn wasn't coming back to her apartment, but was going directly from an afternoon job to Brooklyn Heights. She'd be back before midnight, she had said, and she expected him to be there, but he wrote a note around seven to her, saying.

Darling,
Am worried about tonight and the Reynolds situation. I don't know what will happen. I will call you between 11 and 12. I bought Ajax. Message by telephone for you.

All my love XX
Clare

He left the note on her pillow. The telephone message was from a woman who had a rental service in the Village. She needed a typing job.

Clarence walked up Eighth Avenue to 23rd Street, had a hamburger and coffee, and went to a film on the same street, mainly to kill time. It was after eleven when he came out. He went to a sidewalk telephone booth and rang up the Reynolds.

A woman's voice, not Greta Reynolds's, answered. 'Who is this, please?'

'Patrolman Duhamell. Can I speak to Mr Reynolds if he's there?'

'Oh – you're the policeman who came to see them? ... They're not here now. I expect them back – after midnight.'

Clarence knew what that meant: the Pole had made the date and the Reynolds had kept it. 'I'd like to see them,' Clarence said painfully but with determination. 'Can I phone again – after midnight?'

'Yes. Sure.'

'They went to get the dog, didn't they?'

'Yes.'

'Thank you,' Clarence said. 'I'll ring again.'

The woman hadn't sounded very friendly.

Clarence walked west to Eighth Avenue, then uptown. It was raining slightly, and he was wearing his overcoat, not his raincoat, but he didn't care. At ten of twelve, he telephoned Marylyn. She was in.

'Honey – you saw my note? ... Are you all right?'

She was all right. 'What's with the Reynolds situation?'

'They made the second date – apparently. At eleven tonight. I'm only hoping the dog is delivered at midnight. I want to find out.'

She understood. They had a date tomorrow evening. To see a play. No, Clarence wouldn't forget.

'Where are you? ... Are you coming down later?'

'I don't know. Can I leave it that way?'

'Sure, darling, sure. Look out for yourself.'

Clarence was grateful. She understood. He went into a bar for a beer, and to go to the toilet. And to kill time. He killed time until a quarter to 1 a.m. Now, he thought, he could telephone the Reynolds. Either they had their dog or they hadn't.

Again the strange woman's voice answered. 'They're not back yet. Greta phoned around twelve – a little after. They were going to wait a while.'

Clarence sank. 'All right. I'll be up. Tell them I'll be up – now.' He hung up before she could protest.

Because he saw an uptown bus at once, Clarence took it. What was the hurry? Now, Clarence thought, the thing to do was face Mr Reynolds, admit he'd done the wrong thing in consulting him and giving Rowajinski a chance to escape, and do his best to put things right – to find Rowajinski and get the dog, if she were still alive somewhere, and hopefully get most of the money back, too. By 2 a.m., Clarence thought Mr Reynolds might agree to let his precinct open up on the case, alert all the cops in New York to look for Rowajinski, not to mention looking for his sister.

A white doorman at the Reynolds's apartment house opened the glass front door with a key. Clarence gave his name and said he was expected by the Reynolds.

'Yeah, they just came in.' The doorman picked up the house telephone.

'Did they have their dog with them just now?' Clarence asked, unable to repress the question.

'No. – The dog? The dog's lost. – Mr Reynolds? There's a Mr Dummell – Okay.'

Clarence took the elevator.

Mr Reynolds opened the door. 'Come in.'

'Thank you. I just spoke with the doorman. You didn't get your dog.'

'No.'

There were two other people in the living-room besides Mrs Reynolds – a tall man with grey hair, and a slender dark-blonde woman of about forty, who Clarence supposed was the woman who had answered the phone.

Greta Reynolds introduced them. 'Lilly Brandstrum. And Professor Schaffner. Eric. Officer Duhamell.'

'How do you do?' said Clarence. 'Mrs Reynolds, I am sorry.'

Mrs Reynolds said nothing. She looked about to weep.

'You left money again?' Clarence asked Mr Reynolds.

'Yes, and it was taken again. I waited about an hour after midnight.'

'I told Ed he should have allowed the police to be *there*,' said the tall man, who was standing, restless, by the front windows.

'Well – Mr Duhamell – he's a policeman,' Ed said. 'He wanted the police there, Eric. The kidnapper said no police.'

'When did Rowajinski speak with you?' Clarence asked Ed.

'Last evening around – after seven. After you called me. He made arrangements for the money. I couldn't get anything else out of him.' Ed gave a shrug.

'I found out Rowajinski has one sister named Anna Gottstein.

She lives in Doylestown, Pennsylvania, not in Long Island. But I can have the Pennsylvania police look her up and search her house. The dog might be there. Rowajinski, too. Did it sound like a long-distance call?'

'No,' said Ed. 'All right –' He felt hopeless and tired enough to drop. 'What's there to lose? But I'm pretty sure our dog's dead. Meanwhile – can I offer you a drink? What'll it be?'

'This creep,' the blonde woman said, looking at Clarence. 'If you knew his name and what he looked like, is it so difficult to find him in New York? He's even got a limp, I hear.' She looked at Clarence with obvious hostility and contempt.

Clarence shook his head at the scotch bottle Mr Reynolds was holding. 'No, thanks, sir.' Then to the blonde woman, 'It shouldn't be difficult now. I couldn't put my precinct on to it, because Mr Reynolds was afraid the dog would be killed if the man was picked up.'

'That dog is dead,' Lilly said.

'All right, get the police on to it,' said Ed, as if Clarence weren't the police, or not very good as one. 'He may do the same thing to someone else – with this success.'

'How anyone,' the blonde woman said, 'could find where the guy lives even and then let him escape like that beats me. And what a great dog Lisa was! She didn't deserve *this*!'

'I can't say how sorry I am,' Clarence said to her. 'My mistake was to leave this fellow yesterday for one minute – for twenty minutes while I spoke to Mr Reynolds. That's when he got away.'

'Yes, I heard the story,' said Lilly.

'In this city, anything can happen,' the tall man contributed. He was still on his feet like Ed, like Clarence. 'What a life! Nobody is safe. And yet on the street, in stores these days, all you see is policemen!'

'Isn't it true!' said Lilly.

'No, Lilly, I don't think it's his fault – Officer Duhamell's,' said Greta. 'He told us we had no guarantee that Lisa was still alive. We just took a chance. And we lost.'

'Oh, it's not the money, let's forget that,' Ed Reynolds said. 'It's the goddam shame of it, the unnecessary –'

'Sit down, Eddie,' said his wife. 'Sit down, Mr Duhamell.'

'Thank you,' said Clarence, not sitting down. 'If I can use your telephone, Mr Reynolds –'

'Go ahead.'

Clarence telephoned his precinct. 'Captain MacGregor, please. Patrolman Duhamell here.' MacGregor was available, and Clarence said, 'I would like to start a search – put out a search for Kenneth Rowajinski, sir. I can give you –'

'The one Santini said you were talking about at noon? Come in tonight if you're all steamed up about it. Where are you?'

Clarence said he would come in tonight.

'Well, that's something at least,' said Lilly, who was plainly feeling her drinks.

Clarence looked from Greta to Mr Reynolds. 'If I – If you don't mind, sir, I think it wouldn't hurt now to try the sister in Doylestown. Of course if she's got the dog –' She might kill it at once, Clarence thought. But he was curious. More than curious, he wanted to accomplish something, round them up, get the Pennsylvania police on to it at once, if necessary.

Ed Reynolds again made a casual gesture towards the telephone.

Clarence fumbled out his paper with the sister's telephone number on it. He dialled the number, preceded by a 215, and the others in the room began talking again while Clarence waited for the telephone to answer.

'H'lo?' said a sleepy male voice.

'Hello. I would like to speak with Mrs Anna Gottstein, please.'

'Who's this?'

'Patrolman Clarence Duhamell, New York Metropolitan Police.'

'What's the trouble?'

'I'm not sure, sir. May I please speak with your wife?'

'Just a minute. It's a hell of an hour –'

Now the others in the room had begun to listen, and absolute silence surrounded Clarence.

'Mrs Gottstein? I am sorry to be calling so late. It's about your brother. – Have you had any news from him lately?' Behind him, Clarence heard Lilly groan with deliberate disdain.

'My brother? Paul?'

'No, Kenneth. In New York.'

'Is he dead? What's he done now?'

'No, he's not dead. Do you know anything about a dog?'

'Whose dog?'

'When did you last hear from Kenneth, Mrs Gottstein?'

'Listen, is this a joke? Who're you?'

Clarence identified himself again, and repeated the question.

'I haven't heard from Kenneth in more than two years. And I don't expect to hear from him. He owes us money. He's a good-for-nothing. And if he's done anything wrong, it's not our responsibility.'

'I understand. I'm –' But she had hung up. Clarence put the telephone down, and turned to the room. 'I really think she knows nothing about it. Hasn't heard from her brother in two years.'

Mr Reynolds nodded, uninterested.

Clarence did not dare now to extend his hand to Mr Reynolds. 'Good night, sir. I'm going direct to the precinct house.' With difficulty, Clarence faced the woman called Lilly and said, 'Good night', and also said it to the tall old man, and with less difficulty to Greta. 'Good night, ma'am. I'll be in touch tomorrow.'

'Oh, why bother?' Lilly said.

'Lilly!' Only Greta was kind enough to walk with Clarence to the door.

Clarence felt awful. Catch the bastard Pole, he thought. That would make it up a little bit. He could show the Reynolds that he cared, at least, that he wasn't like what they thought the majority of the New York police force was like. But like Lilly, Clarence had no real hope for the dog's life.

MacGregor was at his desk, neat and alert at 2 a.m. Manzoni was also in the office, in civvies, maybe just going off duty. Manzoni was always smirking, and Clarence hated to tell his story in Manzoni's presence.

'So what's up?' MacGregor asked. 'That Rowinsk – What's he done exactly?'

'He's the one who kidnapped the dog of Edward Reynolds.

If you remember Saturday, sir. Mr Reynolds came in to see us. Well, I found the man Monday and he got away.'

'Got away?' asked MacGregor. 'With the dog?'

'I don't know where the dog is, sir. Mr Reynolds paid a ransom —'

'Oh, yes! The thousand-dollar ransom. You found the man how?'

'I was looking for odd-looking people in this neighbourhood. I happened to hit it right. I asked him to print something, so I know he's the fellow who printed the ransom notes. But he —'

'Got away how?'

'Well, sir, he told me he wanted another thousand from Mr Reynolds before he'd produce the dog. He said the dog was with his sister, but he wouldn't give me her address. I went to check with Mr Reynolds who lives just a couple of blocks away, and Mr Reynolds agreed to pay another thousand, but when I went back to Rowajinski's room, he'd cleared out. This was Monday around 7 p.m.'

MacGregor frowned. 'Why didn't you bring the guy in right away? We could've got the sister's address out of him.'

Clarence had known MacGregor would say this. 'I was afraid the dog would be killed, sir. Mr Reynolds told me he cared more about his dog than the money.'

MacGregor shook his head. 'Dummell — Clarence — you're a cop, you're not with the A.S.P.C.A. And you let the guy get away? He just left his pad *poof*? — Where does he live?'

'He had a room at a Hundred and third and West End.' MacGregor wasn't reaching for a pencil, Clarence noticed, though he had Rowajinski's West End address with him. Manzoni was listening.

'So he collected *more* money?'

'Tonight at eleven. I mean a couple of hours ago. Mr Reynolds insisted that we have no police on the scene.'

MacGregor seemed amused now. 'Who is Mr Reynolds? Is he running the force? He brings his complaints here and doesn't let us follow up? You should have followed up, Dummell, if you were so interested.'

'I realize, sir, I'd like to do what I can now — at least. This

Rowajinski is probably hiding out in a cheap hotel, or maybe with a friend. He's got a definite limp. – If I can write a detailed description, I'd like to get a search going.'

MacGregor motioned to a typewriter. 'Next time, Dummell – communicate.'

'Yes, sir.'

But MacGregor seemed already thinking of something else, and he looked down at a paper on his desk.

'Tsch-tsch,' said Manzoni, and clicked his tongue at Clarence.

Clarence had to look in another office for the right form. He typed out a description of Kenneth Rowajinski, approximate height, weight and age, colour of hair and eyes, a limp in right foot, pink cheeks, lips and nose. Last known address. Clarence added: paranoid type, anonymous letter-writer, furtive, aggressive manner, kidnapper of black female French poodle 'Lisa' owned by Edward Reynolds, etc. in Riverside Park 14th October at 7.30 p.m. Extortioner of $2,000 ransom. From his notebook Clarence got Rowajinski's Social Security number and added it for good measure.

By 5 a.m. Clarence was in Astoria, Long Island. He had drunk another beer in Manhattan, debated going to his own apartment on East 19th Street, then decided to go out and see his parents. He had got off at the Ditmar Boulevard elevated stop. Clarence had spent his childhood in this neighbourhood, and whenever he arrived at Ditmar, he had a flash of recollection of himself at ten or twelve – a gawky blond kid riding a bicycle or roller-skating. bringing home now and then a live miniature turtle that cost thirty-five cents from a pet shop on Ditmar that no longer existed. He'd had a happy childhood with plenty of outdoor life here, plenty of chums, mostly Italian and tough. That was all right, aged twelve. Clarence thought of Santini and Manzoni now. Neither liked him, Clarence felt. Manzoni was a patrolman like himself, but thirty years old and with the cynical, realistic attitude the cops ought to have, Clarence supposed. Manzoni had probably been a cop for six or eight years. Maybe even promotions didn't interest him.

On Ditmar Boulevard now a few trucks were unloading – fish in open boxes of salted ice for a restaurant, and boxes of fresh lettuce, eggplant, and tomatoes for a supermarket. Men in dirty white aprons shouted to each other, wooden beer barrels bumped the pavement, and a garbage truck chewed away noisily. The neighbourhood hadn't changed much since he was a kid. But whatever his parents believed or wanted to believe, his old pals in the neighbourhood (not that there were many, because to an amazing extent the young people had left Astoria) didn't like to have a beer with him any more, even if he wasn't in uniform, and he never was in uniform off duty. The atmosphere was different because he was a cop, a little as if he'd become a priest and might therefore be passing judgement on his friends. 'To be a policeman is surely nothing to be ashamed of,' said his mother, 'or what's New York coming to?' But that wasn't quite the point.

Now Clarence was walking down Hebble, his street, past still sleeping two-storey houses with projecting glass enclosed sunrooms at the front of almost every one. The dawn was starting. His subway-elevated trip had taken ages.

His parents' house was white, trimmed in yellow, with a sunroom in front, and a patch of lawn bordered by a low hedge. Clarence opened the wooden gate gently and went up the short front walk. Through the sunroom's windows he could see the old red leather sofa, the cluttered coffee-table with copies of *Times, McCall's* and *Popular Mechanics*. Clarence suddenly realized he hadn't his key. It was in his apartment in New York. He hesitated, immediately thought that his mother wouldn't mind what the hour was, and he pressed the bell briefly.

Finally his mother emerged in the dimness of the living-room doorway, wearing what looked like a bulky terrycloth robe, and peered across the sunroom. Then recognizing him, she broke into a big smile and flung the door open.

'Clary! Hello, darling! Come in, sweetie! How are you?' She seized his shoulders and kissed his cheek.

'Fine. As usual. Everything okay?'

His mother started coffee in the kitchen – already primed in an electric percolator, so she merely had to plug it in. Questions. They hadn't seen him for six weeks, wasn't it? The red cuckoo clock opened and a bird announced 5.30. The kitchen was smallish, immaculately clean, and full of yellow Formica. And what about his girl-friend, Marion, wasn't it?

'Marylyn,' Clarence said, glad that his mother hadn't got the name right. 'She's all right.' He was in shirtsleeves now, sitting at the kitchen table.

'Did something go wrong?'

Clarence laughed. 'No! Is that the only reason I'd come out, if something went wrong?'

'Why don't you bring Marylyn around? You're hiding her.' His mother turned from the stove, a spatula in her hand. She had insisted on making a brace of eggs – Clarence could sleep afterwards if he wanted to.

'Oh, it's hard for her to find time. Marylyn works freelance. Typing jobs.' He should have had Marylyn meet his parents by now, Clarence supposed, but Marylyn was a bit shy, Astoria was a boring trip, and in short he hadn't arranged it as yet. He hadn't met Marylyn's mother, either, but Marylyn wasn't the type to suggest that. Her parents were divorced.

His mother poured coffee, then turned her attention back to the stove while she chatted with Clarence. Nina was forty-nine, blondish with short, naturally wavy hair that needed little attention. She was practical, but in a sense had never found her *métier*. She had tried running a dress shop, interior decorating, had started a restaurant with a friend, and had stayed with none of these things, though none had been a financial catastrophe either. Now in her spare time, which was at least six hours per day, she did volunteer work for handicapped children, and was unofficially on call day and night.

Clarence's father, hearing the stir in the house, came down in bathrobe and slippers. This was Ralph, fifty-two, an electrical engineer at a turbine factory ten miles away called Maxo-Prop. Clarence had been named for Ralph's brother, whom Ralph had adored and Clarence had never met, who had been killed in France in the Second World War. Clarence disliked his name, but it could have been worse – Percy or Horace. Clarence was not close to his father, but he respected him. Ralph made a decent salary, had a skilled job, and he had got where he was with no college education, merely by taking correspondence courses in engineering and by studying at night. The fact that Clarence had gone to Cornell, an Ivy League university, for four years, was a source of pride to his father, Clarence knew. Not just N.Y.U. or City College, but Cornell, as a boarding student. His family had sacrificed for that, Clarence realized, though it had probably not caused them to buy one overcoat or bottle of whisky less, if they wanted it. But they might have gone to Europe, for instance. A diploma from Cornell was something Clarence had and his father hadn't. His father had never said to him, 'I expect you to work summers, be a waiter or a taxi driver, but pull your weight a little.' Lots of rich families said that to their sons and daughters. Clarence had gone to Cornell like a prince. His parents could have moved, years ago, to a better neighbourhood in Long Island, but they had chosen to stash away their money, bequeathed to Clarence their only child, in case they died. And in case they didn't die, they were going to retire in eight years now, and buy a house in California overlooking the Pacific. Clarence thought his parents hopelessly old-fashioned, but he had to admit they were decent, honest people, and he didn't meet decent, honest people every day in New York. That was why the Reynolds were such an exception for him.

'Well, Patrolman Duhamell, how goes life?' asked his father. 'Are you mingling with delinquent youth, setting them on the right path?'

Clarence groaned. 'Not all of them are young. Lots with grey hairs in their whiskers.' When he had started on the force, he had talked to his parents about making contact with young people in trouble. He had tried to get a job along these lines when he had been at the 23rd Street Precinct, but men already with such jobs (patrolmen with special connections with Bellevue) hadn't wanted to yield place, or there hadn't been a place then for a newcomer. But had he been forceful enough in asking for such work? The matter still bothered him. He could of course try again.

They drank coffee, and his father smoked a cigarette.

'What brings you here at this ungodly hour? You've deprived me of an hour's sleep,' Ralph said.

Clarence said he'd come out on a whim. Clarence realized he couldn't tell them about Rowajinski, because he felt ashamed (at that moment) of his stupidity, therefore he couldn't tell them about the Reynolds. He wanted to talk about the Reynolds, because he liked them.

'I hope you don't have to go to work today, Clary,' said his mother, serving his father a pair of fried eggs flanked by two pieces of neatly buttered toast.

'No,' Clarence said.

'You were on duty tonight?' asked his father.

'No. But I'm off today.' Clarence didn't want to tell them he was on an 8 p.m. to 4 a.m. shift, because they thought it was the most dangerous part of the twenty-four hours, so he was glad that his mother began talking of neighbourhood affairs.

'How's the girl?' asked Ralph. 'When can we meet her?'

'I don't know why you take her so seriously!' Clarence suddenly realized that he was very tired. He felt almost hysterical suddenly, as if something had burst in his heart. He felt on the brink, on some brink, on the edge of a great decision. It was whether he stayed in the police force or not. He wanted to tell his parents this. It concerned Marylyn and the Reynolds. Marylyn didn't like policemen. It concerned the Pole called Rowajinski, the bastard whom he had allowed to escape him. It concerned the fact that Marylyn didn't want to marry a cop, and he was still in the force, even though he could quit any time he wished.

'What is it, Clary?' his mother asked in a kind voice.

Clarence shook his head.

'Our boy is exhausted,' said Nina to Ralph. 'Walking those streets – Come up to your room, Clary.' She extended a small, energetic hand, then as if realizing he was a grown man, she stopped.

'I'll go up,' said Clarence. He was aware that his father was studying his face. Clarence looked straight at his father, ready for his words of well-meant advice or wisdom. But about what? It occurred to Clarence that his father was a little like Edward Reynolds. They were the same height and weight, and their features had a similar rugged handsomeness.

Then his father said with surprising lightness, 'It's logical that you sleep now, isn't it?' He put some home-made jelly on a bit of toast and popped it into his mouth. 'We can talk later. This evening. I hope you'll stay over.'

'Oh, I think so,' Clarence said automatically.

A few minutes later, he was upstairs in his room, having brushed his teeth with his own toothbrush in the bathroom next door. His room had a gabled front window that made two slants in the ceiling. Under one of these, in a corner, was his bed, under the other a long bookcase that still held some boys' adventure books along with college texts on sociology and psychology, plus several novels – Fitzgerald, Kerouac, Bellow, William Golding. On the wall was a picture of the Cornell basketball team, himself third from right in the back row. He really ought to remove that, he thought. Marylyn would laugh: she would think it square, snobbish, and childish, though the picture was only five or six years old. Marylyn would think his parents' house square also, and boring, though not expensive enough to be bourgeois. Well, he and Marylyn would never live in a house like this, in a place like Astoria. They'd have an apartment in Manhattan, maybe a house in northern Connecticut, if he ever got the money together.

The sheets were fresh. Clarence slid into bed and felt himself in a cocoon of safety. Was this another dead end, the police force? Was it like the bank job, in the personnel department? Not the end of the world, of course, even if people like Captain MacGregor and Santini said, 'You're just not cut out for the police, Dummell.' The trouble was that he had tried, was still trying, and presumably had an advantage over most young cops because he had a college degree, but even so, he had goofed in a way the dumbest most primitive cop wouldn't have goofed: he had caught his man and let him go. And Marylyn – she hadn't taken his job seriously, and Clarence knew it would be months before he could get a promotion, even if he went to the Police Academy, which he intended to do. Would Marylyn marry a cop under any circumstances? 'No one bothers marrying these days,' Marylyn had said. Clarence felt he could be loyal to Marylyn for the rest of his life. That was something. That was everything. Odd that in the old days men usually fought shy of marriage, while girls held out for it. Now he wanted marriage and – yes, a kind of security, just what the girls used to fight for ... Must call Marylyn as soon as he woke up. The play tonight ...

'Clary? – Clary?'

Clarence raised himself on an elbow, tense and groggy.

'Clary, I'm sorry to wake you, but it's your precinct on the phone. They want to speak with you.'

Clarence got up. He was wearing only his shorts, and he had to grab his father's bathrobe from the john. His mother had already gone downstairs, and he heard her saying:

'One minute, please. He's coming.'

Clarence glanced at his wrist-watch. A quarter to two. 'Hello? Clarence Duhamell here.'

'Hi Clarence. Santini. We found this Polish guy, Rojinsk – you know.'

'You *did*?'

'Yeah, we did. Listen –' Long pause, while Santini blew his nose, or perhaps spoke to someone else. 'Listen we want to see you. I know it's your day off. Had a hard time finding you.'

'What's the matter?'

'Well – see when you get here. Rowajinski's here. So get here when you can, will you? Say by three, three-thirty?'

'Yes, sir.'

'What is it, Clary?' His mother was standing in the door-way between the sunroom and the living-room.

'I have to go into New York. Right away.'

'Oh, Clary! Without any lunch?'

Clarence ran up the stairs on bare feet. 'They want me there by three, mom.'

When he came down, dressed, his mother said she had cut a slice of roast beef for him. He could eat it standing up, no fuss. Clarence ate half of it. He had taken a hasty shower, scraped at his face with his father's razor. 'This doesn't happen often,' he said to his mother.

Santini's tone had been off-hand, and Clarence felt he had been summoned only because he'd at least seen Rowajinski before and could identify him. The dog had been kidnapped a week ago today. He had let the Reynolds down horribly and unforgivably.

9

Kenneth Rowajinski sat on a bench near the entrance of the precinct house beside a rolling, restless junky whom Kenneth fastidiously avoided touching. It was 2.40 p.m., and Kenneth had been at the station about two hours. He had twice asked to go to the toilet. He was nervous. They had come for him – a single policeman in plain clothes – just after noon. Kenneth still did not know how they had found him. He'd been out that morning around 11 a.m. to pick up some fruit and a hamburger and a couple of cans of beer to take back to his room. Of course there was his limp. And the cop, a black-haired fellow with fat jowls, a nasty grin, had said: I thought you'd be in some crummy hotel, and I sure hit it right, didn't I?' Chatting away while he scribbled in his notebook, standing right in Kenneth's hotel room, the door wide open and a black maid staring open-mouthed from the hall. Invasion! Kenneth's heart had begun to race, and it had not stopped since.

But Kenneth had fixed the bastard young cop who had found him at Mrs Williams's. That was more than a consolation, it was a bit of a triumph. That was hitting back, good and proper. Just wait till he walked in. Kenneth's eyes, darting everywhere, darted most often at the front door on his left, because he knew the blond cop was due.

Across from Kenneth a black cop without a cap sat reading a comic book and chewing gum. His kinky black hair was greying. What a racket the police force was, taking taxpayers' money, taking bonuses and pensions, swaggering around with guns, slapping tickets on cars, taking kickbacks from gambling joints (often in the back rooms of innocent-looking candy stores), and rake-offs from drug-pushers. All well-fed bullies, mainly Italian, though of course there were some Irish, too. The Italian who'd come into Kenneth's hotel room had found his money very soon, counted it and pocketed it. Kenneth had seen the money being handed over in the station to a superior officer (another wop) behind a desk in the room opposite. One thousand one hundred and twenty dollars. It left Kenneth with eleven dollars and some change in his pocket. Kenneth did not know if they had telephoned Edward Reynolds yet, but he assumed so. Kenneth did not look forward to facing Reynolds, in view of his position, but he reminded himself that he had a deep and justified contempt for types like Reynolds, so why should he cringe?

Kenneth glanced at the door, expecting Reynolds as much as the blond cop. Kenneth kept moving a loose lower front tooth back and forth with his tongue and with suction. The tooth gave him slight pain every time he pushed it or sucked it. For at least the sixth time, Kenneth shoved the rolling junky off his left shoulder, and suddenly jumped up, causing the junky to roll all the way over and fall flat on the floor on his face. Kenneth adjusted his new overcoat and averted his eyes.

The coloured guard laughed and got up from his chair, still holding his comic book. 'Hey! Sommun gonna give me a hand here?'

Kenneth refrained from looking. The junky, like an old cockroach, was trying to turn himself over, or something. It occurred to Kenneth to walk out the door, but here was one of the wide-hipped cops – wide-hipped because of the gun and notebook and nightstick and handcuffs under his jacket, and also from sitting on coffee-shop and bar stools – lifting the junky and propping him back on the bench. The cop muttered a joke, the black grinned.

Then the young blond cop, in plain clothes, came up the steps and into the lobby, and saw him at once. Kenneth scowled and held his ground.

The blond cop went into the office opposite.

In a minute or two an older blond officer came out and beckoned to Kenneth.

'You recognize this man, Dummell?' asked the officer.

'Oh, yes, sir.'

'Manzoni picked him up at the Hotel George in the Village.

Just casing hotels for a fifty-year-old man with a limp, you know?'

Manzoni had certainly had luck, Clarence thought, and said nothing.

They were back in the officer's room now.

'Now Rowajinski here –' MacGregor referred to some notes on his desk. 'Found in possession of one thousand one hundred and twenty dollars, all in ten-dollar bills. Just like the ransom, no? Ten-dollar bills? He says you took five hundred to let him go.'

'Yes!' said Kenneth firmly.

'No. I did not,' said Clarence.

'He's bought some clothes, okay. Paid two days' hotel bill, okay.' MacGregor ran his thumbs under his belt. 'Dummell, we're not accusing you, just asking. The five hundred – that's about what's missing from the two thousand, you see.'

The cop's face was red, Kenneth saw, like the face of a guilty man. Kenneth could almost believe he *had* taken it. He might as well believe it, ought to believe it, because he had to stick to his story. 'Yes. And I was to pay him three hundred later. Eight hundred in all!' Kenneth said in a burst of inspiration.

'Captain MacGregor, I give you my word. This fellow – if you'd like to search my apartment – my bank account – I haven't got the money, sir!'

'Now don't get excited, Dummell.'

'I'm not, sir!'

'If you say "no", it's no.'

'Thank you, sir. – Have you spoken to Mr Reynolds, told him we've got Rowajinski?'

MacGregor frowned, looking preoccupied. 'No, not yet. Or I don't know if Pete told him.'

Pete was Manzoni. 'He'd be interested, sir. And the dog. It's the dog, you know – '

'Oh,' said MacGregor. 'Rowajinski says he told you right away the dog was dead. Is that true, Dummell?'

'It certainly isn't true! He said the dog was with his sister in Long Island. That's what I told Mr Reynolds.'

The young officer glared at Kenneth as if he could kill him.

'I told you,' said Kenneth, standing as tall as he could, 'that the dog was dead.'

'You did *not*! Captain — Captain MacGregor, are you going to believe this nut or me?'

'We're not believing anyone yet. Relax, Clarençe.' He pushed a bell on his desk.

Kenneth stood straight and tall, wearing his hat. The young blond cop, Dummell, shifted like a guilty man, afraid to speak. Kenneth sensed a certain victory. He went with good grace with a cop who came to take him away. Pyjamas had been laid out on a cot. All right, a cell. But he'd fixed Dummell!

As the cop closed the cell door, Kenneth said, 'I want a lawyer. I don't have to pay for that, do I?'

The man drawled insolently, 'You-ou'll get one.'

Revolting lot! There were two hooks on the wall, not even a hanger, and a toilet and a basin. He peed. He was hungry. But he put hunger out of his mind and went to the barred door to try to hear something. He did hear what he thought were the voices of the Captain and the young cop, but he could not tell what they were saying. Unfortunate. But Kenneth was pleased that he had focused attention on Dummell and away from Reynolds and the dog. He had told a most convincing story to the cop who had found him about the Monday afternoon talk in his room at Mrs Williams's. The cop had said he was going to call on Mrs Williams, and she could certainly confirm (no matter what nasty remarks she might make against him besides) that Dummell had come twice that afternoon, and had pretended the second time to be completely surprised that Kenneth Rowajinski had disappeared.

10

As soon as Manzoni and the other cop, whose name Clarence didn't know, had left his apartment, Clarence went to his telephone, but stopped before he touched it. He was still shaken, and he didn't want to talk with Mr Reynolds when he sounded nervous. Clarence lit a cigarette, and looked over his living-room – bedroom, not seeing any detail, but conscious of its veil of soot, of the disorder that Manzoni and the other fellow had left after they had searched the place, conscious of his shame. Drawers were half pulled out, shirts mussed. They hadn't turned the place inside out by any means, but that they had come here at all was insulting, especially that Manzoni had come, with his personal touch. 'Did you need some extra money for your girl, Clarence?' How did he know about Marylyn? Or did he mean just any girl? They had asked to see his savings bank passbook. No recent big deposits. Even the pillows on the bed had been stripped of their zipped covers and were in disorder. 'You haven't been here lately,' Manzoni had remarked. 'Where've you been sleeping?' Clarence had said he had spent several nights (or anyway his off-duty time) out at his family's in Astoria. That was another thing: he ought to forewarn his mother to say he'd been out a lot to see them, in case the cops rang her.

Clarence dialled the Reynolds's number. It was just before six. 'Mrs Reynolds? This is Clarence Duhamell. I would like very much to see you ... Yes, there is news, we've caught Rowajinski, in case the precinct house didn't tell you.' (They hadn't.) 'I – I'd rather tell you when I see you,' Clarence said with tortured awkwardness. She had asked about the dog, of course, and he could tell she knew there was no hope. 'I'll come right away, if I may.'

Clarence took the subway, not wanting to arrive too soon,

because he wanted Mr Reynolds to be there. The rush hour was on, worst at Grand Central where he took the shuttle, difficult to breathe due to the pressure of people. Newspapers were crushed under passengers' arms. It was a sea of disgruntled, grim, blank, brooding faces, waiting for the roaring train to spill them into a little more space somewhere. Out of habit, Clarence looked around for pickpockets, then realized that everyone's hands were pinned at the spot they had been in when the last person had been thrust in by a guard, and the door slid shut. Clarence got out at the 103rd Street station, and walked to the Reynolds's apartment house. The coloured doorman was on duty.

By this time it was 6.40 p.m. Mr Reynolds was in.

'So they've caught the Pole again,' Mr Reynolds said after he had greeted Clarence in the foyer. 'And what about the dog?'

'The Pole says now –' Clarence was following Mr Reynolds into the living-room, 'Good evening, Mrs Reynolds.' She was standing by the coffee-table. 'The Pole says that – that he killed the dog the night he caught her. That he hit her on the head with a rock.'

'Oh, Jesus.' Ed turned away. He pulled the palm of one hand down his face.

'All right, Eddie,' said his wife. 'We almost knew, didn't we?'

'What're they going to do with this psychopath?' Mr Reynolds asked.

'I don't know, sir. He ought to be locked up. In a mental institution, I mean.'

'So – he hit her on the head. Then what? He took her away? She wasn't there in the bushes. I looked. No sign of blood. I looked the next morning.'

'He said he carried the dog to his house. His room. He said he wrapped her in something and – left her somewhere. I don't know where.'

'Buried her somewhere?' Ed gave a slight laugh.

'Eddie –' Greta's voice trembled.

'I don't know, sir,' Clarence said.

Ed shoved his hands into his pockets. He walked towards the window, his shoulders hunched.

Clarence said, 'I'm surprised the precinct house hasn't called you. They found most of the money on the fellow. He was in a hotel in the Village.'

'Oh, the hell with the money,' Ed said. He was thinking what a disgusting city New York really was. You had to rub elbows, you did rub elbows with creeps like this one every day of the week, every time you rode a bus or a subway. They looked like ordinary people but they were creeps. His heart was beating rapidly, and he was imagining tearing Rowajinski limb from limb, catching him by the throat and smashing his head against a wall. He could do it, he thought.

Greta was weeping without a sound, wiping her tears from time to time. Almost mechanically she was putting ice into three glasses, pouring scotch.

Clarence accepted the glass she gave him.

Ed Reynolds was wandering about with slow steps, looking at the floor.

'I'm now accused,' Clarence said, 'of having taken five hundred dollars to let Rowajinski escape. Rowajinski accuses me.'

'Oh?' said Ed. It registered, but not much. What if it were true? So what? He glanced at the young cop's serious blue eyes. *Was* he serious? Was he honest? Did it much matter?

'I don't think my precinct Captain thinks I took it. They certainly won't find the money on me at any rate. What I do reproach myself for —' He stopped, realizing that since the dog was dead, Mr Reynolds wouldn't give a damn about his inefficiency, or whether he reproached himself for it. And indeed, Mr Reynolds might not have heard what he said.

Mr Reynolds was talking quietly to his wife. He put his arm around her shoulder and kissed her cheek.

Clarence felt the sooner he left the better. He finished his drink at one draught. The drink hit his stomach and almost came up again, and Clarence tightened his throat, wincing.

Mr Reynolds looked at him with mild surprise.

Just then Clarence remembered that he had to call Marylyn to arrange where to meet tonight. Was the play at 9.30 or

8.30? Since he could not possibly ask the Reynolds to use their telephone for this, Clarence became slightly more rattled.

'Mr Reynolds,' Clarence said, 'I'm going to see that Rowajinski gets the maximum, gets all we can give him.'

Again, Mr Reynolds did not seem too interested.

'Won't you sit down, Mr Duhamell,' said Greta.

Clarence handed her his glass automatically, because she reached for it. He sat down carefully on an upholstered straight chair. Greta returned in no time with a fresh drink for him.

'I have to tell you,' Clarence began, 'that I am very ashamed that I let Rowajinski get away the first time. I told my precinct that. My Captain. I blame myself.'

'I understand,' Ed mumbled, wishing the fellow would leave. 'Just what, frankly, can they do to this Pole? Just lock him up in a mental institution?'

Clarence shrugged. 'I know they're crowded. They can detain him now, anyway. I mean – a fine and imprisonment. It'll be a long time before he's out.' It was not what he had meant to say, and was it true that it would be a long time? 'I'll do my best. It's strange that they suspect me of taking money, when I gave them the most careful description of this fellow, the Pole. A limp, that's already a great help in looking for someone. But Manzoni – the one who found Rowajinski at the hotel in the Village – There's no doubt he was lucky. I wish *I'd* found him. I –' Clarence had started to say he spent many nights in the Village himself.

The telephone rang. Ed seemed not to hear it. Greta answered it, then called her husband.

'Hello?' said Mr Reynolds. 'Yes . . . Yes, thanks. I heard.'

Clarence knew it was his precinct house, that they had waited until Mr Reynolds was home to telephone. Clarence hoped Mr Reynolds would not say he was here. Nervously, he took a swallow of scotch and water.

'Yes, I can do that,' Mr Reynolds was saying in a bored tone.

They wanted him to pick up his money. Clarence was feeling the scotch. How could life get any worse? Clarence stood up when Mr Reynolds put the telephone down.

'I'm supposed to go to the precinct house for the money,'

Ed said. 'Asked them to send a cheque, but they won't. I'm supposed to go now.'

'Sit down, Eddie,' said Greta. 'Relax for a *minute*.'

Ed paid no attention, only walked about.

Clarence thought of offering to accompany Mr Reynolds to the precinct house. But Mr Reynolds might not even want him to. 'I must go now,' Clarence said. 'I want to state my promise again. I will see that some justice is done. To the best of my ability.' He blurted suddenly, 'Don't think I like it, Mr Reynolds, that I'm accused of taking five hundred dollars to let this psycho go! Not accused exactly but suspected.'

'I suppose that'll blow over,' Ed said, bored with it. Lisa, his and Greta's dog, was dead. Ed realized he was enduring grief such as he had endured when he knew definitely that his daughter was dead, had been killed. A dog, a daughter – there should be a great difference, yet the feeling was much the same. At least at that moment. And he could not sit still, he had to walk about, looking at the floor, wishing the cop would go. 'I don't think I want to see this Pole,' Ed said. 'I don't suppose I have to see him, do I?'

Clarence said, 'Not if you don't want to, sir, I'm sure. – Good-bye, Mrs Reynolds. Thank you.'

Clarence went to the door. Even Mrs Reynolds did not say anything except 'good night' as she closed the door behind him. Clarence decided to take a taxi straight to Marylyn's rather than look for a telephone. He felt ashamed, stupid, and somehow weak, as if he had behaved weakly. *I swear I'll make it up to him*, Clarence said to himself.

Ed Reynolds took off his shirt and washed at the bathroom basin. What was he washing off this time? 'Darling, I promise,' Ed shouted over the running water to something Greta was saying, 'they won't keep me more than ten minutes, because I'll refuse to stay there. You can start dinner, really.'

Ed walked to the precinct house. A black policeman, as before, sat on a straight chair at the door and barely glanced at Ed as he came in. Ed had asked him where to go. It was again Captain MacGregor whom he was to see.

There were two or three other police officers in the room

where MacGregor was. 'Edward Reynolds,' Ed said to Mac-Gregor.

'Oh, yes,' said MacGregor. 'Would you have a seat?'

Ed sat reluctantly.

'The kidnapper of your dog, Kenneth Rowajinski, was found today at the Hotel George on University Place. About twelve hundred dollars of the money was found in his room. He seems to have a savings account of about four hundred dollars . . .' MacGregor was consulting a paper on his desk.

Ed was suffering boredom. There were more details.

'. . . tomorrow,' MacGregor was saying. 'At least we hope tomorrow. The psychiatric department is busy these days.'

Ed gathered that someone would come tomorrow to the station here to see the Pole.

Captain MacGregor went to a drawer and unlocked it, pulled out an envelope. 'This is your twelve hundred and twenty dollars, Mr Reynolds. We'll get what we can to make up the rest for you. I am sorry about your dog.' He laid the envelope on the edge of his desk.

'What're you going to do to this fellow, besides have a psychiatrist look at him?' Ed asked.

'Well – he'll be under surveillance for several weeks. Maybe locked up. What they decide to do isn't really for me to say.'

It never was, Ed supposed. There was always somebody just above, someone with more, or different authority, someone you never saw and who didn't even exist in a sense.

'Would you like to speak with Rowajinski? He's in the cage back there.'

Ed got up suddenly. 'No, no, thank you. Serves no purpose, does it? My dog is dead. – How many police patrol Riverside Park, by the way?'

'Oh – a hundred, maybe more. It was very bad luck, Mr Reynolds. I know the Park's a rough place after dark. I know.'

Ed felt his anger rise. He hated it. Anger without purpose, hurting only himself. He tried to appear calm, but his bitterness found another outlet. 'And this young officer – Duhamell? He let the Pole escape?'

'Ah, Patrolman Dummell! Yes. He's new, fairly new on the force. He made a mistake there. It was another officer who picked up Rowajinski, not Dummell. Dummell's got a lot to learn.'

'What's this about his having taken five hundred dollars?'

'You know about that?'

'Dummell just told me.'

'Told you he took it?' The man's small eyes widened.

'Oh, no. He says he didn't. Says the Pole accuses him. But what do you think?'

MacGregor glanced down at his desk and shifted on his feet. 'Dummell telephoned you?'

Ed hesitated, feeling disrespect for all of it, even a curious detachment. 'Yes.'

MacGregor shrugged.

Ed sensed that MacGregor didn't know what to say to be correct, safe. Did the police have to protect the police, Ed wondered, no matter what? Probably.

'About five hundred is missing from what we found on Rowajinski. Nothing that shows how he spent it. We are *asking* Dummell, yes. It seems funny to all of us that Dummell would've caught this guy and then left him for half an hour while he talked to you about a second thousand dollars. Isn't that right?'

'Right,' said Ed dully. He didn't give a damn. To hell with the police. They hadn't even recovered his dog's corpse. 'So I thank you very much, Captain.'

'Oh, don't forget your money, Mr Reynolds! And you're supposed to sign this, if you will.'

Ed did not even read the paper, just signed it.

'That's a receipt for twelve hundred and twenty,' said Mac-Gregor. 'And we'll certainly get the rest. We'll attach this guy's compensation.'

Ed nodded. Nods meant nothing. He walked to the door and out.

Ed took the familiar Avenue homeward, Riverside Drive. What a funny city New York was — eight million people, and no one knew anybody and didn't really want to. It was a conglomeration to make money, not because people were fond of their fellow men. Everyone had a fragile web of friends on the map of New York — friendships that had nothing to do with geography, neighbourhood. Everyone in his way excluded the masses, the unknown, the potential enemy. And Duhamell or Dummell (easy to imagine his name becoming Dummell in another generation), was he honest? Did he need some money just now? Was there a girl in the picture? Ed stopped and turned half around, facing the river, thinking to go back to the precinct and tell them that he didn't care, personally, whether Dummell had taken the five hundred dollars or not. No, even that was dramatic, Ed thought. And the police didn't care, personally, either.

Ed pushed his doorbell and Greta – after looking through the peephole – let him in. Ed embraced her in silence. Then he hung his coat, and seeing the white envelope in the coat pocket, he pulled it out.

'What's that?' Greta asked.

'They gave me twelve hundred dollars back. Said they'd get the rest.' He dropped the envelope on the hall table. Lisa's leash, hanging inside the closet door, made a last tap as it swung and was silent. Ed suddenly remembered that Lisa's water bowl was no longer on the kitchen floor. Greta had removed it one day – Monday? – when he had not been here. Must get rid of the leash, or put it somewhere else, but not just now.

'What do you think of the young cop? Duhamell.'

'Oh? – why do you ask? He's a little strange.'

'Strange?' Greta was intuitive. Ed was interested in what she might say. 'Do you think he's honest?'

'Yes. But a little weak.' Greta was preoccupied, and drifted into the kitchen.

Ed followed her. 'Weak how?' Ed expected her to say, 'Why are you interested?' or 'What does it matter?' Duhamell had twice seen Rowajinski, and that, somehow, was why Ed was interested. Duhamell was, in a sense, a link with this evil.

'I don't know. He's young. Too young,' said Greta, opening the oven door. 'I don't feel much strength from him.' She pulled out a slender, browned loaf of bread that smelled of butter and garlic.

'His precinct captain thinks – seems to think he might've

taken the five hundred bucks. Or they simply don't know. What do you think?' Ed was talking, he realized, to avoid thinking about Lisa.

'No, I don't think so,' said Greta, pronouncing 'think' like 'zink'. She looked tired.

They should go to bed early, Ed thought, and then what, and then what? It was possible to be tired without sleeping. And he ought to read another hour tonight, at least. He had to make his report on two books which bored him, but which he knew C. & D. would publish whatever he said, one on pollution, the other an excruciating four hundred pages called *Horizon with Seagull* (he wished he could forget the title) about a young American girl's first trip to England with ensuing romance. Bilge. Incredibly, C. & D. made a little money on such books. Then he might lie with Greta in his arms, as if she were his mother, his sister, a female comforting him. Ed set his drink down and plunged suddenly into the bathroom. He bent over the basin and pressed his hand against his forehead, grimaced, and let the tears come, turned the water on to drown out a brief, choking sound. Okay, he told himself, one long minute, two, and never again. As with Margaret. He blew his nose on toilet paper, washed his face in cold water, combed his hair, all as quickly as possible. Never again. Good-bye, little Lisa.

Greta had put shrimp cocktails on the table. There was a cool bottle of Riesling already uncorked. Ed turned on WQXR and put the volume low. A Mozart concerto. He had no appetite, but without Greta he would not have eaten at all. She wore a pink blouse with a darker pink flower pattern. Ed suddenly remembered that the night he met her she had been wearing a pink blouse also, at the party given by Leo somebody, down on 8th Street. Greta had looked painfully shy, sitting with a stemmed glass that she was not drinking from, the only person in the room alone, not talking, and Ed had gone towards her. She had been born in Germany, she had told him by way of explaining her accent, and her parents had moved to France when she was four, in 1933. She was half-Jewish. She had come to America when she was eleven. 'I am not *good* at languages, zat is why I have an accent,' she had said, laughing. (But she spoke French perfectly, Ed discovered later.) Ed had a Russian grandmother. That was all he could muster by way of matching her exoticism, the rest was American for some time back. He had been twenty-eight. Less than a year before Ed had been divorced, and he had custody of Margaret, because Lola had left him for another man. Ed had not said anything of that to Greta that evening, nothing about his marriage or his five-year-old daughter, but a new world had opened with Greta. He had entered it cautiously, like Greta herself. He had been living in a small apartment on West 18th Street, working on a novel, earning money by writing articles that didn't always sell, and by reading for publishers. He had had a baby-sitter, a woman who lived in the same street and who could come on short notice, for the times when he had to be out of the house. Greta had changed all that like a fairy queen with a magic wand – effortlessly. She had been busy with concerts in New York, Philadelphia and Boston, but it was amazing the time she had found for him, evenings, week-ends, amazing the way she had transformed his apartment into a home where one could laugh, eat, relax, and be suddenly happy. Greta and Margaret adored each other. 'I am afraid to have children. I have seen too much,' Greta said. Ed never had tried to persuade her to change her mind.

Somehow they talked during dinner, and without forcing their words out. Finally Ed said, quite firmly and matter of factly, 'Darling, we ought to get another dog soon. It's the sensible thing to do.'

'Yes, but not just yet, Eddie.' Dry-eyed too, she began to clear the table.

Yet the sadness remained, the curious emptiness of the house, the curiously ugly silence.

Clarence arrived at Marylyn's apartment just in time to leave with her to go to the theatre on West 3rd Street. Marylyn was annoyed.

'You could've telephoned, no? I was going with Evelyn if you didn't turn up. Now I've got to call her.' So she did. Evelyn was a friend of Marylyn's who lived on Christopher Street.

Clarence waited, chewing his under lip, not sitting down. Two minutes before, he had seen Pete Manzoni at the corner of Bleecker and Sixth Avenue, and Manzoni had happened to glance into his taxi and had seen him. Manzoni's eyes had widened, and he had smiled in an amused way. It was only one street from Marylyn's apartment on Macdougal, and Clarence had the feeling Manzoni had followed the taxi, or tried to, though when Clarence had paid off the taxi, he hadn't taken the time to look around. Now Clarence was afraid Manzoni would be on the sidewalk when he went out with Marylyn.

'I said, are you coming?' Marylyn stood at the door.

Clarence leapt. 'They kept me busy this afternoon. At the station house.'

'Yes, for gosh sake, what happened? I even called your parents.'

'You did? Oh, that's all right,' Clarence said nervously.

'I had to do *something*. They said you'd been there, but you got a call from the pighouse, as usual. Can't they let you alone on your day off or is New York just crawling with crime?'

'They caught the Pole again, the guy who kidnapped the dog.' They were going down the stairs.

'Who caught him?'

Clarence held the door for her. 'A fellow from my precinct house.' He began looking around at once for a taxi, hoping they'd find one on Macdougal and not have to walk down to Houston.

'There's one!' Marylyn said, and raised her arm. 'Taxi!'

Clarence just then saw Manzoni standing across the street, up near the Bleecker corner. Manzoni nodded knowingly and smiled a little. Clarence got into the taxi after Marylyn. Marylyn gave the theatre's address.

Clarence said, 'I'm accused of taking five hundred dollars from that stink of a Pole to let him go. So I'm sorry if I was late. Or I didn't telephone you.' He had thought of not telling Marylyn this, but it was impossible. He couldn't keep it from her.

'Who accuses you?'

'Well – Rowajinski. The man who stole the Reynolds's dog. He killed the dog – right away, he said.'

'Jesus! Really! – And then collected the ransom.'

'Yes. Twice.' Clarence explained the second thousand-dollar payment. 'I just saw the Reynolds. I had to go by to tell them – tell them I'm going to do my best to throw the book at Rowajinski, you see.' But Clarence couldn't tell Marylyn that Manzoni and another cop had searched his apartment today. Or that he'd just seen Manzoni in the street outside her apartment. Marylyn would get into a panic. She had a completely wrong – or maybe completely average – idea of the police force: they were *all* tough, corrupt, fascist, and not above persecuting individuals if they could gain anything from it.

'You seem to be in more of a mess every day,' Marylyn remarked coolly.

'No, that isn't true. Not with Mr Reynolds – he doesn't think I took any money. He knows I want to help him.' But did Mr Reynolds doubt his honesty? Or did his wife?

Clarence did not follow the play at all, could not become interested, even though two of the cast were nude. The damned thing went on for two interminable acts, the second longer than the first. During the intermission, Marylyn met some of her friends and talked away, ignoring Clarence, it seemed to him.

After the show, they had a snack at a near-by Italian restaurant where unfortunately the carafe of red wine was awful.

'What're they going to do to this Polish guy?' Marylyn asked.

'He's locked up. They'll give him a sentence, I suppose. I don't think he's enough of a nut to be put in a loony-bin. But what a creep!'

'What do you expect to run into in your profession?' Marylyn pushed a neatly wrapped forkful of spaghetti into her mouth.

Clarence smiled. Her perfume, which was so expensive even Marylyn was economical with it, came faintly to him across the table, blighted a little by tomato sauce. 'Don't think I'll be a cop for the next twenty years, darling. The fact that I have been a cop a year or two won't hurt me, it might be an asset if I take another kind of job.'

'Oh, you've changed your mind? A couple of months ago you were talking about the great challenge or something – being able to do some good and so forth.'

One of his euphoric moments, no doubt. One of the moments when he was at peace with the world, and could think about fighting the people, the evils that were not on the side of peace. 'I know. I'm thinking of taking some business administration courses. Then I'll see what comes to me.' I haven't really found myself yet, Clarence wanted to add, but was ashamed to. How could he expect a girl to marry a man who hadn't found himself as yet?

And Marylyn wasn't very interested, wasn't looking much at him, as if she found the restaurant's décor, a table across the way, anything, more interesting.

She said at her door, 'Clare, you'd better go to your place tonight. I don't feel like anything.'

He had wanted to stay with her, just sleep in the same bed with her. Marylyn's apartment was more home to him than his apartment, therefore safe, somehow, despite Manzoni. But Clarence didn't want to beg. 'I'm sorry I didn't call you earlier today, really. Can I – I'm not on duty till tomorrow night at eight. Want to have lunch somewhere? Russian Tearoom?' Marylyn liked the food there.

'Tomorrow I'm meeting Evelyn for shopping. Then we're going to a movie at three.'

That let him out. He didn't want to ask to go to the film if Evelyn was going along. Clarence walked to 19th Street via Fifth Avenue. It was just after midnight. The next time he saw Manzoni, he'd have a word with him, Clarence decided. What did Manzoni have against him? What did he have to lose by asking? On the other hand, Clarence didn't want Marylyn dragged into it. Manzoni could have got her name by now, if he cared to get it: a reddish-haired girl at that address. All Manzoni had to do was ask the delicatessen man around the corner, or the coffee-shop fellow downstairs, the blond, wavy-haired fellow Clarence said hello to when he passed the shop, because the blond fellow was often at the door.

Would they, Clarence wondered, say to Marylyn the next time they saw her: 'There was a tough type asking if I knew your name, Marylyn. Thought you ought to know.' She might suspect at once the man was a fuzz, or someone brought on by him, somehow.

Clarence found himself standing in his apartment with the ceiling light on. He had opened his door with his key as if sleep-walking. He put on some chinos and a soiled shirt and started cleaning. He dusted first, then swept. He plumped up his pillows which had covers and were used as sofa cushions when the bed was made up, then he changed the pillowcases to make the bed look fresher. He was too tired to change the sheets. The bathtub was grey with soot, which had come in through a closed, clouded-glass window that didn't fit very well. Clarence turned the shower on, rinsed out the soot, then scoured the tub. *Damn the goddam Pole!* He didn't deserve to be walking the earth, leaving a trail of sadness, of lies, behind him. Bleeding the Government for compensation now, and next it would be the old-age pension. What could he do, Clarence wondered, to make Rowajinski get the maximum? Must look into that tomorrow.

The telephone rang. Clarence darted for it, hoping it was Marylyn, maybe asking him to come down to Macdougal.

'Clare?' said Marylyn's voice. 'I just wanted to know if you got home safely ... I'm sorry I was such a shit ... Yes, I'm in bed.'

She didn't ask him to come down, but Clarence was smiling when he hung up. Marylyn did care something about him. She *did*. Maybe she even loved him.

Clarence slept until 10 a.m. He went down to the grocery store on Second Avenue to buy some things, and meanwhile he was thinking of what he would say, and do, at the precinct house. Clarence was not sure Rowajinski would still be there. Clarence made breakfast, tidied up the dishes, and dressed in grey flannels and a tweed jacket. The day was warm with sunlight.

Captain Rogers was on duty, and looked very busy. Clarence went into another office and found Lieutenant Santini.

'Well, well,' said Santini, surprised to see Clarence.

'Morning, sir. Is Rowajinski still here?'

'Nijinski, Nijinski,' mumbled Santini in mildly facetious manner. 'The Pole! The man about the dog. Yeah.' Santini blew his nose in his handkerchief. 'Yeah, Clarence. One of the fellows was telling me. He got caught again. By Pete.'

'If it's possible, I'd like to talk with Rowajinski.'

'Yeah? Why?'

Clarence hesitated, briefly. 'Because he's accusing me of taking five hundred dollars to let him go.'

'Yeah, I heard that.' Santini sounded indifferent, as if even a lie, a nasty accusation like this was an everyday event. 'Well, I think a shrink's with the Pole now, you'll have to wait.'

'Yes, sir,' Clarence was glad that Santini had no objection to his seeing him.

'Oh, go ahead in, if the shrink doesn't mind,' Santini said.

Clarence went down the hall to the cage. He saw Rowajinski sitting on his bunk and a man in a dark suit opposite on a chair. The man was chuckling, rolling on his chair. Rowajinski looked through the bars at Clarence and said, pointing a finger:

'There! That's the one! The one who took the five hundred!'

The man looked around. 'You're Patrolman –'

'Duhamell. I'd like to speak with Rowajinski when you're finished.'

'Come in now.' He opened the cage door, which had not been locked. He was smiling still. 'We've got a jolly customer here.' He shut the door with a clang behind Clarence.

Rowajinski had stood up, as if to ward off a possible attack.

'This one thinks he's the greatest,' said the psychiatrist.

'Listen,' Clarence said to the Pole, 'you know you didn't offer me any five hundred dollars and I didn't take it. You'd better come clean about that, or someone's going to beat the truth out of you!'

'Bullshit!' said Rowajinski.

'You're just feeding his ego. The more attention he thinks he's going to get, the better he likes it,' said the shrink indulgently, as if he were talking in the presence of someone deaf.

'Well, what the hell're you going to do with him? Do you know besides – besides everything else, he murdered a *dog*, a French poodle, a family pet?'

'Yes, I heard all that. Well – delusions of superiority. Paranoid, too.'

'I suppose he's going to be locked up?'

Rowajinski was following the conversation with birdlike turns of his head as each man spoke.

'Let's hope,' said the shrink somewhat hopelessly.

'Where's he being sent to?'

'Maybe Bellevue – first.' The psychiatrist was putting papers into a briefcase.

'You won't get anything out of me but the truth!' Rowajinski asserted, jutting his unshaven chin forward. His eyes glinted, and there was a shiny pink circle on each cheekbone, also at the end of his nose.

Rowajinski was wearing new shoes, new trousers that he must have bought with Mr Reynolds's money, Clarence noticed. 'Bastard,' Clarence murmured. He said to the psychiatrist, 'At least he admits killing the dog, I suppose.'

'Bye, Kenneth,' the shrink said.

Clarence went out with him, because it was probably more profitable now to speak with the shrink than with Rowajinski. A guard came up and locked the cage at once.

'He's a pain in the ass, sure,' said the psychiatrist, 'but a dog isn't a human being. Like a child. What you're annoyed about is that he accuses you of taking five hundred bucks.'

Clarence didn't want an analysis. 'Can you tell when this guy's lying and when he's telling the truth?'

'Sometimes. Sometimes his boastings are wildly exaggerated. He says he swam the Hudson River back and forth at once.' The man laughed. 'Like Lloyd Brian, he says. He expects me to know Lloyd Brian, some other guy with a limp, he says.'

Good God, he meant Lord Byron, Clarence realized, and what was so damned funny about it? 'I wonder if you or another doctor could make a statement that this man is lying about the five hundred dollars?' Clarence was aware that the psychiatrist wanted to go to see Santini now.

'Um-m,' said the psychiatrist, musingly.

'Where can I call up to find out about him?' Clarence asked.

'Best to try Bellevue.'

'Tomorrow?'

'Maybe tomorrow, yeah.' The man went into Santini's office.

Clarence hesitated, then went back down the hall to Rowajinski's cage.

Rowajinski was on his feet, and he looked at Clarence cockily.

'You'd better knock it off now, Rowajinski. You're in for a long time.'

'That's what *you* think! – I'll tell 'em the *truth*!'

Clarence gave it up and walked back towards the front door. The psychiatrist was just leaving, and turned briskly eastward on the pavement, swinging his briefcase. Clarence was going in the same direction. Ahead of Clarence, approaching him, came Manzoni, walking with his side-to-side but very muscular-looking gait. Manzoni's musing smirk became a grin as he saw Clarence.

'Well, Clarence,' he said.

Clarence could have swung a fist into his teeth. 'Hello, Pete. I saw you in the Village last night.'

'I live there. Jane Street. Just had a talk with your girl-friend. MacGregor's orders, y'know.'

Clarence felt a rush of blood to his face. He was sure Mac-Gregor hadn't ordered any such thing. 'You get around.'

'Been talkin' to Rowinsk? He spilled the beans on yuh, eh Clarence?'

Both of them were slowly moving in opposite directions, and Manzoni waved casually.

Clarence went on towards the subway. Manzoni was prob-ably going to keep the rumour, the story going that he'd taken the five hundred from the Pole. Such malice, and why? Man-zoni would probably also tell the whole precinct about Marylyn Coomes, say that he, Clarence, had needed some extra money because of her. Lies were so much easier than the truth, they hung together so much better sometimes. Manzoni could have found out Marylyn had no regular job, only freelance. Had he talked to her in her apartment? If so, Manzoni had probably looked into her closet and noticed some of his clothes there. If anyone would resent being invaded by an obnoxious pig, asked personal questions by him, it was Marylyn. Clarence looked hectically at his wrist-watch. Twenty-two past twelve. Maybe he could catch Marylyn before she went out shopping with Evelyn. Fumbling for a dime, Clarence went into a cigar store.

Marylyn answered. '*Yes*, there was a stinking pig here and he delayed me badly, so I've got to rush.'

'Marylyn, I'm sorry. I know. Manzoni. He had no reason to come to see you! He wasn't under orders, believe me, what-ever he said.'

'He was harping on the money you took. And what a vul-gar bastard he is!'

Clarence had never heard her so angry. 'The psychiatrists are on to Rowajinski now. They'll find out soon enough I didn't take any money. – Darling, I just saw Manzoni and he told me he saw you. That's why –'

'What did he say? I'd like to know! You'd think I was a whore the way he spoke to me!'

'Honey, he's a bum. Don't let him bug you. Manzoni –'

But Marylyn had hung up.

Clarence went into the next bar for a beer. Sometimes a beer soothed his nerves, made a sort of weight in his stomach that held him down. He had two steins of draught beer, then took the subway to his apartment.

He took off his jacket and shoes and lay on his back on the bed. He realized he didn't dare to turn up at Marylyn's after work tonight, at 4.30 a.m. If she was half asleep and still angry, she might push him right out her door, and Clarence admitted to himself that he wasn't the kind to force his way in, fling a girl on the bed and – well, at least hold her there, which under some circumstances might be the right thing to do. But he could telephone Marylyn tonight around 7 p.m., when she might be back from the film. Maybe she'd be in a better mood. Clarence put his arm across his eyes. He might lose Marylyn because of this. Manzoni might call on her again, just to heckle her. Marylyn would be livid.

He thought of the Reynolds, of their gloom, of his failure there. That Polish turd! A couple of cops could beat the truth out of him, but psychiatrists weren't going to bother. They'd try to classify him, to 'rehabilitate' him – for what? So he could collect more handouts, and maybe start again with a ransom scheme for another dog, maybe even for a child? How long would they keep him locked up at Bellevue? There weren't any laws, Clarence supposed, made specifically for people like Rowajinski.

Clarence knew he should get some sleep for tonight, so he put on pyjamas and got under the covers. Finally he picked up a book because he couldn't sleep.

At 7 o'clock, Marylyn's telephone didn't answer. Marylyn didn't answer at 10 p.m. or just before midnight. Clarence suspected she deliberately wasn't answering her telephone.

12

The next day, Friday, Clarence went to Marylyn's house just before noon. He much wanted to bring her flowers, or a book, but was afraid a present would look as if he were begging her forgiveness, and Marylyn wouldn't like that. He let himself in her front door, and at her apartment door he knocked.

'Marylyn? – It's Clare.'

She opened the door. 'You.' She was in blue jeans and an old shirt, a broom in her hands.

Clarence came in. 'Marylyn, I'm sorry about Manzoni. He's a trouble-maker, and he –'

'He's just a pig. A real pig.'

'That's true. I don't know what he's got against me. You'd think he had something against me.'

'And what do you think people think now, people in my neighbourhood? A flatfoot arriving, staying nearly an hour. He looks like a pig even in his clothes.'

'Nearly an hour?'

'They'll think I'm running a cops' cathouse, that's what. Well, I'm not!'

Clarence could not calm her down. She was on one tack, one note. 'Darling, you must know – it's the worst thing in the world to me if someone's hurt you.'

'He didn't hurt me, he insulted me!'

'I'll punch his nose!'

'What good will that do?'

'Marylyn, darling.' Clarence tried to put his arms around her, but she pushed him back with a strength that startled him. Her force seemed a measure of how much she had turned against him. Clarence was astounded.

'I don't even want to know what this fuzz said to you about me! I can imagine. A fine bunch of people you work with! And him – the pig – futzing around trying to find out from me if you took a bribe! Jesus!'

'He knows I didn't take it. He didn't say anything about you to me.'

'I wish you'd just leave,' Marylyn said.

'Can't we – can't we have some lunch? Out somewhere? And calm down a little?'

'I'm not in the mood to calm down. I'm cleaning the house. Oh, and while we're on that subject, I wish you'd take your things from here.' She gestured to the closet.

After a moment, Clarence moved to the closet, whose door was ajar, and stood there, not seeing. He was startled by Marylyn's tossing two paper shopping bags at his feet.

'These ought to hold everything. Don't forget the ties.'

Clarence folded his things and put them into the shopping bags: trousers, a jacket, a pair of levis, shoes, two ties, finally some striped pyjamas from a hook. He took the bags to the door.

'To think that I'd ever get mixed up with the cops!' Marylyn said. 'I'd rather get *arrested* than have this. No wonder people call them pigs. One thing I'm proud of, I'm not on their side!'

'I'm not a cop when I'm with you. I'm a human being.'

She sighed. 'You're still a cop. Would you go?'

Clarence went, without saying good-bye, without saying he'd telephone tomorrow, because he did not want another negative word from her. He opened the door again before he quite closed it behind him. 'I love you, Marylyn. Really.'

She said nothing, didn't even look at him.

Were women often like this, he wondered, so damned definite-sounding and then – Couldn't they change their minds in a few days? He had to believe she would change. He looked around for Manzoni on the street, not really expecting to see him, but he ought to be prepared for anything from Manzoni. He wondered if Manzoni had tried to get fresh with Marylyn, touched her at all? Probably he had. Clarence's fists tightened on the shopping bags.

Clarence did not call Marylyn the following day, believing

it was wiser not to telephone for several days so that she might begin to miss him, to feel she had been too harsh. However, Clarence was not sure these were the right tactics.

Saturday night after midnight, when he was walking a patrol post that included some of Riverside Drive, a drunk was scraping along the wall of an apartment building, mumbling, ready to fall if the building hadn't held him up. He threw off Clarence's hands and swung a fist at him, missing, and Clarence retaliated with a hard right to the man's jaw. Clarence knocked him out. The act exhilarated Clarence, as if it were some kind of triumph. A passer-by or two stopped to look for a few seconds, then walked on. Clarence's partner that night, a thirty-five-year-old man called Johnson, merely laughed. Clarence radioed for a patrol car and took the man to the station house like a trophy, where he booked him for public drunkenness and resisting arrest.

Sunday noon, Clarence telephoned Bellevue to ask about Rowajinski. It took nearly ten minutes to get through to the right ward or department. Clarence said it was his precinct house telephoning.

'He's to be released Wednesday as an out-patient,' a man's voice said. 'He'll have an out-patients' counsellor visiting him twice a week. To keep an eye on him, y'know.'

'Released? You're talking about Kenneth Rowajinski?'

'Yes. It's him you're talking about, isn't it?'

'Do you know where he's going to be when he's out?'

'The out-patients' department does that. They find these people a room somewhere.'

'We've got to know where that is,' said Clarence.

'You could call back Tuesday. Tuesday afternoon.' The man hung up.

Released. Probably the station house would be informed of Rowajinski's future address as a matter of course, Clarence thought, because surely the law wasn't finished with him. Weren't they going to make him pay the missing eight hundred dollars? Or were they going to believe that he, Clarence, had taken five hundred? Was the precinct waiting for the Bellevue report before bringing that matter up?

It would be a fine thing to tell Mr Reynolds, Clarence

thought, that Rowajinski was going to be back in the world again on Wednesday.

Clarence's mother telephoned around five. Was he coming out Tuesday and Wednesday, or one of those days? Clarence told a small lie and said that his precinct house wanted him closer.

'Oh, Clary! You're just as close if you come to see us. Ralph'll treat you to a taxi to New York, I know.'

Clarence was simply too distressed to go. His mother would keep asking him what was the matter. He emphatically did not want to tell his parents what had happened with Marylyn, even if his mother might, just might give him some sound advice as to how to handle her. 'I can't, Mother, I can't.'

'What's happened now, Clary? I wish you'd tell me.'

'Nothing's happened. Don't make me feel like a child, Mother.'

When they had hung up, Clarence at once telephoned Marylyn.

'It's me,' Clarence said. 'How are you? . . . When can I see you, darling. Please.'

She sighed. 'I don't think I want to see you.'

He could not get anywhere with her.

He tried to sleep, or at least to rest, until he had to leave the house at 7.15. Now it was hardly 5.30. He wanted to see the Reynolds. Yes. He'd try to see them for a few minutes before he went on duty tonight. He dialled the Reynolds's number. There was no answer, and this depressed Clarence further. Around six he tried again, let the telephone ring ten times, and on the eleventh it was answered by Greta.

'Oh, Officer Duhamell!'

'I wonder if I can come and see you? Before I go on duty at eight. Now I mean.'

'Yes, of course you can. We have someone coming for dinner. That is why I am out of breath. I was just running in from shopping when I heard the phone. Ed is out seeing an author but he is due any minute.'

Clarence felt happier when he had hung up. What a nice woman she was! A really nice, warm-hearted woman. Clarence took a taxi.

Greta Reynolds opened the door. Clarence was delighted to see that Mr Reynolds had arrived.

'Hello. Good evening.' Ed was stacking a manuscript on the coffee-table. 'So what's the news?'

'Well – annoying news to me. Bellevue is releasing Rowajinski Wednesday. He's going to be under surveillance. By an out-patients' counsellor.'

'Um. Well. Excuse me a sec.' Ed carried some papers and books into another room.

Mrs Reynolds had gone into the kitchen. The table was set for three, with red candles not yet lighted. Clarence hoped he could stay a few minutes without annoying the Reynolds, wished in fact that he could be the third person at the table, but he supposed he was the most unwelcome person among the Reynolds's acquaintance.

The doorbell rang, and Mrs Reynolds crossed the living-room to answer it. 'Do sit down, Mr Duhamell.'

Clarence sat down in order to be less conspicuous.

'You know Eric, I think,' said Mrs Reynolds. 'Professor Schaffner, Officer Duhamell.'

Clarence stood up. 'Good evening, sir.'

'Good evening. What's the trouble? Any trouble?'

'Oh, no, sir. No trouble.' Clarence was sorry Eric had arrived so soon.

Ed Reynolds came in. 'Hello, Eric, how are you?'

'The same.'

Clarence felt that Eric was equally annoyed by his presence. It was the fact he was a cop, even out of uniform. No one would be completely relaxed until he was gone. Cops stood for trouble. Greta was making a drink for Eric – something like Cinzano. Clarence declined a drink.

'We're going to move,' Ed said to Eric.

'To move?'

'It's –' Greta looked at Clarence. 'We have been through too much here, you see.'

Ed was looking also at Clarence, at his earnest young face. How bright was he? Ed was inclined to think he was honest, and that counted for something. He was well-meaning and not tough. And how long would that last?

'I think I understand why you move,' said Eric.

'You see,' Ed began in a deliberately easy manner to Clarence, 'my daughter Margaret — She was living here with us when she died. A year ago.'

'Oh,' said Clarence.

'It's too much, my husband's daughter, and now this,' Greta said.

'Your daughter,' Clarence said to Ed, 'was ill?' She must have been very young, Clarence was thinking. He imagined a child with some incurable illness.

'No, no,' said Ed. 'She was shot.'

'Eddie!' said Greta.

'She was eighteen,' Ed went on. 'My only child — of my first marriage. She was going around with a rather wild bunch. You know — trying drugs. There was a raid down in the Village. Sort of a nightclub. A police raid. But it wasn't a police bullet that killed her. Someone had a gun, and when the police came in, in the confusion —' Ed stopped with a shrug.

'Eighteen,' Clarence said.

'She was in college,' said Greta. 'Eddie, you mustn't talk about all that.'

'I'm finished,' Ed said. 'This young man is a patrolman. He knows about such things.'

Clarence saw that Eric, as well as Greta, wanted Ed to stop. What a shame, Clarence wanted to say. How long had Ed and Greta been married, he wondered. Mr Reynolds's only child. And now that Mrs Reynolds was at least forty, they probably weren't going to have any children. 'Yes, I can understand that this apartment would depress you,' Clarence said.

'You found another place?' Eric asked.

'We did. Greta did. Down on East Ninth. Practically the Village,' Ed said. 'I was never crazy about this neighbourhood, anyway. It's like a big cemetery.'

A silence.

Clarence composed his farewell, and said, 'By Tuesday I'll be able to find out where Rowajinski's going to live. I intend to keep an eye on him.'

'The one who killed the dog?' Eric asked.

'Yes, sir. He's being released from Bellevue Wednesday. They're going to find a –'

'Released from Bellevue? Then he goes to prison, you mean,' Eric said in his clear, emphatic way.

'I hope so, sir. I'm not sure.'

'You mean, he might *not* go to prison? What kind of justice is that?' Eric asked rhetorically, swinging his arms so that his drink nearly spilled. 'Out on the streets again?'

'So? He's just a little odd,' Ed said and laughed.

'I'm going to do what I can, sir,' Clarence said to Mr Reynolds.

Ed looked at the young policeman. 'Frankly, I don't care where he lives. I don't think I want to know. So don't bother finding out for my sake.'

Clarence nodded. 'All right, sir.'

'I don't deny I'd rather hear he was locked up,' Ed added.

'What kind of justice,' Eric repeated, shaking his head.

'Of course it has hurt *us*. But it is not the same as if a child was kidnapped – or killed,' Greta said, speaking both to her husband and to Eric. 'It just isn't.'

Why wasn't it the same, if people suffered the same from it, Clarence thought. The evil of the deed seemed exactly the same, whether it was a child or a dog. 'Good night, sir. – Mrs Reynolds.' Clarence took his leave awkwardly, feeling Mr Reynolds's eyes on him until the door was closed. Mr Reynolds must think him a complete ass. Inefficient, stupid – and now hanging around, perhaps.

By the time Clarence had walked to the precinct house, his anger against Manzoni had begun to boil again. He wondered if Manzoni was on duty. Manzoni was in the locker room, changing into civvies. Clarence waited for Manzoni in the front hall. When Manzoni came out, Clarence nodded a greeting which was barely acknowledged by Manzoni, then Clarence followed him out on to the pavement.

'Pete?'

Manzoni turned, and a grin started to spread over his face. 'Yeah?'

'I'd like to ask you something. Just what've you got against me? Just tell me straight.'

'Against you? How do I know? If somebody says you took five hundred dollars, I try to find out about it, don't I? That's my business, ain't it?' Manzoni sounded proud of being a cop, confident of his duties.

'You know who said it, that psycho. You go around believing psychos?' Clarence went on calmly. 'There was no reason for you to question my friend, the girl in the Village. It was annoying to her.'

'Aw, college boy! Annoyin'!' Manzoni laughed.

If you speak to her again, I'll report it to MacGregor, Clarence wanted to say, and at once realized that he did not dare do that. He didn't want MacGregor to know that he stayed on Macdougal many nights, though Manzoni might already have told MacGregor this. There might be an actual law against it, though Clarence had never seen such a law. 'Just knock it off, would you, Pete? Check with Bellevue. Maybe the guy's telling the truth now.' Clarence was moving off, back to the precinct house door.

'Aw, bullshit,' said Manzoni.

It reminded Clarence of Rowajinski.

13

Kenneth Rowajinski, with his suitcase, was escorted from Bellevue to his new lodging on Morton Street near Hudson Street on Wednesday morning at 10 a.m. He rode in a white ambulance with two stretcher bunks, on one of which he sat with arms folded, facing a plump intern, or male nurse, in white. Kenneth took an amused attitude towards it all. What a lot of attention he was getting! Really V.I.P. treatment. They'd found a suitable room for him, and they were driving him there, free of charge. But the fact remained they had attached fifty per cent of his compensation, and were taking three hundred dollars of his savings to repay Reynolds, and Kenneth had more or less been compelled to sign a paper saying he was in agreement with this. So Kenneth's sense of importance, of having really won in this story (he wasn't after all behind bars) was in conflict with a certain sense of being hamstrung, supervised, spied upon. A man from Bellevue was going to call on him Friday afternoon at 3 p.m. and see how he was doing, see if he was living in the way Bellevue thought people ought to live.

His second-floor room in the red brick house was medium-sized with a high ceiling, and smelled of dusty carpets, although there was only one small worn-out carpet down, the rest of the floor being covered with linoleum. He had no private toilet, but had to use the one down the hall. There was a basin in the hall with a semi-soiled towel hanging by it. The bathroom door was locked, and one had to ask the landlord, a man named Phil, for the key, Kenneth was told. Under the intern's eye, Kenneth paid out twenty dollars, a week's rent, to the creature called Phil. Now Kenneth had a little bookshelf about two feet long over his bed, but no books to put in it. And no stove. He'd have to eat all his meals out, or eat cold food. Expensive. Kenneth decided he would write a letter on the subject of no stove, and have it ready to present to the Bellevue man on Friday.

Kenneth's first sally from his new abode came twenty minutes after the Bellevue intern had left him. He went out to buy a *Times*. He bought also six cans of beer, some sliced salami, a package of hamburger rolls, and a quarter-pound of butter. When he came back, it struck him that the radiator was not hot enough, so before treating himself to a beer, Kenneth went in search of Phil. He even left his room door unlocked. The door did not lock automatically.

Kenneth could not find Phil, and suspected that he was hiding from him. Kenneth banged on doors, called 'Phil!' and 'Mr Phil!' until the unpleasant voice of a woman upstairs shouted down the stairwell:

'Quiet! Quiet, I say! – What the hell's going on down there?'

And they called Bellevue a madhouse!

Kenneth went back to his own room, churning with frustration, and felt the lukewarm radiator again. He started to open a beer, then the awareness of semi-incarnation came over him again. However, Kenneth had his own two keys, and no one had told him when to be in at night. Kenneth tore off the ring of the can, drank half the beer, then set the can on the window sill inside the room, beside the paper bag of salami and butter. There was a draught through the old ill-fitting window, no need to open it a crack. Kenneth had to go out for a walk, just to feel free. He put on his new overcoat again, and his hat.

On the sidewalk, he looked around for police spies, Bellevue spies. Buildings, dwellings, were not so tall here as in his old neighbourhood of West End. There were more trees along the pavement – they'd have been bigger, Kenneth thought, if they were not peed on hundreds of times a day by filthy dogs – and more small stores and shops. But traffic on Hudson was the same noisy mess as anywhere else, as West End, for example. Then Kenneth saw a man's figure and slowed his steps. Kenneth slightly lifted his chin from his coat collar, and turned his face towards the man like a dog pointing. Yes, surely: it was the bastard of a cop again, the young blond fellow, in ordinary clothes and without a hat. He was on the other side of Hudson Street, on the corner of Morton, and had obviously been waiting for him to come out of his house. He must have learned his address from Bellevue.

Kenneth walked downtown. This left the young cop behind him and on his left, on the other side of Hudson. After some twenty steps, Kenneth glanced over his shoulder. Yes, the cop was following him. Of all the appalling nerve! Kenneth stood still, again facing the distant cop squarely, and by his manner challenging the cop to cross Hudson and speak to him – or whatever he wanted to do. The clear memory of those five hundred going up in smoke in his hotel basin gave Kenneth a massive moral support.

Dummell zigzagged southward and walked into Macdougal Street. Kenneth had barely entered Macdougal, when he saw the cop climbing some front steps, disappearing into a doorway. Kenneth waited a few minutes, then went to the doorway to ascertain its number. Was this where Dummell lived? A rather crummy place, but it was not impossible that Dummell lived here. Kenneth waited across the street, where there was a shop window he could pretend to be looking into, while it gave a fuzzy reflection of the door that Dummell had entered.

After a few minutes, Kenneth crossed the street to read the names on the mail boxes in the open foyer. He gave them a hasty look, not wanting Dummell to come down and find him, but Dummell's name was not among the six or eight names. Kenneth went back across the street. Fifteen minutes or so passed, and Kenneth walked to the corner and back. At last he crossed Macdougal and went into an artsy espresso and snack place almost next door to the house Dummell had entered. He addressed a wavy-haired man behind the counter.

'Excuse me. Is there a police officer living next door? A tall blond fellow?'

The man smiled, not in a nice way. He was arranging little white cups and saucers neatly on a shelf. 'Why?'

'You know him?' Kenneth was sure the man knew whom he meant. Kenneth also sensed that the wavy-haired man disliked him, was suspicious of him.

'*I* dunno,' said the man innocently, and kept polishing his cups.

Kenneth left. There was a delicatessen around the corner, and Kenneth entered it. Kenneth assumed a more polite air. He had to wait a few minutes until a black girl had bought and paid for a sackful of things. 'I was told a policeman lives in this neighbourhood,' Kenneth said. 'I must talk with a policeman right away. Is there a policeman?'

The fat man in the white apron looked at Kenneth with a calm blankness. 'You in a hurry?'

'Yes. Something about my car. Somebody broke in. Somebody said a policeman lives near here. True?'

'There's a policeman visits. I don't know if he's there now. Why doncha use the phone and call the police?' he gestured to the telephone on his counter.

'Visits who?'

The fat man's expression changed. He jerked his thumb towards the door. 'Listen, Mac, go call the cops somewhere. Take my advice.'

Kenneth went.

Kenneth was still determined to wait, and he walked left, crossed Macdougal at a corner, and as soon as he turned and looked towards the house again, he saw Dummell walking in his direction with a long-haired girl in pants. Both were talking and gesturing. Quarrelling? Dummell was completely absorbed in the reddish-haired girl. His girl-friend, of course. Or was he married?

And now they were parting at the corner. The girl waved him away. Dummell shoved his hands into his pockets and walked on uptown, looking down at the sidewalk. Kenneth drifted downtown. The girl was not in sight on the side street. Had she gone into the delicatessen? Would that rude swine behind the counter mention *him* to the girl?

The girl came out of the delicatessen, carrying a bag.

Kenneth crossed Macdougal and followed her. She went up the steps of her house. 'Excuse me, miss,' Kenneth said.

She turned, a little scared looking.

Kenneth limped half-way up the steps. 'You're a friend of the cop's?'

'Who're *you* ? — Get out of here ! *Leave me alone!*'

Kenneth had never seen such fear so quickly. He smiled, excited and pleased. '*I'm* the one who gave your friend five hundred dollars! You're his girl-friend?' Kenneth added a phrase and licked his lips, stammering from his own sudden laughter.

She almost screamed: Kenneth could see her tongue in her open mouth. She looked to right and left, but at that instant there was no one near them. Kenneth stepped backward carefully, holding to the stone balustrade. He didn't want her to scream and cause someone to grab him, question him.

'He's a crook!' Kenneth said. 'He says I'm a crook! *He's* a crook!'

Kenneth slipped away quickly, limping southward, away from the girl and from the young cop — just in case Dummell might have turned back. *Ha! Ha!* Dummell's girl-friend. He could make her feel uncomfortable, all right. Just by being on the sidewalk, for instance, when she came out of her house. The cops couldn't arrest him for that. He had as much right to take a walk on Macdougal as on any other street.

Would the girl call up Dummell now and tell him she'd seen — What did they call him ? Rowajinski ? The Pole?

The day was beginning in a very satisfactory manner.

14

It was Clarence's day off, Wednesday, meaning he had the evening off and didn't have to work until Thursday evening, but now he was without Marylyn. She was adamant, absolutely unbending. However, today at least he had not made himself a bore, hadn't stayed too long in her house. The point was, he had been unsuccessful. 'Can't you get it through your head, I don't like cops? I can't stand the *life*!' she had said, as if 'the life' had some special, horrible meaning for her. Clarence hadn't mentioned the Pole, that he was out today, on the loose again. He had mentioned seeing the Reynolds Sunday evening. He wished Marylyn could meet the Reynolds, but he didn't know how that could be arranged. Was he a friend of theirs? Hardly. Could he ever make them his friends? It was awful to be in the predicament he was in with them, having let them down in the only service he could have rendered – saving their dog. Clarence was on his way home on the Lexington Avenue bus as these thoughts went through his head. Marylyn's stubbornness had left him feeling stunned and tired. He wanted to put on more comfortable clothes, then go to the library on East 23rd Street and change some books.

His telephone was ringing. On the floor below he heard it and went flying up the stairs, thinking it might be Marylyn with a cataclysmic change of mind.

'Hello!' It was Marylyn, speaking before he spoke. 'Listen, that creep – that Pole – He was just on my doorstep!'

'What? You're kidding!'

'The hell I am! He has a limp?'

'Yes.'

'He nearly followed me into the house!' she yelled, her voice cracking. 'Where is safe, I'd like to know? Where? You the great police force!'

'Darling – What did he want?'

'He said you took the five hundred dollars, if you want to know.'

'Marylyn – you're not joking, are you? You're serious?'

'He *spoke* to me. He was almost coming in the door. What've I got to do to be safe, move from here? And you wonder why I don't want to see *you* again?'

'I – I'll report him. The Pole.'

But the next thing Clarence heard was the gentle hum of a dial tone. He put the telephone down, and slammed the back of his fist against his forehead in an agony of shock and shame. 'God!' He took off his tie and opened his collar. He'd go straight to the Pole's pad and scare the hell out of him.

Clarence took a taxi and had the taxi drop him at Hudson and Barrow Street. He glanced around for Rowajinski on the streets, and didn't see him. At Rowajinski's building, one of the five bells (most of them with illegible names) said SUPER, so Clarence pushed this. No answer, and he pushed another, waited a few seconds and tried a third.

Someone buzzed him in.

'Who is it?' a woman's voice yelled from upstairs.

Clarence leapt up the stairs three at a time. He was confronted by a woman of about sixty in a pale-pink dressing-gown. 'I'm looking for the new tenant. The new lodger. Rowajinski,' Clarence said. 'Just moved in today.'

Silence for several seconds. 'Somebody moved in on the second floor.'

'Thanks,' Clarence ran down one flight. There were two doors. He knocked on both. There was silence.

Then a big dark-haired man climbed the stairs slowly behind Clarence. He was in shirtsleeves and houseshoes.

'Excuse me, is this where Rowajinski lives?' asked Clarence.

'Who are you?'

'I'm the police,' Clarence said, pulling out his bill-fold.

The man looked at his police card. 'What's the trouble? Listen, if he's a screwball, I don't have to take him, see? What's the trouble? They told me there wasn't gonna be no trouble.'

'I just want to talk with him,' Clarence said. 'Let me in.'

The man looked at him oddly, then knocked. 'Mr —'

'Rowajinski,' Clarence said.

'Rozinski?' the man yelled at the door.

No answer.

'I would like you to open the door,' Clarence said, with an effort at calmness.

The man pulled a batch of keys from his pocket, and unlocked the door, but it didn't open. 'Bolted on the inside.'

Clarence wanted to smash it with his shoulder, but restrained himself, because the man was calling:

'Mr Rozinski? Would you open the door, please? It's the police!'

Silence. And the man was about to shout again when the bolt slid.

'Police?' said Rowajinski, all innocence.

'Thank you,' said Clarence to the super.

'What's going on?' the man asked the Pole.

Clarence said, 'It's routine. I had to make sure he was here.'

'Are you taking him away?' asked the man.

'No.'

'Not that I'd mind much. I don't have to have weirdos, y'know. I'm doing people a favour. But I don't have to do people no favours.'

'I know. I just have to speak with him for a minute,' Clarence said, pushing his way into Rowajinski's room. He closed the door.

'And what's the idea of this intrusion?' asked Rowajinski.

Clarence tried to back him, by walking forward, into the far side of the room, in case the super was outside the door listening, but Rowajinski circled. 'Among the things you're not supposed to do,' Clarence began, 'is to hang around people's houses and pester them. I just heard about Macdougal Street, Rowajinski. Would you rather be in Bellevue permanently locked up?'

'I got a right to go to Macdougal Street,' said Rowajinski, unruffled. His fists were on his hips.

'I've got the right to book you for loitering and verbal assault!'

Kenneth smirked. 'She's your girl-friend, right? Not your wife, is she?'

Clarence pulled his right fist back.

Kenneth dodged. But obviously the cop wasn't going to hit him. The cop was afraid to. 'You can't come into my house and menace me like this! This is my property here. Get out!'

'Oh, stuff it,' Clarence said. He glanced around quickly at the room – the Pole's cruddy suitcase open on the floor, everything in the room worn out, the seat worn out in the green armchair, metal ashtrays with black gook stuck to them, a bed worse than a cage bed. But it was a trifle cleaner than the Pole's last place.

'I asked you to leave my house!' said Rowajinski.

'Rowajinski –' Clarence spoke between his teeth '– if you hang around Macdougal, I'm going to bust you wide open. I'll fix you. Don't think I can't. It'd be easy for me.'

'Sure, you're a crook! A crook with a gun!' Kenneth said in a proud but martyred tone. 'But I've got *you* fixed! *You* take bribes! You –'

Clarence grabbed the Pole's shirtfront and shook him so that his head bobbed this way and that. 'You can shove that crap right back up your ass, you lousy pollock!'

Kenneth jerked back and squirmed, but could not break the cop's hold on his shirtfront, though the shirt was tearing. 'Crook!'

Clarence gave a shove, and Rowajinski's head banged the wall, then Clarence swung him around and thrust him away. Kenneth fell backward, and sat down on the floor with a thump. Clarence went to the door and out. At first, Clarence did not see the big man at the head of the stairs that went down.

'Now listen, what's all this? What's he done?'

Clarence kept on going, quickly, down the stairs, silent. He went out and turned east, crossed Hudson and had to leap to avoid a taxi that nearly hit him. The taxi driver honked in fury. Clarence wanted to go straight to Marylyn's house. But what good would it do, even if he told *this*, what had just happened?

Kenneth Rowajinski, still on the floor, was finding it impossible to control his bowels. He tensed himself, but it was of no use. At last, miserable, he got up and carefully removed his trousers. No basin in the crummy room! Such a horrible thing! He had heard of such things – due to fright – but it had never happened to *him* before. He removed his underpants, put on other trousers, and went to ask Phil for the key to the bathroom. He would have to wash his underpants in the bathtub, not at the hall basin where anyone could see him.

'Phil! – Mr Phil!' Kenneth shouted in the hall. He went part way downstairs.

'Listen, Mr Rowajinski,' came Phil's voice from the dark hall below. 'I want to know what's going on!' Phil was coming up.

'There is nothing going on. I would like the key to the bathroom,' Kenneth said stiffly.

'Why did that cop want to see you? What've you done? What was all the noise?'

'Mr Phil – the key to the bathroom and I will speak with you later.'

'Oh, yeah? I'm going to speak with Bellevue!'

'Mr Phil! – The key! I want to wash!'

Finally he got the key. Phil fetched it from his own apartment. Kenneth's ablutions took fifteen minutes. And *was* Phil calling up Bellevue? It was probably an empty threat.

But no doubt Phil would snoop on Friday when the Bellevue bastard arrived.

15

On Friday – not at 3 p.m. as promised but after four – a serious, dumpy brunette of about forty called on Kenneth at his Morton Street room. She had a large brown leather handbag, and a large notebook of the kind called ledgers. Her tone was distant and polite, and the words that came out of her might as well have been those of a recorded message.

'You are settling down? . . . What have you been doing?'

'I read. I keep busy.'

'You aret unemployed now.' She sat on the edge of the arm-chair's seat, and kept consulting her notes and writing notes of her own, seldom even looking at him.

'I have not been employed in five years. I had an injury to my foot. My toes.'

'Do you get along all right with your landlord?'

Kenneth thought it best to say he did.

'Where do you have your meals? . . . Do you go out a few times a day?'

Kenneth had been going to complain about the lack of a stove, but he thought it might up his rent if they moved him to another room or to another place with a kitchen.

Soon she looked at her wrist-watch and said she would be going, and would he sign on this line? Kenneth signed in slow but jerky and angular handwriting below the notes she had just taken. He tried to read them, but the writing was dif-ficult and full of abbreviations, and the woman rudely pulled the ledger from him.

'I will call on you again on Tuesday at three. Will you make a note of that so you won't forget?'

She was gone.

No mention of Macdougal Street! So much for Dummell's threats!

In good spirits now, Kenneth put on his hat and overcoat and headed towards Macdougal Street. He had a plan. At the first liquor store he came to, he bought a bottle of wine — not an expensive bottle, only a dollar twenty-nine plus tax, and anyway he intended to keep it. He took one of the business cards of the store, which were in a little box on the counter. On Macdougal he walked more slowly, watching for the girls who might be on the street. He hoped she was on the street, walking away from her house. Then as he stepped on to the kerb of the girl's block, he saw her coming out of her house door, with a dark-haired fellow. She was in blue jeans. From the way the fellow was looking at her, he was another boy-friend. A popular girl! Kenneth at once went into the street where the delicatessen was, and walked as quickly as he could, while still doing his best to conceal his limp. Kenneth circled the block, and when he again approached the house, the girl and the young man were not in sight.

He peered at the names beside the bells in the foyer, and chose one to ring: Malawek. This resulted in a buzz, and Kenneth entered the house.

'Who is it please?' a woman's voice called down.

Kenneth climbed the stairs, not wanting to shout. 'Delivery,' he said. 'Got to deliver a bottle to a young lady who was just in the shop.' He showed the woman the store card. 'The store got her address but not her name. A reddish-haired girl. In pants.'

'Marylyn? Sounds like Marylyn,' said the woman. 'She's third floor front. One up.'

'Marylyn who?'

'Marylyn Coomes.'

'Thank you,' Kenneth said, and climbed the stairs. In case the woman below was listening, he knocked on Marylyn's door. No answer. Kenneth did not want to push his luck too much in case the woman was waiting below (she probably was) to see that he left the house, so he set the bottle on the threshold of the door and went down the stairs.

The woman was waiting, looking through the crack of her own door.

In the foyer, Kenneth looked over the names again and saw

Coomes, and how to spell it. He went out and turned right, away from the direction Miss Coomes and boy-friend had taken. He walked back to his room on Morton Street.

Kenneth bolted his door, got out his writing tablet and his ball-point pen. Now he felt like himself again. He addressed an envelope to Miss Mariline Coomes, then he wrote:

New York

Dear Mariline,

Enjoy the wine! It is too bad you did not seem to like me our first meeting but I am doing you a faver steering you away from that crooked cop boy friend. He will be caught and dishonnerably discharged if he is not allready. Stay away from him and *all cops*! They are crooked pigs, very dangerous men with guns. Better to carry on your busness (ha-ha) without them.

A Friend

He wrote it in his ordinary handwriting. If Dummell ever saw it, what could he do about it? He was warning a young girl to stay away from a crooked pig. Kenneth had a small reserve of stamps, and he stamped his envelope and went out to look for a box. He had not felt so happy in many days. And he found himself glancing at people on the street, wondering if they would make good recipients for an unsigned letter or two — meaning would they scare easily, get upset? Start suspecting the wrong people? Now Phil — *There* was a likely customer and right under his nose, so to speak, meaning Kenneth could watch him. What was Phil's last name? How about worrying Mr Phil with an anonymous threat to set his house on fire? That would drive him nuts.

Kenneth dropped his letter to Mariline in a box.

Clarence, on Monday morning around eleven, found a letter in his mailbox addressed in Marylyn's handwriting. He ripped the envelope open, saw there was another letter besides hers in it, and at a glance thought it was from the Pole, though his was in script. Clarence's stomach seemed to drop several inches. He read Marylyn's letter with close attention.

Dear Clare,

Am sending this to you though I wanted to take it to the first police station but there I thought it might get lost. Since you seem to hate this creep, why don't you work on this? There was a bottle of wine on my doorstep Friday and I mean *inside the house* at my apartment door. Molly tells me the shit said he was a delivery man and asked for my name and she gave it to him. There'll be telephone calls next. Now what am I supposed to do – move from here? I am thinking *seriously* of moving and what a stinking bore that is, finding another place at rent I can afford.

M.

Clarence read Rowajinski's note, then went back upstairs to telephone Marylyn. But he hesitated, not sure of what he was going to say. He could report it to MacGregor, of course. Manzoni would hear about it, no doubt. Clarence didn't want Manzoni hanging around Macdougal. Yet Marylyn deserved protection, his protection. Rowajinski had to be stopped, and locked up.

Or maybe he should take Rowajinski's letter to Bellevue. This seemed a better idea. Clarence dialled Marylyn's number.

'Hello!' Clarence said, delighted that she had answered. 'I just got the letter, darling. I'm going to take it to Bellevue now.'

'Bellevue?'

'Bellevue released him. They're the ones responsible just now. More so than the police.'

'Oh, the *police*,' she groaned.

'I'll try to get him back in,' Clarence said, wishing he could put on a uniform for this errand. 'Darling, I'm sorry. It's awful, it's creepy, I know.'

'Creepy? That guy's nuts! A monster! And walking the streets! I can't understand it. I'm afraid to go out and buy a bottle of milk. A fat lot anybody on the street would do if that guy grabbed my arm – or anything else.'

'I know,' Clarence said miserably.

'I don't go out in the evening now unless I'm with people who'll see me home.'

Men, Clarence thought. He wondered if she had looked up Dannie again, a half-Italian fellow who lived on West 11th

Street and was a ballet dancer. Curiously enough for a ballet dancer, he wasn't queer. 'I'm going to Bellevue, darling. I'll call you back later.'

Clarence went to Bellevue, where he had to wait apparently over a lunch period in order to see the right person, a Dr Stifflin or something like that. Clarence sat in a white-tiled foyer through which interns and nurses went back and forth, and bandaged people were pushed along in wheelchairs or on rolling tables. Other people waited on straight chairs against the walls, and had lugubrious or fearful expressions on their faces. Arms, legs, feet, faces, necks were in bandages or plaster casts. How on earth did so many people get injured, Clarence wondered. And yet, he ought to know. Bellevue, also, wasn't the only hospital in Manhattan. The amount of pain in the world was really appalling. And why did most people want to go on living? This thought shocked Clarence, not for any religious scruples, but simply because to Clarence it had seemed normal to want to live, until this instant.

A nurse told Clarence he could see Dr Stifflin, and took him to a room full of chairs and what looked like sterilizing equipment. Dr Stifflin was young, and wore white.

'Yes, Rowajinski,' he said, consulting a tablet. 'Some organic brain damage. Paranoia, aggression. One of those pain-in-the-neck types but not likely to be really violent. Not a bad I.Q.' He smiled. 'He's being visited twice weekly by an out-patients' psychotherapist.'

'You probably know,' said Clarence, 'that he killed a dog in Riverside Park for no reason and extorted two thousand dollars' ransom for it.'

'No. – Oh, yeah, I heard about that. That's a problem for the police.'

Couldn't he kill a child next, Clarence wanted to ask, but he produced the letter from Marylyn instead. 'Also a poison-pen letter-writer, and this is his latest. Sent to a young woman twenty-two years old named Marylyn Coomes.'

Dr Stifflin read it, then smiled slightly. 'Hates police. Yeah, that follows. How'd you get this?' He handed it back.

'I happen to know Miss Coomes. I'm a police officer,' Clarence added. 'What I would like to ask you, Dr Stifflin, is – can you arrange to have him confined somewhere? He's been out just a few days now, and he's started the same things again.'

'There's no room for him here. Not to sleep here.'

'I understand, but doesn't he need watching? Can't he be put in some other institution?'

Dr Stifflin shrugged slightly. He had appeared to have time to talk at first, but suddenly he wanted to be off. 'That'll depend on the out-patients' psychotherapist's report. We didn't find him violent.'

'Who is he – the psychotherapist?'

'Probably a woman. I can find out –'

'Can't you find out now?'

'Hasn't that been sent to the police? We usually send that kind of information to the precinct that picked the person up.'

'All right. That's my precinct. I'll check.' There were people in straightjackets here at Bellevue, people in cells with barred windows to prevent their jumping out. Compared to them Rowajinski was practically sane, Clarence supposed. 'And if the psychotherapist's report isn't favourable, he can be put away?'

'Sure. Of course.' Dr Stifflin was opening the door to leave. 'I'm on duty now. So long.'

He left the door ajar for Clarence.

Clarence went out into the chill, overcast day. He wanted to ring Marylyn and say something constructive, say that he'd accomplished something. It was Clarence's usual dilemma: when to be persistent, when not to be, and still gain his objective? It was possible to lose by being too persistent, in any situation, Clarence thought. The great wisdom of life seemed to be to judge when to be persistent, and this went for situations involving women, too. If one was not persistent enough, one was considered weak, and if too persistent, uncivilized. Thus one ran the risk of being defeated by men, and dropped by women. It was indeed hard to live. Clarence knew that at the moment he was considered weak by Marylyn and had been therefore dropped. Only temporarily, Clarence hoped.

Like a flash of inspiration, it occurred to him to speak with Edward Reynolds now. It was a quarter to two. Mr Reynolds probably had long business lunches. Clarence went into a coffee-shop on Third Avenue, put in his order, then went to the telephone at the back of the shop. The directory was filthy, the front pages were missing up to the Cs, which themselves were grimy and curled at the corners, but Cross and Dickinson was there, and he memorized the number. He ate his food, then walked uptown. Mr Reynolds's office was in the Forties. Clarence went into a bar on Third Avenue and telephoned.

Mr Reynolds's secretary told Clarence that Mr Reynolds could see him at 3.15.

At three, Clarence went to the Cross and Dickinson offices which occupied three floors of the building. There were books on shelves in the lobby, rubber plants, attractive girl receptionists and secretaries in abundance. Clarence was soon called by a blonde girl who said she was Mr Reynolds's secretary and would show him to his office.

'Hello, Mr Duhamell,' said Mr Reynolds, standing up behind his desk. 'And what's up now? Sit down.'

Clarence sat down in a green leather chair. The office was book-lined, except for tomato-coloured panels that held drawings, and there was also a big Castro poster, not the same one Marylyn had. 'I was just at Bellevue because of a letter written by Rowajinski to a friend of mine,' Clarence said. 'I think it's easier if I show you the letter.' Clarence got up and handed the letter to Mr Reynolds.

Ed read it, standing behind his desk. 'Who's Mariline?' he asked, pronouncing it to rhyme with Caroline.

'Marylyn. He spelt it wrong. She's a friend of mine who lives on Macdougal Street. This is why I went to Bellevue just now, to speak to the doctor who was seeing Rowajinski when he was there. Bellevue has no room for him, they said. My point is, Mr Reynolds, I think if you put in a word with my Captain – especially Captain MacGregor, he's the one you met – and maybe also to someone at Bellevue, we might get this man locked up. Otherwise he's just roaming the streets again. If I mention this – this letter, my Captain might think I'm making too much out of it – just because Marylyn happens to be a friend.'

Ed put the letter on the corner of his desk, where the young man could reach it. 'This man has been watching you? – Apparently.'

'He must've seen me with Marylyn — maybe on Macdougal Street. I'll tell my Captain about it, but you see my point, I hope, Mr Reynolds. If you could back me up a little —'

Ed was reluctant. 'To get him locked up,' Ed said with a sigh, and sat down. 'For how long, I wonder?'

'I don't know. He's not the type who's going to improve, I think. He's fifty-one.'

'I see your point, especially if he's writing letters like this to a friend of yours. But from my point of view — also my wife's — we prefer to drop this thing. Let the law take care of it. Suppose he's locked up for two months and then he's out again? If he knows I've had a hand in it, he'll resent it, maybe try to hit back. What about that aspect of it?'

Clarence understood. Rowajinski needn't know Mr Reynolds had had a hand in it, but Clarence was afraid to promise this.

'I don't even care about the rest of the money this fellow took from me,' Ed added. 'It's life in New York, all right but — Mr Duhamell — What's your first name, by the way?'

'Clarence. Clare.'

'Clarence. If you'll permit me — my wife and I are a lot older than you. What has happened has happened. One can't bring back a life. I don't mean to get sentimental over a dog — but we prefer to let this go by. If you drag us back into it, especially since we want to get another dog — and if this man is let out again —'

Mr Reynolds's words were devastating to Clarence. He was saying what Marylyn had said, and what she meant, in different words. 'But if you made a statement to my precinct — Rowajinski might not ever know it.'

Ed smiled and lit a cigarette.

There was a knock on the door.

The blonde girl who had shown Clarence to the office came in with a tray.

'Coffee, Clarence? Frances, this is Patrolman Duhamell. Or maybe you've introduced yourselves. My secretary Frances Vernon.'

Clarence stood up. 'How do you do?'

'Patrolman Duhamell helped us when Lisa was kidnapped,' Ed said.

'Oh, of course. Ed talked about you. You found the man who did it.'

'Yes,' Clarence said.

'He's just been released from Bellevue,' Ed said.

Frances looked surprised. 'Now what're they going to do with him?'

'I don't know,' Ed said. 'He's living in a room down in the Village, according to Clarence.'

'Really? Just living?'

Clarence saw in her face the same incredulity that he had seen in Eric's. 'I know he should be in prison. He's also still writing anonymous letters and annoying people. A friend of mine just got such a letter.' Clarence stopped abruptly, thinking he had already said too much.

'A man who'd kill someone's dog with a rock,' Frances said. 'Free now. What do you know! That dog – You probably never saw Lisa, did you?' she asked Clarence.

'No.'

'There's a picture of her. Ed wanted to take it down, but I said please leave it up.' She pointed to a framed photograph propped against some books. 'That was at a party here. Fritz's farewell party, wasn't it? Lisa came up to the office lots of times.'

'Oh, a few times,' Ed said.

'She'd make the rounds at a party, greet everybody, and people would give her canapés –' Frances broke off, smiling. 'And she'd always sit up *after* she took anything, just as if she were saying thanks.'

Ed smiled and pushed his hands into his pockets. 'We never taught her to sit up. I don't know where she learned it. She could also wheedle anything out of anyone. Great wheedler!'

'But you know, the idea of a creep killing that dog for no reason,' Frances continued to Clarence. 'It was like a horror story to all of us. We just couldn't believe it here at the office.'

'Have your coffee, Clarence,' Ed said. 'You take sugar?'

'We all wrote Ed a note,' Frances said, 'just as if Lisa was a person. Well, she was a person. – You wouldn't understand unless you'd met her.'

Clarence said nothing. Mr Reynolds gave him a look, smiling.

'Excuse me if I talk like this,' Frances said, glancing at Clarence, suddenly embarrassed. Then she spoke to Mr Reynolds. '. . . at four-thirty. And we don't have to worry about the Boston letter, because they just telephoned and I got that straightened out.'

Clarence drank his coffee. He felt he hadn't accomplished anything. He looked at the plants on the windowsill, the comfortable green leather sofa where probably Ed could flop to read a manuscript, or take a snooze if he wanted to. There was a low table beside it with an ashtray, paper, pencils. The office was like a room in a house.

'I hope you punish that creep,' Frances said as she went out the door. 'The idea that he's living in the Village makes me want to stay clear.'

Clarence took Rowajinski's letter from the corner of the desk.

Ed said, 'Can't you have your friend Marylyn talk to the police? You say you haven't shown that letter at your precinct yet?'

'No, sir. Only to Bellevue. I just got the letter today. I can show it to the precinct house tonight.' But would he, should he? He wasn't sure the precinct would make a move.

'Try to get some action via Marylyn.' Ed drifted towards the door with Clarence. 'She's your girl-friend?'

'Yes. Yes, she is.' Clarence did not dare to say that he hoped Ed would meet her at some time.

Ed opened the door. 'Get her to make a complaint. I wish you luck, Clarence. Can you find your way out?'

'Oh, yes. Thanks, Mr Reynolds.'

16

Clarence went back to his apartment and telephoned Marylyn. He wanted to tell her that he had been to Bellevue, and that he was going to show Rowajinski's letter to his precinct house tonight.

Marylyn didn't answer.

At 5.30, there was still no answer. Marylyn was perhaps out on a job, typing in someone's house, or delivering something. At 7 p.m., he tried Marylyn again. Still no answer. He imagined her going out to dinner, or staying to dinner, with a man, maybe a writer whose work she was typing. Evidently Marylyn didn't care enough about what he was doing in regard to Rowajinski's letter to telephone him in all these hours.

That evening Clarence saw Manzoni in MacGregor's office when he arrived at the station house. Manzoni was going off at eight, Clarence supposed, though he hadn't yet changed out of uniform. Clarence put on his uniform at his locker. Manzoni was coming into the locker room as Clarence went out, and jerked his head in greeting, with a smirk, as if he had something on Clarence, but Manzoni greeted other men going on duty with great heartiness. 'Stevie! How's the missus? Nothin' doin' yet?' Stevie's wife was pregnant, but Clarence felt he didn't know Stevie well enough to ask about his wife.

Clarence went into MacGregor's office and showed him the letter from Rowajinski. He wanted to discuss the letter before the briefing started.

'The girl who got the letter is a friend of mine,' Clarence said.

'Hm-m. Well?'

'Well – he obviously isn't discouraged because he was caught once. He's still annoying people. He even spoke to Miss Coomes on the sidewalk in front of her house. – What do you think they're going to do about him?' The last sentence Clarence had prepared beforehand. 'They' not 'we' and not 'ought to do about him', which would sound personal, but 'are going to do about him', which was routine.

'It depends what Bellevue says. We haven't had the report yet.'

'They found a room for him on Morton Street. He's living there. But isn't he going to have some kind of a trial?'

'Not if Bellevue calls him a nut,' said MacGregor. 'Bellevue's handling him.'

'But he frankly seems to *be* a nut, and Bellevue's let him loose,' Clarence said. 'I spoke with a doctor at Bellevue today. It seems Bellevue is leaving it up to the police what to do with him.'

'You went to Bellevue?'

'Yes, sir. With the letter. I thought that was what I should do, sir.'

'This is the friend of yours on Macdougal Street that Pete was talking about?'

'I suppose. Yes, sir.' Clarence felt the start of a blush.

'Then I see why you're interested. There are more important things on in this precinct than a screwy letter to a girl on Macdougal, Dummell, even if you know her.'

What, Clarence wondered. A couple of junky house robberies? 'I'd feel the same, sir, if I didn't know the girl. It was letters like this that led to the killing of a dog and getting the two thousand dollars' ransom from Edward Reynolds.'

'Oh, that,' said MacGregor, as if it was a little problem of the past. 'All right, Clarence, I'll send the letter on to Bellevue. Didn't they want to keep the letter by the way?'

'No. They didn't ask to.' Shouldn't we at least alert the precinct house nearest Rowajinski to keep an eye on him, Clarence thought, but was shy about suggesting this to his Captain, and maybe it had been done.

'Let's let it ride,' MacGregor said. 'He's being checked on twice a week, Bellevue told me. It's their headache now. Dummell, there was a rape in an apartment hallway on a Hundred and first and Broadway today at four p.m. – reported by a witness, not the girl. The guy got away, natch, but here's his

description. May as well read it now. It's for all you guys tonight.'
He handed Clarence a piece of paper.

Clarence read: Black or black-Puerto Rican, 5 ft 6 to 8, about
35, moustache, stocky build, wearing dark trousers, brown plastic
jacket, brown shoes, dark turtle-neck sweater.

'More important than a dog, that. A kid saw that. His mother
rang us up. We checked with the girl. It's true all right.'

It was already dark when Clarence went out on his patrol.
Tonight he was with Rudin, a heavy-set fellow whom Clarence
hardly knew. On 104th Street, they shooed some kids out of a
basement alley where they were apparently trying to open a door.
One of the kids, about twelve years old, threw the remains of
an apple which hit Clarence in the chest. He brushed the front
of his tunic with one hand and went down the iron steps into
the alley and tried the door. It was locked.

'Who the hell's *that*?' yelled a man's voice from inside.

'Police!' Clarence replied. 'Checking your door. Anything
the matter?'

'Get the hell away! That door's locked!'

Clarence went back up the steps to Rudin. The kids laughed.
('Pigs! Shit pigs!') The man, maybe a super, had been too
afraid to open the door to see if he was a policeman, Clarence
supposed. A year ago, Clarence might have asked for the door
to be opened – just to make sure it was an ordinary apartment
house basement and not a junky shooting gallery or a floating
brothel. A strange anger began to stir in him. It was frustration,
Clarence thought. Nothing seemed to move. Nothing progressed
logically from one point to the next. No one drew logical con-
clusions, and made the next move – like himself just now, not
investigating the voice in the basement. On Broadway, slowly
and dutifully with Rudin they tried the doors they were supposed to try – a hardware shop, several apartment houses too
small to have doormen, a cleaner's shop, a bakery. They walked
westward on 101st, where the rape had taken place at 4 p.m.
Apartment windows glowed with cosy, yellowish lights. Music
and television sounds came faintly. What window was the girl's
who had been raped? He supposed she would be worried about
pregnancy. Rape was not merely humiliation and shock, but
that – possible pregnancy and possible venereal disease. A pity

that New York had been overrun by blacks and Puerto Ricans instead of by some more advanced race that might have improved things. Other countries and cities had had better luck in the past. Clarence especially detested rapists. He had seen at least six brought in since he had been at this precinct house. Like thieves, they avoid looking people in the eye. Clarence was watching out for the five-foot-six-to-eight-inch-tall black or black-Puerto Rican with the plastic jacket. You could never tell.

'You like skin flicks?' asked Rudin.

Clarence thought of Marylyn who actively disliked them. 'No,' said Clarence.

'My wife's brother – he makes 'em. With his friends. Ah, what the hell, you've seen one you've seen 'em all. But he shows 'em every Saturday night at his place in Brooklyn. His house, y'know. Charges admission but it covers the beer. I just thought if you were interested –'

Clarence didn't know what to say to be agreeable. He desperately wanted to speak to Marylyn, now, to hear her voice. 'They're for people maybe who haven't got the real thing, eh?' Clarence said finally.

'That's a point.' Rudin chuckled. He might have been taking a Sunday stroll. His hands behind his back twiddled his nightstick.

Clarence looked at his wrist-watch. His ring time was 17 tonight, seventeen minutes past the hour. Twenty minutes or so till he had to call in. 'Look, uh –'

'What's the matter?'

'Hold the fort while I call my girl-friend? Round the corner.' Clarence meant there was a bar round the corner. Rudin knew.

Rudin waited outside, while Clarence went into the bar to the telephone at the back.

Marylyn answered and Clarence gave a sigh of relief.

'I've been trying to get you since four-thirty!' Clarence said.

'I was walking and I went out for dinner. What's the matter?'

'I went to Bellevue –' Suddenly Clarence didn't want to tell her over the telephone about Bellevue, or about seeing Mr Reynolds at his office. He wanted to see her. And Marylyn was *there*, her voice was there, but she was struggling, Clarence felt, to put a distance between them, pulling herself back.

'Well, what happened? Can't you talk?'

'I want to see you, If I could, I'd come down now.' He was thinking it was remotely possible, but it wasn't. One of the captains or a lieutenant strolled the patrol beats, and you never knew when one would turn up.

'Aren't you on duty now?'

'Yes. Well – Bellevue – isn't very interested. I gave the letter to my precinct. It sort of depends on the Pole's mental status. The legal part of it, I mean. What they'll do with him.' He was telling the truth, but it was so inadequate. 'Marylyn, can I see you tomorrow *night*, if you're busy all day? I'm free tomorrow night. I've got to see you for a few minutes.'

'All right,' with a terrible sigh, more breath than words. 'I have to work tomorrow night. Maybe I'll be finished by nine, nine-thirty. Call me first.'

Clarence went back to Rudin.

That morning at four, Clarence wore his gun when he left the precinct house. Patrolmen were allowed to take their guns, and several men, who had to arrive at the precinct house or go home during night hours, did. Clarence was feeling mistrustful and vaguely scared.

He slept late the next day, because he had not got to sleep until after 7 a.m. He bought groceries, went to the library, and the whole time he was thinking about Marylyn, trying to plan how to make the best of the evening tonight, or of the time she would agree to see him, which might be hardly an hour if she had more work to do tonight, or if she had to get up very early.

Before 9 p.m. he telephoned her, but she didn't answer until 9.35. Yes, he could come down if he wanted to.

Clarence walked to Union Square, took the Canarsie to 14th Street west, then the local to Spring Street. Then it was a short walk to Macdougal. He had been on the look-out the whole way for a flower shop still open, or a street vendor of flowers, and hadn't seen any. Clarence still had Marylyn's keys. At least she hadn't asked for them back, or had she forgotten? Clarence was wearing his gun in its belt. He had a crazy idea of killing himself tonight in case Marylyn wanted to break off with him. Not in her apartment, because that would be too messy and dramatic, but maybe in one of the dark streets that led downtown or west towards the Hudson River.

Marylyn's two windows showed a diffused light behind her green curtains. Clarence hesitated, then used his key to open the downstairs door. He ran up the steps, and knocked at her door.

'Clare?'

'Yes.'

She opened the door. She was wearing a skirt and an old white shirt with its tails hanging out. Some of her long hair hung in front of her shoulders, down to her breasts.

Clarence took her in his arms. He kissed her neck under her ear.

'What's happened?' Gently but firmly she pushed him away.

'Not much. I mainly wanted to see you.' He kept looking at her, but feeling that she was annoyed, he turned away, took a breath and was aware of the familiar smell, faint and mingled, of Marylyn's perfume, of coffee, of books, of the cream-coloured radiators under the window. It seemed he had not been here in six months. Only one lamp was on. Her typewriter was on the round table where she worked.

'And what happened at Bellevue?'

Clarence told her. He told her about visiting Mr Reynolds at his office. 'Bellevue's dumping it on the police and the police are dumping it on Bellevue. I can't get either of them to lock the guy up – as yet.' Clarence removed his topcoat and laid it over the back of a straight chair.

She saw his gun. The belt showed under his unbuttoned jacket. 'You're carrying that thing around?'

'It's allowed. You've see it before.'

'Worse than Texas.'

'I've never used it. Never had to. Except in practice,' Clarence said in a mild self-defence, but he doubted if Marylyn was interested. She wasn't sitting down, and Clarence remained standing too. 'I'm sorry Mr Reynolds isn't willing to back me up a little. I couldn't persuade him to say anything to my precinct. – I don't suppose you would.'

'I'm afraid not,' Marylyn said. 'This is a case of ordinary citizens being pestered, and I don't think the police give a damn.

Do you? – Besides I don't want to be leered at again by that greasy wop.' Marylyn lit a cigarette. 'You came here tonight just to tell me you can't get anywhere? – I can see why Mr Reynolds doesn't want to say any more. He knows it won't do any good. Then the creep's maybe going to hit back at him.'

Clarence sat down on a straight chair by Marylyn's table.

'I'd – I'd like you to meet Mr Reynolds some time. And his wife.'

'I think you said that before. I'm a little fed with all this, Clare. Why should I meet Mr Reynolds? – And that psycho! He could be spying on *all* of us. He probably is. That's how he gets his kicks. And he's as free as the breeze. On Morton Street. That prick!'

'He's not – really free.'

'Why isn't he? Living just a couple of blocks away? I had dinner tonight with Dannie at the Margutta, then he walked me home, even though it's close. You think I'd walk out alone at night now? God, it's sick-making!' Marylyn pulled her curtains so that they would cover more window. 'He could be out there now.' She turned to him. 'You may as well take off now, Clare. I've still got work tonight. I'm sorry.'

'Oh, hell.' Clarence wanted desperately to stay with her, tonight, all night. Tonight, this moment, seemed crucial. 'I'm going to quit the force, Marylyn. Very soon.'

'Quit? I don't believe it.'

'Can I stay with you tonight?' He stood up by the table. 'Please, Marylyn. Don't be angry.'

'I'm just not in the mood. Not to mention –'

'I don't mind if you work. Would you like me to come back later?'

'No-o, Clare.' Gentle but very definite.

'You think I don't do enough about – *this*, but I'm trying.' I have to work within the framework of Bellevue, or of the law, he wanted to say, but he was afraid of her laughter. 'You think I'm not tough enough but –'

'I never said that.'

'You didn't say it, but you think I don't *do* enough.'

Marylyn shook her head slowly, so slowly her hair did not stir. 'You're not cut out for the police, Clare, and that's something. But we're not cut out for each other. We're too unlike. It's like you told me about Cornell – the student demonstrations.'

'Oh, that!' He was suddenly impatient. He had told Marylyn he had balked at wrecking the library and the faculty's offices, having gone along with the anti-war demonstrators, even made a speech or two at the rallies, up to that point, the point where they had talked of destroying what Clarence still remembered he had called 'perfectly innocent, perfectly good and even beautiful books – and furniture!' Marylyn had turned against him because of this: she professed to see a reason why 'everything old' had to be destroyed before something new and better could be built. But it was such an abstract problem, so irrelevant compared to them, standing so close now, people who loved each other, he was sure.

'You'd better go, Clare.'

Clarence felt suddenly weak. He was standing straight, though he felt as if he might faint. 'I do love you.' He was thinking of the night they met, in a bar on Third Avenue of all places, Marylyn with a lot of people he still didn't know, and himself drinking a beer with a college chum. Clarence had approached Marylyn out of the blue, and tried to strike up an acquaintance, and she had given him her telephone number, saying, 'You won't remember it, so what does it matter?' But he remembered it (written it down right away) and things had gone on from there. It was certainly true that they hadn't a friend in common. Clarence embraced her, and kissed her on the lips, a brief kiss, because she pushed him away, a little angry – or was it really anger?

'Go!' she said, smiling a little – perhaps at him.

What the hell did women mean?

Clarence left, buttoning his coat as he went down the stairs, and he nearly fell when his heel caught on the edge of a step. He walked northward, in the direction of his apartment. He'd walk home, he thought.

He saw Rowajinski. Or he thought it was the Pole, a smallish figure that disappeared to the left at the west corner of Bleecker Street. Clarence trotted after him, because it was twenty yards to the corner and Clarence wanted to make sure it was the Pole.

Clarence bumped into a man, and went on with a mumbled 'Sorry.'

Clarence was now at the corner, and he didn't see Rowajinski. There were several stores still open with lighted fronts, cars moving on Bleecker, people on the pavement, but he could not see the limping figure anywhere. Maybe he hadn't seen him. Clarence walked quickly west on Bleecker, trying to keep his eyes on both sides of the street and see ahead in the rather dark distance. The Pole might be heading for home, Clarence thought, because west was the direction of Morton Street.

At Seventh Avenue, Clarence definitely saw him, and his heart gave a thump. Rowajinski was hopping fast across the Avenue to escape the traffic just as the light changed to green. This green held Clarence up, and he danced from foot to foot waiting to cross over. When Rowajinski reached the opposite kerb, Clarence saw him look back, and Clarence knew Rowajinski saw him, and had probably seen him coming out of Marylyn's house, too. Rowajinski dashed westward, but Clarence could not brave the five- or six-lane rush of cars, mostly taxis, down Seventh Avenue. Clarence thought the Pole had gone into the first narrow street west – Commerce, Clarence saw as he ran at last across Seventh Avenue. Commerce was a short street with a small theatre at the end of it. The marquee of the theatre was lighted. Now Clarence had lost Rowajinski again.

Morton Street was parallel with Commerce, one street south. Or had Rowajinski gone ahead into Barrow Street? Commerce made a slight jog to the right and became Barrow Street. Clarence hesitated at the jog, then plunged into Barrow Street, which was dark. Clarence heard the abrupt grate of an ashcan, as if someone had bumped into it, on his side of the street. Now he saw the Pole, or a scurrying figure that looked like him, silhouetted for an instant against the fuzzy yellow lights of Hudson Street, a wide street where traffic flowed. This time he would so scare Rowajinski, maybe even break his nose, that he'd never dare come anywhere near Macdougal Street, Clarence was thinking. Rowajinski ducked into a dark doorway, vanishing. Clarence tried to estimate which door it was, because they all looked alike here: narrow brownstones.

At that instant, Kenneth was pulling closed the sticky front door of a tiny foyer that smelt of urine. There was no light and if the cop hadn't seen him, he was safe. What the hell was the cop so mad about tonight? Kenneth squatted so that he could not be seen through the half-glass door. Kenneth had seen a tall fellow go into Mariline Coomes's building half an hour ago, and he hadn't been sure it was Dummell, but Kenneth had waited, curious whether it really was the cop boy-friend. Kenneth had expected some hell to break lose earlier, Saturday or Sunday, because the girl must have got his letter Saturday, and he had watched her house at various times Saturday (without being seen, he was pretty sure) but nothing had happened. And no one at all had come to see him in regard to his letter, which had been in a way a disappointment, yet a triumph if he cared to look at it that way: people were afraid to come to see him, perhaps, or were plotting something bigger against him than a mere visit with a reprimand. Dummell evidently had been afraid to visit his girl-friend, or she'd chucked him. Then tonight he had turned up.

Kenneth heard running footsteps, and the door that sheltered him was pushed open. The cop's fist hit him in the side of the head.

Clarence yanked the little man up effortlessly by the front of his clothing. Rowajinski's hat fell off, his mouth opened, his eyes goggled and he yelled.

Why do you do it? Clarence wanted to say. He bashed the Pole against the wall and his head gave a crack. Clarence pulled his gun out. He felt it not as a gun but as if it were a weapon like a rock, and he slammed the side of Rowajinski's head with it.

Kenneth, dazed, was aware that his own cries stopped. He was suddenly nothing, limp, vanishing somehow. It was like a mountain falling on him, an avalanche of stones crushing him so that he could not move. Yet it was only one man doing this. That was his last thought. The rest became dream, and the merest ghost of a curse.

Clarence, when one shoe slipped in blood, bumped against a wall and came near falling. In catching himself, he did drop his gun, and groped around on the dark floor for it, as fast as he could, as if Rowajinski would make a grab for it and get it away from him, but he knew the man was knocked out and then some. Clarence opened the door and went out. He went towards Hudson, west.

A young woman with a scarf over her head walked towards him from Hudson Street, glanced at him quickly and passed him. Clarence breathed through his mouth. He was carrying his gun in his right hand and he fumbled under his topcoat and put it away in its holster. In the yellow lights at Hudson Street, he looked at his right hand and saw that it had some blood on it. Carefully, suddenly tired and not thinking, he used his left hand to search for a handkerchief, found one in a back pocket of his trousers, not a handkerchief but a paper tissue. He wiped his right hand. The yellow streetlights made the blood on the tissue look black. There was not much of it. Three or four people walked past him. Clarence did not look at them, and was vaguely aware that he did not care what they thought. He started walking uptown, still getting his breath back, limbering his body like someone who had been cramped. He took the north side of 14th Street and walked to Broadway, then zigzagging without thought made his way to his apartment, dead tired.

17

When Clarence awakened, the events of last evening went tumbling through his mind until he stopped them by deliberate effort. The Pole might be dead, he thought. And if he wasn't dead? He would say it was the cop Dummell who — had attacked him and beaten him nearly to death. Clarence knew that he had flung himself on Rowajinski like a maniac. He had hit Rowajinski with his gun.

Clarence saw the gun belt on one of his straight chairs. He went to the gun, thinking at the same time that he ought to turn the radio on for the news, in case they said anything about Rowajinski. But first check the gun. He couldn't see any blood on it, but he wet a facecloth in the bathroom basin, wrung it out, and wiped the gun carefully. A little pink came off. He opened the cylinder, removed the bullets and washed and dried the chambers and replaced the bullets. At the same time he was wondering if he *could* deny having killed Rowajinski, if a great many facts were against him? Maybe it was hopeless. He was unable to think. But it seemed wisest to get any bloodstains off. He washed his shoes, checked also the soles. He examined his dark brown tweed topcoat in the light by the window. No sign of blood that he could see, either on the front of it or on the cuffs. His trousers. He had hung them, and he went to the closet. On the blue of the left trouser leg, he saw a darker streak about an inch and a half long. He scrubbed at the streak with the wet cloth. The cloth showed a faint pink. He put the topcoat and the trousers on a chair by the door. They should go to the cleaners. Possibly also his jacket. He examined his jacket and saw nothing on the sleeves or its front. Homicide might ask to examine his clothes — all his clothes — and Clarence knew that a microscopic amount of a person's blood somewhere could convict a person.

On the right cuff of his white shirt, there was a smudge two inches long. He soaked the shirt in the basin in cold water, scrubbed for a minute with the nailbrush until it came out, almost. Should he get rid of the shirt? If Homicide questioned him today, it was possible they would look even in the garbage. He scrubbed some more at the cuff, and decided to take it, with a couple of other shirts and a pair of pyjamas, to the laundry on Second Avenue.

The 10 a.m. news had nothing about Rowajinski. Who would find him, unconscious or dead? Surely someone lived in that house, though it was strange no one yelled down at them, considering the noise they must have made. How long had he hit Rowajinski? One minute? Two?

Would Rowajinski have been found last night or this morning – about now? Could he have come to and walked to his place on Morton Street? No, Clarence thought, because he would at once have screamed for justice to be done against the cop Dummell. Rowajinski must be dead. Clarence felt a little faint. He opened a window and began to move just to keep moving, showered, made coffee. He wanted to telephone Marylyn and couldn't, as if something paralysed him for this particular act. Also it was early for her. He realized he wanted to get out of his apartment. Tonight he was off duty. He might go to see his parents. If he felt worse there, he could say he was tired and wanted to sleep in his room. Or he could take a long walk in Astoria. He dialled his parents' number, and was rather surprised that his mother was in. She was delighted that he could come out. Clarence said yes of course he had the house key, if she had to be out. He would be there before noon.

Clarence did not need to take anything with him. He took only a book with him, and the trousers and coat for the cleaners, the bundle for the hand laundry.

His mother was out, as she had said she might be, but came in twenty minutes later with a big bag of groceries. Clarence helped her unload the groceries in the kitchen.

'How is Marylyn? Are things all right?'

'I suppose so. Sure,' Clarence said in a tone that meant of course things were all right and there was nothing to talk about.

'One of our little girls, Edith Freyer – she's ten, a thalidomide case. Mrs Furst, that's our supervisor, made a bad mistake and took her to a centre where kids were being fitted for prosthetic limbs. Sometimes that helps, you know, if they see other kids like themselves. But when she saw all those crippled kids she went hysterical. Mrs Furst was terribly upset, and apologized to Edith's mother. I think Mrs Furst was more upset than the child. Edith was hysterical for hours.'

Clarence understood. He could imagine it exactly and it pained him. 'God what a nightmare.'

'Yes, but how's one to know? Sometimes it's good to go by the book, sometimes by instinct. Edith's not one of my children. I might have known better, but maybe I wouldn't have known better.' Nina was preparing lunch.

The cuckoo clock over the kitchen door came to life: 12.30. Marylyn would detest that clock.

In the afternoon, Clarence felt uncontrollably drowsy, as if he had taken sleeping-pills. His mother told him to take a nap, so Clarence went up to his room intending to read, but he was asleep in five minutes. He slept for three hours, washed his face, and went downstairs. His father had just come home.

'Well, hello Clare! To what do we owe this honour?'

'I'm bored with New York,' Clarence answered smiling.

'You see, Ralph,' said his mother, 'we're less boring than New York!'

'If New York was so fascinating, I'd be living there myself,' said Ralph. 'The air may not be perfect here, but it's a lot better than New York's.'

The usual conversation. They were having steak for dinner, from his mother's favourite butcher, Mueller, on Ditmar. She was sure Clarence never got such good steaks in New York, even in the best restaurants. He looked thinner, they both agreed. How was Marylyn?

'I trust we'll have the pleasure some day,' said Ralph. 'You haven't even showed us a picture. Don't you ever take any snapshots?'

'He's working at night half the time and sleeping in the daytime,' said Nina.

'What about flash cameras?'

At 7 p.m. the TV series was on in the living-room. Clarence

was drinking a pre-dinner beer with his father. Among the last brief items was: 'The body of a man identified as Kenneth Rowajinski, unemployed construction worker aged fifty-one, was discovered today in the hallway of a Greenwich Village apartment house. Death was caused by blows about the head. His attacker is still unknown.' The announcer's voice lowered its tone at the end as if in genuine respect for the dead.

Ralph, not listening any longer, had begun talking during the last words. Clarence had no appetite, to his mother's disappointment. She had made a lemon pie for dessert, Clarence's favourite. Clarence was wondering if the Reynolds had heard the same news? If Marylyn had? She had a TV but seldom turned it on. What would she think of Rowajinski's being killed on Barrow Street, probably some time Tuesday night? Clarence could imagine her glad he had done it, almost admiring him for having the guts to do it, but what if she took the opposite view, that he had been another fuzz with a gun, another brutal pig?

Just after eight, while they were having coffee, the telephone rang. Ralph answered it.

'Yes ... Yes, he is. Just a minute. For you, Clare.' His father handed the telephone to him. 'They never let you alone, do they?'

'Hello, Clarence. Santini here. Listen, did you know that Pole Rowinsk is dead? Somebody clobbered him down on Barrow Street. You know anything about that? Got any ideas?'

'No. I just heard it on the news.'

'Well, Homicide wants to see you. Detective Fenucci. I'll give you his number. Got a pencil?'

Clarence took down the name, number and extension number.

'Mac said you were keeping an eye on this guy and you might know who could've done it. Any ideas?'

'No, I haven't sir. Never saw him with anybody. Except his landlord.'

Santini chuckled. 'I hear his landlord's blowing a gasket. Yeah, I gather he wasn't exactly popular. Listen, Clarence, get on to Homicide right away. They want to see you tonight.'

Clarence turned to his parents and said, 'I've got to go in to New York.'

'Oh, Clare, really?' His mother already looked distressed.

'Your night *off*?' asked his father.

They had been talking while he spoke on the telephone. 'Emergency. It can't be helped.'

'Crime,' murmured Ralph, 'has no days off.'

Clarence picked up the telephone and dialled Fenucci's number. He identified himself. Fenucci wasn't there but was due in less than an hour. Could Clarence come to Fifth Division Headquarters now?

A few minutes later, Clarence was walking towards the Ditmar Boulevard elevated station. He went direct to the Fifth Division Headquarters on West 126th Street. He had a ten-minute wait, then Fenucci arrived with two other men. Detective Fenucci, a paunchy man of about forty, took Clarence into an empty office, sat down behind a desk and opened his brief-case.

'I understand you'd seen this man – Rowajinski – a few times?' asked Fenucci after the preliminary questions about Clarence's precinct and rank and length of time on the force.

Clarence explained how he had seen him, and there was no need to go into the details of the Reynolds's dog and the ransom, because Fenucci had that information, also the Bellevue report. Fenucci also knew about Rowajinski accusing Clarence of having taken five hundred dollars, and asked Clarence was it true.

'No, sir.'

'I understand he was annoying a friend of yours. Marylyn Coomes on Macdougal Street,' said Fenucci, reading.

'Yes, sir. He wrote her an unsigned letter. She gave the letter to me to report. My captain said he was sending it to Bellevue.' Had they spoken already to Marylyn? Probably. How stupid of him not to have telephoned her, not to have tried to before coming here!

'What kind of a man is Reynolds? We're seeing him this evening. I understand you're friendly with him ... Did you ever see Rowajinski talking with anyone in his neighbourhood? ... Is he the kind of man who'd pick a fight with a stranger?'

'It's not impossible.'

'Insult a girl if she was with a man?'

'That's possible.'

Fenucci made a few notes.

What had Marylyn said, Clarence wondered. That he left her apartment around 10.30 p.m. Tuesday? Or that he had spent the whole night with her? Clarence thought it odd, a little frightening, that Fenucci hadn't asked him how he had spent last evening.

'That doorway where he was killed,' said Fenucci, 'it wasn't his house and nobody there knew him. He was running from someone or someone dragged him in there to beat him up. Couple of old ladies live in the house, very poor, you know, on welfare, and an old super lives on the second floor. First floor's empty – derelict, rats. The people claim they didn't hear anything. Matter of fact two out of the three are deaf.' Fenucci laughed, but he looked very tired, and he might have laughed to wake himself up. 'I understand you called on this guy once and got rough with him.' Fenucci consulted a note. 'Just a few days ago, the landlord says.'

'Yes. He'd been loitering around my friend's house on Macdougal Street. I asked him to stop it.'

'You saw him on Macdougal?'

'No. Miss Coomes –'

'Did you hit the guy? The landlord says there was a lot of noise.'

'There wasn't a lot of noise. I did push him and he fell down. I wanted to scare him. I thought if I could scare him once, he'd cut out the heckling.'

Fenucci nodded with an amused air. 'But he didn't.'

'Well – I think he did. My friend didn't mention him loitering in her street after that.' But Clarence realized suddenly that the wine delivery, and the letter to Marylyn, had come after that.

'You haven't seen him since then, since that time you called on him?'

'No,' Clarence said.

'Where were you last night?'

'I had a date with my friend – Marylyn Coomes.'

'Where?'

'At her apartment on Macdougal Street.'

'What time did you get there?'

'About – around ten, I think. She was working before ten.'

'You went out for dinner?'

What had she said? Clarence decided to risk it, and he answered, 'We stayed in.'

'Long? How long were you there?'

'I stayed the night,' Clarence said. He watched for disbelief in Fenucci, but the detective remained perfectly calm, and his slow fingers moved another page of his notes. He made a scribble with his pen.

'How'd you get to the girl's house? Subway –'

'I took the subway from Union Square. I took it to Spring Street.'

'What time did you leave your apartment?'

'I suppose – just after nine-thirty.'

'Did you see – Rowajinski on the street when you arrived?'

'No, sir.'

'What time did you leave the next morning?'

'Oh – I think – seven-thirty or eight.'

'Did you see Rowajinski then?'

'No, sir.'

'What did you do then?'

'I walked home.'

'Rowajinski was killed around midnight last night, give, or take a couple of hours. You were at your girl-friend's at midnight?'

'Yes, sir.'

'Oke-kay.' Fenucci gathered his notes hastily, as if he had to go off somewhere at once – to Mr Reynolds perhaps. Then he said, 'Now we'll go over to your place, if you don't mind, Patrolman Duhamell.'

They went in an unmarked police car, driven by a man in plainclothes. The driver remained in the car, which was parked where it wasn't allowed.

Clarence had made his bed, not neatly but it was made. His gun in its holster and belt lay on the dresser top, and this was the first thing Fenucci commented on.

'You take your gun home with you?'

'Sometimes. At night. Unless I'm going straight to a date somewhere.'

'Did you have it with you last night?'

'No, sir.'

Fenucci pulled out the gun and looked at it, checked that its bullets were all present. He looked at the gun carefully under a standing lamp. 'Rowa – This guy could have been clobbered by a gun. Or a brick. Something pretty solid. He had multiple fractures. We'll take this gun for checking. You'll have it late tomorrow if it's clean.' Fenucci smiled. 'Not afraid to spend twenty-four hours without your gun, are you? Aren't you off tomorrow?'

'Yes, till tomorrow night,' Clarence said.

Fenucci was taking the belt with him also. 'Now – what were you wearing last night? Can I see your closet?'

Clarence opened his closet door. There were three or four suits, odd jackets and trousers, pyjamas and a shirt or two on hooks, shoes in semi-disorder on the floor. The oxblood shoes he had washed were on top on the left – on top of the shoes.

'What were you wearing last night?'

Clarence hesitated. 'These trousers,' he said, indicating the ones he had on, Oxford greys. 'And this sweater – over another sweater, I think.' He had on a V-neck grey sweater.

Fenucci didn't seem interested in what other sweater he meant. He glanced at the clothes Clarence had on, then turned back to the closet. 'Coat?'

'My raincoat,' Clarence said, and touched a dark green waterproof in his closet.

Fenucci pulled the raincoat out, looked at front and back and sleeves. 'Shoes?'

'These shoes.' Clarence indicated the brown loafers he was wearing.

Fenucci nodded.

It wasn't a thorough examination, Clarence knew. Fenucci was counting on the gun. Or maybe he already had his opinions from something Marylyn had said. A real examination would have meant taking Clarence's whole wardrobe to the lab to test for bloodstains.

'You said Reynolds was a nice man, a gentleman. Civilized.' Fenucci smiled a little. 'He couldn't have hired someone to get at this guy, maybe?'

Clarence shook his head. 'I don't think he's that type. Also he told me he wanted to forget about the whole thing. The dog was important to him – and the dog's dead.'

'When did he say to you he wanted to forget the whole thing?'

Clarence remembered the conversation on Monday in Mr Reynolds's office. Clarence didn't want to mention that visit, though Mr Reynolds might mention it. 'He said it to me after he knew his dog was dead.'

'Okay. Okay, Patrolman Duhamell. That's all for now.' Fenucci went to the door. 'You're off till when?'

'Thursday night at eight, sir.'

'Reachable here?'

'Yes.'

'Don't go out of town – for a few days.' Fenucci left, carrying the gun belt.

Clarence took a deep breath and listened to the footsteps of Fenucci fading on the stairway. Half his questions had been calculated, Clarence thought. 'Reynolds couldn't have hired someone to get at this guy?' Had Fenucci expected him to leap at that? Did Fenucci already have everything he needed? And what about the gun? Clarence had washed it well. But the lab tests were fantastic. It'd be yes or no. It was out of his control now. Fenucci might be on his way to see Marylyn or Mr Reynolds, Clarence didn't know, because Fenucci wouldn't be the only man working on the case. Clarence picked up the telephone and looked at his watch: seventeen to eleven.

Marylyn answered, to Clarence's enormous relief.

'Hello, darling. Clare. How are you?'

'Lousy. I'm just about to go out.'

'You're alone?'

'Yes-s.' She sounded impatient and nervous.

'The cops – Homicide was just talking with me. Have they been to see you?'

'Yes. At seven they were here. Would've been here before but I was out all day.'

'What did you tell them?'

'I told them,' Marylyn said, and her rather stiff tone continued, 'that you were here all night.'

Clarence gave a shuddering sigh. 'I said the same thing. Good God. Thanks.'

'You don't have to thank me, it's a pleasure.'

Silence for four or five awful seconds. She meant a pleasure to bollix the cops, to lie to them. 'Are they coming to see you again?'

'I don't know. Probably. But I'm not going to be here. I'm sick of them all. But —'

'But? — What, darling?'

'I gather it was you, right?' she said in a whisper.

He was pressing the phone hard against his ear. 'You said the right thing.'

'I've got to go, Clare. I'm not spending the night here.'

'You're afraid they'll call you at night?'

'I'm just sick of this place, sick of seeing *fuzz* in it!' Now she sounded on the brink of hysteria.

He wanted to ask her where she was spending the night. Probably at Evelyn's on Christopher. 'Would you call me next? Because I won't know where to reach you. — One more thing. I said I left your house around seven-thirty or eight in the morning.'

'I think I said ten. Tennish.'

'I don't think it matters.'

'I've got to go.'

'Promise you'll call me!'

'I'll call you.' She hung up.

At that moment, a little before 11 p.m., Ed and Greta Reynolds were talking with a man from the Homicide Squad, a detective called Morrissey. A different detective had telephoned Ed in his office around 4 p.m., after speaking with Greta and getting his office number, to make an appointment with Ed at his apartment at seven, but Ed had said he had to meet his wife at a funeral parlour on Lexington Avenue: the mother of a friend had died, and he would not be free until after 10 p.m. Ed had been firm. Ed had supposed the police wanted to see him about some detail, a final check-up of some kind in regard to the Lisa business, because the detective had not said he was from Homicide. Lilly Brandstrum's mother had died after a long illness, and Ed and Greta had spent a rather gloomy hour at the funeral home, followed by a gathering, mostly of Lilly's mother's friends, at Lilly's apartment in the East 80s.

Ed and Greta had moved. Since the previous week-end, they had been in their new apartment on East 9th Street, in a building which they both found more cheerful than the Riverside Drive place.

Detective Fred Morrissey explained that Fenucci, who had spoken to Ed in his office, had had to be somewhere else at 11 p.m. 'We have several men working on the same cases,' said Morrissey with a pleasant Irish grin. 'All gathering pieces. It's not much like Sherlock Holmes any more.'

Ed had smiled politely. Ed and Greta had not known about Rowajinski's death until Morrissey told them. Barrow Street. Ed had only a vague idea where it was, west of here, on the other side of Seventh Avenue where streets had names and did not intersect at right angles. They got through the preliminary questions, one of them being where Ed had been last night, Tuesday, between 8 p.m. and the small hours of the morning? Last night he and Greta had intended to go to a film at the Art on 8th Street and hadn't because Ed had had to read a manuscript until close to 1 a.m. He had been out at seven and again at midnight, briefly, to air the new pup Juliette.

'I've never seen Rowajinski by the way,' Ed said.

'No? Not when he was in jail?' Morrissey knew about their dog and the ransom money.

'No. I could've seen him, but I didn't care to. I wanted to forget the whole thing, frankly, because our dog was dead and that was that.' The murder was the final touch; Ed was thinking – sordid and depressing beyond words. Someone had had enough of Rowajinski, and small wonder.

'I see. You don't possibly know of anyone who – Well, the point is, do you know of anyone who might've done it? I can imagine you don't move in the same circles as this guy but –' Morrissey grinned again.

'I don't know of anyone,' Ed said. He looked at Greta who was sitting at the other end of the sofa, calm and attentive and silent.

'I have some notes here – about Patrolman Clarence Duhamell who helped you with the dog thing. You know Patrolman Duhamell?'

'Oh, yes,' said Ed.

'This Rowajinski was annoying his girl-friend –' Morrissey looked at his notes and came up with Marylyn's name and address. 'Patrolman Duhamell also went to Rowajinski's room on Morton Street and roughed him up a little, told him to stop annoying his girl-friend. Do you know about that? Did Duhamell say –'

'No, I don't know anything about it,' Ed said. 'We don't know Duhamell very well.' Ed was thinking, could it have been Clarence who killed the Pole? No, it wasn't possible. Morrissey had said Rowajinski's skull had been fractured in several places.

'It's a funny story,' Morrissey said, 'Rowajinski escaping once after Patrolman Duhamell found him, then Duhamell accused of letting him go for five hundred dollars. That's according to Patrolman Duhamell's precinct.'

'Yes,' said Ed cautiously, 'we heard about that. Duhamell mentioned it. He told us he didn't take it. It was never proven, was it?'

Morrissey consulted his notes before he spoke. 'No. Says here accused by Rowajinski. Just accused. What do you think? – I never met Patrolman Duhamell.'

Greta spoke before Ed. 'Oh, no, I don't zink so. We don't *know,* but Clarence is not like *zat.*'

Ed smiled, suddenly relieved of tension by Greta's frank voice and her accent. 'I doubt if he took a bribe. He's pulling a fast one on us if he did.'

'A fast one? What d'y'mean?' Morrissey asked pleasantly.

Ed knew Morrissey was wondering if Clarence could have killed the Pole because Clarence had been annoyed by the Pole's accusation, true or false. 'I mean I don't think he's the type. He's a nice young fellow, even idealistic. I don't think he'd take a bribe for anything.' Especially in this case, since he hated Rowajinski, Ed wanted to say, but thought he had better not.

'Yeah,' said Morrissey, vaguely. 'Um, you never possibly heard of anyone else this Rowajinski was writing letters to?'

Ed's lips widened in a smile. 'No. We certainly tried to find out during the time our dog was missing. We were trying to find Rowajinski himself then.'

'People don't always report stuff. We're looking for suspects, y'know.'

Ed knew.

Morrissey seemed to be finished. He stood up, putting his pen back in his pocket. 'Thanks, Mr Reynolds. You may hear from us again. I dunno. Good night, Mrs Reynolds.'

'Good night,' said Greta. 'And good luck.'

'That we always need!'

The door closed.

Ed let his arms sag and said, 'Whoosh!' He drifted back to the living-room. 'Well. What do you think of that?'

Greta slipped out of her shoes and picked them up. She was tired. 'Oh, it was bound to happen.'

Ed put an arm around her and hugged her tightly for a moment. 'What a day! Let's go to bed with some hot tea. Or chocolate. Or a hot toddy! A funeral and a murder all at once!'

'Lilly's very upset. She doesn't show it but she's very upset.'

Ed didn't reply. The Rowajinski thing was on his mind. Ed knew it was on Greta's mind too. He glanced at Juliette, who had been unusually quiet on the sofa the whole time. Juliette wagged her cropped tail and looked at him inquiringly.

'Dead,' Ed said, turning towards Greta. 'Funny we didn't hear about it.'

'Ach, we haven't had the TV on for a couple of days.'

Ed thought of the newspapers, which he did see daily. But how important was Rowajinski's demise? If it had been reported, he had missed it. What a wretch the man had been! And the money — Ed wasn't interested in the money that remained owing to him, but the police had taken some of Rowajinski's bank account and had returned three hundred dollars to him. Another five hundred was missing, and who cared?

Burial, Ed supposed, would be at public expense. Ed started to say, *I can't say I'm sorry he's dead*. Instead, he looked at Greta and said, 'I'll pop out with mademoiselle. Let's forget all about it, darling. Fix us a nice brace of toddies.'

'I wonder who —'

'I don't give a damn who did it. He deserved it.'

18

Clarence telephoned Marylyn the next day, Thursday, and on the second try got her, at 3.30 p.m. She didn't want to make a date. She had two urgent typing jobs.

'Marylyn – it's important! Can't you find five minutes? I'll meet you out somewhere – near you.'

The desperate tone in his voice must have had some effect, because she agreed to meet him at O. Henry's at five. It was on Sixth Avenue at West 4th.

Clarence wanted to telephone Edward Reynolds, but he thought he had better not. The Reynolds might be annoyed if he telephoned, and they were probably annoyed already because the police had come to see them in regard to Rowajinski's death. Mr Reynolds would think he was interfering, obsessed by the one subject. Mr Reynolds might even think he had done it, or might suspect it. This had occurred to Clarence earlier. Mr Reynolds could easily say, 'Yes, Clarence had provocation, and it wouldn't surprise me if –' On the other hand, Clarence could more easily imagine Ed saying, 'I hardly know Clarence Duhamell. I have *no* opinion. I want nothing to do with it.'

Clarence arrived early at O. Henry's and managed to get a booth. When Marylyn came in, he stood up so she could see him. She was wearing a long jacket over faded blue jeans, and she walked towards him with her usual short, quick steps – which oddly always made him think of a squaw – not looking at him. Such had been the prelude to many a happy date, but Clarence was not sure about this one.

'Well,' she said when she had sat down. 'What's the latest?'

'Nothing new today.' There was no report as yet re his gun.

Marylyn glanced around, as if expecting to see a cop watching them, or someone in plain clothes keeping an eye on them. Clarence had already looked around.

'Thank you, darling,' Clarence said.

She shrugged.

Clarence glanced up at a waiter who had arrived. 'What'll you have?' he asked Marylyn.

'Oh – a Coke.'

'Not a rum in it?'

'All right. A rum in it.' Her grey-green eyes glanced at the waiter, then she lit one of her Marlboros.

Clarence ordered a beer, and the waiter went away. Clarence had expected Marylyn to be more concerned, to be upset. He didn't know what to make of her eyes that would not look at him. Did you know right away that I did it, he wanted to ask. 'Did you hear it on the news? About the Pole?'

'Dannie heard it and called me up. Yesterday afternoon. He knew where I was working.'

So Dannie knew where she was working. And also about the Pole being a nuisance. Dannie probably knew more about Marylyn's feelings now than he did.

'At least the fuzz last night wasn't the wop cop. Some detective in plain clothes.'

It didn't matter who it was, Clarence supposed. They all shared notes. Clarence refrained from asking was it Fenucci.

The waiter arrived, served them, and departed.

Marylyn relaxed a little, loosened her thick woollen muffler, and said, 'What the hell happened Tuesday night?'

'Well – as soon as I left your place, I saw him. On Macdougal and he turned the corner into Bleecker. I thought he'd been hanging around in your street again, so I followed him with – with an idea of scaring him – but really scaring him. Then he began running because he saw me. He crossed Seventh and I started chasing him. He ran into a doorway. Then I hit him.' Clarence sat forward on the edge of the bench seat. There was a loud juke-box near, and they were whispering besides, hardly able to hear each other.

'Hit him with what?'

'With my gun. I was carrying my gun.'

Marylyn stared at him.

'I know it was with my gun,' Clarence said.

'Well, why shouldn't you know it?'

'Because the rest is sort of vague. I don't mean I blacked out. But I was in a rage. I don't know if I spent three or four minutes there or just thirty seconds. I don't even remember getting home. Just suddenly I was home. Afterward.' He was looking at Marylyn, who still stared at him in a shocked and puzzled way. 'I didn't mean to beat him up – so badly, when I went into that doorway. You know – one of those little houses on Barrow, far west. He didn't even live there.'

'I *don't* know. I only know, Clare, that I want out of this and now. I told the cops you were with me, sure, because I don't give a – a –'

'All right.'

'– about this Pole or about the fuzz. I like lying to them. So it helps you, fine. But this is the end, Clare, the last of it.' Her eyes flashed, and she slapped her hand palm down on the table on the word 'last'.

Clarence wanted to take her hand and didn't dare. He wanted to say: there's nothing to fear and we're all glad the guy is dead, aren't we? By all, he meant the Reynolds also. They must be glad. But he couldn't say a word.

'They asked me if you had your gun that night. I said no, I didn't think so. I thought it was better to be casual about it than to say a definite "no", as if I was trying to protect you.'

'Yep. Right,' Clarence said.

'I can see you're worried.'

'Worried?' The idea of clues went swiftly through his head, but what clues, so far? 'I know I'm a logical suspect. They know I didn't like him. And I was even in the neighbourhood that night.'

'Did anyone see you?'

'Leaving your place?' The juke-box – a gravelly black voice – was in orgasmic agony at the end of a song. 'I don't think so. I don't remember seeing anyone. Not the coffee-shop fellow, for instance.'

'And when you got home? Did anybody see you?'

'No.' Clarence felt better because of her concern. 'Or rather

– I dunno, darling, but I don't think so. – Honey, the number of enemies that guy must've had! Think of that. How many people besides you, for instance, besides Mr Reynolds, who must've hated his guts.'

'Why do you always say "Mr Reynolds" if you like him so much? Hasn't he got a first name?'

Clarence smiled. Marylyn sounded suddenly like herself. 'His name is Ed. Edward. – Marylyn, I adore you.'

'What's going to happen to you?'

'Nothing. I'll bet you nothing.' He reached for her hand that rested on the edge of the table.

She pulled her hand away and gave him a glance of apology. 'I can't stay long.'

Clarence sat back, silent, but he was thinking frantically: she *had* helped him, after all. Surely she didn't hate him. 'This should blow over in a few days. If they haven't a clue, they haven't a clue.' He thought of his gun.

'How did you get home that night? Taxi?'

'I think I walked.'

'You think?'

'I walked.' Clarence swallowed some beer. 'I'll call you in a day or so, darling. I know you're upset.'

'I'm not upset. I don't want to see any more pigs. And I'm not sure I should see you again.' She spoke firmly, not as if she were doubtful or even regretful. 'I'd better go now.'

'You have to be somewhere?'

'Yes.'

He didn't believe her. He paid and they walked out. Marylyn seemed to want to go westward in West 4th, the opposite direction of Macdougal.

'Don't walk me, just leave me here,' she said.

Clarence, pained at leaving her, stopped watching her when she had taken half a dozen steps.

That evening, Manzoni was going off duty when Clarence arrived at the precinct house just before eight. Clarence suspected that Manzoni had lingered in order to see him. Manzoni was leaning against a wall, talking to another patrolman, and he had not yet changed out of uniform.

'Ah, Clarence,' said Manzoni. 'How goes it? You heard about Rowinsk, I think.'

'Yes. Sure I did.' The patrolman with Manzoni was a curly-haired Irishman called Pat, who had always been friendly towards Clarence. Pat was smiling now, and Clarence said 'Hi' to him. The gun, the gun at the lab was on Clarence's mind, and he went into the Captain's office – MacGregor was on duty now – to ask for another gun, or perhaps to hear the result from the lab.

'Ah, Dummell. Clarence,' MacGregor said. 'Your gun just got back.' MacGregor had a pleasant expression on his face.

'Thank you, sir.' Clarence's gun and belt, looking the same as ever, lay on a corner of the Captain's desk.

'Take it.' MacGregor nodded towards the gun. 'What do you think about our friend Rowinsk?'

'I heard about it yesterday.' Clarence picked up his gun and belt. 'Homicide was asking me questions. As you see.' Clarence indicated his gun.

'You were in the Village that night.'

'Yes, sir. On Macdougal.'

'Any ideas who did it?'

'No, sir.'

A telephone rang. MacGregor was interested, and took it from the Desk Officer.

Clarence went to the locker room. MacGregor wouldn't necessarily know, Clarence thought, if the lab had said anything about the gun. Homicide certainly knew where to find him. If they had found blood on the gun, they might simply let him finish his patrol tonight and speak to him later. Manzoni followed Clarence into the locker room, and to Clarence's annoyance seemed to intend to stand there while Clarence changed.

'Who do you think knocked off the Pole?' Manzoni asked.

'I dunno. Could be a lot of people, I suppose.'

'Who, fr'instance?'

Clarence hung his trousers. Around them, ten or fifteen men were dressing or undressing, talking, paying no attention to him and Manzoni.

'You're so often in his neighbourhood. Did you get fed up and clobber him, Clarence?'

Clarence tried to smile as he stuffed the blue shirt into his trousers. 'Aren't you even closer on Jane Street?'

'I heard you spent the night with your girl-friend. All right. But did you take a walk?'

Clarence glanced in the little mirror on his door as he tied his tie. 'Listen, Pete, stop meddling with me. You want to make the Homicide Squad? Go after Rowajinski's killer. Down in the Village. Not me, chum.'

'Could you take a lie detector test?'

Clarence buttoned his tunic. 'Any time.' At least he didn't feel ruffled just then. Maybe his pulse was a bit faster, but it was from annoyance with Manzoni. There was a difference.

Clarence walked in for the briefing. His patrol partner that night was a fellow younger than Clarence named Nolan. Nolan didn't mention the Rowajinski affair. He talked about a forthcoming prize fight. He had a bet on it. Clarence's ring number was 45, and when he called in at 11.45, there was a message for him. Detective Morrissey of Homicide wanted to see him tomorrow morning, and would he be at his apartment?

'Yes,' Clarence said.

Morrissey would be there between eleven and twelve.

When Clarence went off duty at 4 a.m., Captain Smith was at the desk. Nothing was said to Clarence about any message from the lab, so Clarence didn't know what to believe about his gun.

Clarence's mother telephoned the next morning at eleven. 'I hope I haven't waked you, Clary ... A policeman was here to see us yesterday. In the evening, because they wanted to see Ralph, too. What's it all about? This man with the Polish name. He was murdered and you knew him?'

'Well, I didn't know him. I arrested him. He kidnapped a man's dog. Mother, he's a —'

'You never mentioned it.'

'I didn't think it was very important.'

'The detective said you disliked him. He led us to think it was personal. Said the man had been annoying Marylyn.'

'That's true. He annoyed other people, too.' Clarence, still in bed, had raised himself on one elbow.

'You had nothing to do with his killing, did you, Clary? The man said you spent the night at Marylyn's – Tuesday.' Her voice was tense.

Clarence felt a sudden impatience, embarrassment. 'That's true but –'

'Who do you think killed him?'

'I don't know!'

'Well – what're they doing to you, Clary? And why?'

'Nothing, Mother. Naturally they question a lot of people. What was the detective's name?'

'Morrissey. He left his card with us.'

His mother made him promise to telephone her tonight before he went on duty, whether anything had happened or not.

Clarence got out of bed at once and made coffee. Naturally they had put questions to his parents. Had their son seemed upset on Wednesday when he visited them? What had he ever said about Rowajinski? Nothing. Nothing at all. But Clarence hated the lying, especially to his parents. The enormity of what he had done, in their eyes, he could not begin to estimate.

Morrissey arrived just before noon. He was a husky, brown-haired fellow, barely thirty, with a smiling manner and huge hands that could probably knock a man out with a backhand blow.

'Have a seat,' Clarence said.

Morrissey removed his topcoat and sat down. He had his pen and notebook ready. 'Well, you know what this is about, because Detective Fenucci talked with you, I understand.'

'Yes.'

'We're trying to find the man who killed Kenneth Rowajinski Tuesday night. And it seems you knew Rowajinski.' Morrissey looked pleasantly at Clarence.

Clarence sat down on the foot of his bed. 'I suppose you heard about the kidnapped dog, Edward Reynolds's dog. That's how I met Rowajinski.'

'Oh, yes, I saw the Reynolds – Wednesday night it was. Now, number one, where were you Tuesday night?'

'I was staying with my girl-friend on Macdougal Street. Marylyn Coomes.'

'Yes.' Morrissey glanced as his notes. 'What time did you arrive there?'

'About ten.'

'Did you see Rowajinski on the street then? How'd you get to your girl-friend's?'

'The subway. No, I didn't see him. I wasn't looking for him.'

'Rowajinski could've been killed before nine p.m. Just before. It's possible. Where were you before you went to Macdougal?'

'Home. Here. Marylyn wasn't in before nine-thirty or so. I was calling her from here till I knew she was in.'

'Did you go out during the evening?'

'No, we stayed in.'

'Then what?'

'Then I slept there.'

'And then? What time did you leave?'

Repetition. To see if he gave the same answers. 'Around eight, I think.'

Morrissey's brows went up. 'Your girl-friend says around ten. I have it here.'

'It was earlier. She didn't completely wake up when I left. She's a late sleeper.'

'You expect to marry Miss Coomes?'

'I hope so,' Clarence replied, in as pleasant a manner as Morrissey had asked the question.

'The time you went to Rowajinski's house on Morton Street — Why did you go there?'

'Because — Rowajinski said something to my friend, Miss Coomes. He was loitering in her street. He said something unpleasant —'

'What?'

'Something vulgar, I don't know exactly. — Then he wrote a letter to her. But that was afterwards.'

'After what?'

'After I went to see him. I went to see him after Marylyn told me he'd followed her up the front steps of her house and said something nasty. I thought a good scare would stop him. I didn't hurt him. I just wanted to scare him.'

Morrissey was waiting for him to continue. 'And did it stop him?'

Clarence shifted on the foot of his bed. 'Not exactly. The letter came after I saw him. The date's on the letter, you can see it. It's at Bellevue.' Clarence had dated the letter Friday, 30th Oct., in the manner of Edward Reynolds's dating his letters from the Pole.

'Who sent it to Bellevue?'

'Marylyn Coomes showed it to me. I took it to Bellevue.' Clarence didn't want to go into more detail, and didn't think he had to.

'Another thing, Rowajinski accused you of taking five hundred dollars to let him go.'

Clarence explained about Rowajinski's escaping while he went to ask for Edward Reynolds's agreement to the second thousand of ransom money, and Clarence called it a mistake on his part. 'I was searched – my bank account was looked into, I'm sure. I didn't take that money.'

Morrissey nodded. 'But it must've been annoying to you to be accused.'

Clarence shrugged. 'By that nut? Rowajinski liked to annoy people. That's all he did.' Clarence smiled and took a cigarette.

Morrissey asked Clarence about his career so far in the police force. It was a brief story: a year's service, and nothing very interesting had happened to him in that time. Clarence thought Morrissey had very likely already looked into his record.

'You were in the neighbourhood that night,' Morrissey said, 'just about seven blocks away. And you had plenty of reason to dislike this guy. – You're telling me the truth in all your answers here?'

'Yes,' Clare said.

Morrissey smiled. 'Because I'm sure you're going to be questioned some more and some of these guys, you know – a little tougher than I am – they're going to give you a tougher time.'

Tougher than Morrissey, if Morrissey wanted to be tough? 'I can't help that,' Clarence said.

Morrissey nodded, still watching Clarence. 'Of course I

realize Rowajinski's landlord didn't like him and neither did the guy where he bought his groceries, but still.' Morrissey chuckled. 'I doubt if they'd up and clobber him the way he was clobbered.' He lit a cigarette. 'You're getting along all right with your girl-friend?'

Clarence wondered if it was Morrissey who had been to see Marylyn, and it bothered Clarence that he didn't know. 'Yes,' Clarence said.

'She told me she didn't like cops. She didn't have to tell me that, I could see it. How does she feel about your being a cop?' Morrissey's innocent, healthy grin was back.

'Oh, I've told her I wasn't going to be a cop for ever.'

'You have plans for quitting?'

'Not plans. Just that I don't expect to stay in the force for twenty years. The way some do.'

'You look *down* on the force? You don't like it?'

'Of course I don't look down on it.' What else is there even trying to hold the fort, Clarence thought. However he knew what Morrissey was thinking, that he wasn't a typical cop, not one of the brotherhood who stayed in for years and loved it. 'I like it all right.'

Morrissey looked from Clarence to his wrist-watch. 'About Edward Reynolds – He must've hated this guy, too.'

Clarence chose to say nothing. He was standing now, and so was Morrissey, about to leave.

'He wouldn't've paid anybody to knock Rowajinski off, do you think?'

'Absolutely not,' Clarence said.

'You sound as if you're sure.'

'No, that's just my opinion.'

Morrissey nodded. 'So – I thank you. You'll be hearing from us.' Smiling, he put on his coat.

He was gone. Not a word about witnesses. Clarence felt easier.

Clarence telephoned Marylyn. She was in. He did not want to tell her that he had just seen Morrissey, even though it had been a fairly successful interview. He said:

'Can you have an early dinner with me tonight before I go on at eight?'

'No, Clare.'

'Why not ? – You have to work ?'

'I feel a little funny about it.'

She sounded so tense, he wondered if someone was with her, but he didn't want to ask this. 'Funny about me ?'

'Yes, in a way.'

It was agony for Clarence not to be able to find, quickly, the right words. He couldn't say over the telephone such fragile things as, 'But you do care about me, don't you ?' Finally he said, 'When can I see you ? Give me a date, darling.'

'I don't know. I wish you wouldn't count on anything.'

'Oh, Marylyn –'

'What's happening ? Anything ?'

'Nothing, darling.' In a way, he meant it. He wasn't worried. 'There's not going to be any trouble.'

But she didn't want to make any date with him, and she said she would have to work over the week-end.

Clarence went to Columbia and to New York University that afternoon to inquire about courses in business management. N.Y.U. was cheaper and closer to his apartment. He could also take two courses in the afternoons at N.Y.U., while at Columbia the courses would be spread into morning and afternoon, sometimes on the same day. His problem was the police schedule. It was difficult to start any courses if he stayed on in the force, because every three weeks his schedule changed. Tonight and tomorrow were his last nights of the 8 p.m. to 4 a.m. duty, and on Monday, 9 November, he changed to noon to 8 p.m. duty. If he quit the force after Christmas, he could start in the January semester. Clarence thought he should do this.

He wanted to try Marylyn again and didn't dare. Her firmness was devastating to Clarence. It came to him forcefully that what he had done was repellent, shocking to other people. It was shocking to kill a man, pistolwhip him to death, even if the victim was a man who had hurt other people and who deserved worse than the law had given him. To the law, Rowajinski's life was still a human life. Clarence himself was another human being, not a soldier, and not merely a cop in uniform. No one had ordered him to kill Rowajinski. Clarence's thoughts were somewhat vague. He felt nervous and melancholic. He twice dropped his gun Friday and the gun made an awful clatter on the floor. The girl who lived in the apartment below him, a good-looking model who kept odd hours, said when they met in the hall :

'Are you practising karate up there and flinging yourself to the floor ?'

Clarence smiled, embarrassed. 'I dropped something.'

'Not your gun, I hope.'

'I'm afraid you guessed it.'

'Hang on to that gun. New York is counting on you.'

On Saturday morning, Clarence awakened groggy after a series of unpleasant dreams. In one of the dreams he had been a cripple, more crippled than Rowajinski, scorned and avoided by other people. Clarence realized that he wanted to tell Edward Reynolds about Rowajinski. Mr Reynolds would not despise him for it, Clarence thought. Mr Reynolds would understand.

It was 10.20 a.m., and both the Reynolds might be at home. When Clarence dialled their number, a recorded voice said that the number had been changed. Clarence took the new number down, dialled it, and Mr Reynolds answered.

'Hello. This is Clarence Duhamell. You've moved ?'

'Yes,' said Ed cheerily. 'We're on East Ninth.'

'I'd like very much to see you — today if possible. Have you any time ? Fifteen minutes or so ?'

'We're going out to lunch. How is three o'clock ?'

'That's fine. Can I meet you out somewhere ? If you're on East Ninth, there's the Fifth Avenue Hotel —'

Ed agreed.

Clarence was there first, and Ed arrived just after three, hatless, wearing a raincoat. He threw a cigarette out the door before he walked in. Ed smiled.

'Hello, Clarence.' Ed sat down and ordered an imported beer from the waiter who had come at once, and Clarence said he would have the same. 'Beer puts on weight and scotch is too strong,' Ed said. 'There ought to be more coffee-houses. So — what's the trouble ? Marylyn ?'

'No. Well, a little, yes.' Clarence spoke softly. The nearest person, a single man at the bar, was ten feet away. This was a handsome bar with no juke-box, but by the same token it was quiet.

Silence until their beer arrived.

'It's about Rowajinski,' Clarence said.

'Did you kill him?' asked Ed.

Clarence started, as if Ed had clutched his heart and dropped it. 'You guessed that?'

'Not really. I was just – throwing out a guess.' Ed offered Clarence a cigarette, took one himself, and lit them both with his lighter. So Clarence had done it. He and Greta had speculated. *Oh, no*, Greta has said, *Clarence isn't violent*. Ed couldn't digest the fact at once. Now Clarence was suspected, he supposed. Even accused. Or maybe not accused, or he'd be in custody. Why had Clarence wanted to tell him? What did Clarence want? Ed said in a voice that he tried to make quite normal, and quite normally puzzled, 'How'd you come to do it?'

'Well – that Tuesday night – I went down to see Marylyn on Macdougal. When I left around ten-thirty, I saw Rowajinski – turning the corner into Bleecker Street. He'd seen me and he started hurrying away. So I chased him. I thought he'd been hanging around again, snooping. He ducked into a doorway on Barrow Street and I followed him – into the doorway, I mean, and I hit him with my gun. I was carrying my gun. Anyway I lit into him. I hardly remember it. It's not that I'm trying to excuse myself, I certainly am not.' Clarence glanced around, but no one was watching them. 'I felt that I had to tell you this, Mr Reynolds.'

Absently, Ed said, 'You can call me Ed.' He felt dazed by what he'd just heard, as if it somehow weren't real. 'And now you're suspected? Or what?'

'No. Well, yes, they're questioning me. Marylyn told the police that I spent the whole night at her place. She told them that without my asking her to, before I even spoke to her about all this.' Clarence said in a quiet rush, 'What bothers me is that I did it at all. I lost my head. I wanted to tell you, although I know it's got nothing to do with you, Mr Reynolds – Ed.'

And what do you want me to do, Ed wondered. 'Marylyn knew right away that you did it?'

'I suppose she suspected, yes. – She hated the guy too. Not that that's the point. The police weren't really doing anything about him, you see. That sounds absurd because –' Clarence was careful to keep his voice low. 'It's not for me to kill a person just because I don't like him. But I hated him and I lost my head.' He looked into Ed's calm dark eyes, looked away again because he didn't know how Ed was judging him. Clarence forced his heels down on to the floor. His legs were trembling.

Clarence would finally confess to the police also, Ed thought. In a few days probably. Maybe a few hours. Ed wanted to ask if Clarence intended to confess. 'Did anyone see you in the Village? Notice you on Barrow Street?'

'I don't think so.'

'You went back to Marylyn's afterwards?'

'No, to my place. East Nineteenth.'

Silence.

'What's Marylyn's attitude? She intends to protect you?'

'So it seems.' Clarence smiled and took the first sip of his beer. 'She so hates the police – being questioned by them. This is one way to get them off her – to say I spent the night with her and she doesn't know anything about it. Of course, she may want to get rid of me, too.'

'Oh? You really think so?'

'I don't know – at this point. She doesn't want to see me just now.'

So this was a confession simply, Ed thought. Clarence wanted reassurance from someone who had hated Rowajinski also. 'Is there any clue against you?'

'Just – circumstances. No one mentioned any real clue. I've been questioned.'

'And how seriously – questioned?'

'It might get more serious. So far they seem to believe me – and Marylyn. I don't feel like confessing. I really don't.'

Clarence's blue eyes looked steadily at Ed. 'Well, I didn't send any flowers to his funeral. I appreciate your telling me, Clarence.' Ed smiled, wryly, at his own words which seemed absurd, even mad. 'A detective came to see me this week. Morrissey, I think his name was.'

'Yes. He told me. At your apartment or your office?'

'The apartment. He asked if I had any idea who did it. I said no – quite honestly. He asked me about you and the five hundred dollars. I said I hardly knew you, and that you'd tried to help us when Lisa was stolen.'

'And that was all?'

'Yes. He didn't make any remarks against you.'

But Homicide never talked, Clarence knew, only asked questions. Clarence drank more beer. His throat felt half-closed. 'I especially went to see Marylyn to tell her – about this. I wasn't trying to keep it from her.'

Ed was thinking that Marylyn was probably on the point of breaking with Clarence, despite her protecting him. And Ed imagined also that Marylyn, actively or passively, had contributed to the murder. 'Why don't the police *do* something?' Marylyn would have asked. Rowajinski had been annoying Marylyn at her apartment. She must have felt that Clarence had brought Rowajinski down on her himself, which, of course, he had. 'You can trust me not to tell anyone. I won't tell Greta, if you prefer I don't, though she can keep a secret.' But even as he spoke, Ed was aware of an aversion to Clarence, a positively visceral dislike of him. He had killed someone. He looked a pleasant young man, his clothes and his nails were clean, yet he had passed, somehow, that unspeakable border. Ed's thoughts were not clear to himself, because what had come to him was a feeling: Clarence was odd. Or *maybe* he was odd. He just didn't *look* odd. Ed's clearest thought was that he ought not to trust Clarence too far, and that he ought to keep a safe distance from him. But was he right in this? Was his attitude intelligent, really? Did you know the Pole was dead when you left him, Ed wanted to ask. But he felt it was a detail.

Ed had nothing more to say, Clarence supposed. Clarence had had a great deal to say this morning, an hour ago, but where was it all now? 'Thank you for talking with me,' Clarence said.

Clarence suddenly seemed to Ed young and tortured and

honest. Honest to a fault, perhaps. In a curious way that defied all the principles of civilization and rectitude, Clarence had come to speak with him in hope of a word of reassurance, even of praise or gratitude for what he had done — essentially avenged the killing of Lisa. Suddenly to Ed Clarence was a young man who had lost his temper against an evil that no one else was doing anything about. The aura of the sinister left Clarence as if blown away by a wind. Ed said, 'You don't have to thank me for anything. — Would you like to bring Marylyn to the house some evening? For a drink or coffee? Maybe it would help. That's up to you.'

'Yes, I would like to. Thanks.' It would help, if Marylyn would agree to come. Clarence's brain whirled, and he shook his head. He had not finished his beer and certainly wasn't tipsy. It was because he had entered a different world, he felt, a world in which a person like Ed Reynolds shared a dangerous and intimate part of his own world.

'Are you going to tell Marylyn that you talked to me?' Ed asked.

'Yes. I think I would like to. You don't mind?'

Baffled for a second, Ed said, 'No, no,' casually. But what would Marylyn think of him for not reporting it? Or did such things matter any more? Especially to someone anti-fuzz, or revolutionary, as he gathered Marylyn was? 'Want to ask her this evening? I think we have people coming at eight, but six is fine.'

Clarence was afraid tonight would be too short a notice for Marylyn in the mood she was in. 'Could I ask her for tomorrow?'

'Yes, I'm sure. Tomorrow at six, six-thirty?' Ed gave Clarence the address.

'I'll speak to her as soon as I can and confirm it.' Clarence pulled out a five-dollar bill and insisted on paying.

On the street, where the rain came down harder now, Clarence had an impulse to accompany Ed back to his apartment building, but felt he would appear to be clinging if he did.

Ed extended his hand. 'Cheer up. See you tomorrow, maybe.'

Clarence walked home, heedless of the rain. It seemed less

than a minute since he had left Ed when he arrived at his doorway. He had hardly thought of anything during his walk except of the excellence of Ed Reynolds, the rarity of a man like him in New York, of Ed's kindness, and of how lucky he was to have made the acquaintance, possibly the friendship, of two persons like Ed and Greta. He dialled Marylyn's number.

She answered.

'Darling, can you come for a drink at the Reynolds's to-morrow around six? He's asked us.'

'Us?'

'Well, I've told him about you. It's very close to you, on East Ninth. I'll pick you up just before six, all right?'

'It's a party?'

'I don't think so. Just us for a drink. You'll like them both. Just for a few minutes, if you've got work.'

'Can I wear anything?'

'Oh, sure! They're not stuffy!'

19

Clarence went to Marylyn's apartment at 6 p.m. She greeted him casually. She was still putting on make-up, a long process when she bothered with it, because she experimented, and never looked the same twice.

She was wearing bell-bottom black pants, flat yellow shoes, a yellow jersey blouse, and a long necklace that bore a huge oval pendant of pink – probably something that she had picked up at the thrift shop on Macdougal. Some of the furs in this shop looked actively verminous to Clarence. So far, Marylyn had not bought any of the so-called mink coats or jackets which had patches missing in them. All in all, Marylyn looked pretty tonight, not as far out as Clarence had thought she might, and anyway, would the Reynolds mind? No.

'Marylyn, I have to tell you before we go. I told Ed Reynolds about the Pole.'

She turned from the mirror. 'Really?' Her eyes looked especially startled, because of their black outline. 'Was that wise?'

'He understands. He's a wonderful fellow. That's why I want you to meet them. My God, you don't think *he* liked the bastard, do you? He said something like, "Well, I didn't send any flowers to his funeral." He's not going to tell even his wife, he said. But I wanted you to know before we went there.' It was of the greatest importance to Clarence, but he didn't want to hammer the point. Was Marylyn casual and cool about it or not? Should he be calm and unworried also? Life was cheap in New York, in a sense, and Rowajinski had been obnoxious, and yet the police dug and came up with the murderers more times than not. It was the legwork by Homicide that counted, and they expended it on the most worthless corpses. Was he safe? Clarence put the question out of his mind for the moment.

'Are they saying anything at the pig-pen?'

'Not a thing. Otherwise I'd tell you,' Clarence said.

They walked to the Reynolds's apartment house.

'I'm going to take some business management courses at N.Y.U. starting in January,' Clarence said. 'I'll stay on in the force till then and resign after Christmas. Maybe before Christmas or it'll look as if I'm trying to get the bonus.' He smiled, but she didn't see it. 'No tramping the beat in the cold this winter.'

'You've got enough dough?'

'Oh, sure.' Clarence had just enough. It had crossed his mind to give up his apartment and live with his parents. A long subway ride, and he would lose the independence his apartment gave him, but after all, Marylyn had spent only two nights there with him. She didn't like to be away from her own place, from the telephone that brought her jobs. Clarence was hoping he could stay frequently with Marylyn on Macdougal.

The Reynolds's apartment house was a modern one some ten storeys high with a grass terrace in front and a doorman. Greta opened the apartment door for them, and Clarence introduced Marylyn to her.

'Let me take your – cape,' said Greta with her faint accent. 'Oh, how glamorous this is!'

'Thrift shop,' said Marylyn. She stooped to pet a small white poodle who was wriggling around her feet.

The cape was new to Clarence, dark blue and lined with the Vietcong flag, he now noticed.

Greta led Marylyn into the living-room and introduced her to Ed. 'What may I offer you, Marylyn?' Greta said. 'We have whisky, gin, rum, beer, Coca-cola – and wine.'

Ed beckoned Clarence into the hall that led to the front door. 'I told Greta. I hope you don't mind. It's the same as your telling me. I thought things would go better tonight if she knew.'

Clarence nodded, a little startled.

'It won't go any further. Not from this house.'

'All right.' Clarence followed Ed back into the living-room. Greta was giving Marylyn what looked like a gin and tonic.

'I hear you are a freelance typist and you live on Macdougal. Very near here,' Greta said to Marylyn.

It was obvious to Clarence that Greta meant to be friendly.

'What'll you have, Clarence?' Ed asked. 'Not just a beer, I hope. Beer doesn't give a lift.'

'A scotch, thanks.'

The puppy sat on the big sofa between Greta and Marylyn, and her black nose turned from one to the other as they spoke, as if she were following everything they said. This apartment was bigger, lighter, and more cheerful than the Riverside Drive place. Clarence, still standing up, noticed a long wooden table in a front corner of the room that held a buffet spread — platters of cold meats, a salad bowl, wine glasses. He wondered if it was for them?

Greta said in her high, clear voice, 'We were hoping you and Marylyn could have a bite with us, Clarence. I know you haven't much time, so I made a buffet.'

'Really it looks like a banquet!' Marylyn said.

'I'm not on duty tonight,' Clarence said. 'My schedule changes tomorrow and tonight's sort of a bonus.'

'Oh, marvellous!' said Greta. 'When are you on duty now?'

'Noon to 8 p.m. now. Saturdays and Sundays off. Almost normal hours,' Clarence replied.

Ed sat down on a hassock. 'Park yourself somewhere, Clarence.'

'... after our last one,' Greta was saying to Marylyn. 'We had to get another dog very soon, so now we have Juliette. Eddie thought it was best and he's right.'

'I know about your other dog,' Marylyn said. 'Clare told me.'

'Ah, well.' Greta's small figure was settled comfortably in the arm of the big sofa. 'Lisa, yes, she is no more.' She looked at Clarence and said, 'Eddie told me the story, Clarence. About the Polish man. We can keep secrets. I will not tell anyone, even my best friend. I know you know, too, Marylyn.'

Marylyn nodded. 'Yes.'

Clarence felt that Greta, as she looked at him now, was looking through him, not thinking of him but of something in her own past, more complex and important than the present situation.

Greta said, 'I also have some secrets to keep. My family history isn't pretty. Not a bedtime story either!' She laughed with sudden merriment and glanced at Ed.

'One would think she meant things she ought to hide,' Ed said. 'I'm afraid Greta, being half-Jewish, was more on the receiving end than the dishing out.'

'But still,' said Greta, 'some things are too horrible to speak about later, even much later.'

Clarence was silent. He did not know where they were headed. He was more interested in Marylyn's reaction than in anything else. She looked merely polite and serious, and soon she and Greta were discussing a ring. Whose ring on whose finger? Each was showing the other a ring that she wore. Marylyn seemed at ease with Greta, and Clarence realized she had no reason not to be at ease, not to be detached from all this, because she could detach herself from him whenever she wished, starting tonight, starting even now.

'You know, Marylyn,' Ed said, 'if I may call you Marylyn – Clarence told me you were upset by the story of the Pole. It's very understandable. But if ever a man deserved it –'

'Oh, Eddie, don't say that,' said Greta. 'Don't put it that way.'

'Well, why not?' Ed said. 'I mean to say, I might've been capable of it myself, if I'd met him on the street. If like Clarence I'd known he was annoying and deliberately scaring a friend of mine – you, Marylyn – not to mention if he'd accused me of taking money to let him go.' Ed leaned forward with his forearms on his knees. 'I think I might've lit into him for all I was worth, on the street or anywhere, if I'd run into him.'

'Eddie, you'll make yourself upset,' Greta said.

'I'm not upset, darling! I'm just trying to say something. I'm saying what I might've done in anger. I can speak for myself, because I was – furious enough after Lisa, you know that. And why shouldn't I have been? And neither the police nor Bellevue locking him up. I'm not saying it's right to beat him up or kill him, but I'm saying what I might have done. I might've attacked him even with people watching me. And what I wanted to say to you, Marylyn,' Ed went on, trying to finish and not to make too much of an oration of it, 'is that I understand it was a shock for you to hear about. About Clarence killing someone. Just that fact. It might as well have been me, however, and I don't think I'm a murderous type.'

'Oh, murderous !' said Greta. 'Don't say that, Eddie !'

'I said I'm *not* !' Ed said, laughing.

Marylyn's dark-rimmed eyes looked from Greta to Ed. 'It did throw me when I heard it. I suppose I couldn't believe it. Now I do. But when you think —' She hesitated.

'Think what ?' Ed asked.

'Think what kind of a creep he was, I suppose, and the fact that no one was doing anything about it.'

Exactly, Ed thought. But if one wanted to be civilized, one ought to say that punishment by death was barbaric. And murder in anger was inexcusable. Ed didn't care to mention that, and just now didn't even care to think about it. For a while he indulged in feeling primitive. He even glanced at Clarence with a smile, rather a smile of brotherhood. Anyway, the reason for his speaking to Marylyn was to try to make her understand Clarence's actions, if she didn't already, and perhaps he had succeeded.

'There's so much killing everywhere,' Marylyn said, 'not just in New York. Wars everywhere and for what ? Sometimes you want to say, "Stop all of it." I *do* say it. And then this Rowaninsk — whatever it is, his death was still a *death*, somehow — you see. This is what makes it difficult for me to judge, even though I thought he was the worst creep I've ever seen, and I've seen plenty in the Village, believe me.'

'I don't think Clarence should be blamed,' Greta said.

I'm sorry and yet I'm not sorry, Clarence thought, and set his teeth and looked at the floor.

Ed stood up. 'At least Kenneth Rowajinski isn't around to do the same things to other people — or other dogs.' Ed now wanted to end the subject, having started it, and he hoped he had not said too much.

'Darling, did you open the wine ?' Greta asked Ed. 'Is anyone hungry ?'

They moved towards the table, took plates and napkins.

'I go to a lot of meetings,' Marylyn was saying to Greta. 'Do you mean outdoor or indoor?'

'Are things any better?' Ed asked Clarence.

'I don't know.'

'She's an attractive girl,' Ed said.

They sat down, plates on laps or on the coffee-table. Greta and Marylyn were still talking about meetings, Greta mentioning names of people Clarence didn't know – except for Lilly Brandstrum.

'Sometimes I play the piano at the end and we sing,' Greta said. 'What do I play? Vietcong songs, hill-billy, anything. The Battle Hymn of the Republic. We have funny words . . .'

'They should pass the hat for Greta's piano,' Ed said to Clarence. 'It'd help pay the rent.'

'We pass the hat for more important *zings*,' said Greta, who had heard this.

'Gretchen, you take me so seriously!' Ed said.

Greta said, 'Marylyn, you must come to one of our meetings some time. Ours is just a little further east. Wednesday nights. Ours is more a cultural outlet than a political outlet,' Greta said with amusement in her eyes, casting a glance at Ed who was listening. 'We would all rather grab a guitar and sing than talk about politics, really, but it's fun.'

'I don't think she tells them that she has a husband who works for a corporation on Lexington,' Ed put in. 'However it may soon be Long Island if the company moves.'

Marylyn nodded. 'Moving. I know. This city's getting impossible.'

'Not definite, but it's in the air for us,' Ed said, 'moving.'

Marylyn and Greta began to talk again.

'So,' Ed said, turning to Clarence, 'what's the latest?'

'Nothing,' Clarence replied, knowing Ed meant had he been questioned again. 'I may quit the force before Christmas. I want to take some business management courses. At N.Y.U.'

'Oh?'

'Marylyn doesn't like cops.'

'I know. Business management for any particular kind of business?'

'The motivational side. The four-day week. As long as people have to work – I can't explain it now, in a nutshell.' Clarence felt suddenly lost, miserable, weak. He wanted to rush to Marylyn now, seize her in his arms, proclaim that she was his, and spirit her off. Instead he sat like a dolt on the hassock, talking vaguely of business administration, when actually he was as fed up with the whole system as Marylyn, fed up with built-in depreciation, advertising, wage-slaves and their own pilfering dishonesty, as fed up with the whole putrid corpse of it – as Marylyn was. Was it that he didn't have the guts to be a revolutionary?

Ed was thinking that Clarence Duhamell was even more vague and unformed than he had imagined. Or was he dazed, temporarily, by the events of the last few days? 'Are you an only child?'

'Yes.'

Ed had thought so. Clarence was probably spoiled. But spoiled how? Overprotected? 'You joined the police force just after school?'

'No.' Clarence told him about the job in the personnel department of the bank, and of his two years in the army before that, just after Cornell, when he had not been sent to Vietnam because the army had found use for him in the placing of draftees in army jobs. 'I had it lucky,' Clarence said.

'What does your father do?'

'He's an electrical engineer with a firm called Maxo-Prop. A turbine place. It's a nice solid job.' Clarence was aware of a note of apology in his voice.

'Your parents are probably no older than Greta and me. Funny. I'm getting old. Forty-two.'

'Oh, my parents are a little older than that! I'm twenty-four.'

Greta passed the platters for second helpings. Liverwurst, sliced ham, roast beef. 'No begging, Juliette! Don't give her anything!' Then she picked up the little dog and hugged her as if she were a baby.

'Do you go to Marylyn's meetings?' Ed asked Clarence.

'I have been. To two or three. Not in uniform, I assure you!' Clarence laughed. 'I wouldn't get out alive in uniform.

And in civvies my hair's not long enough – to please Marylyn. Personally I don't care how long people's hair is –' As long as it's clean, Clarence started to say. 'I wear mine as long as I can without getting remarks from my captains.'

Then came coffee. Brandy if anyone wanted it.

Marylyn and Greta were looking at a painting.

'You did it?' Marylyn said with surprise.

'I don't sign them,' Greta said. 'For me it spoils the composition.'

Clarence got up to look at the paintings more closely. He hadn't known either that three of the canvases on the walls were Greta's. Two were landscapes, sun-lit white houses, a yellow beach, rather abstract and without people. Clarence was impressed. The paintings appeared to have been quickly done, but perhaps weren't. At any rate, they looked painted by someone who knew exactly what he wanted to do, and Clarence, wanting to say this to Greta, found himself tongue-tied, because it was a compliment.

'Greece. Last summer . . .' Greta was saying to Marylyn.

'I envy you,' Clarence said to Ed.

'Envy me what?'

'Everything.'

Marylyn looked at Clarence with a hint that they should leave, and Clarence indicated that he would leave it up to her.

'It's time we should go, I think. Thank you both – for giving us such a nice evening,' Marylyn said.

'You both must come again. We know *some* young people but not enough. Never enough.' Greta's voice was warm.

Ed helped Marylyn with her cape.

'I'll be in touch about Wednesday night,' Marylyn said to Greta.

'Good-bye and *zank* you !' Greta said.

'Thank *you* !'

Clarence rang for the elevator, smiling at Marylyn, afraid to speak lest he be overheard through the Reynolds's closed door. A certain tension had disappeared, to be replaced by a different one, the one between himself and Marylyn. As they went down in the elevator Clarence said :

'Well, aren't they nice ?'

'Yes. Better than I'd expected. He's very attractive.'

'Ed. Yes.'

'And she paints awfully well. Really those paintings aren't bad for someone as old as she is.'

'They really seem to want us to come back.'

It had become colder. Marylyn sank her chin into her cape collar. Her hair blew straight behind her as they walked into 8th Street.

'Are you free Tuesday night?' Clarence asked. 'I'm free after eight. There's a new Bergman on.' Marylyn adored Bergman.

'It's only Sunday. Give me some time.'

She sounded more friendly, but why couldn't she say a direct 'Yes'? He could have proposed something Monday evening, and he was giving her time by proposing Tuesday. 'It's not late now. Would you –'

'I've still got some work tonight, if I didn't drink too many gin and tonics. But I only had two.'

'Going straight home? Want me to drop you in a taxi?'

'I'm not going home. I'd rather walk.'

Plainly she didn't want him to walk with her, wherever she was going, and he was ashamed to ask where. If it was to Dannie's on West 11th, 8th Street had not been an out-of-the-way route, because Dannie lived far west. They were at Sixth Avenue now. He kissed her cheek before she could draw back – or maybe she would not have drawn back. 'I'll call you about Tuesday. Don't forget.'

He waved good-bye, and did not watch to see which way she walked. His spirits plummeted and he gasped. After the nice evening, after all the effort the Reynolds had made, Marylyn – well, she wasn't with him, now.

At that moment, Ed and Greta were clearing the table, putting things away in the refrigerator.

'You might've gone too far, Eddie,' Greta said. 'Do you have to put all those things into words? I couldn't.'

She didn't mean that at all, Ed thought. She was probably glad he had said what he had. 'I thought it might do some good, my sweet. Clarence – I told you he was worried about what Marylyn thought of it all. – She's nice, don't you think? Better than I'd expected.'

'Better how?'

'More level-headed than I'd expected. To be just twenty-two. I was expecting her to be – dumber, I suppose.'

'Kids these days are quite grown-up.'

'I don't think Clarence is very grown-up, do you? For twenty-four?'

Greta wrapped the roast beef slices neatly in foil. 'With boys it's different. They mature later. And maybe he's the type who sees both sides of every question.' The refrigerator door made a cosy, muffled sound as Greta closed it.

Ed went into the living-room to see if anything was left to put away, and caught sight of Juliette peeing under the table, as if its shadows could hide her. 'Oh, hell, I'm late with mademoiselle! My fault, Juliette!' Ed went for a sponge reserved for this purpose in the bathroom.

He took the puppy out at once anyway. They were trying to train her for between 6.30 and 7 p.m., and tonight they had both forgotten. It was a pleasure for Ed to walk west and find more lights, more people (odd as some of them looked) and less traffic than on Riverside Drive. It was pleasant to think of Marylyn living fairly near, and having a date with Greta next Wednesday night. He hoped Clarence made out with Marylyn, because Clarence was in love. How much did Marylyn love Clarence? He must ask Greta her opinion on that.

20

The next morning, Clarence went to the New York City Ballet Theatre on West 58th Street and bought two tickets for Tuesday evening. Marylyn was quite fond of ballet, and he thought the tickets would please her. He went home and telephoned her from his apartment.

'Oh, it's *you*,' she said, sounding nervous.

'Yes, me. I got tickets for tomorrow for the New York City Ballet. An all-modern programme and one thing is a premiere.'

'Listen, Clare, your wop cop chum paid another visit this morning.'

'Manzoni?'

'I think that's his name. Just rang the bell at nine o'clock so I had to grab a raincoat to talk to him, because I'm not going to talk to that shit in a bathrobe, he'd get ideas! Imagine barging in at that hour without phoning first!'

'Marylyn, he's got no business! He's not Homicide!'

Marylyn cursed. 'He's asking if you really spent the night that night. *You* can imagine. *You* can imagine the nasty questions.'

'Christ, Marylyn, I'm sorry. I'll report him, I swear.'

'And so what if you report him? He was also asking about the five hundred bucks again. Jesus, I'm sick of it, Clare!'

'I'm going to report him.'

'Don't do it for my sake. I'm moving. Now. So I can't talk long and there's nothing to say anyway.'

'Moving where?'

'In with somebody.'

'Who?'

'I don't think I want to tell you, because I'd like to get the police off my back if I can. Evelyn's taking over my place, so don't call here again, will you?'

'But – you've got to tell me where *you're* going.'

'Sorry, Clare.' It was her deeper, more serious tone, and she hung up.

Clarence's heart was beating wildly. He thought of hopping a taxi down to Macdougal. Or would she hate that? Evelyn: a plump drip with glasses. And who was Marylyn moving in with? Dannie? Hadn't Marylyn said he had a big apartment? Clarence took off his shirt and splashed water on his face at the sink. This was the limit. Bastard Manzoni!

He'd give the ballet tickets to the Reynolds, Clarence thought. He'd try the Reynolds now. If Greta wasn't in, he could leave the tickets with the doorman with a note. Clarence walked to 9th Street. It was around 10.30 a.m.

The doorman telephoned the Reynolds's apartment, and someone answered.

'Please tell Mrs Reynolds I just want to give her something. It'll only take a minute.' Clarence wished he had brought flowers also, by way of thanking Greta for last evening.

Greta opened the apartment door.

'Pardon the intrusion,' Clarence said. 'I have two tickets that I –'

'Come in, Clarence.'

Clarence went in. 'For the ballet tomorrow night. I thought maybe you and Ed could use them.' Clarence held the little white envelope in his hand.

'Oh, thank you, Clarence. You're on duty tomorrow night?'

'No. I thought Marylyn was free – frankly.'

'You had some trouble – with Marylyn?'

'Well, yes. A little.'

'Don't you want to sit down?'

'Thank you. I'm on duty at noon, so I can't stay.'

'Something happened? Since last night?'

'Yes, a – a patrolman named Manzoni of my precinct house –' Clarence wished Ed were here, but he plunged on, needing to tell it to someone. 'Manzoni went to see Marylyn this morning. It's the second time he went to see her. Manzoni is the one who found Rowajinski at the Village hotel. So now he's heckling –'

'He dislikes you, this Manzoni?'

Clarence had to ponder the word 'dislikes' for an instant. 'He acts as if he's got something against me. First he was on to me about the five hundred dollars I'm supposed to have taken. Now he's asking Marylyn if I spent the whole night – Tuesday night. The main thing is, she can't stand being quizzed like that. It's not *her* fault.'

'Has he got a reason to think you didn't spend the night?'

A clue, Greta meant. 'I think he's just heckling.'

'How does he know Marylyn?'

'He saw me with her on the street. On Macdougal. Now – Marylyn's so upset she's moving.'

'Moving to where?'

'She wouldn't tell me. I think with a friend somewhere in the Village.' Clarence felt breathless. 'I don't want to bore you with any more of this.'

Greta patted his arm. 'I think she will call me about our date Wednesday night. I'll ask her where she's moved to.'

'But –' Clarence was torn. 'She doesn't seem to want me to know. Thanks anyway. Maybe it's better if I don't know for a while. I've got to take off now.'

As usual when he left the Reynolds's house, Clarence felt a sudden emptiness, an aloneness. He arrived at the station house at ten to twelve, and changed into uniform.

Captain Paul Smith was in charge now, a plump red-faced man with a serious manner. When Clarence went in for briefing, Smith said, 'Patrolman Duhamell?' as if he weren't quite sure. 'Homicide's been trying to reach you this morning. They're out there having coffee. Better go see them.' He gestured in the direction of the back hall.

'Yes, sir.' Clarence went down the hall. Two or three men in plainclothes were standing drinking coffee out of paper cups, talking and laughing.

'Patrolman Duhamell?' one asked.

'Yes, sir.'

'Come in here, please.'

Clarence followed him into an empty room which was more a storeroom than an office, though there was a desk. Another of the men came with them.

'I'm Detective Vesey. Detective Collins there. I know you're on duty now, but this'll just take five minutes. — How're you doing, Duhamell?' Vesey nodded meaninglessly. He looked as if he had all the information he wanted.

'All right, sir.'

'Did you hear the report on your gun?'

'No, sir.' Clarence glanced at the second man who was watching him, smoking. They were all standing.

'Suppose I told you that gun had blood on it? Rowajinski's blood?'

Clarence hesitated a second. 'I wouldn't believe you.'

'Cool,' said Vesey to his colleague.

Clarence was aware of sweating under his arms. He watched Detective Vesey pull some papers from an inside pocket of his overcoat.

'Duhamell, you were the logical suspect and we hit it right. Right?'

Collins gave a nod.

'What're you going to do, Duhamell? Going to admit it? Face up? Come clean? — It'll be easier for you.'

Clarence felt weak, transparent, and deliberately stood straighter. 'No,' he said, in quite a righteous-sounding tone.

Vesey smirked with impatience and nodded again. 'Duhamell, you're going to get a going over. You know what that means.'

Show me the report, Clarence was thinking, show me it, if it's true. Maybe they were putting on an act. And he wouldn't have put it past them to show him a faked report.

'Back to work, Duhamell. We shall see you again.'

They went out first. Clarence walked back to Captain Smith's office. The briefing was still going on, and there were eighteen or twenty patrolmen in the room. Smith was talking about handbag-snatching in the Park. Housewives had been complaining a lot lately. Clarence recalled Santini's voice saying, 'They oughta know better than to carry handbags when they're walkin' the kids. They never learn till they've all had it once.' Clarence got his patrol assignment, picked up his two-way radio, and went out with the rest.

There was a sturdy west wind off the Hudson, and it was rather cold. Clarence waved a greeting to a doorman behind a glass door on Riverside Drive. The doormen were different from the ones Clarence saw on his night shift, but he knew these faces from his former day shifts. Had the detectives been bluffing? They must have been, because if they were trying to break him down, what better start than to show him a report of blood on the gun? However, the working over. That was no bluff. Homicide wanted solutions. They roughed up the innocent with the guilty, Clarence knew. He was wondering if he could stand up to it? The fact he had killed the Pole, in a curious way, didn't count: he felt he ought to stand up to anything, ought to deny his guilt for ever. He felt that he owed it to the Reynolds. Guilt in a moral sense seemed to play no part. Perhaps that was abnormal. But hadn't Ed said, 'I might have done it myself'? And would Ed suffer any guilt if he had? Not much, Clarence thought. Maybe none at all.

Clarence had just turned the corner at Riverside Drive into 105th Street, going east, when two shots sounded ahead of him. He stared for an instant without seeing where the shots had come from, then ran forward towards West End Avenue. At once there were two more shots, tinkles of breaking glass, laughter, and a woman on the sidewalk screamed, and Clarence saw that the shots were coming from a car moving slowly towards him. An arm, a hand with a smoking gun protruded from a window of the car, and there was more wild laughter. Clarence was sprinting for the car. Another shot, and a spatter of glass at the front door of an apartment building. A startled window flew up on Clarence's left, and was immediately banged shut again.

Clarence dashed obliquely into the street towards the car as the next shots exploded. He felt a jolt in his right leg. Glass behind him fell, sounding like treble piano notes, on cement. Clarence grabbed the extended arm with the gun just as the car put on speed. He held on to the arm, the gun fell from the black hand, and Clarence ran to keep up with the car, jerking at the arm of the man who was now yelling with pain. Then the back fender of the car hit Clarence and bounced him off, he landed on his shoulder, rolled a couple of times and was checked against the wheel of a parked car. Clarence pushed himself to a seated position, dazed. To his right, at Riverside

Drive, the car was turning fast around the corner. To his left he saw someone reaching for the gun in the street.

'Don't touch the gun!' Clarence said.

He got up. Two men came forward, hesitated as if he were dangerous, or perhaps they thought he needed no help. Clarence went and got the gun, picked it up by the tip of its barrel. An adolescent boy stared at him wide-eyed from the kerb. A doorman was following him along the pavement.

'You got hit?'

Clarence was limping. He knew the doorman by sight. 'Did you see the licence number?'

'Sorry, I didn't. Look! Lookit what the bastards did to my door! – Hey, you're hit!'

'Anyone get the licence of that car?' Clarence asked, because there were many more people on the street now and several windows had gone up on both sides of the street. Suddenly there were twenty or thirty people standing around, asking questions, cursing the shooters as if their personal property had been destroyed, or as if the gunfire had given them an outlet for pent-up rage.

'Hoodlums!'

'Had an R in it!' said a small boy's voice.

'An old black Cadillac!'

'Blacks! Spades! I saw 'em!'

'Look at that door! Jesus! What's next around here?'

'Foot's bleeding!' said the same boy's voice.

Just as Clarence started to switch on his walky-talky, a patrol car arrived and braked at the kerb, its siren dying down. Two officers got out and, not seeing Clarence at first, began talking to the bystanders. They were talking to a woman Clarence had not seen, whose hand was dripping blood. The woman was holding out her limp hand, gripping its wrist. One of the officers trotted back to his car and started talking on his radio.

Clarence felt faint. He had lost his cap. He looked around on the street for it. No luck. A kid had probably made off with it. Clarence went to speak with the officers. He didn't know either of them, and assumed they were from the Frederick Douglass Park and Amsterdam area just east.

'You were here?' an officer asked Clarence.

'Yes. A black car with three or four men in it. Blacks. I have the gun.' Clarence was carrying it still by the tip of the barrel.

'You're hurt, eh?' The officer looked down at Clarence's feet.

Blood was overflowing his right shoe, and his foot was soaking. Clarence's senses took another lunge. The officer helped him into the patrol car. The other officer said something about waiting till the ambulance came for the woman.

They arrived at Clarence's precinct house.

'Lost your cap?' someone said. 'What's happened?'

Clarence sat on a chair, while someone pulled the leg of his trousers up above his calf.

'Went through,' a voice said.

Clarence started giving his report: time and place, but the scene was dissolving like a spotty, greyish film fading out.

'... old Cadillac, they said ... This officer got the gun ...' Another officer had taken over for him.

Clarence toppled off the chair, and felt himself caught in a slow-motion swoop by the arms of a policeman. He was aware of being laid out flat on a stretcher, and aware of feeling nauseous. Then he arrived at a hospital. They gave him a needle in the arm.

He awakened in a bed, in a room with five or six other beds, a man in each one. His right leg hurt below the knee. His right shoulder was stiff with bandages, his forearm held by an absurdly light-looking cheesecloth sling. The window showed a clear blue sky. Was it today – Monday – or Tuesday? His wrist-watch was gone. It wasn't even on the bed table. A nurse in white scurried into the ward, looking about to drop a tray which appeared excessively heavy.

She said it was 9.30 a.m., Tuesday. His watch was in the table drawer. His shoulder? He had a fractured collarbone.

'And my leg?'

'A flesh wound. Nothing broken. You were lucky.'

Her smile made him feel somehow worse.

Clarence dozed. Then the nurse came back and said:

'Your mother's here.'

His mother came into the room shyly, not seeing him at

first. Clarence raised his left arm. His mother's lips formed a silent 'Oh' as she tiptoed towards him. She had three oranges in a cellophane bag.

The nurse provided a chair and departed.

'Clare, darling, are you in pain?'

'No. I think I'm full of dope. Anyway it's not serious.'

'The nurse said you'd be out in a few days, but you're not to go back to work for three weeks at least. — What happened, Clare? Or don't you want to talk?'

His mother had somehow got hold of his left hand, though she was on the right side of the bed. 'There was a car. They were shooting from the car. Shooting up the doorways. I should've got the licence number but I only got the gun, I remember.'

'Thank goodness, Clary, the bullet didn't hit you in the chest!' His mother was whispering out of courtesy to the other men in the room. 'Ralph's coming to see you around six-thirty.'

'Where is this hospital?'

'It's at Amsterdam and a Hundred and fourteenth Street. It's St Luke's.'

Clarence was thinking of Marylyn. She was an apricot-coloured haze. He could see her lips moving, and she was neither angry nor not angry, but was trying to explain something to him. His mother was putting the oranges on his table, as gently as if they were eggs, saying something about hospitals so seldom having anything fresh.

'You'll come and stay with us, Clary ... The officer who called us said you were very brave. I think the nurse is signalling for me to go. Don't forget Ralph's coming. Tell him I'll be back to meet him here around seven.'

'Mom, can you do something for me?'

'Of course, darling.'

He had been thinking of the Reynolds. Tell the Reynolds where he was. But that would look as if he were asking for attention. His mother didn't even know the Reynolds. 'Nothing.'

'No, tell me, Clary. Something about Marylyn? Does she know you're here?'

'I was dreaming. I made a mistake.'

His mother looked puzzled, kissed his cheek and went away.

Whatever sedatives they had given him, they certainly lingered. Clarence was gradually aware of his father sitting by the bed, of his taut, clear voice, of his smile coming into focus like the emergence of the Cheshire Cat. '... as your mother just told me. Well, things could've been worse! ... stay with us for a couple of weeks, Clary old boy, and get a little V.I.P. treatment ...'

Clarence hoisted himself on his pillow, trying to awaken, and paid for it with pain in his shoulder. 'I'm sorry. I can't seem to wake up.' Why were his thoughts a jumble of Marylyn, Ed, Greta, and not at all of his parents?

'... think you're going to sleep. Don't try to fight it. See you soon, Clary. Bye-bye, son.'

Clarence slept, and awakened when it was dark, except for an unearthly blue light that glowed over the door into the hall. He would have liked to pee, but they wouldn't let him walk and he was shy about asking for a urinal. *I am a failure*, Clarence thought. *I've failed with Marylyn, and failed as a cop, and what can Reynolds think of me? I failed to save their dog, or even all the money they paid for the dog. And Marylyn hates me because of what I brought on her. I have made the mistake of killing a man. Try and get over that one! So I ought to kill myself.* Clarence's body tensed with purpose, and he did not mind the pain. He bared his teeth. To kill himself seemed a decent and logical way out. Thus he could stop making mistakes and being a hardship, even a detested enemy, to so many people.

The nurse scurried in like a fast-moving ghost and pressed both hands on his ribs. 'Sh-h! lie down! You're making a lot of noise!'

The men in the room were mumbling, annoyed also. A needle went into his left arm. God, were they merciless! And what on earth were they giving him?

He had a dream: he was not quite himself and not quite a different person either. He had killed two people, and he disposed of the second corpse, like the first, by stuffing it into a large rubbish bin on a deserted street corner. The second victim was Manzoni (the first was unidentified in his dream). Then Clarence was in a shop or store of some kind, mumbling to himself, and he became aware that several people were glancing at him, thinking that he was an eccentric character, someone to be avoided, and Clarence realized what he had done, killed two people and disposed of their bodies in such a way that they were bound to be discovered fairly soon. 'If a tough detective tries to beat the truth out of me,' he thought, 'I'll certainly crack and tell everything.' Then he suffered guilt, shame, a sense of being cut off from other people, because he had done something that no one else had done or could do. He felt damned, unique and horrible, and he awakened with a dismalness of spirit such as he had never known.

It was dusky in the ward, and only one small lamp glowed where a man was reading in his bed.

The dream and the drugs Clarence tried to shake off by shaking his head. It was not a dream, however. He *had* killed someone. And the way he felt now would last. He would be isolated, living in terror of being found out. Clarence's depression was so shocking to him, he remained a long while propped on his elbow, his lips parted in astonishment. He felt about to scream, yet he didn't.

21

Clarence was to be in the hospital two more days, until Friday evening. MacGregor telephoned on Wednesday, and Clarence spoke with him on the hall telephone. 'We've been in touch with the hospital,' MacGregor said. 'I'm glad things are going all right.' And that was all. Brief, but Clarence was surprised and grateful that MacGregor had troubled.

Around five on Wednesday afternoon Clarence telephoned the Reynolds's apartment. Tonight Greta was supposed to have a date with Marylyn. Greta answered.

'Clarence Duhamell,' Clarence said on a pleasant note. 'How are you? Did you go to the ballet last night?'

'Yes, we did and we enjoyed it very much. Thank you, Clarence.'

'I'm calling – because I'm in hospital just now. Just till Friday and I –'

'The hospital? What happened?'

'Just a flesh wound. A bullet.'

'How terrible! Who shot you?'

'Oh – people on a Hundred and fifth. It's only a little wound in the leg.'

'What hospital? ... Can you have visitors? ... I will come to see you tomorrow. Tomorrow morning, Clarence.'

'Please don't bother, Greta!'

But she was going to bother.

Clarence limped back to his bed feeling infinitely happier. Tomorrow Greta could tell him about her evening with Marylyn, perhaps tell him what Marylyn's attitude was towards him. Clarence closed his eyes and let himself sink into a half-sleep. In the bed on his right a man was talking with the man beyond. They were old fellows.

'... night nurses, all that, when I was in Singapore. British hospital, of course.'

'Singapore?'

'...' A laugh. 'Malaria ... you catch out there. Jap prison camps were full of it ... the worst, cerebral. Some people never shake it off ...'

Greta came the next morning just before eleven, bearing a plastic bag of pale green grapes and a thick book in a new dust jacket. It was a George Orwell anthology of essays and journalism, and included *Homage to Catalonia*.

'Do you like Orwell?' asked Greta. 'Maybe you have read all these.'

'I've read Catalonia. But I don't own it. Thank you. – Is that chair all right?' Clarence was prepared to offer her one of his pillows because the chair looked so uncomfortable. He felt awkward. A ghost of the awful dream still lingered, and he felt as if people could see the dream in his face when they looked at him.

Greta said the chair was quite all right. She wanted to hear what had happened to him. He told her about grabbing the gun, stupidly he said, because he should have got the car's licence number also.

'You saw Marylyn last night?' Clarence asked.

'Oh yes!' Greta's face beamed. 'I hope she enjoyed it. We had two speakers and the last half was poetry. Anyone could read or recite anything.'

'Marylyn looked all right?' He hated it that the man on the right might be listening – eyes closed but that meant nothing. He'd listen for enterainment.

'Oh, I think so. She is living on West Eleventh Street, she said.'

A pang went through Clarence rather like another bullet. West 11th meant Dannie, the ballet dancer. It must mean Dannie. 'She didn't say,' Clarence went on, 'who she was living with?'

Greta for a moment tried to think. 'No. She didn't.'

Greta perhaps suspected that Marylyn had moved in with a man friend. But how unconcerned Greta was, Clarence thought. And what else could he expect? And he hadn't told Greta about Dannie. 'She – Did she say anything about me?'

'Oh! I told her you were in the hospital. I told her it wasn't serious, because you said that.'

Clarence knew Greta must know that Marylyn hadn't even telephoned. He was vaguely embarrassed, or ashamed.

'It's a bad time for you, isn't it, Clarence?'

I wonder sometimes if there's any hope about Marylyn, Clarence wanted to say.

'How long must you be in bandages?'

'Oh, these. I can probably take them off Friday. When I leave. My parents want me to stay with them for a few days. My place on East Nineteenth is a walk-up. Might be a bore with this leg.'

'But of course stay with your family. You need someone to cook your meals.'

The nurse came in then, the smiling Puerto Rican one, to tell Greta that she should leave in a few minutes.

'Marylyn didn't give you her phone number?' Clarence asked.

'No, but she said she would call me again.'

Clarence was abashed by Greta's smile of understanding. He felt Greta knew he had lost with Marylyn, and that Greta was thinking – as all older people would – that he would get over it.

'You know, Clarence, if you would like to stay a few days with us, you are very welcome. We have an extra room. I already mentioned it to Ed.'

Clarence could not quite believe it. 'That's kind of you. But my parents –'

'They're in Long Island. At our place you could see Marylyn more easily.'

That was true. 'I wouldn't want to be trouble to you. I'd rather be a help.'

'Nonsense! I am not so busy.' She was standing up, smiling so that the corners of her eyes as well as her mouth seemed to turn up. 'Maybe Ed can telephone you. Cheer you up. We can call you here?'

'Yes, there's a phone in the hall. – Thank you for coming to see me, Greta. And for the book and the grapes.' Clarence was sitting up and would have accompanied Greta to the door, except that he felt asinine in his nightshirt.

She was gone. The walls were pale-blue blanks again, the room empty of her warmth.

Clarence's parents, who arrived at 6.30 that evening, were astounded that he was thinking of staying with a family he hardly knew.

'Not a family, Mother, just a man and wife.'

Who were the Reynolds? They hadn't heard of them until the detective who called at their house mentioned them.

Clarence explained how he had met the Reynolds last month. 'I didn't mean I'd go straight to them.' But of course he did want to go straight to them. Astoria held no attractions. 'Edward Reynolds works at Cross and Dickinson. He's a senior editor. They're very nice people, Mother.'

'You'll stay with us first,' said his mother. 'You'll want to be feeling stronger before you visit people you don't know so well.'

'We'll come the same time tomorrow and pick you up in the car, Clary old boy,' said Ralph.

There was no way out. 'I ought to get something from my apartment. Check the mail. Bills, maybe.'

'Have you got the keys, Clary?' asked his mother. 'Shall we go by tomorrow night? But you shouldn't climb those stairs . . . I'll bring you some clothes from home meanwhile. You've lots of clothes at home and you like those old clothes.'

Clarence reached for his keyring in the drawer of the bed table. On the ring were Marylyn's two keys, no longer of any use. 'My blue jeans, maybe a shirt or two. Shirts're in the middle drawer. Not the French cuff shirts, the ordinary ones.'

'I know,' said his mother, pleased.

'Marylyn been to see you?' asked his father. 'I was hoping we might run into her.'

Clarence realized that his mother looked younger than Greta, looked very pretty with the fur collar of her black coat still close about her neck and her sturdy face smiling and full of health. But Greta was to him more attractive, even though feature by feature Greta was really uglier. He realized he was a little in love with Greta.

His father was talking about how lucky Clarence had been.

'... twenty-one policemen killed so far this year in New York alone...'

The nurse came in. It was time for his parents to go.

Clarence picked up a book, and felt for a few minutes content. Then he thought of Dannie, of Marylyn on West 11th Street – Marylyn probably cooking his meals, arranging her clothes and her typewriter in his apartment (which Clarence for no real reason imagined rather swank), and he grew tense, and he blinked his eyes. It couldn't last, couldn't be anything serious, Marylyn and Dannie. Dannie knew Marylyn was his girl. And Dannie himself didn't look serious about anything. Clarence had seen him twice. Marylyn could be cool, unfeminine almost, just like another fellow or someone sexless, if she wasn't interested in a man. Clarence had seen it. And what was so marvellous about Dannie? He was twenty-six and not yet a roaring success. His parents were helping him with his rent, he remembered Marylyn saying. Maybe he even had a room-mate, another fellow there. Clarence hoped so.

As Clarence was staring without interest at his dinner tray, a nurse came in and told him there was a telephone call for him. Marylyn, Clarence thought. He got out of bed as quickly as he could, preparing the most casual of remarks about his injuries. And he could say he hoped life was quieter for her on West 11th Street.

'Hello. Clarence?'

Clarence recognized Ed's voice. 'Yes. Hello, Ed. How are you?'

'That's what I'm calling to ask you. Greta thought you looked pretty well, considering.'

'Oh, I'm fine. Out tomorrow. My parents are coming to pick me up.'

'Greta said you might be able to visit us for a few days. I hope you can. How long are you going to be *hors de combat*?'

'Three more weeks, they say. I can get around now. It's just that I can't work for three more weeks.'

Clarence returned to his bed, to the boring tray. He had hoped Ed would mention Marylyn, say something about having seen her Wednesday evening. How absurd it was to grasp like this, Clarence thought, for a word, an impression Ed might have had, assuming Ed had seen Marylyn at all, and possibly he hadn't. Clarence knew he was being unrealistic, hanging on to hopes that were maybe doomed. Marylyn hadn't even telephoned.

22

On Tuesday evening the Reynolds awaited Clarence Duhamell. His parents, or his father anyway, was driving Clarence to Manhattan, and the Reynolds had asked Clarence to bring his parents to the apartment to meet them. Clarence was due around seven. Juliette had been aired. Greta, besides preparing a rather special dinner of roast ducklings, had gone to trouble to make the spare room – really her studio, but her easel had been stuck in a corner and her paints pushed to one end of the long worktable – attractive with a pot of flowering begonia and two or three books, which she thought Clarence might like, on the table by the single bed. She was hoping the Duhamells might stay for dinner.

The telephone rang and Ed picked it up.

'Hello, Mr Reynolds? ... Patrolman Peter Manzoni here. I'm from the same precinct house as Duhamell. You know him, I think. Clarence.'

'Yes?'

'I'd like to see you, Mr Reynolds. I'm in your neighbourhood and I wonder if you've got a few minutes?'

'Tonight I –'

'Or later after dinner? That's okay with me.'

'Tonight isn't good at all. We have guests. Can I ask what this is about?'

'Just that I'd like to ask you some questions about Clarence. Nothing complicated.'

The tough voice irritated Ed. 'Questions you can't ask him?'

The man laughed. 'Not quite. Different questions. How about tomorrow night? Say around six-thirty? Seven?'

Ed hesitated. 'I'd like to know what it's about.'

'I can't tell you over the phone. It's my job, Mr Reynolds.'

It might look worse for Clarence if he dodged the interview, Ed thought. 'All right. Tomorrow? About seven? ... I'll meet you downstairs in the lobby here.' Ed hung up.

'Who was that?' Greta asked.

'That fellow you said Clarence mentioned. Manzoni. Wants to see me tomorrow night.'

'To see you? Why?'

'He says he wants to ask me some questions about Clarence.'

The house telephone buzzed in the kitchen, and Greta turned to go to it.

Ed was wondering if Clarence's precinct house knew that he was going to stay with them for a few days? Probably. The precinct house would want to know where to reach Clarence. 'I'm not going to tell that guy anything,' Ed said to Greta.

The doorbell sounded.

Clarence came in with his father. Clarence stuck his suitcase in a corner of the foyer. 'Ed — Greta — my father. Mr and Mrs Reynolds.'

'How do you do?' said Ralph, bowing to Greta, extending his hand to Ed. 'I'm very happy to meet you, because my son's talked quite a bit about you.'

'Your wife's not with you?' Ed said.

'No, she's got a meeting tonight at eight. She could've come, but she didn't want to make a crowd, I think.'

They went into the living-room.

Ed liked Ralph Duhamell on sight. He looked straightforward, unpretentious, yet sure of himself. His pleasant, full lips Clarence had inherited, but his hair was darker than Clarence's and he was not so tall.

'You feeling better, Clarence?' Greta asked.

'Absolutely all right,' Clarence said.

Ralph accepted a scotch, but said he could not stay for dinner, when Greta said she was hoping that he would. 'Clare told me about your other little dog. That's a terrible story. And the ransom hoax that went with it. That's vicious. — Manhattan's tougher than where we live. No doubt of that. We live in Astoria. Nothing fancy to be sure, but it's a real home there. Clare was brought up there.'

Ed knew from the way he spoke that he didn't know or suspect that Clarence had killed Rowajinski.

'Clare feels he didn't do a good job for you,' Ralph said. 'He's said a good deal about that lately.'

'What could he do?' Ed said. 'The dog was dead from the start, I'm afraid.'

'Yes, I realize. – Clare says you've met Marylyn.'

'Yes, once,' Ed said, glad to change the subject. Greta and Clarence were talking on the other side of the room. 'I thought she was very nice. Quite intelligent.'

'Really?' said Ralph. 'Serious?'

'Oh – yes. Politically.' Ed smiled.

'Because Clare is quite gone on her. At least she works for a living. Doesn't take drugs, I gather. Clare says she doesn't even like smoking pot.'

Clarence showed his father Greta's paintings. Ralph seemed to like one seascape immensely. He declined a second drink.

'Behave yourself, Clare,' Ralph said as he was leaving. At the door he again shook hands with Ed.

'Come and see your room, Clarence,' Greta said. 'Bring your suitcase. Can you carry it all right?'

'Doesn't weigh anything. It's a little suitcase.' Clarence got it and followed her into a hall to the left of the kitchen. His room was on the left with a window on the street side. 'It's a beautiful room,' Clarence said.

There was a solid dark green rug, a bright orange bed-spread, a very practical table, white walls – none of the clutter that ruined most rooms. The Reynolds had good taste. Clar-ence hung up a pair of trousers. He had brought little with him, thinking he ought not to stay more than two nights. He washed his hands and face in the blue-tiled bathroom. Greta had showed him his towels. Clarence went back into the living-room, carrying the bottle of Chateau Neuf du Pape that he had brought in his suitcase.

The dinner was ready.

Later that evening, when Clarence had gone to his room, Ed stood at the living-room window, looking down at a few brownstones squeezed between taller apartment buildings across the street. Greta was out with the pup. Clarence had offered to air Juliette, but Greta had wanted to do it herself. Ed had some reading to do before going to bed. He was thinking of Manzoni tomorrow evening, dreading it. He'd be calm and brief and factual – factual up to a point. Manzoni would probably say, 'I hear Dummell's staying with you now.' Ed might have started his reading, but he waited until he heard the faint click of the elevator door, Greta's step in the hall, and he knew she was safely back. He sat down on the sofa with a nine-page mimeographed bulletin called NON-FICTION: COMPARISON OF CURRENT YEAR WITH LAST YEAR. Advertising, sales by area, returns, all itemized compactly. Ed was gratified to see that two books he had fought for had done quite well. But one book he had been against had done even better. That was life.

'What're Clarence's plans for tomorrow?' Ed asked.

'He wants to help me shopping. And he wants to air the dog.' Greta laughed.

'I don't particularly want him airing the dog,' Ed said in a soft voice. 'We can do it.'

'He wants to be helpful. He –'

'It's that Manzoni,' Ed interrupted. 'I don't know. He might be watching the house. – I don't like it.'

Greta stared at him. 'All right, Eddie.'

'I can tell more about the situation tomorrow.'

The next evening, Ed was downstairs in his apartment house lobby ten minutes before seven. 'Waiting for someone,' Ed said with a smile, by way of explanation to the doorman. Clarence had gone out to a film in the afternoon, but was in now, and he wanted to take Ed and Greta out to dinner. Ed had told Clarence that he had a date with one of his authors in the neighbourhood, and would be back in half an hour.

Manzoni was punctual, and Ed recognized him at once as a cop when the doorman let him in – a man of about five eight, no hat, wavy black hair, a trenchcoat of dark blue, an ambiguous smile on a broad, creased face.

'Mr Reynolds?' he said.

'Yes. Good evening.'

'Well – we'll go out somewhere?'

They found a small bar not far away. Manzoni motioned to a booth at one side. When they had sat down, Manzoni said:

'I heard today Clarence is staying with you. I spoke with his parents today.'

'Yes. For a couple of days. He's just out of the hospital as you probably know.'

'Dummell should've reported where he is. He's still a cop even if he's on sick leave. That's why I phoned his parents. Because his phone didn't answer.'

Ed said nothing.

'Well.' Manzoni smiled. 'What do you know about Rowajinski, Mr Reynolds? That's why I came to see you, to ask what Dummell said about him.'

'I only know he was found dead,' Ed said.

A waiter came. Manzoni mumbled something. Ed ordered a scotch and water.

Manzoni lit a cigarette. He had pudgy strong hands that went with his face. 'You know, Homicide doesn't know who killed Rowajinski, but they have a strong suspicion it was Dummell. Who else, in fact? What do you think yourself?'

'I hadn't thought.'

'No? Really no?'

Ed relaxed, and pulled out his own cigarettes. 'Why should I enjoy thinking about Rowajinski? I don't. I haven't.'

'What I want to ask you frankly is do you think Clarence did it? Has Clarence talked to you?'

'No.' Ed frowned slightly, showed the faintest shock at the question, and realized that he was acting, that he had to act. 'You know as much as I do and probably a lot more.' Since Manzoni was silent, watching him with the speculative smile, Ed asked, 'Are you a detective?'

'No. – I will be.'

Their drinks arrived.

Manzoni took a gulp of his, and ground some ice between his teeth. 'It occurred to me, Mr Reynolds, if Dummell killed that guy, you'd be sort of on Dummell's side, no? After all, you didn't like Rowajinski.'

Again Ed sighed, pretending. 'I didn't hate Rowajinski

enough to want him killed. He was a sick man, sick in the head.'

Manzoni nodded. 'Whatever Dummell said to you – Look, Mr Reynolds, we're sure Dummell did it, and he's going to have to answer a few more questions from us, see? Sure, he's just been in the hospital –'

'Really? You're so sure?'

'Dummell had motive. You know that. This Pole was annoying his girl-friend. He'd accused Dummell of taking a bribe. Something that was never proven yes or no!' Manzoni declared, holding up a thick forefinger. 'Dummell sucks up to people like you, wants to put on a good act for you. Social climber.'

Ed shook his head as if he were bewildered.

'What's the matter?'

'I have no facts to give you. I know you want to get your man, sure.' Ed downed his drink, not so much because he wanted it as because he wanted to leave soon.

'Mr Reynolds, the finger is already on Dummell and we're going to get him. I don't know – just how.' Manzoni subsided in a shrug, almost daydreamed for a few seconds. 'But it's not going to be hard.'

Evidently, Ed supposed, he wasn't quite bold enough to say outright that he, Ed Reynolds, was shielding Dummell. Ed shrugged also, as if to say, 'That's your affair.'

Manzoni looked hard at Ed, still smiling a little, but with the flinty look that Ed had seen in films and in television plays – the tough detective had reached the point of showdown, of crisis, or maybe challenge of some kind. 'What you're saying is, Clarence hasn't said a thing to you.'

'No,' Ed said.

'He just said he spent that night with his girl-friend?'

'That night?'

'The night Rowajinski was killed. Tuesday. That Tuesday.'

'Yes. He did say that.'

'Maybe you know his girl-friend dropped him. Marylyn.'

'Did she?'

'You didn't know?'

'Clarence didn't mention it.'

'You know Marylyn?'

'No. I met her once, that's all.'

'Well, she's fed up. She knows. Nobody thinks Clarence spent the whole night there. His girl-friend says so mainly because she wants to foul up the cops. But she doesn't want a killer for a boy-friend, oh no.'

Ed said calmly, 'I don't know a thing about Marylyn. Clarence hasn't said a thing.' Ed looked at his watch. 'If you don't mind –'

'Oh, of course not. Gotta be somewhere?'

Ed nodded. He pulled out his bill-fold. 'Unless you have any other – Something else?'

'No. Just if Clarence tells you anything, even the smallest thing, let us know, will you? Here's the telephone number.' Manzoni had his bill-fold out also, and pulled half a dozen cards from it, and gave Ed one.

The precinct address and telephone number were stamped crookedly in purple ink on the card. Ed put the card in his overcoat pocket. Manzoni really wanted to pay, but they went dutch, each leaving a sizeable tip.

For Clarence, the day had begun in a princely way. He had awakened at a quarter past nine, when Greta knocked on his door, bringing coffee and orange juice on a tray. Outside, the sun was shining, and Clarence had strolled about the room, barefoot, in pyjamas, sipping his coffee, drinking in also the details of the room which was Greta's workroom – the used but clean brushes in the tall cookie tin, the sketch in dark purple watercolour for a portrait of Ed, a discarded shopping list on which Greta had tried out various shades of yellow. He had heard the hum of a vacuum cleaner and remembered that Greta had said the cleaning woman came this morning.

After a couple of inquiries, Clarence discovered how he might be useful: Greta needed something that might be obtainable in Macy's basement, a kitchen gadget. Clarence set out as if in quest of the Holy Grail. He was not going to return without it, even if the task required A. & S. in Brooklyn. He had made a reservation at a Hungarian restaurant where he wanted to invite Greta and Ed that evening. It was nearly eleven as he approached the West 4th Street subway, an hour at which he could try Marylyn without being afraid of awakening her. He went into a drugstore and looked up Dannie Sheppard's number.

A man's voice answered.

'Hello. This is Clarence Duhamell. Is this Dannie?'

'Ye-eah.'

'Sorry to bother you, but is Marylyn there?'

Brief pause. 'Listen, Clarence, that fuzz is at it again. That wop. He just phoned here. He's still tailing Marylyn and it's a pain in the ass, if you know what I mean. So the least you can do, please, is disappear. Understand? This is my house –'

'Can I speak to Marylyn?' Clarence asked.

'I don't think she wants to speak to you.'

'Why don't you ask her?' Clarence at that point heard Marylyn's voice in the background.

'Hello,' Marylyn said.

'Hello, darling. How are you?'

'How do you think?'

'Marylyn – I do want to see you.'

'That's obviously not such a good idea, is it?'

'But – I must see you. Just for five minutes. I'm very near just now. I'll meet you – even on a street corner. Please, Marylyn!'

Marylyn refused.

Clarence went on in a daze to Macy's. He found the gadget that Greta wanted. He telephoned Greta to say he had succeeded (she was going to stay in and work, painting, that afternoon) and then he went to a film just to take his mind off Marylyn, and also to leave his room free for Greta, although she had said she could work as well in the living-room.

The next day, Thursday, Clarence had thought to leave the Reynolds and go to his apartment, but it happened to be Greta's birthday. Eric Schaffner and Lilly Brandstrum were coming for dinner, and Greta said she hoped Clarence would stay for dinner, too, and it would be silly to go to his apartment late at night, so why not stay another night? So Clarence had agreed. He bought for Greta a silver chain necklace at a shop on 8th Street, a fairly expensive present but not so expensive, Clarence hoped, that it could be considered a wrong thing to do. Buying the present for Greta made him feel more optimistic, and he telephoned Dannie's apartment, hoping a note of cheer in his own voice could make Marylyn agree to see him.

This time she answered.

'I don't want to see you but I will. But just for five minutes.'

They were to meet at once on the corner of 11th Street and Sixth Avenue. Clarence hurried.

Marylyn had only a block or so to walk, and she arrived when he did, on the north-west corner. Her face looked angry and pinched. He didn't recognize her fringed suede jacket, and because it was too big for her, he assumed it was Dannie's.

'Hello,' he said. 'Do you want to go somewhere? Somewhere we can sit?'

'No.' She was restless in her moccasins, hands in her pockets, stiff as if with cold though it was not very cold. She wore no socks. Marylyn was always careless about socks and scarves when it was too cold to go without them. 'There's a fair chance we're being watched anyway, so if we walk or go somewhere, what's the dif?'

'You're cold.'

'Something conked out with the heating at Dannie's this morning.'

'Oh.' Clarence was inwardly glad it wasn't the luxury establishment he had envisaged.

They walked, Marylyn with her stubborn, short steps, her head down. They walked downtown.

'I'm completely sick of this fascist pig,' Marylyn said.

'I know. Dannie said he telephoned.'

'He turned up! Last night. Called up first, all right, but he was there before we could get out of the house. How could we get out and why should we? Dannie had guests. He said he'd just seen Mr Reynolds. Well, how interesting!'

'He's lying. What time did he come?'

'Around eight. He said Mr Reynolds was protecting you and so was I and that you – you know. Seven or eight people heard it. I told him to shove it but what good does *that* do? Dannie'd tried to keep him outside the door, but just because he's a pig, he muscled in. Dannie said have you got a search warrant, and the pig said no, because he wasn't searching for anything. No, he's only heckling. It's a Fascist state, Clare! You can't even fight them. *They've* got the guns! — You're in a spot, I know, but don't drag *me* into it.'

Clarence was thinking that Ed hadn't seen an author last night, he had seen Manzoni. Now Clarence realized that Ed had seemed uneasy, a little cool, at the restaurant last night. Ed had probably had enough, too, like Marylyn.

'I never meant to drag you in.'

'No? I told them you were with me that night, for Christ's sake. You told them that, too. And you didn't mean to drag me in!'

Clarence knew. It was true he had dragged her in.

'I'd be better off in the Bronx or Long Island. But a lot of my work's down here. I've got to stay.'

'I know. I'm sorry, Marylyn.'

'You're always sorry. Let Mr Reynolds protect you, but get it off my back, will you? — Only you can't.' She added sarcastically, 'We shouldn't look like we're quarrelling in case we're being watched. This wop lives on Jane, you know, God knows when he's off duty. We ought to be just casual friends. Medium-like.'

Marylyn's sarcasm was something new. They had stopped at the corner of the Women's House of Detention, where five busy streets met.

'Maybe they're letting you recuperate,' Marylyn said, 'but that cop said they're going to question you again.'

'Look, Marylyn, I'm going to pull through this, I'm sure of it.'

'Really? I've heard they beat people up.'

'I can take it.'

Marylyn turned to the right, into Greenwich Avenue, walking slowly back uptown. Clarence walked beside her.

'It's not that I want to be a bitch, Clare. But you can't blame me if I can't take it, can you?'

He understood. He wanted to say words of comfort and strength and couldn't find them. 'But you will see me later, I hope – when this has blown over.'

She shrugged evasively. 'Sure, maybe. Now and then.'

Less than a minute later – Marylyn did not want him to walk back with her to 11th Street – Clarence was alone, walking back down Greenwich Avenue towards the Reynolds's. *Now and then.* It was somehow worse than if Marylyn had broken off completely. She neither loved nor hated him. She was in between. What it seemed to mean was that she had never loved him and never would.

Greta was busy with her dinner much of that afternoon, and Ed came home at four to do some work. He said he worked the entire day at home two or three days a month. Clarence was happy to go out, twice, for something that Greta had forgotten to buy at the grocery store. Greta in the afternoon went to the piano and began to play a Chopin waltz, and when Clarence came to listen at closer range, she smiled mischievously and launched into 'Second-hand Rose' which she sang, making Clarence laugh.

'What we sing,' Greta explained, pounding away, 'when one lousy poet after another gets up to read his stuff.'

This was followed by 'Somebody Else is Taking My Place', until Ed yelled, 'What is this, old Sammy's on the Bowery? She's going to break the lease!'

'On my birthday I can risk to break the lease!' Greta retorted.

The apartment filled with the aroma of baking ham, cloves and brown sugar. By seven, the sparkling table held a plate of rollmops in sour cream.

The guests arrived, by accident in the same elevator. Eric brought flowers, Lilly a large flat box of chocolates, and there were wrapped presents as well. Greta told them that Clarence was staying until tomorrow, as their house guest. Lilly and Eric greeted him in quite a friendly way. Cocktails and canapés. Greta opened her presents. From Lilly, a box to hold paints and brushes which seemed to please Greta enormously, and Lilly explained that it was the latest and most efficient paint box, designed in Denmark, to hold the maximum in minimum space. Eric's present was a pair of Italian candlesticks of wrought iron. Ed's gift was a startling jacket of silvery green which shimmered with sequins — for evening wear. Greta exclaimed over each gift. It was a pleasure for Clarence to watch her. Of Clarence's necklace she said, 'Oh, Clarence! It's so glamorous!' And she put the necklace on.

Clarence began to feel easier. They were evidently not going to refer to the Rowajinski affair. But also he felt like an outsider looking in. The Reynolds and the other two were such old friends, like a family, despite the German accents of Greta and Eric versus the New York accents of Ed and Lilly. They were all pleasant to Clarence. The difference was only in Ed: Clarence felt that Ed avoided looking at him.

'Oh, Greta said you were in the hospital,' Lilly said to Clarence during dinner. 'I haven't extended sympathies. Wounded in the course of duty, Greta said.' She wasn't cynical now. She was merry on the dinner and the wine.

'What we call a little shoot-up,' Clarence said. 'Nothing serious.'

'Some people were shooting up glass doorways,' Ed said. 'Uptown in our old neighbourhood.'

'And what's the news about the man with the Polish name? Didn't you say he was murdered, Greta? Yes!' said Lilly, as if it had slipped her mind.

'Yes,' said Greta, and bit into a celery heart. 'I told you that a couple of weeks ago.'

'Of course. I heard,' Eric said. 'I heard it on the TV before Greta told me.'

'Do they know who did it?' Lilly asked.

'No,' Greta said. 'Someone on the street. Who knows?'

'That *Verrückter*! He was asking for it!' Eric declared.

'Did you say stabbed or shot?' Lilly asked.

'Just beaten up,' Greta said.

'Clobbered,' Ed added.

'What a subject,' Eric said, 'what a subject for a birthday party!'

'More wine!' Greta got up to fetch another bottle from the kitchen.

Ed took a long time lighting a cigar. The subject was not

exactly changed by anyone, but it drifted off to something else. Lilly remembered that she had brought an electronic record for them to hear. They played it while they had coffee. Eric chuckled and made comments. The few words, said in German by a female voice, were interspersed by eerie, owl-like moaning and screeching. Clarence's thoughts drifted. He saw a garden of metal flowers, then a dark tunnel, an airless hell in which anything could happen, or spring out. It was an unknown world, yet completely known, as one knew one's own dreams, and yet did not know them – because one could not completely interpret them, but not because one did not know them and their peculiar atmosphere. Clarence was thinking of Marylyn : she had her way of life, and suppose it was essentially incomprehensible to him? If she had a lurking doubt that her life was incomprehensible to him, she would sense it and reject it, Clarence was thinking. She would reject him. As perhaps she had already done. He wished he had seized her in his arms that morning and somehow impressed upon her – how? – that they must be together and stay together. As usual, he had not done the right thing at the right time.

Eric was the first to leave, kissing Greta on both hands, exchanging German pleasantries with her. Then Lilly left, bearing her mysterious record under her arm.

It was nearly midnight. Clarence complimented Greta on her dinner and said good night to her and Ed, thinking that they might want to be alone.

Ed knocked on Clarence's door half an hour later. Ed was in pyjamas and dressing-gown. 'Hello, Clarence. I saw your light.'

'Come in !' Clarence had been reading in bed.

Ed sat down. 'Well. All this – I gather you're not out of the woods yet ?'

'No.' Clarence sat up higher in bed. 'I heard you saw Manzoni last evening.'

'Oh ?'

'Marylyn told me. I saw her this morning.'

'How did she know ?' Ed asked, and at once knew how.

'Manzoni came to see her. Where she's living. She's fed up with the police questioning, of course. I hate it – for her.'

'There'll be more questions, I understand.'

'Yes. And they'll try to break Marylyn down, too. I don't mean they'll be rough but – It's mainly because I said I spent the night there, you know, and Marylyn said so, too.'

'I know. Of course.' Ed's mind formed sentences, then they disappeared and he was lost again.

'I'm sure Manzoni wasn't pleasant,' Clarence said, 'because he knows I'm staying here.'

'True, and I was thinking – for your own good it might be better if you didn't appear to be too friendly with us. For obvious reasons. If it isn't already too late.' Until it blows over, Ed thought of adding, but would it blow over? If they kept hammering at Clarence, wouldn't he finally break? Didn't people always break? 'I certainly don't mind your staying here now. Neither does Greta. But I mean in the future –'

'I understand.' Clarence felt wretched, unable to get out of the house, now, because of the hour, because it would be awkward. And even tomorrow morning, at best, would be a retreat because of what Ed had just said.

'Marylyn's friendly?' Ed asked.

Clarence almost choked. 'She doesn't like Manzoni visiting her. In fact, she's furious about it. So I won't be visiting her, seeing her either. That's inevitable.'

Ed stood up, unable to look at Clarence's unhappiness any longer, unable also to find any reassuring words to say. 'Yes, inevitable. For the time. I'm tired. I'll say good night.'

'Good night, Ed.'

In the bedroom, to Greta, Ed said, 'I've made the worst mistake of my life.'

'It is not so serious. Think about it tomorrow, Eddie.'

Ed lay in bed with his eyes open in the darkness. 'It's not just tonight that I think about it. I've thought about it days ago.' He spoke softly, imagining Clarence in the room across the hall. 'I can't stand the sight of him. I don't know what it is. – Yet I do know what it is. I don't trust him.'

'Why? Eddie –' Greta found his hand, patted it and held it.

'I don't know what went wrong. I should never have said – It was that time in the bar of the Fifth Avenue Hotel. I had the feeling then. Keep away, I thought. There's something odd about him. And here I am protecting him, just as this — this Manzoni said.'

'What's odd about him? He got angry, Eddie.'

Ed closed his eyes. Angry. It was something more than that. Greta's attitude was a funny one for a woman to have, Ed thought. But Greta often saw things in a different way from him. She had seen more than he. More brutality. It had struck close in her family. All right, but had she ever had one of the cool killers as a guest in her house? Or had possibly one of her own family retaliated in like manner against a German killer? Had Greta heard about it with maybe a sense of justice? Maybe. But Ed couldn't completely fathom it. That had been war, anyway. This wasn't.

23

Clarence went to his 19th Street apartment by taxi on Friday morning. He had been up and dressed in time to say his thanks and good-bye to Ed before Ed went to work. He had drunk two or three cups of coffee with Greta (she had a passion for coffee) in the course of his packing. Greta had been cheerful, optimistic, and also realistic. Thinking over their conversation as he rode in the taxi, Clarence wondered how she had managed it. 'Marylyn might not be the girl for you ... You are in a state of shock, you can't realize it all yet ... Never mind Eddie. He is complicated ... So? Yes. If you have such a temper, you must control it, really.' Clarence had devoured her words, weighed them, savoured them, and it was no effort for him to commit them to memory. He felt that Greta was wise. Not because she was on his side, in fact she wasn't entirely. He had said his temper got the better of him. He had said his temper had been bad enough the time he called on Rowajinski at his Morton Street room. 'You must not let it ruin your life ... Look at the murders in New York! Who cares? They say the cops do their best. Maybe they do, but what about the people the cops kill? Who does their best for *them* – if one speaks about human life?' Clarence had pointed out that he killed Rowajinski for a personal reason, and that he hadn't been shooting a robber in the act of running from the scene.

The conversation with Greta, inconclusive as it may have been, was of the greatest comfort to Clarence. He felt he would have collapsed – maybe not confessed, but somehow collapsed – if he had not been able to talk about his problems to someone like Greta.

Because of Greta, he now had morale.

Clarence turned on his radio for company and set about unpacking, straightening his apartment, dusting and sweeping, shopping, starting the fridge which his mother had evidently cut off. Larry Summerfield, a college chum who lived in Manhattan, had written a note: where was he? His telephone wasn't answering. And Nolan, of all people, had written a friendly note on a postcard with a soppy picture of a pair of brindle kittens in a basket: 'Get well soon. The old shithouse misses you. Bert.' The postcard had been enclosed in an envelope.

Clarence picked up his laundry, which included the shirt he had worn the night of Rowajinski. Clarence did not examine the shirt but put it with his others in a drawer. He was thinking that he ought to ring his parents today. They wanted him to come out for Thanksgiving next Thursday. His leave lasted till 4 December, which was three weeks after his hospital discharge.

His telephone rang around 3 p.m. A man's voice said that he was Detective somebody of Fifth Division, and could Clarence come tomorrow morning, Saturday, to the Fifth Division Headquarters at 10 a.m.? Clarence said he could come.

Clarence was there at 9.50 a.m., and was asked to wait. He had brought the *Times* and a book, and he read for half an hour. Just after 11 a.m., Clarence was ushered into a room with Detectives Morrissey and Fenucci, Fenucci appearing to have other things to do, because he paid no attention to Clarence. Fenucci gathered papers from the desk in the room. Clarence was offered a seat on a straight chair. Morrissey wore a dirty shirt, Clarence noticed, and looked as if he had been up all night – Clarence was pretty sure not because of him.

'Waiting for someone,' said Morrissey to Clarence, and helped Fenucci assemble the papers he was looking for.

It occurred to Clarence that he hadn't called his mother, and that this was an absurd thing to be thinking of now. He would have called his parents last evening, but he had not wanted to tell them he had been summoned for another police interview this morning, and he might have told them, if his mother had pressed him to come out to Astoria at once for the week-end, and to stay through Thanksgiving.

Just before noon, a big man whom Clarence didn't recognize at first – the landlord of Rowajinski on Morton Street – came into the room, looking frightened and aggressive. His eyes fixed on Clarence's face for a couple of seconds, then he did not look at Clarence again.

'Well,' said Morrissey, rubbing his hands together. 'Mr –' He faced the landlord. 'Philip –'

'Liebowitz,' said the man.

'Philip Liebowitz. And this is Clarence Duhamell. Patrolman Duhamell. Mr Liebowitz says,' Morrissey said, addressing Clarence, 'that you came to his house on Morton Street Wednesday, October twenty-eighth to see Kenneth Rowajinski. Right?'

'That's true,' said Clarence, not sure of the date.

'Mr Liebowitz is the landlord there, as you may know. Mr Liebowitz says you beat Rowajinski up. True?'

'I told you,' Clarence said, 'that I shook him. I wanted to scare him. I did push him and he fell on the floor. I did not beat him up.'

'That is not the way Mr Liebowitz reported it,' Morrissey said with a tired, wide grin. 'Tell him, Mr Liebowitz, maybe he's forgot.'

'Well, there was a lot of scuffling like. I heard it. I was right in the hall. I heard a thud. This guy Rawinsk –'

'Rowajinski,' said Morrissey, who was standing up between them.

'Rowajinski, he was all upset, wanting to use the bathroom just afterwards, I remember.'

'How long did Patrolman Duhamell stay?' asked Morrissey.

'Oh, a good ten, fifteen minutes.'

More like five, Clarence thought. Clarence blinked his eyes, watching Liebowitz. Had Liebowitz been told what to say? The interview was probably being taped, Clarence thought, by a machine in some part of the desk.

Morrissey began politely in tone, 'Patrolman Duhamell, to repeat the circumstances which you already know, you had reason to dislike Rowajinski, he accused you of taking five hundred dollars to let him escape in October, and when he was recaptured, charged, and released on probation, he began annoying your friend Marylyn Coomes and wrote her an unsigned letter saying things against you. You were in the neighbourhood of Barrow Street the night Rowajinski was beaten about the head and left dead in the foyer of a house on Barrow Street near Hudson Street. You had already called on Rowajinski for no apparent reason except personal resentment, and knocked him down on the floor. The only support you have for your story of having spent all night in a house on Macdougal is your own statement plus that of your friend Marylyn Coomes. She might be expected to back you up, no? It's natural. We offer you a chance, Patrolman Duhamell, to tell us what you really did that night. So what have you got to say?'

'I have nothing more to say. No changes in my statements,' Clarence said.

Someone brought in coffee, awful coffee in limp paper cups.

The blond fellow who ran the coffee-shop below Marylyn's arrived. He greeted Clarence with a nod and a flicker of a smile. He was in bell-bottom black trousers, and a fur jacket. Teddie his name was, Clarence remembered.

'Theodore Hackensack,' he said to Morrissey.

Morrissey established his residence, place of work, the fact that he knew Marylyn Coomes at least by sight, and also Clarence Duhamell by sight.

'You have said ...'

Morrissey had evidently already questioned Teddie, and Teddie had said he had not seen, or couldn't remember seeing Clarence leaving Marylyn's house the evening of 3 November, Tuesday, around 10.30 or midnight or any other time that evening. He also hadn't seen him arrive. Teddie looked unshaken and unshakable.

'Do you remember ever seeing Rowajinski, that evening or any other time?'

'Yeah, I told you about his coming into my shop and asking if there was a cop living next door.'

'Yes. I think we established that as around twenty-eighth October,' said Morrissey. 'And you told him what?'

'I told him I didn't know,' Teddie said, squirming in his chair, irritated by the questioning or the memory of Rowajinski. 'Why should I give him any information? I didn't like his looks.'

'But you knew Patrolman Duhamell came frequently to Marylyn Coomes's house?'

'Oh, sure. I've seen him around.'

'For how long? How long a time has he been visiting Miss Coomes?'

Teddie shook his head, amused. 'I really didn't keep track.'

'Do you know Miss Coomes well?'

'No,' said Teddie.

'How well? She's just an acquaintance or what?'

'She's just a neighbour. A couple of times she's come in for coffee. We say hello.'

'She never said anything about marrying Patrolman Duhamell?'

Teddie shook his head tolerantly. 'Now why would she tell me that?'

'Or that she's broken off with this man now?' He indicated Clarence.

'No,' said Teddie, bored. He looked in another direction and reached for his cigarettes.

'She has. – Have you any reason to fear Patrolman Duhamell, Theodore?' asked Morrissey.

Teddie's blue eyes showed annoyance, then he smiled again.

'A shakedown? I don't cater to junkies or pushers. They may come *in*. They're not my chums. If you know what I mean.' He added, 'I mind my own business. So far I don't have to take guff. From cops or anybody else.'

Morrissey nodded. He had removed his jacket and loosened his tie. The room was overheated. 'Did you ever talk alone with Patrolman Duhamell? Face to face?'

Teddie and Morrissey looked at each other. Morrissey was still smiling, but the smile had become nothing more than a slightly open mouth.

'No,' Teddie said. 'I'd remember that.'

Clarence realized that Morrissey was trying to get Teddie to say he'd accepted some kind of a rake-off, and to imply that for this reason Teddie might be afraid to say anything against him. Morrissey finally got nothing out of Teddie but scowls and silence. Teddie was allowed to leave.

'Miss Coomes is arriving soon,' said Morrissey, and took

the telephone and ordered sandwiches and coffee. 'Oh – four, I suppose.'

Philip Liebowitz sat like a forgotten heap on a straight chair, frowning and looking puzzled.

Morrissey turned to Liebowitz and said, 'Any other people you ever get in a hassle with Rowajinski, Mr Liebowitz ?'

'No, I told you. Just this fellow.'

'Patrolman Duhamell, we'll see how your story holds up when your girl-friend arrives. We know you're not telling the truth and neither is she. But you wouldn't want to put her through a lot of unpleasant questioning, would you – even if she has broken it off with you ?'

Clarence wanted to ask who had said she had broken it off ? But he reminded himself that the less he said the better, and that to become angry might be disastrous.

'She's due any minute,' said Morrissey with his smile that had now become ghoulish. 'There's time for you to say now – yes, I took a walk. Came *back* to Macdougal maybe. But you went out and clobbered that guy round about midnight, no ? So why not admit it, Duhamell, and save yourself a lot of trouble – pain in the ass questions ?' Morrissey took a cigarette, holding it between his teeth.

Clarence felt unpleasantly warm, shifted slightly, and said nothing.

'She's not the only one turning up. Your friend Edward Reynolds is coming too. Just after Miss Coomes.' Morrissey looked at his wrist-watch. 'At three-thirty.'

'Fine,' Clarence said.

But 2 o'clock came, and still Marylyn hadn't arrived. Liebowitz had been dismissed with hearty and phoney thanks from Morrissey.

'You told Detective Fenucci you didn't have your gun with you that night,' Morrissey said when he and Clarence were alone. 'We think you did. We think you used it to clobber Rowajinski. Isn't that true ?'

'That gun was examined. That gun wasn't used for anything,' Clarence said, feeling on safe ground – or if the ground wasn't safe it was time they told him.

'Oh, you could've washed the gun. Why did you have it at home, if you weren't carrying it that night?'

'I take my gun occasionally when I leave the precinct house after 4 a.m. So do a lot of patrolmen.'

'Patrolmen,' Morrissey said in a mocking way. 'You're the polite type, eh Dummell? Nasty subject murder, no? Not used to talking about it, eh Dummell?'

Clarence said nothing. He wanted a cigarette and didn't take one.

Marylyn arrived at ten to three. Now she wore a skirt, a wide, longish black skirt embroidered in red at the hem. She nodded and gave a faint smile to Clarence who was still sitting on the straight chair.

'Do sit down, Miss Coomes,' said Morrissey. 'Is that chair comfortable?'

'Yes, but it's full of smoke here,' Marylyn said.

Morrissey opened a window, pulling it with difficulty down from the top. 'Well now, Miss Coomes – we are making progress. Are you still prepared to say that Clarence Duhamell spent the entire night of November third-fourth at your house on Macdougal Street? Never went out even briefly – and maybe came back?' He smiled.

Marylyn, looking tense, took a deep breath and answered quite calmly, 'He spent the whole night. Why should I change my story?'

'Your story? Is it true?'

'I wouldn't bother lying,' Marylyn said with superb contempt, and Clarence imagined 'to pigs' that might have ended her statement.

'I understand you've broken off with Duhamell, Miss Coomes. Isn't it because you know he's guilty – guilty of having bashed a man to death?'

'And who said I've broken off? I'm perfectly friendly with Clare. As friendly as ever. After all, we're not married. And what business is it of yours?' She got out her cigarettes. 'I gather it's okay if I smoke,' she said, casting an eye up at the murky ceiling.

'Pete Manzoni told me you'd broken off,' said Morrissey.

'Clarence Duhamell hasn't spent any nights on Macdougal since the –'

'Manzoni can shove himself. He's a fascist pig – a – disgrace! You issue uniforms and guns to people like that? I intend to report that wop pig but I'm still gathering my dossier so I can really slam him. I wouldn't be proud, if I were you, to have such shit as a colleague.'

Morrissey was momentarily silenced, and Marylyn added:

'This wop is a heckler and he's the kind who feels women up. Crime, we've plenty of it, so why doesn't he go after it instead of knocking on my door and crashing in, hoping he can find me in the middle of dressing – or undressing. This whole bloody town,' she said, looking straight at Morrissey, 'is rolling in dope and the pigs are rolling in dough from it, and you waste your time trying to find out who killed a creep. What side are you on, anyway? I'll tell you. The cops are on the *creeps'* side!'

The insults plainly rolled off Morrissey. 'Why a creep? Rowajinski was a human being.'

'Ho-hum,' said Marylyn.

Morrissey smiled. 'Aren't you saying that because you –'

'I have no further comment on that *creep*. He was no better and no worse than the wop cop, for instance.'

There was a knock on the door, an arm in a uniform sleeve came into Clarence's view, and then Ed Reynolds entered. He nodded to Morrissey, and said 'Hello' to Clarence and to Marylyn. Morrissey, who was half sitting most of the time now on the edge of the desk, pulled another straight chair from the wall for Ed.

'Thank you for coming, Mr Reynolds,' Morrissey said. 'We've been going over the circumstances of the night of November third–fourth last. And we are going to get to the bottom of it. And we already have, I think. Miss Coomes here –' Morrissey stopped, because the door was opening again.

Fenucci came in, and after a glance went out and returned at once with another chair for himself. He signalled for Morrissey to continue.

'I was saying,' Morrissey resumed, 'Miss Coomes here continues to say that Dummell spent the entire night with her.'

He was mainly addressing Ed Reynolds. 'But that's understandable since Dummell is a friend of hers. Mr Reynolds, we don't believe this story and that's why we're here – to get the truth out, now or later.'

Ed glanced at Clarence, an assessing glance, Clarence felt, as if to try to estimate how much questioning he had been through already. Clarence felt perfectly fit, and reminded himself again to keep calm and to save his energy. Morrissey wasn't going to keep Marylyn or Ed all night, but he himself might be for it.

'I wonder, Mr Reynolds, if you share Miss Coomes's dislike of the police force?' Morrissey asked pleasantly.

Ed smiled slightly, and hesitated. 'I haven't given it much thought.'

'I imagine you disliked Rowajinski even more,' said Morrissey.

A nasty slant, Ed thought. He kept the blank, agreeable expression on his face. He also kept silent, even though Morrissey was awaiting a reply. So was Fenucci waiting.

'Dummell has said,' Morrissey went on, 'that he spent the entire night of November third–fourth at the apartment of Miss Coomes from ten p.m. to around eight the next morning – or ten, there're two different stories there from each of these people, because neither is true. Dummell says he didn't go out even for half an hour. Says he didn't have his gun with him, and Miss Coomes doesn't remember seeing it, although his gun was later found at his apartment because he'd taken it from his precinct house. We think the gun was the murder weapon and that Dummell washed it well, which was why no blood was found on it. We also know Dummell took a pair of pants and a topcoat to his local cleaners the morning after Rowajinski's death. Strange, no?' Morrissey glanced at Clarence.

Clarence kept his cool. He had supposed that Homicide would check at his local cleaners.

'And so the evidence mounts up,' Morrissey said with satisfaction. 'Now –'

Ed slowly got his cigarettes out, and in his effort to appear relaxed was so relaxed that his lighter slipped from his fingers. Morrissey retrieved it for him, because it was closer to his feet than Ed's. 'Thanks,' Ed said.

'You say, Mr Reynolds, that Dummell said nothing to you at any time about wanting to hit back at Rowajinski?'

'That is correct,' Ed said.

'Even after Bellevue wasn't doing anything, wasn't doing enough, in Dummell's opinion? Didn't he say to you something like – "Somebody ought to do something"?'

Ed inhaled smoke. 'He thought Bellevue ought to do something.'

'And when they didn't?'

'That's all he said – to me.'

'Don't you really know, Mr Reynolds, that Patrolman Dummell is responsible for Rowajinski's death?' (Marylyn gave a bored moan.) 'And that it's something so plain it doesn't need to be put into words maybe?'

'No,' said Ed, hating it. He hated Morrissey's manner. He hated his own lying. He realized he couldn't look at either Marylyn or Clarence, couldn't even glance at them. Ed looked at the floor, or at the cuffs of Morrissey's trousers. Morrissey was leaning against the desk.

'Don't you suspect, Mr Reynolds, that Clarence Duhamell killed that man? You're an intelligent man. How could you not suspect it?'

Ed didn't want to reply anything, yet realized that he ought to reply something. 'I have no real reason,' he said finally, 'to suspect it. That's why I don't.'

'Your goodwill – naïveté – I'm afraid they don't much apply here, Mr Reynolds. We're going to get the truth out of Clarence Duhamell.' He added more heatedly, 'No reason to suspect, even, when he's the only person in the whole picture who had motive – who had the means at hand, a gun with which –'

'So did I have motive,' Ed interrupted, smiling.

'Mr Reynolds, you're a different temperament from this man . . .' Morrissey went on for a few minutes. It was boring.

'Don't leave me out. I had motive,' Marylyn said.

Morrissey waved a hand at her. He looked vague for an instant, then said, 'Excuse me for a minute,' and went out.

Fenucci, who had been listening attentively, got up also, and paying no mind to the others in the room, went out and closed the door.

Ed gave a sigh, and glanced at Marylyn and Clarence, knowing without even thinking about it that the office must be bugged, and that he had best not say a word.

Clarence stretched his legs out in front of him and reached for a cigarette. He smiled at Marylyn, but didn't catch her eye. Ed evidently suspected also that a recording was being made, Clarence thought, and that was why Ed was silent.

Then Marylyn said, 'This is so we can all yak and spill the beans,' and Clarence and Ed laughed. Marylyn almost laughed, and pursed her lips to control her smile. 'Why don't we sing a hymn ? I –' Then she stopped.

How long do you think they'll keep you? Ed wanted to ask Clarence, but even this question, or Clarence's answer, might for some reason be inadvisable. Held against Clarence.

Morrissey came back. How Morrissey had changed since that first affable evening interview, Ed thought. Now he looked weary, mechanical, no longer human. He was doing a job. Ed felt that he was on no side at all. He was neutral. Or a blank. Except that he wanted to nail *somebody*.

Morrissey was leaning against the desk again, drumming with his finger-tips as he composed his next words. 'Mr Reynolds, we're going to get the truth from this man,' he said, indicating Clarence. 'It's only a question of time. You can help us, if you will. Just tell us what you know. Tell us the truth – please.' The tone was politely pleading.

It irritated Ed more than anything else. It implied that he hadn't been telling the truth, and that he was protecting Clarence because Clarence was a friend. 'I have nothing more to say. And if you haven't any other questions, I wouldn't mind taking off.'

Morrissey nodded. He looked disappointed. 'Very well, sir. I thank you for coming.' He pushed himself off the desk.

Ed had stood up. 'Bye-bye, Marylyn. Bye-bye, Clarence.'

'Good-bye, sir,' Clarence said. The 'sir' was a slip. 'Thanks for troubling to come.'

Morrissey gave Clarence a smirk as he opened the door for Ed.

Ed went out of the building and took a deep breath of cold air. The dismalness! Suddenly even the ugly buildings on the street, a row of four ashcans, looked better, nicer than what he had just left. He wanted to telephone Greta at once, just to hear her voice. Instead he got the first taxi he saw and headed for 9th Street.

By 5.30 p.m. Clarence was feeling sleepy and also a little angry, but he was still repressing his anger. Marylyn had been told that she could go some ten minutes after Ed had left. Morrissey's dismissal of her had been rather off-hand, and Marylyn had said, 'This is my last visit here, by the way, because I have better ways of spending my time. I intend to report the wop pig whether he visits me again or not, and if he's dumb enough to visit me again, I'll resort to that famous weapon – screaming. The whole neighbourhood's going to know about his next visit.'

Morrissey, rude as stone, had nodded absently, not looking at her, not replying anything.

Morrissey had heard worse, Clarence supposed. The following hour, Morrissey went over the same things – the gun in Clarence's apartment, the fact that Rowajinski had accused him of taking five hundred dollars, his friendship with the Reynolds. He was sucking up to the Reynolds, wasn't he? He thought they were upper class, didn't he? Swank? Clarence made no reply. It was more like a lecture than a questioning, anyway.

'Am I the only person who ever wanted to take a swat at Rowajinski?' Clarence said to Morrissey.

'No. No,' Morrissey said, happy at some response. 'No, we had a guy a few days ago – Andrew something. A janitor in one of the buildings where Rowajinski used to live. He hated Rowajinski. Rowajinski's landlady told us about him. Okay, they had some kind of feud, because he once bumped Rowajinski when he was rolling out ashcans or something. They once had a fistfight on the street. All right. But Andrew didn't come down to Barrow that night. He didn't know where Rowajinski was living.'

Clarence twice got up and walked around the room. The straight chair had become painful, a chore to go back to, but Clarence was afraid they might keep him standing all night. Surely the rough stuff would take place in the basement, or somewhere else. And they would try to make him angry, because now he had the reputation of a bad temper.

'Getting tired of the subject, eh?' Morrissey said, sitting on the edge of the desk, munching a sandwich.

Clarence had not been listening.

'You'll get plenty tired of it. Look what you're putting your friends through, Clarence. They're not going to be your friends any longer. You know that.'

Clarence calmly sipped the bad coffee. There was a ham and cheese sandwich on a paper plate on the desk, but he wasn't hungry. He imagined Ed Reynolds and Marylyn trying to telephone him this evening, getting no answer at his apartment, and immediately realized that neither would telephone, probably. For different reasons, neither would telephone. Ed had looked fed up, depressed by it all. Were they going to speak with Ed again? But Morrissey, at some point, had already said they would. Was that true? Perhaps they were going to grill Ed, in a way, as they were grilling him. Bore him into admitting what he knew. As Morrissey said, Clarence hated that, would do anything to save Ed from it. But no, he hadn't said that, Morrissey had said it. Clarence was becoming weary. He wanted to take a walk. Or a nap. The room was stuffy again.

'You want to make a telephone call, go ahead,' said Morrissey, indicating the telephone on the desk. 'Just press the green button before you dial.' Morrissey went to the door. 'Somebody else'll be here in just a minute.'

Alone, Clarence went to the window and opened it ten inches from the bottom. Then he slumped in a different chair, a swivel chair behind the desk, and put his feet up on the radiator under the window. He tried to sleep, his head back on the wood of the chair.

Fenucci came in. Clarence looked at his watch and saw that it was 7.44 p.m.

By a quarter to 10 p.m., Fenucci was droning on in a soporific way: '. . . just the facts. That's all I'm telling you, Clarence. No rough stuff. Not my style.' Fenucci strolled about, hands in his pockets. 'Feeling sleepy? Stand up.'

Clarence stood up. 'I want to open the window a little.'

Fenucci had closed it.

'Don't jump out,' Fenucci said, smiling.

Clarence was too tired to react. For some reason, perhaps tension, his injured collarbone had begun hurting, hours ago, and it hurt worse as he lifted the window.

'No rough stuff except this,' said Fenucci, slapping or jabbing Clarence's face suddenly as Clarence turned from the window. 'That's an insult. You deserve it. Or this.' Fenucci jabbed at the pit of Clarence's stomach.

It did not hurt much, but it was a shock. Clarence felt a cool film of perspiration break out over his face. His eyes widened. The atmosphere changed suddenly. This was what Clarence had expected.

Fenucci now stamped on his toe.

That didn't hurt much either, and Clarence almost smiled. Stamping on toes was silly. One had to see things in perspective. Clarence walked around, feeling awake now.

'. . . a matter of time, Clarence. There're several of us and only one of you . . . if not tonight then another night, eh? Tomorrow night or the next night. Or the third morning, who knows? There won't be any let-up, Clarence, until you spill the beans.'

Clarence remained calm. He felt it might be an advantage to feel tired, therefore relaxed. Mustn't let his nerves 'wear thin' however. Fenucci seemed to be talking just to be saying something, and Clarence also let his thoughts ramble where they would. Marylyn, maybe at a pleasure dinner party tonight, regaling her friends about police methods. Ed, reading, or maybe at a film with Greta, Ed no doubt trying to forget the minutes with Morrissey.

'Call up Mr Reynolds. I insist.'

Fenucci's words caught Clarence's attention. 'I don't care to call him up. For what?'

'I insist. You're taking *my* orders. Call him up, Clarence.' He nodded at the telephone.

'But I have no reason to call him up.'

'Afraid you'll annoy him? Fine. The reason is, I order you to call him up!' Fenucci lit a cigarette viciously, as if he were very angry. 'So go ahead.'

'I don't know his number.' It was true, Clarence at that moment wasn't sure of Ed's new number.

Fenucci pressed a button on the desk, scowled absently at the scattered papers before him, then a cop in uniform appeared at the door. Fenucci asked him to bring a Manhattan telephone directory. Clarence had to look up the old number, dial it, and get the new number. This he dialled.

Greta answered.

'Hello. It's Clarence. I'm sorry to bother you. I —'

'Are you — Do you want to speak with Ed ?'

'It's not that I want to, they're —'

Fenucci swatted Clarence on the back of the head. Clarence gripped the telephone and wanted to slam it down, but Fenucci would only make him ring again, Clarence realized.

'Tell him you *wanted* to call him,' Fenucci said.

'Hello, Ed,' Clarence said. 'Please excuse me for —' He received another swat on the back of the head. 'They are making me telephone you !' Clarence shouted. 'I wish to excuse my —'

Fenucci yanked the telephone from Clarence's hand. 'Hello, Mr Reynolds ? Detective Fenucci here. I think Dummel is going to confess for us. He wanted to talk with you.'

'I did *not* !' Clarence yelled.

'I'll pass you to Clarence.' Fenucci handed the telephone to Clarence.

'Ed —'

'What's up ?'

'I am not confessing anything ! I want to say I'm sorry that I bothered you at this hour but I was not able —'

This time Fenucci delivered a harder punch in the stomach, almost casually, and took the telephone from Clarence and dropped it into the cradle.

Clarence's heart was pounding. He couldn't speak for a few seconds, because the blow had knocked some breath out of him. 'And what — what's the purpose of that crap ?'

Fenucci smiled thinly. 'Just to show your chum Ed what a sap you are. We succeeded. Now you can call up your ex-girl-friend.'

Clarence could breathe again. 'No, I can't. I don't know where to reach her.'

'We do. We've got the number.' But it took Fenucci a ludicrously long time to find it, thumbing through notebooks and scraps.

Clarence recognized it as Dannie's number. He dialled this. To his joy, there was no answer.

Around 1 o'clock, Fenucci said, 'Okay, you can go home.'

Clarence was startled out of a semi-daze, although he was on his feet. He stood straighter. He had been standing, at Fenucci's request.

'Go, I said. Home. See you tomorrow. Say around two in the afternoon? Give you a chance to get some sleep,' said Fenucci.

Clarence pulled on his coat, started to close his shirt collar and tie and gave it up.

'You are disgusting,' Fenucci said.

Clarence went out. He let the cold air chill him awake. The air blew down his shirt collar, icy against his sweat. He caught a taxi. At his apartment, he took off his shirt and washed, brushed his teeth and drank two glasses of water. He was thinking of calling Ed, explaining, despite the hour. Then he decided against it: wouldn't it be more annoying to ring at this hour, when perhaps they were asleep? Clarence wanted to take a shower. Then he thought, no, ring the Reynolds now, before the shower, because after the shower it will be even later. Yes, he had to apologize, and tonight, otherwise he wouldn't be able to sleep for thinking about it. Clarence dialled their number which he now recalled exactly.

Ed answered.

'It's Clarence again. I'm home. I hope I didn't wake you.'

'That's all right. What's the trouble now?'

'They forced me to telephone you. I didn't want to call you at all!' The rise in Clarence's voice shocked him, and he tried to control it. 'I am sorry, Ed. They were at me all day, you know. I did *not* confess.' It suddenly occurred to him that his telephone could be bugged also, same as the room where he'd spent all day. Clarence laughed a little crazily. 'I have no intention of confessing. It's absurd! But I – I wanted to apologize for disturbing you in a – a way I never would have done.'

'That's all right,' Ed said, thinking Clarence was a bit hysterical. 'Get some sleep.'

'You didn't possibly see Marylyn?'

'No,' said Ed.

'They made me telephone her, too. Fortunately she wasn't in. Down on Eleventh Street.' Clarence felt that Ed wanted to wind up the conversation, and Clarence desperately wanted to hang on, to explain, above all to make sure that Ed was still on his side. 'Thank you for today, Ed. Thank you.'

'No need to thank me. – But I really hope it's the last of it. I'm not coming to see them again. I don't know if I can refuse to let them in the house again, but I'm going to be too busy to come to see them again. Enough is enough.'

Words, in a surge, rose in Clarence's mind. He couldn't get them out, couldn't decide which words to say first. Gratitude. Shame. Failure. Regret. And the fact that he blamed no one, certainly not Ed. The fact that he understood why Ed, why Marylyn – and really maybe everyone except Greta – considered him a pariah, because he had killed someone.

'Better try to get some sleep, Clarence.'

'Can I – I don't suppose I can see you some time tomorrow? I've got to see them again at two but –'

'Clarence – no. It's for your own good. Can't you understand that? Do you want them to think we're in conspiracy? They'll be watching you, won't they? Or mightn't they?'

'Yes, sir,' Clarence said, exhausted. 'It's true I'm upset. – Good night, sir.'

Ed hung up. 'Good God,' he whispered.

Greta was awake. She had been almost asleep, and Ed had been reading by the lamp on his side of the bed. 'What's happened?'

Ed walked on bare feet to the window, and turned around. 'He says he hasn't confessed. He must've had twelve hours' questioning today – questioning or worse.'

'Where was he calling from?'

'From his apartment. He says it's not finished yet. He's going to see them at two tomorrow. But he's surely going to confess. They mostly do. Don't they?'

Greta didn't answer at once.

'Sure they do,' Ed said. 'Well, I really don't care. I've lied. Clarence will say he told me – days ago. So I've lied.'

'And so have I then. I was questioned too. I am not sorry. I really am *not* sorry.'

Ed wished he could see it as simply as Greta did. She must be right, he thought. Yet he couldn't see it. At the same time he didn't think he had been completely wrong. Was there such a thing as being half right and half wrong? No. 'I only know I –'

'Come to bed, Eddie. Talk in bed.'

Ed was walking about. 'I can't stand the sight of him. I ought to be – more tolerant. Stronger. I don't know.'

'You know zomezing,' Greta said, yawning a little, but giving her attention to what Ed was saying, 'I am not sure he will confess.'

That was a possibility, a strange one. It might be true. Yet somehow it wasn't the point. The point was not even that he had protected Clarence Duhamell. It was that he simply and profoundly disliked him now.

24

The ringing of his telephone awakened Clarence. He was groggy, and reached slowly for the phone, dropped it in the darkness and found it again on the floor.

'Hello?'

'Hello. This is Pete. How are you, Clarence?'

Manzoni's voice shocked Clarence awake, to a pained alertness.

'I hear you're cracking up,' said Manzoni.

Clarence's anger rose only slightly. He put the telephone down, and fell back on the bed. Slowly he grew more awake, and blinked his eyes quickly in the black of his room. What had Manzoni found out? Maybe nothing. He hadn't come anywhere near cracking up. He wouldn't. He damned well wouldn't. Clarence made himself close his eyes and breathe regularly. The dawn was beginning.

Clarence was half awake when the telephone rang again. But now it was a quarter to 10 a.m.

'Hello, Clare? It's Mother. How are you, darling? We've been trying to reach you. Are you all right?'

'Yes, I'm all right.'

'Why didn't you telephone us? We didn't want to ring the Reynolds because – I wasn't sure you'd still be there.'

'No.' Clarence shook his head to try to wake up. 'No, I left Friday.'

'You're sleepy. I woke you. I'm sorry. Are you feeling all right? Not hurting anywhere? . . . Why don't you come out, Clare? You've still got so many days of leave.'

Clarence struggled inwardly. He could lie, insist that he wanted to spend the time alone in his apartment. Or he could tell the truth which was so much easier.

'Clare?'

'Mom, they're questioning me. On the Pole thing. They want me here in town.'

'Really? Do you know so much about it?...'

He ended by lying after all. He had seen the Pole several times, he said. Yes, he would call her as soon as he knew when he had any free time.

Clarence tried to sleep again.

By 2 p.m. Clarence was at the 126th Street Headquarters. He wore tennis shoes, a turtle-neck sweater. He had breakfasted on two eggs and as much toast as he could manage. Again he had to wait a long while, and it became 3.10 p.m. Clarence had brought the Sunday *Times* and a paperback of short stories by Ben Hecht, which he had read twice before.

Morrissey arrived, looking fresh, and gave Clarence a preoccupied glance as he strode past and went to the same room (Clarence thought) as the one he had been in yesterday. Another twenty minutes passed, and Clarence put his head against the wall and fell asleep. It seemed a better sleep than he had had all the preceding night, but when a middle-aged cop shook him awake, Clarence saw that only ten minutes had passed. Clarence was ushered to a room, the same room as yesterday, where Morrissey awaited him behind the desk.

'So Dummell – it's only a matter of time now. Isn't it? Minutes, maybe. Sit down.' Morrissey was seated. 'We've spoken with Edward Reynolds. He sounds no longer so ready to defend you – protect you.' Morrissey smiled. 'You have nothing to say to that?'

'No.'

'And Miss Coomes – she won't be turning up either. You're all alone today. No chums. Let's go to another room for a change.'

Morrissey led the way, leftward in the hall to another door. It seemed to Clarence that a couple of cops in the hall looked at him with a strange amusement, but he might have been mistaken. They went down some stairs, then into a larger square room with a desk in its centre. There were no windows in the room, and there was a whirr of an electric ventilating machine, or maybe the heating system, which evidently operated by means of the grilled vents near the ceiling. There were two straight chairs, and Morrissey took one, but he said to Clarence:

'Walk around a little. You look sleepy.'

Clarence did not feel sleepy. He laid his coat on the other chair and walked around, slowly. He was still walking an hour later, circling the desk widely, reversing when he wished. This was what he had expected. This could go on until he dropped. Clarence did his best not to listen. He thought this a good precaution against becoming angry.

It was, of course, true that the Reynolds would not stand by him. Wasn't it true? Ed had declined to see him today, not refused exactly, but said it wasn't a good idea. Marylyn was — in a way unreachable. Clarence's right leg had begun to hurt. It was the leg in which he had had the bullet wound. He took a breath and glanced at the pale grey walls as he made a turn.

'. . . in the face of the clearest evidence I've ever seen . . . wasting people's time . . . Admit it, Dummell! What's all this jazz? You're trying to be a hero? The very . . .'

Morrissey's voice shut off again as if by magic. Clarence looked at the grey walls which blended to near charcoal in the upper corners. He held his head higher. Morrissey was calling him a lying piece of shit. Worse. In a curious way that seemed comical now to Clarence, he was censoring Morrissey's unending speech. Clarence felt separate from it, untouchable. That was the word (Morrissey had used it) untouchable, and so what the hell? He was different, fine. But did Morrissey expect him to cringe? Morrissey could think again!

Morrissey sat drinking from a paper cup of coffee. Clarence had not been offered any coffee. (The coffee was muck anyway.) The coffee had arrived via a uniformed lackey some minutes ago, along with a piece of pie. It was 5.37.

Clarence stopped and faced Morrissey with a slight smile.

'. . . not the guts to —' Morrissey's voice ground to a halt like an old phonograph record.

Not the guts to what? Clarence felt that he could face anything. They could pull his fingernails out tonight, his teeth — which he was now clenching. Morrissey was awaiting a word from him. Clarence wasn't going to give it. He stared at Morrissey, who was becoming angrier.

'So?' said Morrissey finally.

Clarence was silent. He stared at Morrissey until Morrissey's eyes flickered and looked down at the papers before him. Morrissey looked even a trifle frightened, Clarence noticed, though there was a telephone and the usual box of buttons on the desk so Morrissey could summon a couple of strong men in a trice if he wished. There was probably a gun somewhere, too, maybe in a drawer.

'So? Can we have it now, Clarence? Just a simple statement, "I clobbered the guy on *Barrow* Street." – Let's have it.'

Clarence almost closed his eyes, but otherwise he did not move.

'Walk,' said Morrissey.

Clarence didn't walk, and Morrissey got up and hit him in the jaw. It was quick, more with closed fingers than a fist, but Clarence felt Morrissey's anger in its sting. Slowly Clarence walked, just as before. He wasn't angry. He felt in fact marvellous, and stood taller.

Morrissey was on the phone now. The telephone on his desk had buzzed. Clarence was not curious, but he listened just to have a change.

'No, not yet,' said Morrissey. 'No, I'm fine ... You can tell him he's here, sure ... Okay ... Okay.' He hung up. 'Your precinct. Want to know if you're here. If you've talked yet.' He gave a short laugh and lit a cigarette. 'You probably thought it was Mr Reynolds wondering about your health.'

Clarence tried to turn Morrissey's voice off again. Maybe it had been Ed. Morrissey had spoken with a cop, not the person who had telephoned. But probably it hadn't been Ed. Very probably not. Clarence reminded himself of his new-found strength: he didn't need Ed any more. Not that he didn't like Ed. That wasn't the point, but he didn't need him, or Marylyn. And the night was young.

'Like a sandwich?'

This question from Morrissey came many minutes later. Clarence was deliberately not looking at his watch any longer. But Morrissey said:

'It's nearly nine o'clock.'

Clarence was still in a mood not to say anything, so he didn't.

Morrissey got up and was about to swat nim again, so Clarence said:

'A sandwich and milk.'

'Milk? No coffee?'

The coffee, like Morrissey, like everything, was so disgusting, why say so?

Clarence was allowed to sit down while he ate most of a liverwurst sandwich and drank milk through a straw. Then he was told to walk again.

Morrissey was more tense. He wanted to wind things up tonight. Clarence felt ready to take on Morrissey's replacement, to walk on and on until he dropped, and even if he dropped, they wouldn't get anything out of him. How could they get anything out of him, if he didn't choose to say anything? Now was the time for a lie detector test, Clarence thought with sudden joy: he felt he wouldn't have the least reaction. For hours now, Morrissey's monologue had been rolling off him like — like —

The telephone rang, or something buzzed, and Clarence tripped and had to catch himself. He was a bit tired, he had to admit. Morrissey was talking, laughing. What time was it? Clarence did not look at his watch. It didn't matter.

'Yeah, you *have* got a nerve,' Morrissey was saying. 'Well, all right, all right, you're excused.' Morrissey looked at Clarence. 'Your other chum, Manzoni.'

Clarence faced Morrissey, who was not looking at him now, but talking into the telephone again, joshing with Manzoni. *I'll talk with the bastard,* Clarence wanted to say, suddenly angry as if Manzoni had intruded on what had been a pleasant atmosphere.

'Okay. Do you want to talk to him?' Morrissey said, extending the telephone towards Clarence.

Had he spoken out loud? Clarence didn't know, but he took the telephone. 'Manzoni!' Clarence said, a little gaily.

'Dummell. Clarence. I hear you're getting the treatment! Cracking up, hey Clarence? So they tell me.'

Manzoni's ugly voice was suddenly a focal point for Clarence. Clarence cursed him. Clarence was fluent.

Morrissey's laughter made Clarence stop.

'. . . cracking up!' Manzoni was laughing too.

Clarence put the telephone down.

'Why'd you put the phone down?' asked Morrissey, grinning. '*I* didn't tell you to put the phone down.' Morrissey swung at Clarence, not meaning to hit him, and his hand was inches short.

Clarence resumed his slow walking about the room. Yes, he'd made a mistake losing his temper like that with Manzoni. Still, not a serious mistake. It could be overcome.

'You don't like the police, do you, Dummell? You're an outsider.'

'How do you mean *that*? I wouldn't have —'

'You're not one of us, so I'm told. You look down on the police force.'

It was too complicated to explain. Also Morrissey didn't want clarification from him. Things would've gone better for him, Clarence supposed, if he'd been 'one of them', one of the kickback-takers, one of the boys. Was that what Morrissey meant? Even though Morrissey had the rank of detective and wore plainclothes, he was one of the boys, Clarence supposed.

'I didn't —' Clarence stopped, too exhausted to begin.

'What?'

'I didn't join the force to be a spy, to look —'

'Who said anything about being a spy?' Morrissey laughed.

'I thought a great deal of the police force. That's why I joined up.' To be of some service, Clarence thought, but he didn't want to be met with more laughter.

Morrissey nodded with an attitude of contempt.

Cops had protected cops in his situation, Clarence was thinking. He'd heard of it. It was common knowledge. But they weren't protecting him. Clarence felt anger and self-pity rise in him. He tried to fight it down. *This* was what Morrissey wanted him to feel.

Morrissey was saying something else.

Clarence put his hands over his face. He was tired, angry, frustrated. He heard Morrissey cursing to himself.

Morrissey left the room, impatient because his replacement had not turned up. Morrissey had been yelling into the telephone about it. Clarence flung himself into the straight chair, on top of his coat, put his head back and stretched his legs out, like a boxer resting between rounds. Clarence fell asleep as if being sucked down a black, spiralling hole. Then a hand shook him vigorously on the shoulder, and he looked up into a dark, smiling face. A rugged Italian type of face, a strange face.

'Get up, mac,' the man said in a deep voice, and walked towards the desk.

Clarence got up.

The two men looked at each other. It was plain to Clarence that the man was assessing him: how tired was he, how hostile? Clarence was so tired as to feel mushy; at that moment, no doubt his face looked mushy too, but he wasn't weaving on his feet.

'Well, it seems – Yeah. Hm m,' said the dark man, looking at his notes.

In the next minutes, it was the same rehash of the Rowajinski story. The man was limbering up. It had a faintly soporific effect on Clarence. Clarence sat down. He remained seated four or five minutes until the man told him to get up again.

'Keep walking,' he said. 'You said in one place here your girl-friend Marylyn is a sound sleeper, she didn't hear you leave in the morning. Maybe she didn't hear you that night when you left her apartment and came back. When you went out and found Rowajinski ... Isn't that possible? What've you got to *say*?'

'I didn't go out – that night.'

The man continued. Dates. The visit to Bellevue. His effort to start a friendship with the Reynolds. His attempt at friendship. '... nothing to say?'

'No, sir.' Clarence was walking about, circling slowly. A while ago he had wanted to pee, and now he didn't. Strange. The toilet was down the hall to the right.

'... and now your friends have walked out on you ... Would you stand up straighter? You can make things a lot easier for yourself if you admit these facts which I've got right in front of my eyes! If you admit that – that you left your girl-friend maybe around eleven or twelve that night, went straight to Rowajinski's neighbourhood and found him and beat him up! Admit it!'

'I did not!'

'You're going on trial, you know, and if you plead not guilty, they're going to slam you!'

'That's too bad!'

It went on.

'... mustn't think your girl-friend's going to keep on protecting you. She'll have a limit just like you, just like everybody ... our guys aren't finished with her either ...'

Clarence dropped to the floor. The dark-green cement seemed to come up and hit him like a punch in the cheek, and he was instantly alert, pushed himself up and stood up, facing the desk over which there was a light. There was a buzzing which seemed to be in the very crown of his head. Or was it the telephone? No. The dark-haired man was half twisted round in his chair, yelling something at him.

'... going! Keep going! Are you going to talk for me?'

Now a punch in the stomach. The man was suddenly right in front of him. Clarence blinked, hurting.

'The time-wasting! For Christ's sake, give it! ... Save yourself ...'

Clarence asked to go to the toilet. He realized he was mumbling. Exasperated, the man accompanied him, asking him to leave the door open so he could see him, just as Morrissey had done. There was a basin. Clarence wet his head, drank out of his hands water that tasted of the liquid soap he had washed with. When they came back into the room, Clarence went to the chair and sat down on his coat.

'Get up!'

Clarence got up. 'I am not saying anything else tonight, not to you or anyone.' Now he was weaving a little, and his feet felt damp with sweat. But he was chilly now, not warm.

The dark man, angry, started to say something and didn't. His lips had started to form words. Then he went to the telephone. Clarence didn't bother listening. The conversation seemed to go on for five minutes or more. Clarence looked at his watch, with difficulty focused his eyes, and saw that the watch said 3.22. He felt the knob of the watch to see if it had pulled out and caused the time to be wrong, but it hadn't. It was 3.22 a.m. Monday.

'Do you want this to go on and on?' asked the dark man who had hung up. 'Tomorrow and the next day? Let's have it now! ... We can give you a shot ...'

A shot to keep him awake or to make him talk? Clarence was wilting again. His eyes stung.

The man went again to the telephone and yanked it up, pressed a button. He had loosened his collar and tie, and looked quite a different person from the one who had arrived several hours ago.

'I dunno if I need any help here or not ... No, no, not that.' He was muttering, sullenly.

Clarence turned off his voice as if it were a language he couldn't understand. Let them bring up reinforcements, fine! Let them give him shots to pick him up, bennies so he couldn't sleep for days! He wasn't going to talk for them. They could kill him, and he still wouldn't talk. As torture went, what he was going through now was nothing, and Clarence didn't feel sorry for himself. He felt brave. It was exhilarating.

'Let's go, I said!' yelled the dark man.

Clarence turned around.

The man was walking towards the door, jerking his thumb. 'Get your coat.'

Clarence supposed that they were going to another room. They climbed the stairs, walked down the hall towards the front door. Out into the cool air. There was a taxi, evidently summoned by the patrolman on the pavement.

The dark-haired man opened the door and said, 'You're going home. Nineteenth, isn't it? ... Don't try to go anywhere else. We can always find you.'

The taxi door slammed. The driver had the address.

Clarence got up his stairs. He took off his tennis shoes and his trousers, washed his hands and face perfunctorily, and fell into bed. It was very dark. His ears rang in a pulsing way. Minutes later, he woke up with a terrible sense of falling, and sat up in bed. He fell back on the pillow again, tense, and not at all sleepy now. His brain was spinning. Morrissey, Marylyn,

Ed Reynolds, Greta. They were not doing or saying anything, only whizzing . . . And there was a ringing.

The ringing was real. Clarence groped for his telephone, then realized it was his doorbell. Who was it? Marylyn maybe? No, the cops, certainly, making sure he was home. Clarence didn't want to let them in, but they'd break in if he didn't, he supposed. He found a light, and pushed the release button. Then he opened his door a little. He heard a single pair of feet on the stairs, not climbing fast, a man's tread.

There was a dim light in the stairwell, and Manzoni's figure came into view. Clarence started to shut the door, then hesitated. Manzoni smiled a little, seeing Clarence.

'Hyah,' Manzoni said. 'Just checkin'. Can I come in?'

'No. Checking on what?'

Manzoni, stocky and determined, smilingly pushed the door wider and came in. 'That you're here. I heard you're very tired but you didn't talk yet.'

'Piss off, Pete.' Clarence picked up his trousers from a chair and put them on, keeping an eye on Manzoni.

Manzoni had lit a cigarette. He was hatless, his coat unbuttoned now. Clarence thought he might have his gun with him. Clarence looked at his watch. It was twelve minutes to six.

'Y'know, Clarence, I talked with your two chums today, Marylyn and Reynolds. It's only a matter of time till Marylyn's going to tell the truth – and also Reynolds.'

Manzoni's hesitation about Ed made Clarence not believe any of it. Marylyn wouldn't help the cops, and certainly not Manzoni. Clarence had no doubt at all about Ed: Ed had given him his word, and besides Ed was sick of all of it. But the great thing was, it didn't matter now to Clarence. And he was not afraid of Manzoni, even if Manzoni had a gun.

'Let's have it straight, Clarence.' Manzoni sat down and grinned up at Clarence. 'What're you going to *do* when your ex-chums spill the beans on yuh?' He chuckled. 'You're finished already. So why don't you just say it? You wasted that Rowinsk.'

Clarence lit a cigarette. Manzoni was here to scoop his 'confession' after Homicide had worn him down. Manzoni wanted his promotion, wanted to be a detective! Manzoni had hoped to find him in a weak moment, Clarence supposed. Here was the stinking wop right in the middle of his apartment! The same bum who had infuriated and insulted Marylyn and made her break with him! 'Just get out, Pete.' He took a step towards Manzoni.

'Oh, no.' Manzoni drew his head and shoulders back, and kept his seat. 'I've got a gun here, so watch out. – Clarence, *I* found that Rowajinski when you let him go. *I* was the –'

Clarence pulled his fist back.

Just as quickly, Manzoni drew his gun and pointed it at Clarence. Manzoni was still seated.

'I'm not afraid of your gun. I said get out!'

'You oughta be afraid. I can plug you and say you put up a fight. You think anybody's gonna worry about *your* life?'

Clarence smiled slightly.

The gun was just inches from him now, pointing at his stomach. Clarence advanced with an intention of knocking Manzoni off the chair.

Manzoni jumped up, and the straight chair went over backwards. In his dark, creased face was sudden terror, a fear for his life. Clarence saw the terror. Clarence took a step back.

Manzoni looked scared and puzzled.

I've won, Clarence was thinking, and it's because I have nothing to lose. How simple! How obvious!

'Come on, take a walk,' Manzoni said, gesturing with his gun towards the door.

'A walk why?'

'I feel like it. S'matter? You scared?'

'I have no reason to take a walk. Just leave me.'

'I asked you to!'

Clarence felt well, very well, no longer tired. He had won over the little scum, and he knew he ought to let it go at that. It was crazy to take a walk – just so Manzoni could pull something on the street, a phoney fight between them so Manzoni could use his gun. 'I've been walking all day,' Clarence said. 'No, thanks, Pete, just –'

The gun went off and Clarence felt a thin jolt in the stomach. He stared at Manzoni, who curiously looked just as frightened as he had a few minutes ago, but now there was anticipation and anxiety in his face also. Whether to fire another shot? Manzoni was waiting for him to drop. And Clarence wilted.

Clarence was on the floor. Manzoni was briskly departing but Clarence's thoughts ran even faster. He was thinking Manzoni would say he had put up a fight – therefore in self-defence – That was, if Manzoni had to say anything. Any way you looked at it, Manzoni was safe. And he thought of Marylyn, a glimpse of the impossible, the unattainable. What a pity she had never understood, really, what it was all about. And Ed, and Greta – they never understood that he would practically have died for them. *I had wished for so much better.*

Manzoni's brisk departure was achieved. A door closed.